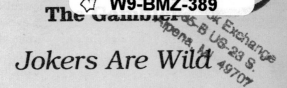

Jokers Are Wild

"My name is Brady Hawkes, and I have invested a lot more of my nights around the gaming tables of some muddy-water, stray-dog town saloon than I have in the back-row deacon's pew of a traveling salvation tent. The games are sometimes as crooked as the roads I ride, but crooked games don't bother me if they're the only games in town. The man with a cheating heart hasn't figured out that I know which cards are missing, which cards he's gonna play, and how nervous he gets. . . . A man with sweaty hands can't palm an ace. The graveyards are full of those who thought the hand was quicker than the eye. And the poorhouse is crammed with those who didn't have the guts to try. A man can lose his life or his fortune on one turn of the cards. I've taken their money. It's what I do. . . ."

JOKERS ARE WILD

CALEB PIRTLE III & FRANK Q. DOBBS

BOULEVARD BOOKS, NEW YORK

KENNY ROGERS' THE GAMBLER: JOKERS ARE WILD

A Boulevard Book / published by arrangement with
Kenny Rogers Productions

PRINTING HISTORY
Boulevard edition / March 1996

The Putnam Berkley World Wide Web site address is
http://www.berkley.com

ISBN: 1-57297-053-7

BOULEVARD
Boulevard Books are published by The Berkley Publishing Group,
200 Madison Avenue, New York, New York 10016.
BOULEVARD and its logo are trademarks
belonging to Berkley Publishing Corporation.

PRINTED IN THE UNITED STATES OF AMERICA

10 9 8 7 6 5 4 3 2 1

♠
♥ 1 ♦
♣

The first day is always the worst.

Old Preacher Blasingame wanted to kill me, and now he couldn't find me. If I were a betting man, which I am, I would have wagered my last queen-high dollar that he was out there on the dust-caked streets of Fort Smith, poking the barrel of his sawed-off shotgun into every unoccupied nook and cranny he could find. He'd be praying silently with an unrepentant heart that he would stumble across my face staring back at him from one of the whiskey-stained shadows in a back-alley brothel and send me, without any pomp and damn little circumstance, on a one-way journey to the promised land as only he could promise it.

My name is Brady Hawkes, and I have invested a lot more of my nights around the gaming tables of some muddy-water, stray-dog town saloon than I have in the back-row deacon's pew of a traveling salvation tent. The games are sometimes as crooked as the roads I ride, but crooked games don't bother me if they're the only games in town. The man with a cheating heart hasn't figured out that I know which cards are missing, which cards he's gonna play, how much money he can afford to lose, and how nervous he gets when he tries to draw to an inside straight. It's easier for a camel to go through the eye of a needle than it is for a cowboy with a hole in his pocket to get an inside straight in a crooked game. A man with sweaty hands can't palm an ace. The graveyards are full of those who thought the hand was quicker than the eye. And the poorhouse is crammed with those who didn't have the guts to try. A man can lose his life or his fortune on one turn of the cards. I've taken their money. It's what I do. Whether a man lives or he dies is entirely up to him, which is pretty much the same message the Reverend Blasingame kept on preaching night after night, obviously deciding there was no sane reason to change sermons until somebody had paid attention to the first one.

The preacher knew a lot about the Hereafter, especially the lake of burning fire that smoldered as red as the flecks of brimstone that swam in his eyes when he flailed away on the sawdust floor beneath his revival tent, battling the demons that came to torment him with the Good Book in one hand and a bottle of cheap communion wine in the other. He was as thin as broomstraw, with white, unruly hair. He was dressed in black, the long tails of his mourner's coat collecting dust as he chased the devil around the tent. The color of his clothes matched the circles beneath his eyes, which kept darting from sinner to sinner like a hungry turkey vulture. And his gnarled, bony fingers gripped the words of Matthew, Mark, Luke, and John as tightly as a drowning man holds on to the frayed end of a rope.

The preacher spent most of every evening trying to save a few lost souls from the pits of hell where men, and a few soiled doves from Miss Bonnie Claxton's bawdy house, would never die, and their thirsts would never be quenched, and they would wail and gnash their teeth throughout all eternity, which, I'm told, is even longer than it sometimes takes to get a good soaking rain in south Texas.

Some he saved. A few he condemned.

Hell, he swore, had been created by the hands of God Himself for fools like me. Vengeance is mine, saith the Lord, and the righteous Preacher Blasingame was never one to stand idly by and make the good Lord do all the work when a couple of well-placed shotgun shells could damn well do it for him.

I have never gone out of my way to invoke the wrath of a man of God. There's just not that many of them out here where the sinners outnumber the horned toads two to one. The preachers, be they holy or huckster, have their reason for being. They marry the beloved, comfort the bereaved, and bury the ones who depart this earth.

Preacher Blasingame would probably have never known my name or even seen my face if it had not been for the lovely countenance of Amy Sue. He was standing there beneath that ragged old tent, preaching hell so hot you could feel the heat in a stifling August wind. But her voice, when she sang "Amazing Grace," made me want to lie down beside still waters, which was the only Scripture I remembered from my Sunday School days back a long time ago in the Shenandoah Valley, back before I realized a king beat just about everything in your hand except a good bluff.

Amy Sue's voice was as clear as a bell on a cold night, and I spent three nights with Preacher Blasingame trying to wash me in the blood of the Lamb just so I could catch the first, third and last verse of "Amazing Grace," silently cursing because the man who wrote it hadn't had the decency to add a few more verses, which could have gotten me as close to heaven as I've been in a while. Amy Sue might have been twenty, or she could have been thirty. It was difficult to tell since she was draped by that long,

blue-checked gingham dress, cut so large that every curve of
her body was carefully hidden, if she had any curves at all.
It was one of those mysteries that every man wants to solve.
Her hair was auburn, but it looked black in the flickering
light of a coal-oil lamp that set beside her on the piano, a
scarred, battered refugee from some mining camp saloon
that had gone out of business about the same time the creek
ran dry of nuggets. When she sang about saving a wretch
like me, a wayward curl fell out from beneath a blue-
checked gingham bonnet, and, at that glorious moment, I
gave my soul to Jesus but my heart to Amy Sue.

The night was old and weary, probably approaching the
midnight hour, and the good Preacher Blasingame was still
on his knees, pounding the sawdust with both fists, wrestling with whichever devil happened to wander in out of the
darkness, praying with a few repentant old reprobates who
had been hauled to the revival by their sanctified, God-
fearing wives. Amy Sue, with the face of a porcelain doll,
had packed up her hymnal, shoved her stray curl back
beneath that blue-checked bonnet, and was stepping out of
the last faint glow of the coal-oil lamp when I decided that
no young lady in a strange land surrounded by strangers
should be permitted to go back to the hotel without being
told how her songs had touched more than the hearts of Fort
Smith. It was the least I could do.

I smiled my best Brady Hawkes smile, tipped my hat,
stepped out of the shadows, and tried to think of something
clever to say, which is usually fairly easy to do unless you
think about it too hard.

"Ma'am," was all I managed to say.

"Yes?"

"I don't go to church too often," I told her. "In fact, I've
been in a dozen towns in the last four months, and the only
crosses I saw in any of them were out in the cemetery. We

don't get a lot of preaching out here, and the men I run across figure God either has mercy on their souls or He doesn't. But I can guarantee you one thing. If you were singing every Sunday morning, I don't believe I'd ever miss a service."

I thought I saw the corners of her mouth turn up into a faint smile. "Why, thank you," she replied softly. "That's very gracious of you."

She had no idea how gracious I could really be.

She held out her hand and I took it. "My name's Amy Sue."

I nodded. "Hawkes. Brady Hawkes."

"You live here, Mr. Hawkes?"

"I generally live wherever I happen to be at the moment, and at the moment Fort Smith's got a stall for my horse, which means I can't think of a better place to be."

"You must be a very religious man," Amy Sue said.

"I know most of the Ten Commandments."

"And I'm sure you've never broken any of them."

"Only when they've tried to break me."

Her laughter was as musical as her songs had been. "I've seen you at the revival meeting for the last three nights running," she said. "The preacher's good. But I never thought he was that good."

"I know a good song when I hear one."

The laugh in her throat was repeated in her eyes, and Amy Sue turned up the wooden sidewalk that led toward the Chapman Hotel. The dark street was deserted, and the only sound, outside of the wailing and gnashing of teeth down beside the tear stains of Preacher Blasingame's altar, came from a honky-tonk piano, whose disjointed notes echoed through the swinging doors of the Crazy Water Saloon.

"How long are you planning on being in Fort Smith?" I asked.

"Till all the lost souls are saved," she replied matter-of-factly, "or until the collection plate starts coming back empty."

At least she was honest.

"How did you and the preacher do tonight?" I wanted to know, primarily because I just wanted to keep her talking.

"We got just over three dollars, if you count Archie Madison's IOU," she said. "And Brother Blasingame talked two cowboys and a Mexican sheepherder into confessing their sins, so I guess you could say we just about broke even."

"That's something I could never do."

"What's that?"

"Confess my sins. Not out loud and in public anyway. There are some things I'd just as soon the world didn't know."

"The Lord will forgive you."

"Maybe." I shrugged. "But the Lord's not on the grand jury."

Her green eyes were black in the moonlight, and I thought I saw them twinkle, but it was probably just my imagination.

She didn't speak, so I did, which was a better alternative than the silence. "It appears to me that all you and the preacher are making is about a dollar a soul, less if old Archie runs out on his IOU," I told her.

"Sometimes it's a dollar a week."

"The Lord buys his souls pretty cheap these days."

"He can afford to," Amy Sue said. "He doesn't keep them very long. About the only way most of the converted sinners ever get to heaven is if they're struck dead while being baptized in the river. By the time they dry off, they're back out drinking, smoking, cavorting, and gambling again. Preacher

Blasingame says that whiskey, tobacco, and women are the only trinity any of them will ever worship for long anyway."

"The Preacher Blasingame knows his cowboys."

"He should. He was the meanest man in Arizona till the Lord reached down and saved him."

"What turned him to preaching?"

"His picture on a wanted poster."

"Dead or alive?"

"I don't think anybody wanted him alive."

We walked along the wooden sidewalk past Harvey Smither's blacksmith shop and paused a minute or two for Amy Sue to look with envy at the red satin dress, trimmed with white lace, that hung in the far corner window of the widow Ferry's mercantile. The wind had died away, and the August heat wrapped itself around our shoulders like a wool blanket. Sweat glistened on Amy Sue's face, and that wayward curl of hers lay plastered against her wet forehead.

I tried to decide if the perfume she was wearing had the fragrance of lilacs or dried roses. A breeze swept across us, but it was as hot as the furnace behind Harvey Smither's anvil. A splintered moon shed its thunderhead, and a pale light touched her eyes. Her lips were moist when she smiled. It was definitely the fragrance of lilacs.

From the far end of the street, Judge Isaac Parker's prison wagon came rolling around the livery stable, its wheels disturbing the night with a clatter and a clank, headed toward the territorial jail, hauling its cargo of the cursed and the damned, men on the run who thought no one was tough enough or mean enough to chase them west of the Talimena Mountains, men too stubborn or too ornery to look over their shoulder until the final sound that woke them was the dull, metallic click of a hammer being cocked in their ear. It's too late to run and too useless to crawl, and their only hope is to die in their sleep before they come face to face

with the judge's hangman, a meeting that seldom lasts more
than a minute or two and ends with a crack louder than the
cocking of the hammer. They lay in the wagon, crumpled
lumps of humanity, asleep, drunk, or dead—sometimes it
was difficult to tell the difference—smelling like sour hog
swill.

The territorial marshal and his shotgun guards were
slumped with weary shoulders, staring ahead with numb
eyes and windburned faces. They had gone a thousand
crooked miles, straight into those same pits of hell the
Preacher Blasingame kept sermonizing about, and come
back out again. A good night's sleep, a hot cup of coffee, a
bath over at Miss Bonnie Claxton's, and they would be gone
again. Sunrise kept them in Fort Smith. The sundown
couldn't hold them.

A white-haired albino pressed his pale, angular face
against the bars as the wagon bounced past. His eyes were
those of a wild dog. His mouth frothed like a mad dog. An
Indian, his face scarred by the slash of a hunting knife,
threw back his head and howled like a coyote. A cowboy
groaned. A buffalo hunter lay in his own vomit, too tired,
too sick, too stubborn to move. The Indian tore at his chest
with broken fingernails. An old man with gray whiskers and
a soggy face grinned. His teeth were gone, his gums were
bloody, a piece of his ear was missing. The albino spat at
Amy Sue and promised to do things to her that would have
even shamed the girls who occupied the second-floor
boudoir of Miss Bonnie Claxton's place.

Amy Sue watched in hypnotic fascination until the old
wagon creaked around the corner of the Crazy Water
Saloon, pulled along by a pair of sore-shouldered horses
more dead than alive.

"My God!" she whispered.

"I don't think He's got much use for them," I said quietly.

"They are headed straight for hell."

"I'm not sure the devil wants them either."

"What's gonna become of them?"

I shrugged nonchalantly. "The lucky ones die," I said at last. "The rest rot beneath Judge Parker's jail. They've got a grave. They just don't have a coffin yet."

Amy Sue had turned ashen. She placed her hand in mine. It was cold, coiled into a knot. Her shoulders trembled. We could still hear the rattle, the clatter, of the prison wagon in the distance, but her head was bowed, and she chose not to look back. We crossed the street toward the hotel, and I felt her gently rub the palm of my hand. She looked up at me, and a touch of color had returned to her eyes.

"You're not a working man, are you, Mr. Hawkes?" she asked. "There are no blisters or calluses in your hand."

"There are those who say I work pretty hard at what I do."

"But not with your hands."

I smiled at her. "Always with my hands," I said.

I pulled a new deck of cards from my coat pocket and shuffled them slowly as we reached the front doorway of the Chapman Hotel.

"A gambling man," was all she said.

"Poor men gamble," I told her. "I merely play the odds and read the faces of those poor lost souls who sit at the same table with me."

"Then you and Brother Blasingame are in the same business."

"We both take their money, yes, ma'am. He just plays for higher stakes."

"And if you lose?"

"I just head on down the road to another town and another table of lost souls. I guess the preacher does pretty much the same thing."

Amy Sue stood in the glow of the gaslight that illuminated the hotel sign offering a bed, a bath, a barber, and a good meal for those discriminating gentlemen who were considerate enough to kick the mud and horse manure off their boots before entering the "Most Luxurious Hostelry and Eating Establishment West of the Mississippi River." The yellow light fell across her face, pale and young and innocent.

"We'll be leaving day after tomorrow," she said.

"Then I guess I'm running out of chances to hear you sing."

She reached up and touched my face with her fingertips, and they were as hot as a running iron at roundup time.

"I can sing for you tonight," she whispered. "Or I can do the best I can to save your soul."

At the moment, it was definitely lost and longing for a little salvation.

I looked at Amy Sue's face in the yellow light again, only inches from mine now. Pale and young, maybe. But not nearly as innocent as I had thought.

"What about the preacher?" I asked.

"His sermons take a long time. His praying takes even longer."

"I've broken a few of the commandments in my time," I told her, "but I've always managed to say away from coveting my neighbor's wife."

"Is that what you think?"

"You do belong to the preacher, don't you."

Amy Sue was indignant. "I'm certainly not his wife," she said.

She took my hand and led me across the hotel lobby toward the carpeted stairway. The desk clerk was asleep. So was the long-eared dog that lay at his feet. Our footsteps were the only sounds in the place. The clock with gold numbers and ebony hands, hanging above the fireplace, read twelve-seventeen. And Amy Sue tightened her grip on my hand as we reached the landing on the second floor.

Her room was dim and sweltering, splintered by a ray of moonlight that spilled through the window overlooking the streets of Fort Smith. She removed her bonnet and tossed it onto the bed behind her. The curls fell softly down around her oval face where they belonged. And a thin line of perspiration was beginning to glisten upon her forehead. Her eyes were moist, larger than I realized.

She had unloosened the top button of her long gingham dress.

I was fumbling with the second button, and the breeze brushed her hair against my face, when the door came suddenly crashing open, and I saw the face of Beelzebub himself reflected in the smoldering brimstone eyes of Preacher Blasingame. His was the growl of a mad dog, low and mean, and somewhere between the revival tent and room 28 of the Chapman Hotel, he had traded his trusty old Bible for a trusty old double-barreled shotgun.

I had heard him preach about damnation.

Now I knew what the hell he had been talking about.

Amy Sue screamed, which meant I didn't have to. "Daddy," she yelled.

Holy Mother of God.

Given the choice between an irate father and the wrath of God, I'd just as soon take my chances with my Maker. He forgives.

At least that's what the Preacher Blasingame said. And at the time he had not had any reason to lie to me.

"You son of a bitch," he growled, which I did not recall as being scriptural at all, and the preacher's long white hair whirled around a gaunt, twisted face that belonged to the grim reaper.

The first blast from the shotgun shattered the mirror

beside my head. The flash of fire leapt from the end of the
barrel like lightning trying to strike. Broken shards of glass
tore at my face, and my reflection in the mirror fell in small,
misshapen pieces around my feet. Amy Sue fell across the
bed crying, and I don't think her tears had anything at all to
do with my particular plight at the moment.

There was no reason for me to hang around long enough
to find out what the second blast would shatter. The window
was open, so I took the easy way out, scrambling down the
wooden fire escape while the Preacher Blasingame cut loose
again, hitting only the red velvet drapes that fluttered in
the darkness where I had been and had no yearning to ever
be again.

Thunder had never been so ominous.

Or close.

The preacher's ghostly face, as white as his hair, was at
the window, snarling like a judge on Judgment Day. He
dropped one shell. It bounced on the sidewalk behind me.
He was on the fire escape by the time he had jammed
another one into the chamber.

I've never been a man to run.

But then, I've never thrown away good money on bad
cards either, especially not when I know the man sitting
across from me has a loaded hand.

The preacher's was definitely loaded.

You don't really have time to think in moments like this.
You just react and try to make sense of what you've done
later. One man with a shotgun was doing his dead level best
to end what he considered a pretty worthless life. It seemed
unreasonable to me that another man, carrying a shotgun
just as lethal, an honest, judicial sort who wasn't holding
any particular grudges, might be able to keep me alive long
enough to witness another sunrise, provided the sun wanted
to get up early the next morning.

Judge Parker's territorial marshal was dragging his grizzled cargo out of the wagon, clamping leg irons around their ankles and shoving them through a narrow brick doorway that led into the whitewashed walls of the prison yard. They were yawning and cursing softly, wiping sleep from their eyes and drool from their mouths, men who had too many notches on their revolvers and too much blood on their hands, hard men who had taken the only lives they had and wasted them, bitter men without faces or names, and none of them seemed to mind at all when I stepped in line behind them.

Preacher Blasingame was stomping down the street toward me, a skeletal shadow with white hair and crooked legs. The light of the moon cast a dull glint off the barrel of the shotgun. Both hammers were cocked.

Our eyes locked.

And he grinned. I could almost hear him cackling, if he was making any sound at all. His knuckles were white from gripping the shotgun so tightly, and his face was as thin, as lethal as a double-edged ax.

Vengeance is mine.

The shotgun was leveled at my belly. We were separated only by the narrow width of a dirt alley behind the blacksmith shop.

The territorial marshal grabbed my shoulder and shoved me toward the prison yard. I stumbled and fell against the wall while someone ripped the boot off my right foot, and I felt the leg irons behind clamped hard on my ankle, tight and heavy, digging into the flesh, and my leg was suddenly slippery, and I didn't know whether it was from sweat or blood. The pain did not last as long as the confusion.

"How come this sumbitch ain't barefooted like the rest of 'em?" the marshal snapped. "Nobody gets this far wearin' boots."

"Must've been dark when we picked him up." The voice was tired and raspy.

"It ain't never that dark. You can tell if a man's barefooted with your damned eyes shut. Nobody runs on J. C. Flagg, and nobody sure as hell don't run in this godforsaken prickly-pear country barefoot."

I turned and faced him for the first time. "I don't belong here," I said.

"Nobody does." He was tired and irritable and in no mood to talk. The brim on his hat hung low over his eyes, which were sunk back in his head as though trying to get as far away from the misery around him as possible. His granite face was square and tough as boot leather, over-grown by three days of whiskers that probably wouldn't see a razor until the week ended, unless, of course, Miss Bonnie Claxton had mercy on him before morning.

"I'm afraid there's been a mistake," I said.

"The only mistake I make is when I shoot 'em instead of haulin' 'em back," the marshal said. "I don't get paid for the ones I don't haul back."

"You didn't haul me back."

"Don't make no difference. I'll get paid for it anyway."

"I'd like to see the judge."

"You'll get your chance."

"When's that?"

"When he's ready to hang you."

The marshal dragged me into the prison yard, and all I could hear was the loud, cackling laugh of Preacher Blasingame as they slammed the big wooden gate shut behind me. The night was so black even the moon was hiding its face behind a thunderhead, and the preacher's eyes burned through the darkness like a pair of coals in the blacksmith's forge. He fired his final blast into the air, and

I swear the ground shook beneath my feet. The marshal did not even bother to look around.

The cell was even smaller than Amy Sue's hotel room and not nearly as promising. It was crowded, even though there were only three of us, if you count the rat, and he took up as much space as I did. Fraley was the only company I had. He did not have a first name, or if he did, he said he had forgotten it. He must have been in his sixties, or maybe he had just led a hard life and aged in a hurry. The hair on the top of his head was almost all gone, and his round, jolly face supported a gray beard that he did not bother to comb anymore. His flannel shirt was faded white, and a pair of stretched suspenders did the best they could to hold up his khaki trousers over a round, pudgy body that looked swollen.

The straw beneath our feet was wet and rotting, the window above my bunk had been boarded up to make sure we were never disturbed by anything resembling fresh air, and the heat was oppressive. It crawled down your throat and tried to squeeze it shut. I could barely breathe. The stench was so bad I wouldn't have breathed at all if the alternative had not been so damn depressing.

The old man kept grinning.

And whistling, and he never whistled the same tune twice, and he never whistled any tune I had ever heard before.

"It ain't so bad," he said. "It don't rain on you. Nobody wakes you up early or makes you do any work around here. And they bring you three meals a day, and it don't cost you nothin'."

"What kind of meals?"

"Stew mostly. Sometimes it's got potatoes in it. Sometimes it don't."

"What about meat?"

"Sure. You can have meat anytime you want it." He winked and stroked his gray beard. "Of course, you have to kill the rat first," he said.

The first day is always the worst.

I just didn't know if it would end, and I'm not sure it ever did.

♠

♥ 2 ♦

♣

Old Fraley had seen the best of them and the worst of them, primarily the worst of them, come and go into the dark, dank, godforsaken bowels of Fort Smith, down where the damp air was thick with the stench of sweat and urine and rotting food, and men prayed to die, if death was the only escape they had, and struggled to hang on to every breath of life as though it might be their last.

"They drag most of 'em in kickin' and screamin'," he told me as we wasted the rest of the night, or maybe it was morning, or maybe the sun just figured it no longer had any reason to shine down into the innards of an Arkansas hellhole. "They don't make so much noise when they leave."

He grinned and tossed a crumb from the green mold of an old chunk of cornbread toward the rat who kept watching me with curious little beady eyes as though he was jealous of every inch of space I'd stolen from him and every meal I was bound to eat when I got hungry, if I ever got hungry, and a man's stomach seldom growls too loudly until his nose comes to terms with the sweet, sickly odor of decaying humanity.

I slumped down on a mattress that had been wadded up
and shoved against the wall out of old Fraley's way. Lumps
of wet, mildewed straw were clotted together with the
horsehair, and they offered little relief from the clammy
stones embedded in the foot-worn bedrock floor. At times
like these, a man clings to only two thoughts. Part of him is
searching for a way out, and the rest of him knows there is
no way out, and I lay there wondering if life and its
consequences would have been easier to take had Preacher
Blasingame been a better shot.

Old Fraley opened his good eye wider, staring hard at me,
probably trying to figure out if I was as harmless as I looked
or if looks might be deceiving, which they usually are. The
other eye merely darted around the cell, too nervous to light
anywhere for any length of time.

"You kill anybody?" he wanted to know.

"Not that anybody's aware of."

"What they got you in for?"

"Being in the wrong place at obviously the wrong time."

"Just what in Hades were you doin' at the wrong place
when it'd been a damn sight smarter to be someplace else?"

"Tryin' to keep myself from getting killed."

"Up till now you've been real lucky, but a man's luck
tends to change when he gets thrown into the only place left
on earth that preachers forget to pray about and the devil's
outnumbered." Old Fraley spoke with a drawl that reminded
me of Georgia, his voice devoid of any emotion.

"We've all got hell to pay," I told him. "Sometimes it just
costs a little more."

"A redheaded woman got me in this mess," the old man
said. "God shouldn't have made redheaded women. All of
'em's trouble, every dadblamed one of 'em."

"You run out on one?"

"I tried, but dadgummit, I didn't run far enough or fast enough."

"Hell hath no fury like a scorned woman, I'm told."

"Especially not a redheaded woman." He sighed in a forlorn sort of way. "I sure loved that woman," he said. "And she loved ever' man in town. And I loved ever' redheaded woman, an' she got mad, an' I got mad, an' now she owns her own little piece of Arkansas, an' I'm in here, an' I don't even know what day it is."

"Friday."

"Any particular month?"

"June or July. I don't recall. It just gets hot in these parts, and when the weather cools down a little I know it's not summer anymore."

"In here, it don't ever change." Old Fraley shrugged. "You'll get used to it," he said softly. "You won't like it, but after a while it won't matter."

"Don't worry about me," I said, forcing a grin. "I'm just passing through."

"You ain't plannin' on leavin' very soon are you?" he asked.

"As soon as the judge finds out there's been a mistake."

I stood and tried to stretch in the narrow confines of the eight-by-ten-foot space that I had inherited from the old man. The rat backed away cautiously between the shelter and comfort of old Fraley's feet. He was looking at me pretty much the same way I was looking at him, with loathing and contempt.

"I'll be out of here by this time tomorrow," I said, wondering if some semblance of light was actually beginning to penetrate the gloom, or if my eyes were merely growing accustomed to the darkness.

Old Fraley shuddered, and his voice was no louder than

a whisper. "There ain't but one way out of this place," he said at last.

"Which way's that?"

"In a pine box." He paused, and there was a dry rattle in his throat. "There ain't but one thing worse than a pine box," he said.

"What's that?"

"A redheaded woman, an' you can't remember her name."

The cell seemed darker than it had before, and the rat sank back into the shadows, and old Fraley began whistling again. It was either a dirge or a lullaby, and I felt as misplaced, as misput, as lonesome as a stray who found out his best friend had died, then realized he hadn't had any friends anyway. Not now. Maybe not ever.

The name of Judge Isaac Parker had been cursed and damned, condemned and blasphemed at every gaming hall that huddled throughout the far reaches of the Ozarks, particularly over in the Indian Territory where men holed up in hollows that the maps forgot to mark and sometimes wound up with rope burns around their neck just thinking about him.

Parker was an enigma all right. He should have been a preacher, some whispered. Judge Isaac Parker didn't save men's souls, perhaps. And he couldn't forgive them of the dastardly deeds they had done in the past. But he sure knew how to send them packing across the River Jordan before they were able to do anything worse than they had already done.

The only man overworked in Fort Smith was the hangman. He seldom got a night off and seldom wanted one.

President Ulysses S. Grant had shipped Parker out beyond the Arkansas River to tame lawless land where a good killing was easier to come by than a good poker game.

Grant had looked at Judge Parker with those stern eyes of his and said, "Clean up that cesspool, and I don't give a damn how you do it, as long as it's legal."

Judge Parker used the gallows.

"I've never killed a man in my life," the judge liked to say, and when he said it you knew he believed it. "The outlaws, the murderers, the thieves, the renegades, the rapists, the dregs of society, they all kill themselves. I simply provide the rope."

A day passed. Or maybe it was an hour.

I wasn't so sure anymore. Old Fraley had either run out of tunes to whistle, or his lips were chapped and his mouth was dry.

A key rattled in the lock, and the big wooden door creaked open. A thick-shouldered, potbellied deputy filled the doorway, a shotgun cradled in his arms. His black eyes shifted from old Fraley to me, and his face was as grim as smallpox.

Old Fraley crept back against the wall and pulled the shadows in around him. His good eye never left the deputy. Neither did his bad one. There was no sound from the shadows. Old Fraley was afraid to breathe.

Methuselah the rat disappeared into the wet straw.

"Hawkes," the deputy said. "Brady Hawkes."

I stood to face him, straightening my vest as old Fraley caught his breath again with a whimper. The deputy didn't blink, and his finger never left the trigger of his long-barreled shotgun. Both were worn from use, the finger as well as the shotgun.

"The judge wants to see you," he said in a flat, nasal voice.

"I thought he'd forgotten me."

"The judge don't forget nobody till they put a stone over his grave, then he don't have to."

He waved me out into a narrow hallway, and I heard old Fraley whisper, "May God have mercy on your soul."

The door slammed shut before I could tell him good-bye, and we walked toward the flickering light of a miner's lamp that was doing its best to cut through the heavy darkness at the far end of the hall. It wasn't enough.

The courtroom was streaked with sunshine. It was day after all, and the light hurt my eyes, and I shielded my face from sun I had wondered if I would ever see again. I had no idea what time it was. The old clock was broken; it hadn't chimed for anyone in years. A dozen tabernacle pews were wedged into the courtroom, scarred and covered in dust and no doubt reserved for the families of men whose families had lost touch with them years ago, men who measured time in miles, never years, mostly the miles that carried them from home. It was just as well. The dreams mothers have for their sons never have anything to do with Judge Parker's court or his rope.

The unmistakable figure of Judge Isaac Parker loomed above the bench. He was a big man, at least six feet tall, maybe taller, with his broad shoulders straining against a black suit that too many washings had faded gray. His face was chiseled granite, virtually hidden behind a white mustache and well-manicured goatee. He stared at the prisoner with piercing blue eyes, his meaty hands clasped together upon an aging Bible where such unnecessary judicial words as love, mercy, and forgiveness had been scratched out, or so the rumors went.

The prisoner's hands and feet were heavily manacled. A month's growth of unkempt whiskers patched his baby face, and his shoulders were trembling. A deputy grasped his arms tightly to keep the prisoner's feet steady.

Judge Parker spoke softly, but his words had the impact of low, rumbling thunder before a summer storm. "The sword of human justice is about to fall upon your head, Billy Bascomb."

The prisoner squared his shoulders.

"You have taken a human life," the judge continued. "You have sent a soul unprepared to its Maker. You have set at defiance God's law."

Billy Bascomb's breaths were coming in short, uneasy bursts.

"Your fate is inevitable," said Parker. "Let me, therefore, beg of you to fly to your Maker for that mercy and that pardon which you cannot expect for mortals and endeavor to seize upon the salvation of His cross."

The prisoner's hands had turned white to match the color of his face.

"Farewell forever until the court and you and all here today shall meet together in the general resurrection."

Billy Bascomb, not quite a man but about to die like one, kept twisting his neck as the deputy dragged him from the courtroom. Already his throat was tightening, and he was beginning to choke and he had not yet felt the stinging touch of a well-oiled rope.

The judge remained silent, his face as hard as granite, staring intently after Billy Bascomb until the boy had been shoved roughly past a metal door that, when shut, prevented the sounds of any weeping, wailing, or gnashing of teeth to interrupt or interfere with Judge Isaac Parker's courtroom.

The courtroom was empty, save for the young man with hard, unflinching eyes who sat between two guards at a table beside the bench and two elderly little ladies who huddled close together on the front row, nervously twisting their lace handkerchiefs with wrinkled hands, afraid the judge was going to hang every poor soul who was hauled in front of him and afraid he might not. Their cheeks were painted a shade too red, and the consequences of age had begun to wither them. One wore a dress with faded roses, and the other was dressed in subdued white that, in an earlier time, may have even been a pale yellow.

The lady in roses dabbed at what she hoped was a tear in her eyes and whispered in a quavering voice, "He's just a boy."

Subdued white shook her head. "Not anymore. The judge growed him up today."

"He's too young to hang."

"He wasn't too young to pull the trigger."

"He could be your son, you know."

Subdued white turned haughtily away. "I don't see how," she snapped under her breath. "I was never married nor did I want to be."

Judge Isaac Parker shifted his weight and slumped heavily against the woven cane of his high-backed chair. He motioned for the young man with hard, unflinching eyes to be brought before him. The prisoner stood gun-barrel straight, and he walked forward with the grace of a cat. His features were dark and finely molded, and his drooping black mustache made him appear older than he really was. His shirt was white and trimmed with lace, his black trousers worn slick by too many years in the saddle. His arms hung loosely at his side like those of a hired gunfighter, and his hands were soft, unaccustomed to common labor. He could have been a schoolteacher, a scholarly and gentle man, but his eyes betrayed him. The eyes always do.

The judge and the young man stared across the bench that separated them for several minutes, sizing each other up, a duel of wills that both were determined to fight but neither would win, their faces grim, their gaze unbroken. I had seen the looks a thousand times before, strangers around a gaming table trying to decide who's lying and who's bluffing and who just ran up on a streak of bad luck.

Judge Parker spoke at last. "It says here, Mr. Earp, that you were apprehended riding a brown horse with three white feet and the Diamond H brand," he said, ignoring the pretense of any formality.

"It says right."

"It also says the horse didn't belong to you."

"I bought it."

Judge Parker leaned forward and lowered his voice. "Did the man who owned the horse know you had bought it?"

"He would have as soon as I paid him for it."

"How much was the horse gonna cost you?"

"We never talked money."

"You and Mr. Harley Hamilton hadn't talked at all, had you Mr. Earp?"

"I met him once."

"You talk horses?"

"We talked poker."

"There's not much to say about poker."

"There is when he's got three queens, and I have a pair of queens, and that's one queen too many in anybody's deck, and he was dealin' the cards."

"Was Mr. Hamilton crooked, or careless?"

"They generally bury one as deep as they do the other."

Judge Parker glanced through the legal papers once more and scratched his chin. "Where were you apprehended, sir?"

"About six miles west of Crandall's Crossing."

"On the Red River?"

"Near as I could tell."

"Mr. Earp, there's one basic question that needs to be answered, and it has a great deal to do with the disposition of this case," Judge Parker said, choosing his words carefully. "If you bought the horse from Harley Hamilton, and you were committed to pay him for the horse as you told the court you were going to do, then why in the good Lord's name were you runnin' hell-bent toward Texas?"

"I wasn't ridin' to Texas at the time."

"Then where were you headed?"

"Nowhere. I was asleep at the time." The young man called Earp grinned sardonically. "If I had been in the saddle, I'd a' been gone, and your gunslingers wouldn't have known where to look because there wouldn't have been anybody to find."

"Fast horse?"

"I've had horses run faster, but not many of 'em."

Judge Parker tossed the legal papers into a crumpled heap on top of the desk, leaning back and watching a spider spin her web on the ceiling above him. "You know what I think, Mr. Earp?" he said in a voice so low I had to lean forward to hear him. "I think you stole Harley Hamilton's horse either because you were on foot or still mad because he beat you playin' cards, and you figured the horse was probably worth what you lost, and maybe it was. I think you're a thief, Mr. Earp."

The young man's jaw tightened, but his expression never changed. There was a slight hint of anger in his eyes, but he had never been introduced to fear and probably wouldn't have recognized it if fear walked into the room and sat down beside him.

"You're entitled to an opinion, Judge."

"Fortunately, or unfortunately, son, mine is the only opinion that counts in here." Judge Parker glanced out the window and toward the white plank gallows that rose up in the prison courtyard. They were long and narrow, crudely fashioned, just wide enough to send a half dozen men to the grave at the same time. And six freshly oiled ropes dangled above the trapdoors, swinging lazily in the stiff Arkansas breeze. An old man in a brown derby hat was on his knees, nailing one of the thirteen steps back in place.

Judge Parker waited until the final nail had been hammered into place, then turned again to the young prisoner whose face was as stoic as stone. "Mr. Earp," he said, "you're damn lucky you didn't reach Texas soil. In Texas, they hang you for stealing a man's horse. Sometimes they hang you if you even look at a man's horse the wrong way. I reserve my gallows for those who have taken someone's life and owe a life, and life, even in Arkansas, is worth more than a horse."

He paused long enough to unbutton his coat and begin fanning himself with a well-worn funeral-home fan that had been lying on the desk, doing what he could to chase away an unforgiving summer heat. "I'm not going to hang you, Mr. Earp," the judge continued, "unless, of course, the hangman's having a real slow day, and the sun stays up longer than normal, and we've got time to do unto thieves what ought to be done to them. No, Mr. Earp, I'm going to fine you two hundred dollars for stealing Harley Hamilton's horse—no, make that two hundred and fifty dollars because you said he was a real fast horse—and another two hundred and fifty dollars for court costs, and I am keeping you in jail where I can keep an eye on you until you can pay that five-hundred-dollar fine. It's not that I believe you'll run away if I let you out on bail, Mr. Earp, it's just my way of making sure you don't."

The young man with hard, unflinching eyes frowned for the first time. "Where in hell do you expect me to get five hundred dollars?" he asked.

Judge Parker shrugged. "I don't even know where you got the horse," he said.

The gavel sounded like a pistol shot when it hit the desk.

The lady in roses watched the prisoner march gracefully

toward the metal door on bare feet. She shed no tear for thieves, only for the condemned. Her friend in subdued white pinched her lips together in obvious distaste for the judge's decision. The thought of death horrified them. The thought of not hearing a death sentence was even worse.

Judge Parker turned his attention to me. I was the only one left in the courtroom with an armed guard. I stood before he called my name and began walking toward the bench. The handcuffs had been clamped so tightly around my wrists that my fingers had turned white and lost their feeling.

"Mr. Brady Hawkes," he said slowly. "I've got you in my jail and I don't know why you're here, and that troubles me a great deal."

"It's a simple misunderstanding, Your Honor."

He nodded. "Life's full of misunderstandings," he said. "So is my jail. One man shoots another. It's a misunderstanding. One man steals another's horse. It's a misunderstanding. A man beats his wife. It's a misunderstanding. Perhaps you can make me understand why you, above all others, have been so damn misunderstood."

The cloud must have passed on by, which is what I should have done when I rode into Fort Smith. A thread of sunlight inched its way back past the window behind Judge Parker's head and fell awkwardly across his shoulder.

I felt the numbness leave my fingers and begin crawling up my arms as I answered him. "A preacher thought I'd be better off in hell," I said.

"That's the opinion of most preachers, I'd say."

"This one wanted to send me there personally, and he loaded up both barrels of a shotgun to get the job done. He didn't ask me if I wanted to take the trip, and if he had, I'd a' told him I'd just as soon head on up north where the climate's not so warm."

"You messing with his wife, Mr. Hawkes?"

I sighed. "His daughter, Your Honor."

The lady in roses gasped and leaned forward to make sure she caught every sordid word, praying silently under her breath that no one would leave any sordid words out of my plight. Subdued white began tapping her shoe angrily on the floor. She'd never had a daughter, or so she said, but, more than likely, once upon a time she'd been one. And I couldn't tell if she was mad because I did or didn't wind up with the daughter.

A slight grin played at the corners of Judge Parker's mouth. "Mr. Hawkes," he said, "I'm not sure that's a capital crime."

"It is if the shotgun's leveled at your belly, Your Honor."

I followed his gaze toward the ceiling where the spider was lying in wait, dangling from his web, watching a fly crawl toward a trap from which there would be no escape, and I wanted to yell for the fly to get the hell out of there. But nobody warned me, and I was as foolish as the fly, so I turned back toward the judge, not wanting to see that terrible moment when it occurred. And the spider kept waiting, and the fly kept crawling. . . .

Judge Parker broke the stilted silence. "So why is it that you wound up in my jail instead of hell, if there's any difference?" he asked.

"I could have stood there in the streets of Fort Smith and be shot, or fall in line with the prisoners your marshal hauled in last night, and, for some reason that escapes me now, I thought your man with a shotgun looked somewhat more friendlier than the preacher man did."

"That's not a misunderstanding, Mr. Hawkes."

"No?"

"That's a mistake."

"That's what I tried to tell the marshal."

"And he didn't listen."

"He didn't give a damn."

"He shouldn't. That wasn't his mistake, Mr. Hawkes. It was yours." The judge was smiling, but his eyes weren't. They could chill a hot room, and they did. He stood for a moment and walked to the nearest window, opening it wider and letting a gentle breeze blow against his face. It offered little relief, and the sunlight ran away behind a cloud and hid once more.

"What's your profession, Mr. Hawkes?"

"I'm a gambling man."

"With women or cards?"

I shrugged. "I've had a good deal more luck with one than the other," I answered.

"You deal a crooked game?" the judge wanted to know.

"The games are never crooked, only those who bet money they can't lose on cards that can't win and haven't figured out the difference."

The judge opened his desk drawer and pulled out a cigar, chewing hard on one end without bothering to light the other. "How long have you been in Fort Smith, Mr. Hawkes?" he asked.

"Five days, not counting today, since I'm not quite sure what today is."

"Where were you, say, seven days ago?"

"Fort Worth, Texas."

"What caused you to leave Fort Worth, Texas?"

"A high-stakes poker game."

"You lose, Mr. Hawkes?"

"I'm afraid the man who bet the last dollar he had on the one-eyed jack he pulled out of his sleeve lost, Your Honor."

"Was that the first time he cheated you?"

"It was the first time he got caught."

"You kill him?"

"No, sir. But I politely stepped out of the way of the man who did."

"I believe I would have shot him, Mr. Hawkes."

"I'm a card player, Your Honor, not a gunman."

I glanced back toward the ceiling, and the fly was nowhere to be seen. The web was empty. Even the spider had left.

"What brought you to Fort Smith?" the judge wanted to know.

"A high-stakes poker game."

"You win, Mr. Hawkes?"

"Maybe. I haven't seen the last card yet."

"Maybe you wagered all you had on the preacher's daughter and came up with a losing hand."

"We all pick our games. Sometimes we don't pick so wisely."

Judge Parker's face reddened. I don't think he particularly liked what I said or the way I said it. "For the record, let me get this straight now, Mr. Hawkes," he drawled. "You expect me to believe that a preacher of God chased you through the streets of Fort Smith last night, doing his dead level best to blow your head off with a double-barreled shotgun, and you got away from him by walking into this prison along with the outlaws, renegades, and cutthroats that Marshal Thompson dragged out of the hills and gullies and blackjack forests of the Indian Territory, and you're standing before me this morning as an innocent man who's the victim of some misunderstanding?"

"That pretty well describes it as near as I can remember it, Your Honor."

"Marshal J. C. Thompson never thrown anybody in this jail who didn't deserve to be here. But I'll vouch my good name and reputation that you're guilty of something. I just don't know what it is yet." Judge Parker leaned toward me and propped himself up on the bench with his elbows. "You know what I wish?" he asked, twisting the end of his mustache, biting off the end of his cigar and spitting in on the floor beside him.

"What's that?"

"I wish the preacher had shot you, then I wouldn't have you in my jail, wondering why you're in here and if you're lying and if I ought to let you out or stick you so far back in one of those cells on the back side of this place that the sunshine couldn't reach you if you opened the window. And I can make damn sure you don't have a window."

The judge dismissed me with the wave of his hand and turned his face back toward the window.

"What do you want me to do with him?" the deputy asked.

"Hold Mr. Hawkes over for trial, unless, of course, he's got two hundred dollars to pay his bail."

"What's the two hundred dollars for?" I demanded.

"Room and board, if nothing else." The judge raised his voice angrily as the deputy shoved me toward the metal room that led back into those damnable pits of purgatory. "Get him out of here, and don't let him out of your sight, and if he kills old Fraley's rat, I'm gonna hang the son of the bitch for murder."

The lady in roses laughed out loud, and I was shoved into a hallway where laughter was a stranger, and I wished I could hear her one more time, even if she was laughing at me. The metal door sounded like a shotgun blast when it slammed shut, and I thought for a moment I was dead, then realized I wasn't that fortunate.

♠

♥ 3 ♦

♣

The cell had grown much smaller by the time I retuned.

Old Fraley had not moved from his cot. he was simply sitting there, a gleam in his good eye, a glaze over his bad one, maybe dreaming about a redheaded woman, maybe not, watching to see what I might do, if I did anything at all. His face was a gray mask in the dim light that had found its way into the cell, and, like the rest of us, had not found a way back out. It was difficult to tell if old Fraley was smiling, or if his face, in some bar fight long ago, had been permanently hammered into a scar that merely resembled a crooked grin.

Methuselah, the rat, had scampered back beneath the old man's feet for safety. His eyes were red dots in the darkness, his yellowed teeth clenched, wary and uncertain and frightened. The rat had the same feelings that possessed us all at a time like this.

Rats don't lie.

A slight tremble crawled down my back.

It may have been fear, maybe anger. It didn't matter. It was there, and then it was gone, and old Fraley chuckled, or maybe he coughed.

"Nobody didn't think you was comin' back," he said. "When the judge takes 'em out of here, don't many of 'em come back, an' them that do are already dead an' just ain't figured it out yet."

This time there was no mistake. It was a laugh, hard and cynical.

"Then again, it could be you're already dead," old Fraley said, "an' I just ain't figured it out yet."

The laugh was louder. Even the rat scurried out of sight.

The tall, lanky young horse thief with hard, unflinching eyes lay sprawled across a mattress that, until a couple of hours ago, had been worn with wrinkles to match those in my own aching back. He frowned when he looked up, and bristled with a bad case of indignation. I've seen prairie dogs look kinder upon rattlesnakes that had burrowed into their holes. The cell was dark and brooding, and the young horse thief that the honorable Judge Parker had addressed as Mr. Earp spit out the straw he was chewing. An uncertain silence clouded the distance between us.

"I hope you aren't making any plans to sleep on this mattress tonight," he drawled, clenching his fist as he slowly rose to his feet.

I tried to read his eyes, but the shadows that swarmed the cell kept getting in the way. "It was mine when I walked out of here," I replied. "I kind of figured it would still be mine when I got back."

His eyes turned cold, and he folded his arms in defiance.

Old Fraley was on his hands and knees, his eyes swinging from me to the horse thief, then back to me again. "The mattress don't belong to nobody but the horse," he said with a cackle. "It's crammed plumb full of his hair anyways. I guess by all rights the dadgummed old horse ought to get it back."

"He can have it as far as I'm concerned," I said.

"Can't." Old Fraley's laughter was raised an octave, and his voice cracked. "We ate the horse."

"Where I come from," the horse thief said slowly, "a man stakes out his territory, and he owns what he homesteads, and it's his, good and legal, and, mister, where I'm standin' is what I own in this cell."

I did my best to smile and failed miserably. "What a man gets is his as long as he can keep it," I said.

His stern, bitter gaze met mine, and I waited for him to blink.

Men are born with a certain bravado. Life may scare the hell out of them. But they are bound and determined to face a showdown—sometimes against a loaded gun, a stacked deck, an angry husband, a redheaded woman, whatever— with grace and stoicism, even though the hammer is cocked and a bullet to their gut is only a hair trigger away. I've sat at poker tables and watched them wager their last flake of gold on the turn of a card, praying rather than gambling that Dame Fortune has not turned her back on them, knowing they have one shot to survive, and it's a long shot, doing their damnedest to hide, or at least mask, the doubt and disappointment that creeps into their eyes.

The losers blink.

The seconds passed. They became minutes.

All I could hear was the calm, even rhythm of his breathing. The lace on his white shirt had been soiled. His black mustache was crooked, his shoulders square and broader than they had looked in the courtroom. Old Fraley coughed, not daring to move. Methuselah was nowhere to be seen.

The horse thief's eyes had hardened into molten balls. His arms hung loosely at his side, and the shadows gave his face a ragged edge.

Nobody blinked.

The stillness was oppressive, as stifling as the heat. If a man took a deep breath, he could have choked on it.

Old Fraley began to whistle again, an old tune, a sad tune, a tune as frayed as our nerves. The horse thief glanced toward the old man for just a moment, but moments are what gets a man killed or keeps him alive.

I hit him.

The best time to hit a man is when he least expects it, and the best way to hit him is with the metal barrel of a long-barreled rifle, or maybe a hoe handle that's been seasoned by the sun. But since I didn't have a rifle and the cell didn't have any hoe handles lying around loose, I hit him with my fist.

His head jerked back, and a sharp pain bolted up my arm, lodging in my elbow. The bullet beneath my collarbone hadn't hurt nearly as bad. He grunted and slammed heavily against the back wall of the cell. I waited for his legs to go limp, and when they didn't I hit him again and wondered if the blow pained him as much as it did me.

He slumped to one knee, and blood was running freely from the crack in his lip. He wiped it away with the back of his sleeve, steadying himself with both hands on the floor until the dense smoke in his eyes turned to fire.

And he grinned, which was not what I had hoped he would do. I've been around a long time and witnessed down-and-dirty, stomp-'em-in-the-face-till-they-can't-get-up street brawls from Galveston to Fort Worth to Denver to Dodge City, and I've never known a man to grin when he was whipped.

He charged, bellowing like a wild Mexican bull, and I slammed him in the face with the old horsehair mattress, popping him again and again as though it were a poor man's bullhide whip, and he fell backward, choking on the dust and blood, the spittle and urine, the vomit and dried whiskey stains, the lumps of rotting straw and rat dung that had been shoved against his face, then up his nose.

His scream was one of rage. And frustration. He pawed at his eyes, blinded by the dust, as upset as a camp-meeting preacher with the devil perched in his outhouse. He gagged and spit dried blood, not all of it his.

I hit him again with the only good fist I had left, and we both fell to the wet, rotting straw, eyeball to eyeball, separated only by the width of the horsehair mattress.

His stare was a rifle shot. But still he hadn't blinked.

"You're the craziest son of a bitch I've ever seen," he said.

"I've been in places where that's the nicest thing any-body's said to me," I replied.

"Nobody in his right mind would fight over a filthy, stinking mattress."

"I didn't want the damned old mattress," I spit out. "I just didn't want anybody telling me I couldn't have it."

The horse thief started to grin, then thought better of it and laughed out loud. He picked up the mattress, torn at the seams with the last of the twisted, knotted horsehair spilling out in flea-infested clumps onto the damp, decaying floor between us. "It ain't much, is it?" he said.

"I tried to sleep on it last night," I told him, "and it damn near made a cripple out of me."

The horse thief sat back and leaned against the wall of the cell. Blood had dried on his chin. His lower lip was swelling, but the anger had packed up and left his eyes. "When you walked in here, you didn't look like a fightin' man to me," he said.

"Nobody looks like a fightin' man when he's standing there with bare feet, tired and sleepy and as mad as a rained-on rooster, a sore back, an aching head, and his legs itching from being gnawed on by a gaggle of strange little critters he can damn well feel but can't see."

"A smart man would have wagered good money on you backin' down," the horse thief said, his bruised lips barely moving. "I figured you to be just a little too refined, too intelligent, to do something stupid like fighting."

"I choose my fights very carefully."

"When you think you can win?"

"When I've got no other choice." I shrugged wearily. "I'm a gambling man, sir, and I'm afraid that all I know how to do is simply play the cards that are dealt me. And when my life's at stake I do what I never do when I'm merely dealing cards for money."

"What's that?"

"I cheat."

"Cheatin' can get you killed," he said, rubbing his jaw.

"Not as quickly as playing fair when the odds are stacked against you." There was no reflection of triumph in my eyes, no sign of defeat in his. "Tonight, it was your game and you were dealing your cards, but I had the advantage," I said.

"How do you figure that?"

"I knew for dead certain you would kill me if you got the chance. You had no idea what I would do, and I did, so I simply played my hand before you had a chance to look at yours."

"You got anything left in your hand?"

This time it was my turn to laugh. "A busted knuckle," was the only answer I could give him.

The glow began to dim in old Fraley's eyes. He settled back down on his cot and scratched the unruly corners of his beard, looking for all the world like a beaten cur. "I'm disappointed in you boys," he said. "I didn't think either one of you was the kind to quit."

"Nobody quit," I answered him, folding up what was left of the hollow horsehair mattress and tossing it at his feet. "It's just that we don't have anything left to fight for."

Old Fraley's fragile voice was a whisper of discontent. "I've seen a better fight between two earthworms," he said.

The horse thief's grin had lost its bitterness. "Maybe you'd have liked it better if one of us had been beaten to death," he said.

"Hell, I'd a'liked it better if both of you had been beaten to death." Old Fraley closed his eyes, and his voice trailed off. "Then me and Methuselah would have had this cell to ourselves like it was before, the way God meant for it to be."

He turned his face away as the rat scampered up onto the cot beside him. The old man reached down and gently stroked Methuselah's furry gray head, gently picking up the rat and dropping him in the frazzled pocket of his faded flannel shirt, missing as many buttons as old Fraley was teeth.

The horse thief looked back at me, and his sigh was one of hollow resignation. "If it makes any difference," he said, "my name's Wyatt Earp."

It didn't. "Hawkes," I replied. "Brady Hawkes. I'd shake your hand, but I'm afraid mine hurts too much."

His eyebrows were raised in thought. "The face is a lot more familiar when you put a name to it," he said. "I watched you clean out a bank in Joplin one night without ever looking at your hole card."

"Sometimes you don't have to look. You know what's there."

"You ran the best bluff I ever saw with that much money ridin' on the table."

"I wasn't bluffing."

"You really have that straight flush?"

"He thought I did."

Time has no meaning when there is no day and no night, and the shade of gray that hovers in the cell around you never changes and never moves. A man becomes lost in his own thoughts, and the thoughts are always of home, except for the drifters who have no home and no memories of one. The drifters long for the glimpse of another sunrise, of wind ruffling the leaves of a cottonwood tree, a full moon riding low on the mountaintops, the howl of a coyote, the smell of a woman, the road out of town, especially the road out of town. The direction didn't make any difference.

The sound of a key rattling the lock startled me. The cell door creaked open, and two guards, armed with small-bore shotguns shuffled quietly inside, as reverently as if they had entered the holy sanctuary of a church. One, with a thick black beard and high cheekbones, was obviously the man in charge. He had manacles and leg irons thrown over his shoulder. His partner was as thin as a rail with beady little eyes that sank back into the creases of a hawk face. He kept licking his lips, a nervous habit that reminded me of a coiled rattlesnake waiting to strike. A third man, much smaller, his head bowed, quietly mumbling a mouthful of words that sounded pretty much like an unknown tongue to me, was virtually lost in the veil of darkness behind them. Neither was carrying the bucket of swill, which was just fine with me.

Black Beard studied each of us for a few fleeting moments that seemed like eternity, then he turned his attention to old Fraley. "It's time," he said with a voice as desolate as his eyes.

"It ain't mornin' yet." Old Fraley shut his good eye, and the bad one began to softly cry.

"It's close enough."

"Judge Parker don't hang nobody till mornin'."

"The hangman can't wait around here forever."

"He can wait till mornin'." Old Fraley's thin voice trailed off into a whimper.

"By mornin' you'll be eatin' breakfast with the devil."

Old Fraley suddenly laughed. "By gawd," he said, "it'll be the first hot breakfast I've had in years."

The taste of nausea hung thick in my throat. I glanced at Wyatt Earp. His eyes were like mine, stunned and disbelieving. By the time I got to my feet, Hawk Face had jammed the barrel of his shotgun under my chin, and I could smell the powder where it had been recently fired.

"I don't understand what's going on," I blurted out.

"There's not that much to understand," Black Beard said dryly. "Four months and sixteen days ago, the Honorable Judge Parker sentenced Jarvis H. Fraley to hang by the neck until he was legally dead, and when his time comes, he pays for what he did. An eye for an eye, you know."

Hawk Face kept digging the barrel of his shotgun into my throat, and I think he was beginning to enjoy my discomfort. I backed away and heard him snicker.

"But he's just an old man," Earp said. "He's harmless."

"That's not what Miss Bonnie Claxton testified to the grand jury," Black Beard said. "Old Fraley had a penchant for redheaded woman."

"There's no sin against that," Earp said.

"There is when you do to 'em what old Fraley did to 'em."

The manacles were clamped on the old man's gnarled and knotted hands, visibly trembling in the dim light.

"He used a knife," Hawk Face whispered aloud.

"We found their bodies stuffed in old whiskey barrels out in the alley behind the saloon," Black Beard said.

"We never did find their heads," Hawk Face finished.

"Jesus," Earp said. It was a prayer.

"How many women?" I asked slowly.

"Just them with red hair," old Fraley answered.

"How many?" I asked again.

"Three," old Fraley answered, although he was choking on every word. "There would have been four, but only three of 'em had red hair, an' I was in love with ever' one of 'em, an' I told 'em not to go seein' any more gentlemen callers whilst I was in Fort Smith, an' they promised they wouldn't, but they lied to old Fraley, an' Mama always told me this world ain't got no use for a lyin', redheaded woman, an' my mama, she ain't never been wrong about nothin'."

The shiver in my gut was a knot of ice that would not melt.

Black Beard took old Fraley's arm, and the old man who loved redheaded women began shuffling his way toward the darkened hallway. He suddenly stopped and turned back toward me.

"Hawkes," he called out.

I stepped forward and nodded.

"I'd be real obliged if you'd take Methuselah out of my shirt pocket and keep an eye on him for me." Old Fraley brushed a tear out of his good eye with the back of his hand, although it was all he could do to raise his manacled hand that high. "He's all I got, and I guess he's the only one left who'll miss me. He don't eat much an' don't cause any trouble to speak of. If you ever get out, take him with you. He ain't never done anything wrong and don't belong in nobody's jail, especially not one run by the hangin' judge."

I reached into his pocket and carefully removed the rat. Methuselah was trembling, too.

Old Fraley smiled one last time, and I held the rat close enough for the old man to stroke his gray, furry coat. "You're a good man," he told me. "The next time you get close to a redheaded woman, think about old Fraley." He laughed. "I'll flat be thinking about you."

The ice in my gut grew even colder.

The door slammed shut and jarred the tiny cell, the noise rumbling down the hallways like thunder from a summer storm. The thunder died away, and all I could hear was the faint clanging and rattling of the leg chains that followed every hesistant step the old man took. Another door slammed, far away. And the clanging stopped. Silence wormed its way back into the cell.

Maybe old Fraley had been right after all. There was only one avenue of escape from Judge Parker's jail. A pine box.

Old Fraley knew Judge Parker was having one built for him. He just forgot to mention it. Or maybe he simply slept better at night if he just forgot what a sane man had rather not remember.

I pitched Methuselah onto the straw and scrambled up on top of the old man's cot, clawing at the boards nailed across a narrow opening that had once served as a window. I silently cursed the pain shooting up my arm, and, in an instant, Wyatt Earp was on the cot beside me, fighting the rusted spikes that defied him, peeling back the splintered planks with broken fingernails until his hands were raw and bleeding. One board split along a rotten seam and gave way.

And a shred of sunlight, no wider than a dagger's blade, cut sharply into the cell.

It pierced my eyes, and the sudden, throbbing pain made me forget my busted fist. I squinted and pressed my face against the opening. It was like trying to look through the eye of a needle.

"What the hell's going on out there?" Earp wanted to know.

"They're hanging a man."

"How's he takin' it?"

"Better than I am."

The old man was standing on the gallows, weighted down by chains. His knees were bent, his head bowed, but I doubted he was praying. A black hood fell across his face, and the knot of the rope lay gently upon his left shoulder.

Wyatt Earp sighed as though to exorcise any sentiment he may or may not have felt at the moment. "We've all got to go sometime," he said.

"I wish I'd remembered to tell him good-bye."

The God-Fearing folks of Fort Smith crowded around the gallows, a mob pushing against itself, surging forward for one last curious look at a man that nobody knew or wanted to know. The crowd had no faces. No names. Save one.

Amy Sue had climbed her way to the third of the thirteen steps, her face framed in a blue-checked gingham bonnet, a stray curl dangling against her cheek. Her hands were clasped prayerfully and reverently beneath her chin, her voice lifted in song. Her grace was as amazing as it ever was.

The glow of the late evening sun touched her face with gold. And it tinted the color of her hair red. I wondered if the old man had taken notice before he closed his eyes for good.

♠

♥ 4 ♦

♣

I kept staring through the eye in the needle, watching the gallows until darkness finally came to mercifully hide them. They were simply gnarled slabs of wood, standing like a gaunt, anguished skeleton silhouetted against the fiery streaks of a day's end, ax-hewn pine and oak that soaked up man's last tears, rebutted the last curse word or prayer to ever drip like spittle from his blasphemous lips, felt the last tremble in his knees and witness the final snap of his neck. I don't recall ever hearing, or even hearing of a man who screamed on the gallows. Maybe God gives him the courage to stand strong and face that ultimate moment in silence. Maybe the scream tries its damndest but never quite escapes the tightening of the rope.

Old Fraley looked so small and harmless, his killing didn't seem real. He was just a wisp of a man, broken by time and circumstance, a loner who loved redheaded women and rats, and did a better job of keeping his rats alive. The crowd lost interest in him as soon as he drew his final breath, and the courtyard was virtually devoid of humanity by the time the black hearse, drawn by a pair of sloth-footed mules, came to haul him away in a pine box to the burying ground, a special place for paupers and prisoners and at least three redheaded women.

"It must have been a slow day," Wyatt Earp drawled, sitting against the back wall.

I looked at him, puzzled.

"The judge said he'd hang anybody on a slow day, even horse thieves and old men and probably the likes of you, Brady Hawkes."

"That is different," I told him.

"The judge gets himself a new rope and don't want to waste it."

"Old Fraley was convicted of murder."

Earp grinned, leaned his head back and closed his eyes. "I've known a redheaded woman or two," he said. "I think what old Fraley did was probably justifiable."

"The jury didn't agree with you."

"Hell, the jury's not in jail, sittin' here, watchin' that rope swing back and forth, wonderin' whose neck it's been sized for next."

"You don't have anything to worry about."

"Not if I get out of here, I don't."

"All the judge wants out of you," I said, "is five hundred dollars, then you'll be on your way, and, by fall, you won't even remember where you've been."

"There are some folks who'll tell you my life's not worth five hundred dollars, and others who'll swear I've never had five hundred dollars in my life, and a dance-hall girl in Abilene who knows I damn sure had it tucked away in my bedroll at least once in my life because she owned it all by the time I sobered up and figured out where I was and realized she didn't dance in Abilene anymore."

The pale light of a Comanche moon returned an innocent specter of peace to the innards of Judge Parker's jail. An old man had left with no one, with the possible exception of a slightly overweight rat, to mourn his passing.

I had not expected to see Judge Isaac Parker so soon and certainly not standing at the doorway to our particular corner of Hades, his eyes grim, deep shadows darkening the weary lines that time, and probably a hanging or two, had chiseled rather harshly into his somber face. His black tailored long coat was wrinkled and creased with sweat. He was not nearly as tall nor as gun-barrel straight as I remembered or thought he would be, and he was leaning heavily on a cane hand carved from red cedar.

Seated in his courtroom, staring down upon the just and the unjust, Judge Parker had the omniscient power and appearance of the Almighty Himself. Down among men, he looked almost like a man himself. Stroking his beard with the gold handle of his cane, he strode into the cell, nodding at Earp then looking directly at me with the same callous interest a butcher gives a bloody carcass of a renegade steer. They say Judge Parker's stare can wither a rose, or at least give it second thoughts about blooming.

A shotgun guard with a whiskey face and a big belly that stretched a pair of leather suspenders over a white cotton shirt, yellowed by too many washings with too little soap, waited in the hallway, absentmindedly tossing a shotgun shell into the air and catching it, as the judge gently closed the door behind him.

"Gentlemen," he said, "I hope you don't mind if I come in." The anger in his voice had calmed.

"As long as you're not carrying a rope," Earp spit out.

The judge forced a grin. "You shouldn't worry, sir, if you don't deserve to wear one," he answered.

"An old man was hanged yesterday," Earp said, glowering at the judge. "He was a good old man. Hell, I liked that old man."

Judge Parker nodded, removed his coat, folded it neatly, and sat down on the cot where old Farley had slept a restless sleep the night before, laying the coat across his lap. "I can understand your sense of grieving," he said with no remorse and only a slight hint of compassion. "That, I'm afraid, is the curse of human nature. Of course I would have felt a lot better if you had been here to grieve the loss Betsy Graham, Katy Chandler, and Scarlett Witherspoon."

"I didn't know them."

"Unfortunately, old Farley did."

"They were nothing but whores," Earp said defiantly.

"Once they had been little girls playing on the rug at their mother's feet." The judge smiled sadly. "That's the way I prefer to remember them," he said.

Wyatt Earp pushed his hat down over his eyes and looked away. A wise man knows when an argument is lost, and I doubt seriously if Isaac Parker had lost an argument in years, maybe never. He turned his attention back to me.

"Brady Hawkes," he continued, "I seem to recall your telling me that you are a gambling man."

"I've played my share of cards."

"I've done some checking," he said. "And it seems like every two-bit card shark from here to yonder and back again is familiar with your name."

"You meet a lot of people in my profession."

"And most of them owe you money." The faint glimmer of a smile began creeping into the dark recesses of his eyes.

I shrugged. "We all have our debts," I told him. "Some you collect. Some are more trouble than they're worth. Some you forget."

Judge Parker leaned back and squared his shoulders as the only shaft of sunlight we had turned the color of his unruly beard from gray to white. "I'm in the market for the best gambling man I can find," he said softly. "From what people who have no reason to lie to me tell me, you're that man."

"I didn't know I had that many friends."

The judge laughed out loud. "I didn't say they liked you," he said. "I said they liked the way you handle yourself at a gambling table. You know which cards to play and which ones to throw away, and, perhaps more importantly, when it's not wise to play any of them at all."

"I don't always win."

"Maybe not. But then, in the long run, you seldom lose."

"I make it a point to leave while there's still money in my pocket." I raised an eyebrow to make a point. "That means I've got a chance to play again tomorrow. A gambling man never keeps records of his winnings or his losings. He just does what he can to guarantee he hasn't played his last hand. Tonight's game is never as important as tomorrow's game. That's all."

Judge Parker brushed the dust and straw from the collar of his coat, picked it up, reached into the left inside breast pocket and pulled out an unopened deck of cards, the high-priced kind that's cost a lot of good men their money and some of them their lives. He tossed the deck to me. "Show me," he said.

"Show you what, sir?"

"How good you are."

My gaze never left his. I shuffled the deck twice, cut it once and slowly began to deal, placing the cards slowly and deliberately face down in front of him.

"The first card is a king of hearts," I said. "The second, a queen of spades. The third, a five of diamonds. The fourth, an ace of clubs." I paused and nodded toward the cards. "You have any interest in seeing if I'm right?"

The judge turned them over one at a time, just as slowly, just as deliberately, although his eyes never left me.

A king of hearts. A queen of spades. A five of diamonds. An ace of clubs.

He glanced over the four cards, shaking his head in disbelief. The muscles in his jaw quivered slightly, and his eyes flickered red in the fading glow of sunlight like those of old Methuselah. "Go ahead and tell me," he said.

"Tell you what, sir?"

"That was a new deck. You hadn't seen those cards before, much less touched them. They weren't marked. I made sure of it. How'd you do it?"

I sat for a moment, waiting for his frustration to grow as strong as his curiosity. With a gavel in his hand and a shotgun guard standing at either shoulder, the judge made the rules. He was boss. But this time I was holding the cards, and he was empty-handed. For the first time in a long time the illustrious Judge Isaac Parker had lost the advantage.

"It's no parlor trick," I told him. "I simply read the cards before I deal them."

"But you didn't look at the cards. You couldn't even see them. I watched you the whole time."

"I use my fingertips."

Perplexity darkened his face like the shadow of a cloud that gets in the way of a new moon. He leaned forward, propping his elbows on his knees to get a better look at the cards. Even Wyatt Earp stepped closer to the cot.

"How can you read those blasted cards with your fingertips?" the judge asked.

"We all have the sense of feel," I told him. "For some, that particular sense is merely sharpened. Maybe it's a blessing. Maybe it's a curse. Maybe it just comes from years of holding cards. I don't rightly know. I simply knew I had dealt you the king of hearts because the king has a grizzled face, and I can feel the heart pulsating between my fingers. The queen has a softer face, and the spade, as you can see, is sharp on the end. It pricks the fingertip. The five of diamonds? The diamond is cold, not unlike ice, and this one had five distinct points. An ace always has the texture of money, and a club, for whatever reason, doesn't have any feel at all."

Judge Parker stared at me, trying to decide whether to digest what I had told him or merely spit it out, which is what any sane man would have done. His eyes narrowed, and he gingerly rubbed his short, thick fingertips over each of the four cards lying on the soiled, lumpy cot before him, searching for the king's grizzled face, the sharp end of the spade, the five points on an icy diamond. He studied the deck, then he studied me. The only thing any of us could hear in the cell was the raspy, uneven sound of his breathing.

"Can you really feel all of that with your fingertips?" he asked at last.

I picked the cards up, shuffled the deck, and handed it back to Judge Parker. "I've been accused of it," I replied. "And I don't call any man a liar to his face unless he or I is ready to die."

Judge Parker took a deep breath, stood, and slung the long coat around his broad, thick shoulders. "A day or so ago, I told you I didn't know what to do with you," he said. "I'm not in that quandary any longer. I've got a job for you, Mr. Hawkes."

"Does it pay well?"

He shrugged his broad shoulders, and a faint grin played curiously about his lips. "That, sir," he answered, "depends entirely on you."

The judge walked to the door and knocked twice, then waited for his whiskey-faced shotgun guard to open it. I heard the click in the lock, and Judge Parker glanced over his shoulder. "You coming with me?" he asked.

"You turning me loose?"

"I can do with you what I want," the judge said, a sudden hardness returning to his voice. "Your freedom is certainly one plausible option. Another, Mr. Hawkes, is that tonight just may be the last time you ever suck the fresh air of the outside world into your lungs. If I were you, sir, I would make the most of any opportunity offered me. It knocks but once, I'm told."

I turned to Wyatt Earp, leaning against the far corner of the cell, his hat pushed back, both hands jammed nonchalantly into the pockets of his dust-creased trousers. "I don't guess I'm coming back," I said.

"When they leave here they seldom do."

"It looks like you inherit the cot now."

"I'm not sure I want it anymore."

"I got some advice for you."

"What's that?"

"There's not a damn thing in here worth fighting for."

The swelling of Earp's bottom lip had turned his grin into a crooked scar. "It's just as well," he said, eyeing the empty cell. "There's nobody left to fight."

I picked up my hat, dusted it off, and followed Judge Parker through the door. "If I get there first," I told him, "I'll have a good, stiff drink waiting on you. If I don't, I'll at least have a drink for you before I leave."

"Have another for old Fraley," Earp answered, not bothering to move. "Of course, where you're goin', old Fraley may be pouring the drinks."

The door slammed, and we trailed the thin, jittery light of Whiskey Face's lantern down the narrow hallway, its thick, mud-clicked walls lined with planks ripped from the bottoms of old, decrepit teamster wagons and reinforced with logs. Around us were the sounds of men singing and snoring, vomiting and dying, men who had wasted their last chance, and the odds were not good at all they would ever be given another. If Judge Parker heard them, his emotions did not betray him. He marched with his shoulders stiff and erect, not unlike a Philadelphia mortician at a politician's funeral, his face chiseled from stone, his eyes unflinching. He had been down into the tombs of hell before, and only he and God had any idea of why he had come back down into them for me.

A dozen more steps and we were through the mildewed door and out onto a back street of Fort Smith. The singing, the dying, had been left to those who had nothing better to do. A dry wind slapped my face, and the air smelled of fresh straw, lathered horses, old leather, lilac perfume, stale cigar smoke, the hint of rain, and horse manure. It was good to breathe again. But the sweet and sour stench of sweat and urine and day-old swill hung in my nostrils, and I wondered if I would ever be able to outrun it, or if I would even be able to try.

The judge straightened his long coat and pointed down the street to the dim light that crept through the soiled windows of the Crazy Water Saloon. The faint sounds of a player piano spilled through an open doorway, and a drunken cowboy staggered out onto the wooden sidewalk, holding tightly to a tiny, dark-haired woman in a faded red satin dress who was doing her best to guide him, or at least drag him, in the general direction of Miss Bonnie Claxton's bawdy house. He wanted love, and all she had to offer him was her frail little body, but the hour was too late, and the cowboy too drunk, to quarrel about the difference.

The judge cast his eyes toward me. "I assume that you are familiar with a drinking establishment here known as the Crazy Water Saloon," he said.

I had frequented the bar a time or two.

Judge Parker continued with the same thunderous voice he used to condemn the guilty and beg for God to have mercy on their souls: "In the back, so I'm told, Horace P. Garfield, the proprietor, has a high-stakes poker game where there are no limits, and fortunes can be made or lost depending on the luck of the cards or the skill of the men who play them." Judge Parker paused to make sure I was listening, then asked, "Have you ever had the privilege to sit at Horace P. Garfield's personal gaming table?"

"Mr. Garfield only welcomes men of considerable means to the inner sanctum of his back room," I said.

"Did you win as much as you lost?"

"I always left with money in my pocket."

Judge Parker stepped forward, and his face was illuminated by a gaslight hanging above the courthouse. "Do you feel as though you can leave Horace P. Garfield's with money in your pocket tonight? Not just walking-around money, mind you. A lot of money. A helluva lot of money, if God will forgive the expression."

"It depends on how the cards run."

Judge Parker's eyes narrowed until they were the size of bullet holes and almost as lethal. "I was under the impression, Mr. Hawkes, that you could read each card with your fingertips," he said.

"Unfortunately, they don't allow me to deal every hand," I told him.

"How often are you allowed to deal?"

"Usually often enough."

The drunken cowboy had reached the gilded front door of Miss Bonnie Claxton's place, leaning heavily on the tiny woman in red satin. Her thin, pretty face, aglow in the dancing lights of a gas lamp on the corner, was young and unblemished, her eyes aged and worn. He had a heart full of love. She had a fistful of dollars. His shoulders bent forward, and his head slumped against her bosom. She dropped him, and the cowboy was asleep by the time he crumpled face down onto the wooden sidewalk. It wasn't what he came for, but it was all he got, which, I guess, is pretty much the way we all lead our lives.

"We presently have a serious problem at the First Church of the Holy Sepulcher," Judge Parker said.

"What kind of problem?"

"It had to do with money, or, more accurately, the lack of money." Judge Parker frowned. "During the last three years and four months, we had raised seven thousand two hundred sixteen dollars and thirty-two cents, if I recollect correctly, to build a new sanctuary out on Arbor Hill, a peaceful kind of place, as far as we can possibly remove ourselves from these dens of iniquity that blaspheme the streets of Fort Smith."

"That's odd," I remarked.

"How's that?"

"I was always under the impression that churches were put here to save the sinners, not run from them."

Judge Parker scratched his chin, his eyes cutting sharply through the darkness, trying to determine whether or not I was mocking him. He was obviously able to read the Scriptures much more clearly than he did a man's face. He started to answer me, then thought better of it.

Instead, the judge said, "The money was placed under the care of the church's most able and trusted deacon, Basil Redfin, a godly man, a beloved husband and father, a merchant of fine clothing for refined women, if you believe the sign in his window, who came to Arkansas when Fort Smith was little more than a wilderness crossroads, with neither road leading anywhere of particular importance."

Judge Parker looked away and slowly shook his head. "I would have trusted Deacon Redfin with my life," he said.

"But not your money."

His deep breath was filled with anguish. "No," he answered, "not our money, if I had only known then what I know now."

"That happens a lot in your business."

"What's that?"

"Most every man who hangs from your gallows wouldn't be hanging there if he had only known then what he knows just before the trapdoor drops out from beneath his bare feet."

"'I guess you're right."

"What did Deacon Redfin do with your hard-earned money?"

"Mr. Hawkes," the Judge began, "we all have our weaknesses. For some it's whiskey. For others, it's women. Some steal. Some cheat. A few just like to roll up their sleeves and have a good fight."

"What's your weakness, Judge?"

He shrugged with a deeper sigh of resignation, and his broad shoulders seemed to weaken beneath the weight of his long coat. "I trusted Basil Redfin with seven thousand two hundred sixteen dollars and thirty-two cents," his answered, his voice barely audible, his words lost like dried leaves in the dry, stiff wind.

"And what was Deacon Redfin's weakness."

"Cards, Mr. Hawkes. I knew he had a tendency to gamble a little from time to time, but never more than a few dollars. It was his pastime, his avocation. But he lost more than usual one night to Horace P. Garfield in the back room of the Crazy Water Saloon, more than he could afford to lose, actually. In his desperation to win it back, Deacon Redfin dipped into the church's holy treasury. By the time he had played his last card, I'm afraid Mr. Garfield had taken our last dollar. He still has it, Mr. Hawkes."

"And you want me to get the money back."

"I understand that's what you do best."

"And if I win?"

"I will be more than lenient on you when your case comes to trial," he replied.

"And if I lose?"

"Your case may never come to trial." The judge brushed away a layer of sweat that was glistening on his forehead.

"It's not much of a choice you give me," I said.

"It's the only choice you have, Mr. Hawkes."

"As you yourself said," I reminded him, "it's a high-dollar game that Mr. Garfield plays in his back room. A man doesn't sit down at the table with empty pockets. I trust the church passed the collection plate enough times to stake me."

The judge was not amused. He pulled a leather pouch from his coat pocket, and I could hear the crisp jingle of silver. "Here's a hundred dollars," he said. "I fear it's all the money that remains in the church's treasury."

My grin, as pleasant as it was, only seemed to antagonize him. "If I lose it, what'll you use to pay the preacher?" I asked.

"If you lose," the judge answered gruffly, "we'll only have to pay the preacher to conduct a funeral."

"I may be wrong, judge, but I don't believe the honorable Mr. Garfield allows men to sit at his table with bare feet."

He frowned as he considered the thought of my trying to enter the back room of the Crazy Water Saloon, looking more like a drifter asking for a handout than a gambler with money in his pocket. Finally, his frown became a bemused grin, and the hanging judge turned toward Whiskey Face. "Get him some boots," he snapped.

The shotgun guard opened the mildewed back door, picked up a pair of old, rundown boots sitting beside the steps and threw them defiantly at my feet.

"Those aren't my boots," I said.

"They'll do," Whiskey Face said, draping his shotgun over his right shoulder.

"Who'd they belong to?" I wanted to know.

"He won't be needing them anymore," the judge answered.

"They look suspiciously to me like old Fraley's boots," I mused.

"We don't bury anybody out here with their boots on," Whiskey Face replied.

They were too small. They were so old the eagle imprinted on the side looked more like a one-eyed jaybird. The soles had holes in them, big ones. But they kept the mud from getting between my toes, which, I guess, was the best I could hope for under the circumstances.

I reached for the pouch that was straining beneath the sagging weight of silver, but Judge Parker was reluctant to hand it over. "Shall I carry it," I asked, "or will you be carrying the money for me?"

"I won't be accompanying you," he replied, finally placing the bag of silver dollars in my hand. "It wouldn't be wise for a justice of the law and a deacon of the First Church of the Holy Sepulcher to be seen partaking of the pleasures of the Crazy Water Saloon."

"It didn't seem to concern Deacon Redfin."

"Brother Redfin is no longer a deacon. In fact, no one at the First Church has seen Brother Redfin in Fort Smith since he had the misfortune of separating God from the money that was rightly His."

"You run him out of town?"

Judge Parker smiled. "I gave him a bottle," he said. "You

see, whiskey is Brother Redfin's other weakness, and, I'm afraid, his every waking hour since that tragic moment has been spent trying to keep those snakes in his cell from choking him to death." The judge ambled slowly away. "Poor man," I heard him say. "His wife thinks he ran off with a bare-legged dancer from Dr. Jarvis Pearson's traveling show. She told me she never wanted to see him again, and I guess it's my unfortunate lot in life to make sure she gets her wish."

As I stepped into the street, Judge Parker glanced slowly around and yelled at the whiskey-faced shotgun guard, who was hanging closer to me than a drunk man's shadow. "Coleman," he said, "don't let Mr. Hawkes out of your sight. He's our guest, and I don't want him to spend the night on the town alone. If he tries to run with the money, any of it or all of it, please inform me of the funeral arrangements. The court will reimburse you for the shells."

♠
♥ 5 ♦
♣

The Crazy Water Saloon, though packed with trail hands, ranch hands, rail hands and a general assortment of drunks, malingerers, guns for hire, teamsters and riders just passing through, had no particularly distinguishing nor redeeming features. It could have been any saloon on any trail town in any territory west of the Mississippi River. The bar, situated beneath the painting of a slightly overweight naked woman being serenaded by angels the size of fireflies strumming on gold harps, was long and fashioned from roughhewn lumber, well scarred with cigar butts, rifle butts, knife blades, and splintered by a few well-placed bullet holes.

A few of the regulars stood leaning against the bar, men with neither faces nor names worthy of remembering. The player piano banged out a happy tune, which meant the player piano had no memory at all. Two brunettes from Miss Bonnie Claxton's place hung sensually on the side of the piano, one tall and willowy, the other short and either plump or a lot of woman, depending on what appealed to you. And, before morning, she would certainly be appealing to someone. She winked at Whiskey Face, and his knees almost buckled. I think there was something about the long double barrel of his shotgun that grabbed her attention, and Whiskey Face, if he had not been acting under the strict orders of Judge Isaac Parker, would have considered shooting me on the spot, stuffing the silver dollars in his pockets and running away with temptation in a bright red dress. But, alas, duty stood in his way.

I knocked twice on the door to Horace P. Garfield's back room, saw it inch open, and waited for a pair of nervous, darting eyes to recognize me. Those eyes knew every face in town, perhaps every face in the territory, that belonged to fools, fancy Dans, and other gambling men who had money to play and money to lose, which had always been Horace P. Garfield's favorite kind of customer.

There was always a lot of money stashed on the table, probably more than had been stuck honorably into the vaults of the First State Bank, separated from the Crazy Water Saloon by a single brick wall with several of the bricks missing. Horace P. was never afraid of losing his money to a straight-dealing gambling man. Sooner or later he would always get it back from the player who, sooner or later, took it from somebody else. His pockets were deep, and the house odds, since time began, have favored those who have deep pockets and the nerve to bet their last dollar before they've seen their last card. What Horace P. feared most was some band of two-bit, half-drunk, crooked-eyed outlaws bursting in on him and taking everything he owned, including, more than likely, what was left of his life.

Harry the Eyes did not let any strange face through the doorway.

Jefferson the Gun was waiting if they came through anyway. Jefferson, big and fleshy, was not the brightest of men. He had neither scruples nor a conscience, but he could shoot straight, which made him a perfect employee for Horace P. Garfield. He simply sat in the corner, one shotgun in his lap, another at his feet, a third propped up against his straight-backed chair, and if Horace P. yelled Shoot, he shot, and he kept shooting until Horace P. told him it wasn't necessary anymore.

"Harry," I said, "it's Brady Hawkes."

The nervous eyes softened, and the door eased open. "It's good to see you, my man," Harry said. "I thought you'd done gone and rode out of town without coming by to tell old Harry good-bye." He was ancient and wiry, a broad toothless smile plastered on his kindly black face. If Harry ever had two nickels to rub together at the same time, he would give you one if you were broke, and it seems like just about all of Harry's friend's were always broke.

Harry wrinkled his nose when I stepped closer to him. "I don't want to insult you, Mr. Hawkes," he said, "but you smell like you been sleepin' with the pigs."

"You didn't insult me, Harry." I grinned. "But you may have hurt the feelings of a few pigs in town."

His smile faded into a frown when he saw Whiskey Face stroll into the room behind me. "He with you?" Harry asked.

I nodded that he was.

"Jefferson don't allow nobody else in here with a shot-gun," he said.

I turned to Whiskey Face. "You heard the man," I said. "Let Harry have your shotgun. It'll save all of us a lot of trouble."

Whiskey Face balked, a sneer forming a scar beneath his black mustache. "There ain't no man alive gonna take my shotgun away from me," he said with a scowl.

I shrugged and placed an arm around Harry's frail shoulders. "I tried to tell the gentlemen what he ought to do," I said.

"That you did, sir," Harry answered.

"And I'm afraid he refused."

"That he did, sir."

"So I guess there's only one thing left to do."

"Whatever you say, sir."

"Jefferson's gonna have to blow his fool head off."

"Jefferson's gonna enjoy that, sir."

Whiskey Face, without argument or debate, being of sound mind and body, decided he had rather face the wrath of Judge Isaac Parker than the judgment of Jefferson the Gun.

He gently laid his shotgun on the floor beside his boots.

Harry kicked it rather unceremoniously into the corner.

Horace P. Garfield, his face soft and pudgy, reached beneath the table and calmly pulled out a new deck of playing cards, as though there had been no disturbance of any kind at all. "I'm honored, Mr. Hawkes," he said. "I believe the last time you sat down with us, Lady Luck did not choose to bless you at all. I wondered how long it would take for you to return and try to exact a certain measure of monetary revenge."

He laughed heartily, as did everyone else who sat at the table. There was no animosity in the laughter, just genuine pleasure. Garfield could have easily passed for an eastern banker. But, for the last three decades or so, he had chosen to invest his considerable wealth in the Crazy Water Saloon. "Why not?" Garfield always asked those God-fearing, back-row deacons who thought one of Fort Smith's most influential backers should be involved in an enterprise that did not cater to drunks, gamblers, and prostitutes. "The Crazy Water makes more money than the bank."

I poured the silver coins on the table, and Garfield waited until he found his gold-rimmed spectacles and put them on before counting it. He was a very precise man, a self-styled impresario who conducted his back-room poker games with the fastidiousness of a Wells Fargo accountant.

"I presume you know everyone here," he said, without bothering to look up until he shoved the last of my chips across the table.

I did, by face and reputation if not by name.

The Rancher had taken his first herd to Abilene without incident, came home and bought every piece of land he could find between the Ozark and Wichita mountains. The Rancher settled down, married the youngest fledgling in Miss Bonnie Claxton's bawdy house, and spent enough money to make them both respectable.

The Merchant drove his team into Fort Smith late one night, knocked on Jasper Flanagan's door, and found the old man dying with a .45 slug in his chest. By morning he had taken Flanagan's name out of the store window, hung up a sign that bore his own name, sold his wagon, and served as mayor of the town. No one ever found the killer of Jasper Flanagan.

The Lawyer had been a hired gun. But that was long ago, somewhere in south Texas where hired guns were as commonplace as ticks on a cow's belly and almost as dangerous. He was better with words than guns, and a good attorney could get rich representing the guilty who were destined to stand before the harsh, lethal stare of Judge Isaac Parker. His clients did not win many cases, but the Lawyer did not appear to have lost in years.

Miss Bonnie Claxton herself sat across from me. Age had not stolen her beauty, but the business she ran had left her eyes with a hard, defiant edge. The cut of her satin dress was as distracting as the cigar clamped between her lips. She had been a rancher's wife, and, as was the fate of many ranchers' wives, she ended up a widow. She definitely possessed what men were willing to pay for, and what she had to sell carried a very high price tag. She was much better suited to be a businesswoman than a widow.

"You must not be plannin' on stayin' very long tonight, Hawkes," the Lawyer said, loosening the black string tie around his neck.

"A hundred dollars don't last long around here," the Merchant chimed in.

"It's a chance I'll take," I replied.

"It looks to me," Garfield said softly, "like Mr. Hawkes has fallen on hard times."

"He sure smells like hard times," Miss Bonnie said, a slight grin curving around the unlit cigar jammed into the corner of a dainty little mouth.

There are times when a man is better off not talking. This was one of them. I smiled at the Lawyer, winked at Miss Bonnie, kept my eye on the Rancher, ignored the Merchant, and waited for Horace P. Garfield to deal me my first card.

It was a two of clubs.

It looked like a loser's hand, unless of course Horace P. tossed me another deuce, which he did, the two of diamonds.

It was time to forget the cards. I either got them or I didn't. They were either good or bad. It didn't make any difference. Cards, when the night grew old and the whiskey grew stale and cigar smoke hovered like a late summer fog above the chips, hardly ever won or lost. Men and, in this case, a little lady did.

They were much easier to read and a lot more fascinating than the hands being dealt. Faces on cards never change. Those facts across from me never stayed the same.

Cards aren't predictable. People are.

And when a man is foolish enough to sit down at a high-dollar poker game with only a hundred dollars in his pocket, knowing he has to walk away with seven thousand two hundred sixteen dollars and thirty-two cents or there's no sense even trying to walk away at all, he needs every advantage he can get.

The Merchant was and had always been an opportunist. When he was satisfied he could not lose, he bet and bet big. When there were any doubts at all, he threw his cards in early and poured himself a stiff drink of sour mash whiskey. The later it got, the stiffer the drinks became. Along about midnight, his eyes and his mind had a sour mash haze, and every hand looked like a winner, and he had trouble remembering what he had won and what he had lost or whether he was playing stud poker, straight poker, or buckshot in the river, which nobody in his right mind played unless he was with the wrong crowd on the wrong side of town with a cocked revolver lying in his lap.

The Rancher was a tough old man. He made his fortune rounding up strays and driving them hell-for-leather north, and damn anyone or anything that was ignorant enough or stubborn enough to stand in his way. The Rancher played his cards the same way. He never figured on losing, so he always bet he would win, openly daring anyone to oppose him, spitting and sputtering as mad as a wet hornet when his two of a kind wasn't good enough to beat a full house, knowing damn well nobody would ever be able to beat two of a kind again.

Miss Bonnie played with reckless abandon. Somewhere along the way, money had lost its value. She had plenty. If she lost plenty, she had ways, damn interesting ways so I'm told, of earning it back. For every thousand dollars she squandered that night, her girls were taking in another thousand, maybe more. To Miss Bonnie, gambling was simply a gamble. She had no idea what she needed in her hand until she saw what she had, and sometimes it was enough, and sometimes it wasn't. And she believed, "You can't win if you don't play, and you can't win if you throw in your cards, and you can't win if you're scared," and Miss Bonnie had not been afraid of either bad luck or poverty in a long time.

The Lawyer still had the mentality of a hired gun, one that hid in the shadows and made it a habit of sneaking up on his victim, quickly and quietly, putting a bullet in the back of the man's neck, then vanishing into the night, gone before anyone knew he had been around. Hand after hand, the Lawyer lay in wait, losing an ante but seldom anything more, watching his victims, never in any hurry, realizing that all he needed to strike was one good hand and one big pot, and he would be a richer man when he strode like a proud peacock out of Horace P. Garfield's back room. His nerves were cocked, but he had not yet pulled the trigger and wouldn't unless he was holding four of a kind and all of them wore royal faces.

There are no secrets at the table.

The Rancher raised an eyebrow when he had two of a kind or better. He squinted when the cards turned cold. He clenched his jaw tightly, and his facial muscles quivered slightly when he was bluffing.

The Merchant leaned back in his chair when the cards were good to him. He sat forward on the edge of his chair when he raised somebody's bet even though he knew he shouldn't.

Miss Bonnie held her cigar in the left corner of her mouth when she had a hand worth keeping. The cigar hung out of the right corner of her mouth when it was time to fold, which she seldom did.

The Lawyer studied his cards when there was reasonable doubt in his mind. He studied our faces when he thought it was time to pull the trigger.

It's bad manners to count your money at the table.

I had no other choice.

The judge was expecting seven thousand two hundred sixteen dollars and thirty-two cents, and I did not believe he would be willing to settle for a nickel less. I glanced again at my hole card, and the room began to smell of sweat and stale urine and soured swill, and I knew I couldn't go back to the tombs that Judge Parker had reserved for the living. Rats, then snakes, and I heard the faint, faraway sound of old Fraley whistling on his way to meet his Maker.

Slightly more than six thousand dollars were stacked in front of me. And at least another thousand lay scattered on the green-velvet-covered table. Money from the sale of cattle, clothing, men's necks, and women's bodies.

I checked the clock above Garfield's head. It was seven minutes past five. The sun would be climbing above the Ozarks in another hour, and Judge Isaac Parker would gavel his courtroom in order. A man's life would be hanging in the balance. Somewhere a wife, or a mother, was weeping. The hangman was tying the last knot in his noose. And the poor old judge would be thinking only of me and my all-night efforts to atone for the last deadly sin of Deacon Basil Redfin.

The Merchant folded, as we all knew he would.

The Lawyer had one big pot left, and it was staring him in the face. It was the chance he had been waiting for all night, but his eyes never left his cards. I dismissed him as though he did not exist.

The Rancher had an eyebrow raised, but his jaw was quivering. He studied the pot, then his hand once more, and the eyebrow fell into a sober squint.

Miss Bonnie's eyes were full of hope and laughter, but the cigar hung loosely in the right corner of her mouth.

Horace P. Garfield glanced down at his cards, neatly assembled on the table, grinned at me, and lightly rubbed the palms of his hands together. His meaning was clear.

Those who sat around us were only pretenders. They no longer concerned him. And, he was sure, I had also lost interest in them and whatever threat, if any, they might possess.

It had come down to this, Garfield and me. Winner take all. Loser weep. At stud poker.

The five cards lying in front of him against the five cards that lay beneath my fingertips, nothing wild, the rest of the table be damned.

Garfield had three kings showing.

I had a two and a ten and a queen.

He raised a hundred dollars.

The Lawyer turned pale. The Rancher cursed slightly under his breath. Miss Bonnie threw her cigar on the floor.

"I don't like the way you dealt these cards, Garfield," she snapped.

"If there's one thing you know about me, Miss Bonnie," Garfield replied softly, "it's that I don't cheat."

"I'm not callin' you a cheat," she said, "I'm just sayin' you're doin' a damn good job of keepin' all the good cards to yourself."

"It'll cost you another hundred dollars to find out if you're right."

"You willin' to take it out in trade?"

"It's certainly appealin' to my basic male instincts, Miss Bonnie," Garfield said with a grin. "But I can't speak for the other gentlemen here tonight, so I guess it's best if we stick strictly to cash."

"You know I only brought two thousand, and I'm down to my last fifty dollars." Miss Bonnie threw up her arms in despair.

"You know the rules, my dear."

"Damn your rules."

She disgustedly threw her cards down on the floor

alongside her cigar and crossed her legs. Garfield poured her a snifter of brandy, and a hint of fire touched her eyes. Miss Bonnie was not angry because she had lost her money. She was upset because she could not play out the hand. And Miss Bonnie would rather die than quit.

The Lawyer stood as gracefully as he could under the circumstances, bowed slightly, and fastened the buttons on his coat. "Gentlemen," he said, "as much I would like to remain for another hand, I'm afraid that I have a court date in slightly less than an hour, and I would hate to see my client hang for the sake of a game of cards."

The Lawyer strode like a proud peacock out of the back room, broke for the time being, but unbowed. He would be back at another time on another night. Men who are easily parted from their money always come back.

"Mr. Hawkes," Garfield said, "I believe you're the only one left. It will cost you a hundred hard-earned dollars to see what I'm holding."

"Besides the three kings?"

"There may be a fourth, Mr. Hawkes." He looked at my two, my ten, and my queen and made no attempt to hide the grin that broke out of his face.

"It's a cheap price to pay." I tossed another hundred onto the pile. "But the price keeps getting higher every minute."

Garfield laughed. "You think you can bluff me, don't you?" he said.

"I think it's getting late."

"I'll call, Mr. Hawkes, and we'll see how late it really is."

There wasn't really anything special in my hand. A two, a ten, a queen showing. A five and an ace face down. With more than a thousand dollars on the table, they would have been a fool's hand, a pauper's hand, if they hadn't all been diamonds.

Horace P. Garfield's three kings paled by comparison.

And that's all he had. Three. The color drained from his face. He bit his lower lip and glanced again from my cards to his. "How did you know?" he asked.

"How did I know what?"

"I didn't have a fourth king."

"Call it instinct, Mr. Garfield," I said. "Sometimes we follow a hunch, and it pays off. And sometimes we follow out hunches straight to the poorhouse." I shrugged. "Besides, the Lawyer had the other king."

Horace P. Garfield reached across the table and turned the Lawyer's hole card over. It was a king of hearts.

"He show it to you?" Garfield wanted to know.

"In a sense he did. For whatever reason, the Lawyer has a fascination for face cards. A queen makes his eyes flicker. A jack makes them nervous. When he has a king, the pupil's began to dilate."

"I thought he was just gettin' drunk," Miss Bonnie said with a stifled laugh. Her powdered face had lost its softness beneath the harsh glare of an unforgiving lamp, and there was the faint hint of a knife scar along the crease of her chin. They say she looks younger with her clothes off. I'll have to take their word for it.

"That was my mistake, Mr. Hawkes," Garfield said softly, leaning back in his chair and touching a lighted match to a pipe. "I was watching you when I should have been watching him."

"Tonight, the right cards fell at the right time," I said, sitting forward and counting out the money that had been stacked in front of me. "But they're fickle. Tomorrow, they may desert me for some other fool."

"Somehow," Garfield mused, "I don't think you'll be here tomorrow."

I felt Whiskey Face's bony hand on my shoulder, and his

breath had the stench of cheap whiskey, raw onions, and turpentine.

"He ain't leavin'," Whiskey Face spit out. "But he ain't gonna be here either." His grip tightened my arm, and his broken fingernails dug into the fabric of my coat.

Slowly, deliberately, I stacked, then set aside, the money that had been lost by Deacon Basil Redfin, wondering if God, the judge, or anybody would ever have mercy on his soul. The judge wouldn't for certain, and the judge had him buried so deep that God had quit looking for him, and nobody else counted. I shoved the pile of money toward Whiskey Face.

Seven thousand. Two hundred. Sixteen dollars. And thirty-two cents.

Whiskey Face's grip loosened, and he began filling his hat with the contributions of a Rancher, Merchant, Lawyer, Impresario, and bawdy-house Madame. I motioned for the old man beside the door to come closer, and he did with a crooked grin working its way around the wrinkles on his face.

"Harry, I got a job for you to do," I said.

"Whatever you say, boss."

I handed him five hundred dollars. "Take this to the honorable Judge Parker," I continued.

"You in debt to the judge?"

"The judge is holding an acquaintance of mine. All that's standing between him and the road out of town is five hundred dollars. That's not the case anymore."

"This acquaintance of yours got a name?"

"Earp. Wyatt Earp."

"Where will this Mr. Earp find you?"

"He won't."

"Where you gonna be?"

Whiskey Face grunted. "He's gonna be in the same

hellhole he was in when this mornin' caught up with him," he growled.

"And Harry?" I said.

He raised an expectant eyebrow. I placed an extra twenty bucks in his hand. "When I hire a man to do a job, I pay for it."

He beamed. "Thank you, boss," he whispered.

"I got one more thing to ask, Harry."

"You name it an' it gets done. You know that."

"Give this fifty to Jefferson. Tell him I'm walking out of here, and I'm walking out by myself. If this whiskey-faced son of a bitch tries to follow me, tell Jefferson I would regard it as a personal favor if he shot the bastard's head off."

Whiskey Face's hat hit the polished hardwood floor, and seven thousand two hundred sixteen dollars and thirty-two cents scattered from one end of the room to the other. His ruddy face turned white.

Miss Bonnie squealed with laughter, and, after gnawing on it for most the night, finally bit the end off her cigar.

Horace P. Garfield cut his eyes sharply toward my custodian, who had the option of either facing the consternation of Judge Parker or the last rites of St. Peter, courtesy of Jefferson the Gun.

"Please sit down and stay awhile," Garfield said, his mood darkening. "It's been a bad enough night without having to wash your damn blood off the floor."

Whiskey Face looked for an empty chair.

"You can have mine, sir," I said, rising and walking briskly across the floor, putting the last four hundred and sixty-eight dollars in the vest pocket of my coat. I patted Harry on the back, nodded at Jefferson as he cocked the hammer on his shotgun, and let the door close by itself behind me. By the time I reached the street, I still had not

heard the eruptive blast of a shotgun so decided that
Whiskey Face was not coming after me. Perhaps Judge
Parker would not be so hard on him once he delivered the
missing funds from Deacon Redfin's poker game to the First
Church and Wyatt Earp's five-hundred-dollar fine to the
court.

The only train leaving Forth Smith at midnight was
pointed south and almost six hours late. I bought a ticket,
not quite sure where it was going nor caring how long it
would take to get there, and I was asleep before the first
gnarled fingers of daylight timidly touched the top of the
pines.

♠

♥ 6 ♦

♣

Fort Griffin, Texas, was the end of the line, a ramshackle collection of slab-board buildings and adobe huts where painted women would dance with a cowboy to the tune of a single fiddle, as long as he bought two very short beers at cutthroat prices, and soggy-faced bartenders served up bottles of Mexican tarantula juice that would draw blisters on a rawhide boot. It was the final resting place, with no law and no one tough enough to uphold it, for those renegades, deadbeats, buffalo hunters, drovers, outlaws, gamblers, army deserters, and misfits who gathered to live out the frazzled end of a misspent life.

They all looked the same, these men who had ridden a long, crooked trail that brought them to their own personal purgatory on the Texas prairie. They were earthy, unlearned, and generally illiterate, with few wants, other than a bad whiskey and a good woman, or vice versa, and their only ambition was staying alive long enough to drink one more whiskey and dance with one more woman, knowing that each time could very well be the last time. They were the fortune hunters who had long ago given up on finding a fortune west of Bitter Creek. They could raise more hell than a terrapin when the tank goes dry, and a few of them were convinced they had come to Texas so long ago that the sun wasn't no bigger than a saucer, and there wasn't any moon at all.

They wore hand-me-down flannel shirts, as long as the undertaker patched up the bullet holes and bleached out the bloodstains, with a faded handkerchief to keep the sun from blistering their necks, butternut pants, and a sombrero with high crown and brim of enormous proportions. And, I'm convinced, they strapped on their revolvers before they put on their pants each morning. The pants only kept them decent. The revolvers kept them alive. And decency among either men or women was not one of the more admired attributes of Fort Griffin, Texas.

The train never tarried for very long in Fort Griffin, and it stopped only on rare occasions and always reluctantly and this time because I had a ticket that wouldn't allow me to ride any farther west.

The streets were empty.

The town, for all practical purposes, had given up the ghost. Other than myself, the only living, breathing creature in Fort Griffin was an aging station master with a bald head, ragged white beard, stooped shoulders, and crippled right leg that still bore a load of cannon shot from the Battle of Shiloh. He called himself Ezra Bodine, and he swore that someday he would be leaving Fort Griffin. But, in the meantime, he was content to wear his black wrinkled suit, sit by the side of the track, and sell tickets to those poor devils who needed to get out of town worse than he did.

"It looks like everybody's already left," I remarked, watching the train fade into the purple shadows that had crept down out of the foothills, slowly spreading across the sage and shinnery prairie that fenced in the miseries of Fort Griffin. The sun was hanging low in the sky like a prospector's last gold dollar, there for the taking but always just out of reach.

"They ain't gone far," Ezra Bodine said, rubbing his bald head with a ragged bandana and adjusting the bent wire-rimmed spectacles before they slipped down onto the tip of his nose again. "They ain't got no real preacher with 'em, so it won't take 'em long to do what they gotta do."

Ezra Bodine read my blank stare and realized I had no idea what he was talking about. He continued, "They're putting Miss Dottie away, God rest her soul. Miss Dottie runs the Double Eagle Saloon, or at least she did till about this time yesterday."

"Miss Dottie must have had a lot of friends."

"She treated 'em all fair and square, the rich and the poor alike, an' so did her girls. Wasn't nobody who didn't like Miss Dottie, except Ike Rigby, of course."

"Who's Ike Rigby?"

"A buffalo hunter who comes into town when he's killed off ever' buffalo he can find and needs some place to wash the blood off. Meaner'n eight acres of rattlesnakes, he is. Ain't got no fear of man or beast, and I've seen him curse the good God Almighty in the middle of a lightnin' storm. I've seen a lot of bad ones. Hell, there ain't no kind out here but bad ones. An' he's the worst of the lot."

"What did Ike have against Miss Dottie?" I wondered.

"She threw him out of the Double Eagle, or at least she tried to." Ezra fell silent for a moment, and the color drained slowly from his aging face. "Miss Dottie was a big woman, a pretty woman, but a big woman just the same, an' she did a pretty damn good job of keeping the peace over in her place," he said. "She never had no bouncer, never needed one. She just rolled up her sleeves an' did her own fightin'. Ike, he wanted his whiskey without payin' for it, an' he wanted the best-lookin' gal in the place, and Miss Dottie knew he wouldn't pay her nothin' for either one of 'em. So she did what any saloon keep worth his salt would have done. She jerked the bottle out of old Ike's hand, told him to get the hell out and stay out."

"I don't guess Ike appreciated her particular brand of hospitality."

"Ike took a knife to her." Ezra shuddered and held his hands tightly beneath his chin to keep them from trembling. "He's a buffalo hunter, you know. He kills 'em. He skins 'em. He did things to Miss Dottie I ain't never seen no human bein' do to another one. You could hear her screamin' plumb to Buffalo Gap. God, we were glad when she quit screamin'." He paused a moment and stared out the window, and I knew that down somewhere in the recesses of his mind, Ezra Bodine could still hear the screams. He waited until they had at last died away, then whispered harshly, "So now they've all taken her down to put her away, what's left of her."

"An' you're the only one left in town."

"Me an' Ike Rigby. I had to meet the train. An' he's over at the Double Eagle tryin' to drink all the hard whiskey he can, now that there's nobody around to try and make him pay for it."

His story was almost too incredible to believe. I knew Fort Griffin didn't have a soul. But I thought at least it had nerve. "Nobody tried to help her?" I asked.

"Nobody messes with Ike Rigby when he's got his buffalo gun in one hand an' his skinnin' knife in the other. He's a mean one, I told you, meaner'n hell with the hide off."

"What about the sheriff? I presume you do have a sheriff that hangs around here, don't you?"

"He took one look at Miss Dottie. She was beggin' Ike not to cut her anymore. An' he took one look at Ike. Ike was licking her blood off the knife. An' the sheriff said he had suddenly been called by the Good Lord to be preacher man, and it'd be a sure sin to get himself involved with anything pertaining to violence. He turned in his badge, ran down to the church, and hid for the rest of the night. I ain't seen him this mornin'. He may be down prayin' over the remains of Miss Dottie, or he may be ridin' south on the fastest horse he could steal. The job's open, stranger, if you're interested."

"I'm just passing through."

"That's what they all say. Nobody comes to Fort Griffin to stay for very long. Ever'body's just passin' through. That's the trouble with civilization. It's just passin' through, an' it don't leave us no better off than it found us." Ezra Bodine grunted with a feeling of despair and helplessness.

Ezra Bodine rolled his chair a shade closer to the station window and waved his hand toward the distant prairie, almost swallowed by the evening shadows, slowly turning from a deep purple to black. "Just look at all of that land," he said with both pride and defiance.

I did.

"We ain't never gonna run out of room to dig graves," he said.

A blast of hot wind bounced off the prairie and slapped me in the face as I walked out of the depot and stepped down upon the only street that had the misfortune of running through downtown Fort Griffin. It was hard clay, baked by an unforgiving sun and hardly ever disturbed by a good rain. The weathered doors on the collection of ramshackle slab-board buildings were closed, and dust-stained, tattered curtains had been drawn in shame across the windows.

The town was quiet. I crossed the street and pushed open the swinging doors of the Double Eagle. The room was dark, though no cooler, devoid of any artificial light. Only a slender thread of wayward sunlight managed to work its way through a crack in the hall window, above the stairway, resting gently on a mangled spider web that hung from a hand-scrawled sign, making mention of whiskey, mineral baths, rooms to let, and the girls who went with the rooms, referring to each girl by name. Unless the prices had changed, a dance or a night with Ruby Marie would break a man much quicker than the time he spent with Victoria, Sally Mae, or Sarah Jane.

In the darkest corner of the room, the hulking figure of an unwashed buffalo hunter leaned heavily against the bar, holding a half-empty bottle in his hand, gnawing the raw flesh off a chicken bone and staring hard at me with eyes as cold and deadly as the muzzle of the buffalo gun that lay atop the bar and beneath his arms. He was the size of a mountain, with black, unruly hair hanging in long, matted clumps over the collar of a beaded leather coat, handmade by a Mescalero Apache. He shoved the chicken bone in his mouth and I heard it crack between his teeth.

"You lookin' for me?" he snarled.

"I don't even know who you are," I said since Man Mountain and I had not been formally introduced.

"How come you ain't at the funeral?"

"I wasn't aware that anyone had died." Running a bluff was usually what I did best, especially when faced with a buffalo hunter who used the same knife to dig out bullets, mash ticks, castrate cattle, skin buffalo, kill a woman every now and then, and pick his teeth.

"The bar's closed," he said.

"I'm just looking for a bath," I told him.

"There ain't no girls here."

"I can bathe myself if that's what it takes."

"It's gonna cost you."

"It almost always does."

"Six bits for the hot water, another quarter for the soap, if you can find any."

I tossed a dollar onto the bar in front of him. "Fair enough," I said. My eyes were slowly becoming adjusted to the darkness, and I could see his face clearer now. It was big and flat, full of scars and whiskers. A necklace made of buffalo teeth dangled around his neck. His eyebrows were bushy and as black as his hair. He never looked the same direction at the same time out of either eye. He jammed his knife into the top of the bar as he reached over and picked up the silver dollar. He studied it for a moment in the dim light, then dropped it in the pocket of his leather coat. Satisfied, Ike Rigby turned back to his bottle and dismissed me as though I did not exist.

The tub in the back room was streaked with rust. The water was only lukewarm. And I had paid a quarter too much for the soap. But the bath was wet enough and hot enough to wash away a week's worth of sweat, dust, stale urine and soured swill. So I guess it was a bargain after all.

I closed my eyes and wondered what Judge Isaac Parker would do with the likes of Ike Rigby and whether anyone had invented a rope strong enough to keep his kicking, convulsive body attached to the gallows. Then I was a struck by a more troublesome thought. What in God's name was I going to do about Ike Rigby?

In Fort Griffin, nothing builds a good thirst quite like the weeping and wailing at the funeral of a saintly woman who was taken from this life long before her time. No one spoke ill of Miss Dottie Dembo that night. They simply drank her whiskey, both cheap and expensive, until it was gone, while her girls, the whole chorus line, stayed behind locked doors and asked God's mercy on their own souls, suggesting that no one would terribly mind if the good Lord could find the time in his busy schedule to strike Ike Rigby down dead. It was obvious that no one else in Fort Griffin was willing to try it.

The mercantile stayed open long enough for me to purchase a new suit of clothes and a pair of boots that had been ordered by a Texas drover who trailed a herd of cattle to Kansas and never came riding back through town again. The Indians must have got him, the store owner told me. Or maybe it was a stampede, or even a swollen river. Perhaps some handsome lady had taken the drover's last dollar before he left Abilene. A handsome lady could put that kind of spell on a poor, old, deadbeat cowboy, he said as though he had the craving for a similar kind of spell himself.

I carried old Fraley's boots out behind the livery stable and buried them, hoping they would catch up with the old man someday. Somehow, I couldn't see him stumbling barefoot through all of eternity, especially not walking on brimstone and hot coals, which is what old Fraley was probably doing at the moment.

A somber mood prevailed over the Double Eagle Saloon. Bad whiskey was in much greater supply than laughter. No one was mourning the loss of Miss Dottie Dembo. They only knew that Ike Rigby had not yet left Fort Griffin, and no one among them was safe as long as he remained in town. He had departed the Double Eagle before any of the wayward and repentant returned from the burying ground, and now no one knew where he was or what he was planning to do next. Ike Rigby had become part of the night, and mankind has always feared what it could not see.

I found a seat beside a lanky, sullen-eyed drifter from Palacios, who sat with his back to the wall, a Sharp's rifle spread across his lap. The legs of his faded blue trousers had been shoved into his boots, and a red bandana was wound tightly around his neck. His short beard was the color of rust, and it matched the deep burn an unforgiving sun had given his face. He regarded me as a nuisance when I said, "I've been told from one end of this state to the other that Fort Griffin just may be the toughest town in Texas."

"What you heard was probably right," he answered, his voice flat and distant.

"It looks to me like everybody in town's running scared."

"They ain't runnin'. They just sittin' here, mindin' their own business."

"Scared half to death." I glanced around me, and every eye was staring out toward the street. "You've got men in here who had just as soon shoot somebody as wring a rooster's neck for Sunday dinner. I know some of them by face, some by name, a few by reputation. If this Ike Rigby fellow is making you so dadgum nervous, why don't some of you just walk out there and take care of him?"

The drifter shrugged his bony shoulders. "Cause there would be some of who wouldn't be walking back in here when the shootin' was over," he said. "Look, mister, around here we don't fight nobody who ain't done nothin' to us, and Ike Rigby ain't done nothin' to nobody 'cept Miss Dottie. If he comes lookin' for me, I'll blast away until me or him, one, falls. Right now, I'm just bein' cautious. A man stays alive a lot longer around here if he's cautious."

Only one person had knelt to wipe away Miss Dottie's bloodstains. She looked twenty-five, but was probably younger, with long black hair twisted around an oval, olive-complexioned face. Her eyes were black and moist, and they reflected the sadness that gnawed at her insides. Her features were soft and delicate, and her long, thin fingers pulled a rag back out of a bucket of hot, soapy water. She began to scrub the floor that held the last visible evidence of Miss Dottie Dembo. She worked alone, generally ignored by the drifters and drovers, teamsters, and soldiers who would stay and mourn at Miss Dottie's wake until the whiskey was finally gone.

I knelt down beside her, gently took the rag from her hand and attacked the dark, rusty stains as vigorously as I could. She smiled through her tears. "Thank you, sir," she said in a voice that conveyed unmistakable pain and sadness.

"Don't mention it."

"She was a good woman," the young lady said softly, reaching up to make sure the top button on her high-collared gray cotton dress was fastened securely.

"I'm sure she was."

"Did you ever meet Miss Dottie?"

"I never had the pleasure."

"She was everybody's friend."

"So I gathered."

I leaned against the bar and pitched the rag back into the bucket, studying her face, so full of wide-eyed innocence. It was without blemish. "Were you one of Miss Dottie's girls?" I asked, wishing I hadn't the moment the words tumbled out of my mouth.

"I'm an actress," she replied, holding out her tiny hand to shake mine. "My name is Dora Hand. I do light comedy and some drama, of course, but what I like best is a Shakespearean tragedy."

"I wasn't aware that Fort Griffin had a theater."

Dora Hand shrugged her frail shoulders, and her eyes twinkled in the soft glow of the overhead lamp. "I'm on my way to California," she said. "I was only working for Miss Dottie until the next theatrical troupe comes by headed west. I'm quite good, you know."

That was another point I couldn't argue.

"You don't look like you belong in Fort Griffin either," she said.

Before I could answer, the silence of the fearful little

town, too weary to be awake and too frightened to sleep, was abruptly shattered by the tumultuous ringing of the church bells, clanging nervously from the tower of an old wooden chapel whose doors had been closed and locked for years.

Louder, they rang, as though hammered unmercifully by an angry fist.

Dora Hand grabbed my arm. "It's the judgment of God," she whispered.

It was Judgment Day, all right, but I doubted seriously if God had anything to do with it unless God wore an Apache shaman's beaded leather coat and carried a skinning knife in his belt.

There was no sign of any movement from man or beast on the dirt street outside the Double Eagle Saloon. Even the dry Indian summer winds had fallen with grace upon the barren countryside. The jittery flame of a candle flickered in the darkened window of the chapel, staring back at us from the far end of town.

And the bells kept ringing.

They were almost deafening now, defying anyone who heard them, and everyone heard them, and the whole town was awake. Some were on their knees in prayer, others cursed and blasphemed the darkness, and the rest of us fools were running madly down the street toward the church, not knowing what to expect or what we would find.

But the bells were tolling. They were maddening, growing louder, more ominous, with each step we took.

I kicked the door open, and we rushed inside.

The chapel was virtually deserted. Only the preacher was there, older than his years, dressed formally for a wedding, or maybe a funeral, his thick black hair falling recklessly upon a handsome face tanned deeply by the sun. His empty eyes stared past me, and a curious, inquisitive smile lay beneath a neatly trimmed mustache. His hands were raised toward heaven in praise, and his hands were tied savagely to the bell ropes. He dangled there, swaying gently up and down, the weight of his body continuing to ring the bells, even though the preacher did not hear them anymore.

His throat had been cut. The blood dripped down his naked chest and onto an open Bible that lay upon the weather-worn boards of a rotting floor. The Scriptures had been distorted by the ugly stain.

The pin of his sheriff's badge, thrown away in fear the night before, had been shoved deeply into the middle of his forehead, and the five-pointed star hung loosely between his pale, translucent eyes.

"Oh, my God," Dora Hand whispered, crumpling at my feet.

"The sonuvabitch is gonna kill us all," I heard somebody say as fevered men with crazed eyes ran out into the streets, shooting wildly at moving shadows, and the moving shadows kept firing back. Renegades. Deadbeats. Drovers. Outlaws. Gamblers. Army deserters. Misfits. And not a buffalo hunter among them.

Someone yelled in anger.

A bullet slammed into the bell tower overhead.

Someone else screamed in fear.

Another in pain.

The three bells had been fashioned from gun metal melted down by the survivors of the Conroy Expedition in '64, and now they were pealing as frantically, as irrationally, as the pulse of the entire town, loud enough to wake the dead. But the dead couldn't hear them for the explosion of gunfire.

A riderless horse darted from a back alley and ran through the street, the dark, unmistakable stain of fresh blood splashed on his saddle. Darkness reached down to drape itself around Fort Griffin, penetrated only by an occasional string of fire spit by a revolver and disturbed by the ricocheting thunderclap of a rifle shot.

I held a trembling Dora Hand close and wondered how many of them would be dead by morning.

♠

♥ 7 ♦

♣

Dora Hand was a petite, dark-haired beauty whose life had taken a wrong road somewhere west of the Alleghenies, then followed a bad road to Fort Griffin, which was where most people wound up when they had ruined their names everyplace else and had no place left to go. Like myself, Dora Hand was just passing through. Unlike myself, she had no idea when, or if, she would ever leave, riding lavishly away atop the brightly colored wagon of a theatrical troupe that would never have a chance of finding her at all unless it was hopelessly lost. She just kept smiling, even when it hurt to smile, and told herself with the rising of each new sun, "Well, I'm one day closer to getting out of here than I've ever been before."

The sun, though partially hidden by an angry cloud that hung in the sky like a swollen bruise, brought a curious, though desperate, calm to Fort Griffin. The sporadic gunfire that interfered with anyone getting a good night's sleep had finally been silenced. It was just as well. Daylight had chased away the most ominous of shadows, and there was nothing left to shoot at.

I had cut down the lifeless carcass of Fort Griffin's dearly

departed preacher man as soon as the gunplay erupted
throughout town, and laid him out on the pew closest to the
communion table, placing his Bible beneath his head. He
had probably never used the Bible for a pillow before. But
then, I doubted that he had spent a great deal of time reading
it either. It was the most religious thing I could think of
doing at the moment.

The three bells gradually grew silent, rattled only by a
frail easterly wind that, like a few other wayward strangers
in town, was just passing through. By morning, it was gone,
leaving Dora Hand and me behind.

She slept in the church that night. Since it was too
dangerous to step outside, I chose to stay with her, watching
as the splinter of pale light from a full coyote moon fell
gently on her face. Hers was not nearly as peaceful and free
of worry as the still, rigid face belonging to the preacher
man. Her nerves twitched convulsively every time a gun
fired, and she groaned out loud. She reminded me of a rose
doing its damnedest to grow on rocky ground. It would
bloom once, maybe twice, then wither away and die. And,
after a while, no one would remember it had ever bloomed
at all.

When the sun came again to Fort Griffin, and the
shadows had all been gathered up and herded out of town,
and the renegades, deadbeats, drovers, outlaws, gamblers,
army deserters, and misfits had not been able to pry Ike
Rigby from wherever the night had taken him, I escorted
Dora Hand back down the street to the Double Eagle
Saloon. She moved cautiously toward the far sidewalk, her
eyes darting from one end of town to the other, afraid to let
go of my arm. Her breath was coming in short bursts. The
color had been drained from her face. She pulled the white
collar of her dress tightly around her neck.

"You don't have to stay here any longer," I told her.

"Where else could I go?"

I didn't have an answer. I didn't even know where I was headed, only that I was going and the sooner the better. Fort Griffin did not need Ike Rigby to kill it. Fort Griffin was merely a reflection of an earlier time when towns were run by the man who had the most money and owned the most guns. The money had already fled Fort Griffin. The guns that remained were scared guns, and men with scared guns died a little every time the sun rose anew. They got old in a hurry, and old men did not last very long in a town that had grown as decrepit as they were. Civilization was carving another rut in the road west, a rut that had no reason and no invitation to go to Fort Griffin.

"How often does the train run?" I wanted to know.

"When it gets here," was all she said. "Why?"

"A smart lady would sit on the front steps of the station and wait for the train no matter how long it took to get here," I said. "And when it left, she'd be on it."

"If I were a smart lady," Dora Hand answered softly, "I wouldn't have been here in the first place."

"What gets you in trouble is not nearly as important as what takes you away from it," was really the only advice I had to give her.

She looked up at me and did her damnedest to smile.

"Are you going to be on the train?" she asked.

"I may be gone before it gets here."

"Are you afraid, Brady Hawkes?"

"Broke is probably a better word. A gambling man in a town that's dying on the vine is a man sitting on the front porch of the poorhouse, trying to figure out how's he gonna get enough money to buy himself a room for the night."

She tried to laugh, then decided there was nothing to laugh at after all.

The street was deserted. A lone tumbleweed bounced

along beside us until it ricocheted off the edge of a water trough and abruptly changed direction. Even the tumbleweeds were leaving town. High overhead a hawk reached out and caught the wind with its wings, slowly circling above the town, riding one current until it was swept away by another. Or maybe it was a vulture.

Dora's room was on the third floor, but she stopped me at the swinging doors. "I'm all right now," she said softly, wiping the last trace of sleep from her eyes. "I can go the rest of the way by myself."

"I've brought you this far," I told her, squeezing her hand with the assurance that she no longer had to face the day alone. "I sure don't mind going the rest of the way."

"I'm afraid I can't let you do that."

"Why not?"

"It's ten dollars if you go up the stairs," she said, trying to stifle a yawn, "and another ten if you go in my room. Those are Miss Dottie's rules, you know."

"Miss Dottie's not here anymore," I answered as gently as I knew how.

"Maybe not. But the rules are."

I stared at Dora Hand, trying to figure her out, watching her brush a loose curl back into place. There were dark circles under her eyes that her powder was no longer able to hide. "I didn't think you were one of Miss Dottie's girls," I said, remembering our conversation from the night before.

"I'm an actress," she replied demurely, and I thought I saw the hint of a teardrop moisten her eye. "Actresses live in a make-believe world, and, most of all, actresses try to make believe their world does not exist. I've learned to do it pretty well. The men who come calling and pay their respects to Dora Hand are entertained by an actress, a very good actress, I must admit. Dora Hand would never do the things she does."

She smiled. It was a sad smile, but a sincere smile. And she stroked my hand, an apologetic gesture. Nothing else.

I started to answer, but she reached up and put a finger to my lips to stop me.

"You are not the kind of man who wants to be entertained by an actress," she said. "Your world is real. I know. I lived there once."

Dora Hand turned abruptly and walked briskly across the empty dance floor of the Double Eagle Saloon. She looked smaller than I remembered, a child, really, a child that became a woman and made her living the only way the woman knew how in the perfumed back rooms of Fort Griffin. I watched her until she climbed the stairs and disappeared beyond the grandfather clock that had died when a bullet slammed into its face at exactly thirty-four minutes past two. I had no idea whether it was A.M. or P.M., last night or the year before. Nothing stayed alive for very long in Fort Griffin, Texas.

Charley Moseby, the gravedigger, sauntered down the hard clay street, dragging his well-worn shovel in the dirt behind him. His shoulders were bent, and it appeared as though he had gone at least a week, maybe two, without a shave. His whiskers were black and stuck to his face like a prickly pear. The sleeves of his undershirt, stained the color of Red River mud, had been ripped off at both elbows. And the legs of his brown trousers drug in the dust beneath the boots he had probably taken from some poor customer who happened to wear the same size and certainly would no longer need them down where he had been planted in the alkali caliche soil. Charley Moseby was as thin as the barrel of an army carbine, and if he was awake, you could bet on his mouth being stuffed with a wad of chewing tobacco.

There were some in Fort Griffin who swore that Charley was a rich man. He only looked the way he did because so much of his time was spent with corpses, and corpses didn't care what he was wearing or how much money he had. Charley Moseby had made a deal with the city fathers of Fort Griffin years ago, long before the city fathers loaded up their wagons and moved out, turning their town over to renegades, drovers, gamblers, buffalo hunters, army deserters, and misfits to run. Charley took care of their dead, dug the graves and packed the deceased away for good, and, in return, he was allowed to keep whatever he found in their pockets. He treated his customers all alike. The rich weren't buried any deeper than the poor. Their coffins all came from the same pine slabs, and Charley figured two nails were enough to keep any self-respecting corpse from getting out once the final amen had been said above his unfortunate head. Four nails just meant more work. And six were out of the question.

"You're a busy man this morning," I said, stepping off the front porch of the Double Eagle Saloon.

"That's the way it is around here," he answered, turning his head to spit a thin, brown stream of tobacco juice into the dust. "Seems like I always got more work than I can do. And if I don't, all I got to do is sit around and wait till Saturday night, and some poor fool will be needin' me again."

"What's the count this time?"

"Three, if you count the preacher." He wiped the spittle off his mouth with the back of his hand. "I found another one in the alley over there. He had been shot twice. And some fellow who came in on Friday's train ran into a double barrel's worth of buckshot. I think he'd a' made it if he didn't bleed to death. Jesus, he was worse than a stuck hog."

"The last two have names?"

"Damned if I know."

"They have Christian burials?"

"Didn't need one. Near as I can tell, weren't none of 'em Christians. The preacher thought he was. But he was just scared, and the Good Book says, 'Verily, verily, them that run from heaven ain't got no business runnin' toward it,' or something like that."

The bruised cloud that threatened rain had been burned away by a sun dead set on blistering everything it touched, including me and the gravedigger. Sweat was beading up on my forehead, and the dry, probing heat seared the back of my neck like a running iron branding maverick calves. Charley Moseby was dry as a bone if you didn't pay any attention to the spittle dripping down his chin.

"It seems to me they at least deserved a funeral, no matter how mean or ornery or hypocritical they may have been," I said.

"Couldn't do that." Charley jammed the head of his shovel in the hard clay, and leaned on it for support. "Didn't have a preacher. He was the first one in the ground." He looked up at me and squinted his eyes. "We got an openin' for a preacher, mister, if you're interested."

"Just passing through."

"That's the best way I know of to stay alive."

Charley Moseby rolled his wad of tobacco from one side of his mouth to the other and trudged slowly away, his shovel bouncing in the dirt behind him. His pockets looked stuffed.

Everybody in Fort Griffin knew everything there was to know about Ike Rigby, and nobody knew a damn thing about him. He had ridden in astride a stolen horse almost a decade ago, stricken with a bad disposition and nursing an ugly gunshot wound just above his right nipple.

The first sergeant for a cavalry patrol that spent most of its time hunting down feminine companionship at the

Double Eagle bit the end off a well-chewed cigar and said in a soft Georgia drawl, "Didn't nobody shoot Ike Rigby. He shot himself. From what I was told, a Comanche raiding party had him cornered in a narrow little old box canyon down on the Pecos. Ike knew they only wanted him for his scalp. He's got a damn big head of hair. Make a damn impressive sight hangin' on some warrior's belt."

The sergeant paused to pick up a candle on the Double Eagle bar and touch the flame to his cigar. He puffed once, then twice, closing his eyes and filling his lungs as full of smoke as possible. He exhaled slowly, continuing, "Some of these tribes runnin' loose out here are real superstitious, and Ike had heard that the Commanches wouldn't take the hair off anybody who'd committed suicide. They believe one of them evil spirits lurks inside anybody crazy enough to take his own life. An' if you scalp him, you unloosen the evil spirit, an' it escapes out the top of the fellow's head and enters your own body. It's a chance none of them Comanches want to take. Ike decided death was preferable to losin' his hair, but he only did a half-decent job of shooting himself. He was about half-ashamed of himself when he didn't die. Always swore it was the worst damn shot he'd ever made."

The buffalo hunter had reached town just before the last remnants of daylight scattered behind the hills that rolled on west of jackrabbit-mesa country. He headed straight for Asa Hatcher's blacksmith shop, stumbled inside without nary a hello-how're-you-doin'-or-get-the-hell-out-of-my-way, and pulled a red-hot poker out of Asa's blazing furnace. Ike Rigby rammed the poker into the gaping bullet hole and seared the wound, and the whole shop was overcome with the sickening odor of burning flesh.

Asa said Ike Rigby didn't scream.

He didn't even flinch.

But his square, bewhiskered face was awash with sweat, grime, gunpowder, and traces of blood that had splattered onto his chin. He wore a sardonic grin as though he had defied the devil one more time without paying the consequences. Ike Rigby didn't believe in paying for anything. His basic philosophy about life, particularly his own, was a simple one. The West, he always said, was made up of takers and givers. Those who were strong enough took what they wanted. The rest, sooner or later, gave up everything they had. Sooner or later, Ike Rigby wanted it all.

He had marched into the Gold Nugget Saloon, forced his way behind the bar, took three bottles of Bill Buford's best sour mash down from the shelf, knocked the tops off with the ivory handle of his skinning knife, and poured all three of them down his throat as though he was a thirsty man trying to prime his pump, only stopping long enough to belch every now and then. It took three bottles of tarantula juice to numb the pain, Ike said, but he needed a fourth bottle and probably a fifth to be sociable, and Fort Griffin was the first place where he had felt the need to be sociable in a long time.

It was Bill Buford's untimely misfortune to be tending bar that night. He ran a clean place that sold a good whiskey for a good price, and he expected to be paid for it. A preacher man had once sermonized that charity begins at home, Buford always said, and he never intended for the Gold Nugget be anybody's home, especially not when they poured one drop too many into their gullet and started fighting, belching, and vomiting on the dance hall floor.

When Ike Rigby reached behind the bar to take his fourth bottle down from the shelf, he found the long, metal barrel of Bill Buford's hunting rifle jammed rather rudely in his face.

"Mister, you ain't paid for the first three bottles yet," the bartender said, carefully measuring his words. He was not overly concerned. He had dealt with drunks before, big ones, mean ones, tough ones, wild ones, drunks who did not feel that going to town was worth the trouble unless they whipped somebody or got whipped.

Bill Buford had never dealt with Ike Rigby before.

"I hope you ain't thinkin' about shootin' me with that little old rifle you got there," Ike said, a dry laugh choking loose from his throat. "If you did, an' I sobered up long enough to find out about it, it might upset me a little, an' old Ike don't like gettin' upset."

Buford cocked the rifle. "You owe me six dollars and twenty-five cents, an' you ain't tastin' another drop till I get paid. I can either shoot you where you stand or let the sheriff haul you off to jail. It don't make no difference to me."

That's how Fort Griffin lost a good bartender.

Those who were sitting in the Gold Nugget that night, and just about everybody in Fort Griffin swore they were, said that Ike Rigby was quicker with his skinning knife than a hired gunslinger was with his revolver.

Bill Buford was dead before he could squeeze the trigger.

Ike Rigby went ahead and drank his fourth bottle of sour mash for the night and chased it down with a tall, cracked glass of straight tequila. But, for the life of him, Ike Rigby could not find anybody, male or female, in the Gold Nugget who cared anything at all about being sociable, even though the drinks were on him.

He drank until the whiskey lost its taste.

He took Abigail Jenkins to be his lawful wedded wife. A ceremony was merely a waste of time.

And Ike Rigby left the Gold Nugget crackling in flames, spiting the darkness, when he rode out of Fort Griffin. In the charred, smoldering ruins the next morning, Asa Hatcher uncovered Bill Buford's gold tooth in the ashes, but nothing else. Three days later, a wagon train hauling supplies to El Paso found Abigail Jenkins wandering naked on the prairie, those long, brown curls shaved from her head and only a pair of bloody scars where her nipples had been. The Baptist Women's Missionary Union took up a collection and sent her away to an asylum somewhere near St. Louis. Ike Rigby fell off the flat edge of the earth.

Ike Rigby ventured back once to swap horses. His dun had come up lame, but the buffalo hunter could not see the wisdom of putting one horse out of its misery with a Sharp's rifle ball to the head before he had another one under his saddle.

In August of '71, he stayed in town just long enough to nail up a couple of wanted posters that prominently featured his own likeness, courtesy of some newspaper printer in Fort Davis, bragging that his worthless life had been valued at five thousand dollars. He doubted seriously if there was another life west of the Trinity River as valuable as his.

Ike Rigby had become something of a celebrity, and he was damn proud of it.

Fort Griffin had always been troubled by the likes of Ike Rigby. Some were afraid of him. Others thought he was a nuisance. The rest just made sure they weren't in town when he was, and came riding home when Ike grew weary of civilization and rode away again to the mesa country, a desolate yet sanctimonious place fit only for coyotes, tumbleweeds, sidewinders, prairie dogs, and, of course, Ike Rigby. They did not try to drink from his bottle, steal whichever painted woman he set his eyes and put his hands on, or occupy the same side of the street darkened by the buffalo hunter's shadow and haunted by his presence. They did not look his way, and had the decency to turn away whenever he cast a glance at them.

Through the years, Fort Griffin discovered that Ike Rigby

wasn't too particularly difficult to get along with, as long as nobody crossed him and everybody got out of his way and stayed there. He would show up in town and fill his belly with sour mash and tequila until he had satisfied his thirst, usually riding away in a week, maybe two, leaving the rag doll remains of a battered woman in some upstairs room of Miss Dottie's Double Eagle Saloon when he felt the urge to follow the buffalo again. There was no offense in mistreating a lady of the night. It was part of the pleasure that some men were willing to pay for, except Ike Rigby, and he did not pay for anything. He took it, and what he took was hardly ever worth giving back.

Fort Griffin and Ike Rigby had an uneasy truce.

The town was his as long as he chose to stay there.

And he hardly ever troubled anybody, unless you counted the bruised and beaten whores in the Double Eagle brothel and nobody ever did, until Miss Dottie Dembo finally grew weary of watching Ike Rigby drink up her profits and had the audacity to jerk the bottle out of his hand. Ike did not pay that night either. Miss Dottie did, and the price was a lot higher than she and the preacher man could afford.

♠

♥ 8 ♦

♣

The night sat down heavily atop the shacks and makeshift buildings that clustered haphazardly around the foot of Government Hill and threatened to stay there the rest of the week. The moon went elsewhere, or maybe it was just stuck somewhere up there behind the shank of an angry thunderhead that grew darker by the minute, rumbling in the far distance like a hungry man's belly and occasionally sending bolts of twisted lightning shooting across the flatland prairie.

Along about midnight, the cattle quit their bawling, the coyotes grew tired of howling at a moon that had slipped out of sight, and Fort Griffin doused its gas lamps, settling down to another few hours of restless slumber. Only the Double Eagle Saloon stayed open past the witching hour. Miss Dottie would have wanted it no other way. Her girls would have it no other way. They still had to make a living, even if Miss Dottie was no longer among them, and business had been rather brisk ever since that ragged black cloud in the west swallowed up the sun. There's nothing like a little uncertainty in the wind to make a man need the touch of a woman, or at least be willing to pay for one.

Only the lone figure of one man was visible in the incessant flashes of lightning that left the earth an ashen gray and the sky purple. He came limping toward the Double Eagle, dragging a crippled leg across the ruts that army wagons had cut in the hard clay street. He paused to catch his breath, coughing to clear his throat and running a moist handkerchief across his bald head to wipe the sweat away.

"Looks like rain," I said as Ezra Bodine stepped up onto the porch of the saloon.

He sniffed the air, then shook his head. "Don't smell like rain," he replied.

The thunder growled in defiance.

"Sounds like it's getting closer."

Ezra Bodine chuckled. "Just because this country promises rain don't mean it's gonna deliver any rain," he said. "When this ground gets desperate, the rain always goes someplace else. When water gets axle deep in the streets, you can bet on it rainin' one more time 'fore the sun goes down. Sometimes, I get to thinkin' that God don't like Fort Griffin. Sometimes I get to thinkin' that I don't blame him."

The wind picked up a little, but it was as dry as the caliche dust that boiled off the prairie around us. A horseman passed by, slumped in the saddle, his hat pulled down low to shield his eyes. He may have been riding into Fort Griffin, or leaving. He was in no hurry to do either.

"You calling it quits for the night?" I asked Ezra Bodine.

"The one-twenty from Fort Worth is due in about an hour," he answered, stifling a yawn. "But it never gets here on time, and usually it don't bother to come at all. I used to wait on it, but I got tired of waitin' up by myself. So now I come by and get me a shot or two of nerve relaxer and go on home. Nobody from the Santa Fe Flyer gives a damn, and I pretty much feel the same way they do."

Ezra Bodine leaned wearily against the doorway of the saloon, his wizened old face caught for a fading moment in the aftermath of a runaway lightning bolt that lit up the whole sky and most of downtown Fort Griffin. "One of these days," he said, "the last train's gonna be leavin' out of here, and when it goes, I'm gonna be on it."

"Where to?"

"It don't make no difference, Hawkes. Not anymore, it don't." He took one step into the Double Eagle, then turned back to look at me over the swinging doors, his pale eyes squinting wearily into the darkness. "You got a place to stay for the night?"

I nodded. "Third door to the right. Second floor. Right now it's occupied."

"Who's up there?"

"Sarah Jane, I believe."

"The man got a name?"

"Probably."

Ezra Bodine grinned. "You're all right, Brady Hawkes," he said. "I'd ride the river with you anytime, 'cept I'm too old, an' the river's too deep, an' I sold my saddle years ago." He glanced into the Double Eagle, and his eyes traveled slowly around the room. "Don't worry about waitin' too long for the room," Ezra continued. "Sarah Jane don't waste no time with none of 'em. Whoever's up there with her, she'll give him what he paid for and kick him out 'fore he knows he ain't gonna get nothin' else. I been with Sarah Jane a time or two myself. That's why I stick to whiskey. It lasts longer."

"Take care of yourself," I told the old man as I settled back down on the worn church pew that had been shoved up against the outside wall of the Double Eagle. "And if you see Ike Rigby coming your way, you may want to go ahead and catch the next train out of town. It doesn't matter whether it's the last one or not."

Ezra Bodine stuck his bald head back out the doorway.

"You heard anybody around here screamin' that shouldn't be screamin'?" he asked.

"Not since we found the preacher man."

"He's gone."

"You seem pretty sure of yourself."

Ezra Bodine waited until the low rumble of thunder tumbled down the western slopes of Green Onion Mesa, then said cautiously, "I been here a long time, Hawkes. This ain't the first time I seen Ike Rigby. It's not the first time I seen him hurt somebody. He comes to town. He gets his supplies. He stays by himself. If nobody gets in his way, he comes and goes peaceful-like. An' when you don't see him no more, he ain't here. The fact you didn't see him goin' don't mean he didn't go."

I did not feel nearly as certain about Ike Rigby's quiet, sudden departure as Ezra Bodine did. "I'd like to ask you a question," I told him.

"Shoot."

"You see the moon anywhere?"

For a few moments, Ezra Bodine's gaze nervously studied the black abyss that formed the sky. "Not tonight, I don't," he answered.

"It's still up there," I said.

"What are you tryin' to say, Hawkes?"

"The fact you don't see the moon doesn't mean it's gone."

Ezra Bodine blinked, his face grew whiter and his shoulder twitched. "You give me the willies, Hawkes," he said. "If you ain't got something good to say, then I'd just as soon you do your talkin' to somebody else."

"Be careful," I whispered.

Ezra Bodine did not hear me. He had already made his

way to the bar and was drinking straight whiskey from the first bottle he could reach. Sarah Jane came leading the foreman of the Rocking B Ranch down the staircase. His shirttail was hanging out, his boots were stuck under his arm, and he held his hat limply in his hand. The cowboy slumped into the leather-backed chair beside the stairway and began pulling on his boots. Sarah Jane's skin was alabaster white, and her long red hair fell loosely upon her bare, fleshy shoulders.

God, I'm glad old Fraley's not around, was my first thought. He would be in love before morning, and the Good Lord only knows what would happen to Sarah Jane. She smiled down at the cowboy, then glanced up at me as I ambled across the scuffled dance floor of the Double Eagle.

"The room is all yours," she said softly, placing the key on the bar in front of me. Her dancing dress was lavender and lace, and it fit a little too tight, held loosely together by a single braided belt. A man could see just enough of Sarah Jane to want to see more, which is why she did as much business as the bartender in the Double Eagle.

"Thanks." I picked up the key.

"That'll be a dollar and six bits."

I paid her.

"For another dollar and six bits, you can have me along with the room."

I smiled and nodded politely. Another time I might have been tempted to find out what old Fraley had found so captivating about redheaded women. Sarah Jane wore the fragrance of wild roses, and the green of her eyes was as enticing as her smile. "It's been a long day," I said. "If I were looking for female companionship, I assure you that I'd be knocking on your door. But right now, all I need is a little sleep."

"What if I come knocking on your door?"

"I'm a heavy sleeper."

She pouted. I wondered how many times Sarah Jane had practiced that pout to get it just right, and she had it down just right. "You don't know what you're missing." she said.

She was absolutely right.

It gave me something to think about when I lay down upon a pillow that bore the distinct fragrance of wild roses, and listened to the wind beat sharply against the shutters outside my window. Thunder crackled near and above the distant mountains. Lightning played hide-and-seek through the cracks in the wall. And the last thing I remembered was the sound of a summer rain falling gently upon wild roses in a harsh, uncivilized country where everything was wild and nothing, absolutely nothing, as gentle as a rose.

I heard the noise before I realized what it was, faint at first, then frantic, birthed, it seemed, from deep within the bowels of a thunderclap that exploded out of the night and hammered the sky into submission.

I lay there and noticed immediately that the room was still black as pitch. I had no idea what time it was, nor did I particularly care. No hint of daylight had yet found its way to Fort Griffin, and it could wait the rest of the night as far as I was concerned. A fly buzzed about my face, and the air was thick and muggy, difficult to breathe.

Again, the thunder.

Again, the scream. A wail, really. Or was it the wind? An evil wind does that sometimes, play deadly tricks on a mind that's been numbed by spending too much time in places where it does not belong. A revival tent for one. A jail for another. And finally a dying town paralyzed by the unspeakable deeds of a buffalo hunter who may damn well be a spook but certainly wasn't acting like one.

A knife of lightning pierced my room, throwing strange shadows on the wall: a hat too wide, boots too high, a gunbelt that hung like the silhouette of a lifeless diamond-back rattler on a farmer's broken-down fence.

There it was again.

The wail of a frightened animal, or wounded one. The wind had never sounded so miserable before. No wind, not even a blue norther rolling out of the panhandle like a runaway locomotive, had ever been so desperate.

Rain had cut tiny canals through the dust that clung to the cracked panes of my second-floor window. I pressed my face against the glass.

For a moment, I saw nothing but the rain.

The street was empty.

The last light had been snuffled out in the Gold Nugget Saloon, a rotting hull that found itself wedged between the jail and the old blacksmith shop. The jail was as empty as the street. With the exception of Ike Rigby, troublemakers were riding elsewhere to make their trouble.

Again, the thunder. The window rattled, and the old boards that held the Double Eagle together shook precariously beneath my feet. Lightning tore a ragged seam in an ominous sky, then tumbled out of the clouds and fell upon Fort Griffin in a rage. For a moment, no more than the blinking of an eye, the whole town was as light as midday, pale and yellow.

That's when I saw her.

She stood in the street, down in front of the old abandoned army livery stable, her black hair plastered against her olive skin by the downpour. Her drawn face was awash with tears and the rain. And her eyes were wide, and wild, as though she had come face to face with the devil himself. The bodice of her gray dress had been ripped open, and the torn fabric fell off her shoulders, also soaked by the rain. She threw her head back, and a scream was muffled, then forever lost, in the thunderous voice of the storm.

A horsehair rope had been attached to Dora Hand's tiny waist and tied loosely around the thick, muscled neck of a stallion that bore the U.S. Army brand, the crazed animal dancing nervously as the heavy rainfall pounded without mercy into the hard clay ruts beside him. His eyes were as wide and wild as those belonging to the actress who journeyed west searching for a vaudeville stage but performed her one-act plays only in the upstairs bedrooms of the Double Eagle Saloon.

Dora Hand's fingers were frantically, feverishly clawing at the knots of a wet rope that tore like a dull knifeblade into the skin of her bare midriff. She clenched her jaw tightly in grim determination, and her bare feet dug into the mud. She glanced up toward the sky, her lips moving as though praying for redemption or perhaps cursing her very existence. Then she was gone.

The lightning gave up its ghost, and the darkness dropped its curtain around her once more. It was as though Dora Hand had merely been an illusion, not real, surely not flesh and blood, only the passing caricature of a nightmare that the enigmatic winds of summer had blown into town and would surely blow out again before morning.

I reached for my boots, not daring to take my eyes off the window. Thunder coughed overhead as though the sky was stricken with consumption, and a driving rain kept rattling the shutters outside my room.

The lightning brought a new scream again.

The sky fairly crackled with a sudden surge of electricity leaping from cloud to cloud, and the stallion's scream was louder, even more frightened, than the one spilling from the throat of Dora Hand.

The horse reared abruptly on his hind legs, fighting the air and almost losing his balance, jerking Dora Hand hard to the ground. As she grabbed for the rope, the big stallion bolted forward, racing madly down the street, dragging the help-less woman behind him.

She tried one final time to scream. Nothing. She lost her grasp of the rope, bouncing like a child's rag doll behind the runaway horse, clawing the ground, fighting to breathe, battling to survive, a battle she must surely lose, pitched from rut to rut, the raw earth peeling away her soft, velvet skin in patches, then ribbons. She choked back a scream. The only sound she made was the pain that wracked her flesh. And the ground spit mud in her face. Dora Hand knew what it was like to feel the specter of death take her throat and slowly begin to squeeze with its cold and bony fingers. Her eyes closed, and her body went limp. The mud on her face was replaced by slender threads of blood oozing from the holes torn in her skin.

Dora Hand was dying. She might already be dead.

And I had done nothing but watch with a curious horror, the likes of which I had never experienced before. I was as helpless as she. Dora Hand was so small, so far away, thrown at the mercy of a wild horse that only wanted to escape the frail, unwanted cargo bouncing savagely down the street behind him and those cruel eruptions of lightning that turned a dark night into day.

At first the blast sounded like thunder. But it was too sharp, too crisp. From the porch below, a single splinter of fire corroded the darkness.

The carbine only shot once.

The rope snapped.

And Dora Hand lay motionless at an odd angle, face down in the street, not daring to move, not able to move. It was as though she had been an old rag, nothing more, worn out, cast aside, then thrown away. The frightened stallion raced on into the night without her, his hoofbeats drowned out by the low growl of thunder that waited until it passed the far reaches of the mesa country before running out of anything else to say.

The rain washed away the mud. And the blood.

Her face, illuminated by erratic flashes of lightning, was that of a corpse, pale, drained of all color.

A tall, thin shootist, a second-hand army carbine cradled in his arms, stepped out into the street and hurried toward the fallen Dora Hand, his sad, yet lethal, eyes sweeping the sidewalk that held the far side of town together. His clothes, like his hat, were black, heavily creased with wrinkles, and his gaunt face was virtually hidden behind a dropping, blond mustache that gave him the appearance of a starving walrus.

Until those stormy predawn hours when someone tried to drag the lovely Dora Hand through the gates of eternity, all I knew about Wyatt Earp was that he was a damn good fighter, a damn poor loser and probably the worst excuse for a horse thief on either side of the Red River.

Now I knew he could handle a rifle well enough to shoot the left eye out of a running jackrabbit if necessary. The only odds a shootist like Wyatt Earp ever wanted, or needed, was the chance to get off one shot. That's all. If he missed, he could live with the consequences, if he were still living at all.

Earp knelt on one knee beside Dora Hand and gingerly brushed the clumps of wet black hair away from her face. Around him, Fort Griffin began to show hesitant signs of life, awakened from a dead sleep by the rifle shot. The faint glow of a kerosene lamp spilled out past the swinging doors of the Double Eagle.

Someone shouted, "What the hell's goin' on out there?" It sounded a lot like Ben Carson, the bartender. It could have been anybody. Nobody sounds like himself when he's scared and half-asleep, and the blast of a gunshot knocks him out of bed before the first hint of daylight cracks the sky.

Wyatt Earp ignored him. He placed the carbine on the ground beside him and cradled Dora Hand in his arms. She tilted her head and looked up at him, not quite sure who he was or what he was doing there, a little surprised to find herself still breathing, even though each breath was a painful struggle.

She started to speak. But a soft moan was all she could manage.

Wyatt Earp wiped the mud from her face with the tail of his white shirt. Dora Hand tried to smile but broke down in an awful fit of coughing, spitting blood and dirt, holding her bruised ribs with both hands in a feeble attempt to keep the dull pain from cutting through her innards like the heated blade of Ike Rigby's skinning knife.

He lifted her gently off the ground. Dora Hand gritted her teeth to keep the scream from forcing its way back out of her throat.

The blast of a double-barreled shotgun kicked the mud up at his feet.

And from deep within the shadows that cloaked the Gold Nugget Saloon, I could hear the guttural roar of Ike Rigby's laughter.

Another shotgun blast tore past Wyatt Earp and Dora, splattering into the outside wall of the Double Eagle. The shootist turned slowly to face the insane sound of laughter, his face as expressionless as if he were running a bluff with his last dollar on the table and a pair of deuces in his hand, nothing wild.

"You ain't got no business interferin' with me and my woman," Ike Rigby yelled from the doorway of the Gold Nugget. He had stepped outside now, clenching a double barrel, a pair of Mr. Colt's .45s jammed into his belt. The skinning knife hung from a rope tied around his neck. It cast off a deadly glint in the lightning, which had begun to lose interest in Fort Griffin.

Wyatt Earp stared hard into Ike Rigby's muddy eyes. "I don't know who you are," he drawled, "an' I've never seen your woman before. But I've got no use for any man who mistreats a lady this way."

"I'll treat her any damn way I want to."

"Not while I'm here, you won't."

Ike Rigby laughed again. It was more of a howl. "It looks to me, stranger, like you ain't in much of a position to do a damn thing about it," he said, giving each word a sharp edge.

Wyatt Earp had probably never been more vulnerable in his life. He was facing a mad-dog killer, eyeball to eyeball, separated only by a narrow ribbon of darkness, with his arms full of a woman and his old army carbine still lying in the dirt at his feet. Dora Hand was scarcely able to breathe. Her eyes reflected the fear that boiled inside of her. Every muscle in her slender body was tensed, and her hands, clasped prayerfully beneath her chin, were quivering uncontrollably.

"She's hurt pretty bad," Wyatt Earp told him in a calm, even voice, his distaste for the mad man in the shadows beginning to simmer. "I need to get this woman to whoever practices as the town doctor, then you and I, sir, can settle any differences we have in the morning."

He started to walk back toward the Double Eagle.

A shotgun blast stopped him in his tracks.

"You don't understand, stranger." Ike Rigby snorted. "I don't give a damn if she's hurt. I don't give a damn if she dies. An' if you take one more step, you're gonna die like a stray dog in the street with her."

"She's done nothin' to you," Wyatt Earp said.

"She don't want me," Ike Rigby said, a sullen anger

creeping into his voice. "An' she don't want my money even if I'd a given it to her. There's only one thing to do with a damned old whore that turns down Ike Rigby, an' that's bury the bitch."

He broke open both barrels of his shotgun, slowly, deliberately tossed away the spent casings and reloaded. His eyes never left Wyatt Earp and the girl, and neither did the muzzle of his sawed-off belly blaster, the kind street ruffians and cowards prefer to use in close quarters when all they need to do is point in somebody's general direction and fire. Ike Rigby chuckled and faded back into the line of shadows until he was one of them. I knew he was there. I could no longer see him.

A stray splinter of lightning ricocheted off Wyatt Earp's face.

It was made of stone.

Dora Hand had begun to cry softly again.

I took the stairs two at a time until I reached the barroom of the Double Eagle. The lone kerosene lamp was flickering in a wind unloosed by the storm. Ben Carson had found shelter down behind the player piano. It had stopped bullets before, especially on the night it played its last tune, and Ben Carson was in no mood for music on this night either. He had at least found out what was happening out there and who was causing all the racket, and he had been better off when he was ignorant.

Sarah Jane sat on the bottom stair, her face buried in her hands. When she looked up, I saw the nasty slash of a knife wound down her face and another one across her chin. Her torn lavender dress bore the dark stains of dried blood. Sarah Jane had beautiful red hair and the softest, whitest skin I had ever seen. But Sarah Jane would never be pretty again. In the dark, perhaps. But never in the sunlight. Ike

Rigby made sure of it. Dora Hand had not been the only girl to reject him that night.

Charley Moseby was asleep on a bench in the back of the bar, unaware that business appeared to be picking up for him. His sweat-stained, tobacco-plugged hat covered his face. I picked it up and slapped him sharply. He awoke with a start and the ill temper of a bear with the bellyache.

"The last man that did that ain't around no more," he grunted.

"Get your boots on."

"Why the hell should I get up? It ain't daylight yet, and I ain't seen the sun come up since I was knee high to a grasshopper."

I had neither the time nor the temperament to argue with him. "We've got a job to do," I said.

"I don't work for you or nobody else," he snapped. "I dig graves."

"You may have to by morning."

I hurried to the back door, and Charley Moseby followed, probably because he was already awake, up on his feet, and had nothing better to do. He was unaware that Ike Rigby was on the prowl again, that Dora Hand and a stranger named Wyatt Earp would be shotgunned down in the street outside if we didn't act and act fast, and I wasn't sure there was sufficient time left to act at all.

"What you plannin' on doin'?" he asked as we stepped out in the narrow alleyway that ran behind the saloon.

I told him.

It seemed simple enough.

"What's gonna happen if your idea is as dadblamed deranged as I think it is?" Charley wanted to know.

"Then Fort Griffin may have to find itself another gravedigger," I told him.

The teamster's wagon yard lay just down the muddy

street to the east of town. I ran toward it, bending low, keeping myself as close to the shacks as possible. The rain had turned into a fine mist, and the low-hangiing clouds provided all the cover of darkness I needed. Ike Rigby couldn't see me even if he were looking, which he wasn't. His eyes still held Wyatt Earp and Dora Hand captive. Around him, Fort Griffin was either still asleep or dead drunk. Sometimes it was difficult to tell the difference.

Behind me I could hear the booming voice of the buffalo hunter. "You should have kept on moving when you hit town," he yelled at Wyatt Earp, still motionless, Dora Hand sobbing in his arms, looking more like a statue than a man, "especially if you ain't got no more sense than to mess with Ike Rigby. I'd rather face a hungry mountain lion with my bare hands than face Ike Rigby when he's mad, and, stranger, I'm gettin' madder by the minute, and by daylight I may be mad enough to tear this whole damn town apart and get rid of ever'thing that still's movin' after I rip the last damn board off the last damn building."

Wyatt Earp's voice was as clear, as unhurried, and calm as if he were discussing which way he wanted the cook to serve up his eggs for breakfast. "Mister," he said, "it appears to me that you were mad when you reached town." The flicker of a smile crossed Wyatt's face. "It wouldn't surprise me to find out you were mad as a hornet with his stinger missin' the day you were born," he said.

Ike Rigby threw back his head and roared with laughter. "I still got my stinger," he bellowed. "I got a stinger in both hands, and you're gonna feel the sting of both these sumbitches soon's I get ready to show you what happens when somebody sticks his nose in Ike Rigby's business. You ain't gonna just lose a nose, stranger. You gonna lose your whole damn face."

I thought I could hear the soft, muffled whine of Dora

Hand crying, but it may have just been the rain blowing on the window panes above me. The night had always been a good hiding place. The darkness consumed me totally. I wouldn't have even known where I was if I had not been breathing so hard.

I had reached the wagon yard, wondering if Charley Moseby had made it to the livery stable, or if he had squatted down in the darkness behind some building, deciding that gravediggers weren't cut out for fighting. They just went to work when the fighting had ended. Whatever, I wouldn't think any more or any less of Charley regardless of what he was doing.

The mule team tied to the corral post was still hitched to an old Rocking B chuck wagon. They slept on their feet, preferring the warm outpouring of rain to the August sun that blisters the prairie. One was a nuisance, the other deadly.

I hastily threw saddle blankets into the wagon, buffalo skins, flour sacks, a bag of oats, two old hats and a shirt that had been torn into rags, anything in the teamster's shack that would burn. I doused it all thoroughly with kerosene, then lit a lamp hanging on the fence and pitched it on top of the pile. The blaze erupted, defying the mist and engulfing the wagon. The frightened mules fought at the ropes that kept them tethered to the post, and I untied them, pointing them toward the western side of town. A sharp slap on the rump and the mules were off in a dead run, weaving wildly down the street, trying to free themselves of the fire that was licking at their tails.

Wyatt Earp saw the blaze heading his way before he knew what it was, a pillar of fire weaving drunkenly through town. The mules heed and they hawed as loudly as they could, the bent, battered wheels of the wagon straining and groaning on rusty axles.

On it came. Closer. Always closer. A movable fire from the brimstone pits of hell itself, fearfully lighting up a night too wet to burn. The red glow of the flames danced across Wyatt Earp's solemn face, piercing the black pupils of his expressionless eyes.

Dora Hand stared at the blaze, mesmerized, as the mules tried desperately, then frantically, to outrun the fire chasing them.

Ike Rigby stepped out of the shadows and onto the rotting front porch of the Gold Nugget. He only had a brief moment to look at the flames reaching toward a soggy sky with long, skeletal fingers before hearing the pounding hooves of a running horse racing up the street behind him, almost on top of him.

He wheeled around and fired instinctively at the blazing Comanche blanket that Charley Moseby had tied with a rope to the tail of a crazed stallion. A fiery wagon bore down upon him from one side, a runaway horse from the other.

A second blast roared, and the sawed-off shotgun jerked convulsively beneath Ike Rigby's arm.

He was distracted just for the tick of a clock. No more. That was all it took. Wyatt Earp's Smith & Wesson fairly leapt into his hand. Ike Rigby never saw it.

His eyes, like a pendulum, were swinging back and forth between the pillars of fire. He had no time to think about where he was going or how fast he would get there. The first bullet caught him just above the right eyebrow. He staggered forward, and the laughter died with a gurgle in his throat. The light went out of his eyes. The second tore open his throat. Ike Rigby did not feel the second slug.

Dora Hand screamed both times.

♠

♥ 9 ♦

♣

The burning wagon tore loose from the terrified team of horses just beyond the crooked arroyo that wound its way into the scrawny live oak stand behind Fort Griffin. It rolled into the dry wash, end over end, and the last of the flames made one final effort to consume everything within their reach before dying away in a shower of sparks and alkali dust. And when Charley Moseby's crazed horse finally outran the Comanche blanket, leaving the fire to sputter and finally drown in pools of rainwater that filled the ruts, the street that separated the Gold Nugget and Double Eagle Saloons darkened as if somebody had tied a blindfold around our eyes.

Wyatt Earp watched me step out of the livery stable and begin ambling up the muddy alleyway toward him. His Smith & Wesson had four shots left—three if he kept one chamber empty the way most shootists did—and it was pointed somewhere between my belt buckle and breastbone. Earp stood calm and relaxed. Three shots were plenty if he decided the man marching up the alley with no face and less of a name deserved a good shooting. Three shots were two more than he needed.

He stood slightly slouched to balance himself beneath the weight of Dora Hand. His eyes and his trigger finger were both wired to the same nerve, and it had every reason to be frayed. What his eyes told him, he did instinctively. He did not hesitate or cloud his mind with unnecessary questions. That's what kept Wyatt Earp alive.

"Getting rid of Ike Rigby will get you elected mayor around here," I called out. "Shooting me will get you a date with Isaac Parker and probably breakfast with old Fraley, provided, of course, your throat's not squeezed too tight to handle the devil's ham and eggs."

The silence was as thick as the darkness between us.

I waited for him to answer and kept walking.

Finally he said, "They told me I'd find you here, Hawkes." Wyatt Earp turned his head toward the fallen Ike Rigby and nodded. "It's just that nobody told me I'd find him."

His revolver slid into its scarred leather holster as quickly, as easily, as it had leapt into his gun hand. He still held the limp form of Dora Hand firmly in his arms. Her face was buried in his shoulder, and I could hear her whimpering softly as I walked closer to him.

"Who is he?" the shootist wanted to know. "I detest killing a man if I don't know who he is or why I killed him."

"A buffalo hunter named Ike Rigby," I told him.

"I can't say as I've ever heard of him."

"Those who did wished to God they hadn't."

Wyatt Earp frowned as he moved closer to the fallen hulk of Ike Rigby, who died without having the decency to close his eyes. There was still a haunting look of disbelief etched on the big man's face, his beard matted with blood. Some people know they are going to die, and they're ready for it, even if they don't like it, whenever it comes. Others don't expect to ever die. And it's a real disappointment to them when they do. Ike Rigby went down a disappointed man.

"What was he doing with the girl?" Wyatt Earp asked.

"The buffalo had gotten a little too tame for him," I answered the best I could. "Ike preferred hunting people, especially pretty ladies who never seem to look the same when he leaves town."

"What reason did he have to hurt this one?"

"Ike didn't need a reason, just an opportunity."

The sound I heard behind me was a familiar sound. Good old Charley Moseby was shuffling up the street, dragging his shovel in the dirt behind him.

Ezra Bodine had limped across the street and was on his hands and knees, trying to get up enough nerve to close Ike Rigby's eyes. His hands trembled. It was as though he feared the buffalo hunter would start breathing again at any minute and maybe even reach up and bite off his fingers if Ezra did not pull them back quickly enough.

"Bury him deep, Charley," Ezra Bodine said.

"I'll do the best I can."

"I got some dynamite down in the station house," Ezra told him. "We can blast a hole so damn deep that sonuvabitch can't ever climb back out."

Around us, one by one, a nervous army of flickering lights began to appear in the windows overlooking Wyatt Earp, the actress who had her arms wound tightly around his neck and showed no intentions of letting go, and the rest of us, who just happened to be at the right cross section of time to watch a man who needed killing get what he deserved.

A hush settled down on Fort Griffin like one of those strange autumn fogs that rises up out of the alkali flats and rolls across the prairie like a windblown tumbleweed.

"You responsible for the burning wagon?" Wyatt Earp wanted to know.

I nodded. "Charley Moseby set the blanket on fire and damn near scared a good horse to death."

"I guess you saved my life." A wry grin touched his face. "It's getting to be a habit, one I'm not particularly accustomed to."

"I just bought you a little time," I told him. "Mr. Smith and Mr. Wesson saved your life. They pack a lot more firepower than I do."

The thunder was only a diffident growl in the west, and the lightning tried one final time to sear the sky but fell helplessly beyond the mesas. The storm had grown weary of Fort Griffin and, like most of us, sooner or later, had left to see what lay at the far end of the railroad tracks. This time, Ike Rigby wouldn't be going along with it.

"I didn't know how long it'd take me, Hawkes," Wyatt Earp said after a moment or two of awkward silence, "but I knew I'd find you sooner or later."

"I didn't know I was worth looking for."

"Most men aren't." Wyatt Earp glanced skyward. The moon poked its head through a break in the clouds briefly, then the warm rain began to fall around us again. "But I owe you, Hawkes. You bailed me out when I didn't have a penny to my name, nobody to bet with and tryin' to run a bluff without a hole card."

"Forget it," I said.

"I can forget about somebody cheatin' me, shootin' at me, or stealin' from me." Wyatt Earp's stone face cracked with a faint grin. "Hell, out in this country they do it all the time. After a while, as long as they miss and don't take too much of your money, you just don't pay much attention to it. But if my daddy taught me anything in life, he taught me to pay my debts. He damn sure did even when he didn't have nothin' but a handful of seeds, a sore-legged mule, and a secondhand plow. The only difference between his debts and mine is the amount due. To him, ten dollars was all the money in the world. I don't even set down at a table with a man if he don't have more than ten dollars. But when I die, you can carve it on that tombstone that I paid ever'body what I owed 'em 'fore I cashed in my chips. That includes the devil. Isaac Parker. Half of Texas. Damn near all of Arkansas. And by gawd, Brady Hawkes, that includes you, too."

"You must have had a run of luck," I said.

"What makes you say that?"

"It didn't take you long to turn up the two hundred and fifty dollars."

Wyatt Earp's face turned solemn again. "I ain't got two hundred and fifty dollars," he said quietly. "I tracked you down, Brady Hawkes, so's me an' you can settle this debt fair and square. I'll draw you high card for the full amount."

"Sounds fair enough," I told him, since the two hundred and fifty dollars in question had come from Judge Parker's pockets, not mine.

"We'll get us a new deck." Wyatt Earp said. "I'll shuffle. You cut. If I win, we'll call the debt even."

"What happens if you lose?" I asked.

Wyatt Earp stared at me for a long time, carefully contemplating the question. At last he shrugged indignantly and said, "I don't rightly know. I never gave any thought to me not winning."

He glanced down at the woman in his arms, then looked back toward me, bewilderment embedded in his eyes. "What's the lady's name?" he asked.

"Dora Hand."

"She work here?"

I smiled. "She's just passing through," I said.

Wyatt Earp nodded and carried Dora Hand into the Double Eagle Saloon and up the flight of stairs to her room, last door on the left.

♠

♥ 10 ♦

♣

Charley Moseby was older than his years, as thin as a reed
and almost as brittle. His eyes were sullen and sunk back
into the dark hollows of his face, his shoulders bent from
digging too many holes in a grim earth that had been
parched and packed hard by wind and sun and the hooves of
a million longhorn steers treading toward a faraway land
that lay somewhere beneath the north star. He never got in
a hurry. He never had to. His customers were never in a
hurry. Charley Moseby could take all the time he wanted, as
far as they were concerned. And he seldom had to put up
with the weeping, the wailing, or the grievances of some
grieving relative, which is what appealed to him about the
job in the first place. Charley Moseby did not like confron-
tations of any kind. He had no objections about putting a
man in his grave as long as he was not personally responsible for the deceased needing one.

The unfortunates who drew their last breaths in the streets
and alleyways and sultry little back rooms of Fort Griffin,
for whatever reason, hardly ever had any next of kin or
anyone else to mourn their departure. They were generally
accompanied to the burying ground by a few acquaintances

who felt an obligation to pay their last respects and a handful of enemies who wanted to make damn sure they were in the box and the box was in the hole.

Ike Rigby took his final journey the same way he chose to live, alone. Charley Moseby went with him, of course. But a genuine, certified gravedigger who had been called to duty by God and the town council did not have any other choice.

Charley Moseby, if nothing else, was a thorough man. From the body of Ike Rigby he took the buffalo hunter's skinning knife, which he sold to Ezra Bodine for two dollars and thirty-four cents, and Ezra, being schooled in the mysteries of commerce, promptly placed the knife on display down in the station house where he was building a little corner museum. Someday, he said, travelers to the West would pay good money, or at least a dime apiece, to view the fragments of history he had managed to preserve and stuff in a glass case he bought from a candy peddler who had spent his last dollar with Miss Dottie Dembo and did not have the fare back to Fort Worth.

Ike Rigby's pockets yielded two Mexican gold pieces, a faded New Testament with a bullet hole through the Gospel of Luke and most of Acts, the captain's insignia off a military uniform, an Indian bearclaw necklace, and the yellowed photograph of a naked dancing girl, clipped from the magazine advertisement of a traveling St. Louis burlesque show. Charley Moseby could barely conceal his grin. The Mexican gold pieces alone made burying Ike Rigby a worthwhile chore, even if the hint of daybreak promised to be hot enough to make Ike Rigby break out in a sweat, and the buffalo hunter had not been known to sweat too many times when he was alive.

The lanky gravedigger had already pocketed two dollars and thirty four cents, thanks to Ezra Bodine's lust for a

bloody skinning knife. Charley Moseby would try to get the
buffalo hunter in the ground by sunrise, then auction off
both the shotguns before night came crawling back to Fort
Griffin. The death of Ike Rigby had been quite a bonanza,
the best haul he had made since a gang of Kiamichi bandits
ambushed the Butterfield stage with the president of two
banks and a Wells Fargo attorney aboard. But that had been
ten years ago.

Charley Moseby was laughing at his good fortune,
making no sound but laughing just the same, while a pair of
sawed-off mules hauled him and the last remains of Ike
Rigby down past the mesquite stand, beside a little garden
that Dottie Dembo had lost to the weeds, and up the hill
toward a barren mound of wooden crosses that, as fate
would deem it, had been chosen to serve as the buffalo
hunter's final resting place.

A reluctant sun had just creased the sky when I heard the
first dynamite blast and felt it shake the ground beneath my
feet.

The rest of Fort Griffin was awake and had their curious
heads sticking out the windows by the time the second blast
rattled their windows. Ike Rigby would be famous now, not
for his deeds, but for being sunk down in the deepest grave
in Texas, maybe the world, or at least as far north as
Montana.

May he rest in peace.

Amen.

The bar of the Double Eagle was closed, although Ben
Carson would pour you a drink if you woke him up and had
four bits to pay for a shot glass of whiskey imported by
mule from Jacksboro. Carson preferred sleeping, but he
hated to see a grown man go thirsty in a land where thirst
was as common as cow chips and almost as dry. Sarah Jane
was frying eggs, and she had a thick slab of bacon the size

of a beefsteak that she was throwing into the grease by the time I reached the staircase. An old carpetbag, covered with huge flowers that had lost their bloom, lay on the floor beside the stove.

"You hungry?" she asked.

Ben Carson was snoring on a mourner's bench behind the bar. A good killing always wore him out, whether or not he was involved, and the brushy-headed, red-faced bartender would walk a block out of the way to keep from being involved in anything that required a man to pull a weapon of any make or model and either stand behind it or in front of it.

"I hadn't given it much of a thought till I smelled the bacon frying," I answered, doing my best to smile pleasantly as I backed down the stairs.

"There's plenty of breakfast here for the both of us," Sarah Jane said. "And I don't feel like eating alone."

It was curious. Sarah Jane had the longest legs and the fairest skin in all of Fort Griffin, and she did not know what it was like being alone. She usually had the pleasure of one customer, while another rogue or renegade was waiting outside, playing solitaire, which he would not have to be playing much longer. But now, her cheeks were flushed and puffy. She had been crying, probably most of the night, but the tears had been unable to wash away or dim the red, ragged gashes that Ike Rigby's skinning knife had carved on her face. These were the least of her injuries. They would be with her a long time, and Sarah Jane would never get rid of the memories of Ike Rigby. The mirrors would not let her.

"I'd be honored to join you for breakfast," I said. "A body that don't get up early around here don't know what he's missing."

She tried hard to smile but did not have much luck. "I'm sure gonna miss this place," Sarah Jane said.

"I didn't know you were leaving."

"Ike Rigby didn't give me much choice."

"Ike Rigby's gone now."

Sarah Jane nodded, and her sigh was one of defeat. "He took my looks with him," she said.

"Running's not always the right thing to do," I said, wondering why a man who was always wandering from town to town, changing directions as often as a west Texas wind, would give her such narrow-minded advice.

"If I stay here, ever'body that sees me will say, Why that's the woman old Ike Rigby carved up. A woman with a pretty face has a hard time earning a living out here anymore," Sarah Jane said matter of factly. "Nobody wants the services of a woman who's gotten too old and too tired and been carved up by old Ike Rigby."

"People will forget. They always do."

"But ever'body who comes to town will want to see the woman whose face was whittled by Ike Rigby." Sarah Jane sighed from a terrible depth. "I might as well buy me a tent on the edge of town and put up a sign that says, 'See the woman carved by Ike Rigby. She walks. She talks. She bleeds for a nickel.'"

Sarah Jane had filled the room with self-pity. Now she was wallowing in it.

"Where you headed?" I wanted to know.

"Dodge, I guess."

"That's a tough town."

"They're all tough towns."

I could not argue that point. "Why Dodge?"

"That's where the next train is headed."

"From what I hear," I cautioned, "Dodge is not a safe place for a lady."

"Maybe not for a lady. But from what I hear," Sarah Jane said, "whores do just fine."

She mopped the last crumbs of a well-done egg from her plate with a chunk of sourdough bread and had just finished chewing when she rose abruptly and began to straighten her hair. "It's time," she said.

I nodded and picked up the carpetbag that held her clothes. "I'll carry this to the station for you," I said.

"You don't have to do that, Mr. Hawkes."

"It's the least I can do." I shrugged and nodded toward the empty plate I was leaving. "You cook up a real good batch of eggs."

"Don't thank me," she replied. "The chicken did all the work."

The railroad station lay at the western end of town, a small one-room building painted yellow. A single wooden bench sat outside. Another one waited inside. Ezra Bodine had planted petunias in a small box beneath the station window. But the sun had burned most of them off at the stems. Only a white bloom and a withered purple one were still managing to hold on. That's the way it was in the harsh, barren land that rolled endlessly west of Fort Griffin. It was inhospitable. It could sometimes be downright cruel. But someone—or some thing—always managed to hold on and take his rightful, even if it was unlawful, place beside the rattlesnakes and horned toads, which almost always made better neighbors than did the human species.

Sarah Jane stepped up on the station platform and I set her carpetbag next to the bench beside her. She turned and looked back over the collection of weather-worn shacks and slab-board buildings she was leaving behind. They were virtually lost behind a veil of heat and dust shimmering up off the prairie between town and the tracks. The town had looked old and decrepit the day it was nailed together, primarily to serve the wayward soldiers of a misbegotten army outpost who fought most of their skirmishes and all of their battles among themselves and within the whiskey-stained walls of the Double Eagle and Gold Nugget saloons. The village should have been condemned. Those who came and never found the road out of town certainly were.

"The first time I saw Fort Griffin, I thought it was the ugliest town I had ever seen," she said. "Nothing's changed."

The faraway whistle of a train rode the south wind into Fort Griffin, and Ezra Bodine carted an armload of cotton sacks out onto the platform. He, too, was wiping the sweat off his face, and his white shirt was plastered to his soft, round body.

"It must be early," I said to him.

"What?"

"The train."

Ezra Bodine shook his head no. "That's yesterday's train," he said. "Today's train won't be here till day after tomorrow. A hard rain messes up the tracks real bad. We're still waitin' on the train that was due in June sixteenth. Nobody never did tell me what happened to that one."

"What's the fare to Dodge, Mr. Bodine?" Sarah Jane asked.

"Thirty-three dollars flat. Another two dollars if you want one of them cars with a bed in it."

Sarah Jane kneeled down and opened up her carpetbag. From a little leather purse she pulled out thirty-five dollars and slowly handed them one at a time to Ezra Bodine. "I want the best you got," she said.

With her own Pullman car, I figured Sarah Jane would probably be in a position to earn that thirty-five dollars back at least twice before she reached Dodge, provided, of course, it got dark in a hurry, stayed dark a long time, and there were men on the train who did not care what Ike Rigby carved on her face.

Sarah Jane kissed Ezra Bodine good-bye, just a peck on the cheek, and he patted her back awkwardly.

"It's not gonna be the same without you," the old man said.

"Yes, it will," Sarah Jane told him.

And we all knew she was right. For a few days, the men down at the Double Eagle would drink a little, fold a few hands of cards, and remark, "I wonder whatever happened to Sarah Jane." And nobody would know. And after a while, nobody would ask the question anymore. She would be as nameless as those wooden crosses up on the barren hill that had recently been disturbed by the addition of Ike Rigby.

Yesterday's train was moving out by the time Ezra Bodine had thrown the last cotton sack into the baggage car. It had no time to waste. It was desperately trying to reach the Red River before today's train caught up with it. A matter of pride, I guess.

I heard the sound of the shovel dragging in the dirt before I saw Charley Moseby come around the corner of the station, dragging a burlap bag behind him. "Damn it all to hell," he said as he sat down on the edge of the platform. "It's so dadblamed hot up there I saw a dog chasin' a rabbit, and they was both walkin'."

"You get it done?" Ezra Bodine asked.

"He's down as deep as he'll go."

"You don't think he'll climb out of that grave and come back to haunt us, do you?"

"If he does, he's gonna have a helluva time locatin' Fort Griffin."

"What makes you say that, Charley?"

Charley Moseby held up the burlap bag and tossed it onto the platform floor at Ezra Bodine's feet. It landed with a soft, hollow thud. "He's gonna have to find his head first," Charley Moseby said. "Ike Rigby can't find a good place to shit without his head."

♠

♥ 11 ♦

♣

On the second day after his two well-placed bullets rid Fort Griffin of Ike Rigby, Wyatt Earp came back out of Dora Hand's room and swaggered down the staircase, his cold, emotionless eyes sweeping the bar, studying each face that turned his way, trying to determine who his friends were, if he had any friends at all. He was alone, not counting Mr. Smith and Mr. Wesson, who rode comfortably in the holster on his right hip. Wyatt Earp was still wearing the black garb preferred by most professional gamblers, although I had never seen him play a game of cards or deal any faro. Maybe he wasn't a gambler. Maybe he had just found the garb, or taken it from some gambling man whose aim was as crooked as the hand he dealt. He was wearing a black, long-tailed coat, even though the rest of us in the Double Eagle were sweating, and the expression on his face was as detached, as cool, as though he was impervious to the heat. His hat sat low over his forehead, shading his eyes in a barroom lit by only two gas lamps, and one of them was flickering weakly.

Dora Hand slipped out of her room and moved to the top of the stairs as Wyatt Earp descended them. She had never

appeared more elegant. A long green satin dress flowed off
her bare shoulders, and the hem brushed the floor. Her dark
hair was pulled back and braided in layers on top of her
head. She held her chin high, clutching a single red rose bud
in her hand, and for a moment it was easy to forget what the
elegant and lovely Dora Hand really was. She actually
might have been an actress, a misplaced songbird in a
misplaced land, searching for a stage. Maybe she had
already found one in her bawdy house boudoir. At least she
had her leading man.

Wyatt Earp paused beside the bar and tapped it twice
without bothering to look around at Ben Carson. The
stoop-shouldered bartender dried his hands on a dirty towel
draped around his waist and reached under the counter
where, it was rumored, he kept his finest whiskey, the rare
bottles that came from Kentucky instead of Jacksboro.

Dottie Dembo had paid top dollar for the whiskey, and
Ben Carson charged top dollar. He did not charge Wyatt
Earp anything.

Tennessee McClosky, thick shouldered and a little too
paunchy, stood leaning against the bar beside the shootist,
carefully examining the double-barreled shotgun, one of the
few worldly possessions left behind by the late Ike Rigby.
McClosky was one of those men who grew old quickly and
stayed that way for a long time. His features were chiseled
by too much wind and not enough rain. He looked to be in
his forties, but his hair was beginning to gray at the temples.
And the sunburn had left a festered sore that would not heal
just beneath his right eyes. He wore faded blue trousers and
a yellow checked vest that hung loosely over a white shirt
that had not been really white since it was washed the first
time in Alkali Creek. He had been busting wild horses for
the Half Moon Ranch for almost a decade, and the older he
got the more Tennessee McClosky hurt when it rained.

He had never been a shotgun man, said he could cut down any rattlesnake on the Half Moon with his .44 carbine. Besides, he hunted coyotes from time to time, but never any kind of beast resembling man, and he politely stayed out of the way of those who might have a reason for hunting him. Yet Tennessee McClosky could not take his hands off the pair of shotguns. The long one was heavy, and the stock had been carved by hand from an old hickory tree, but it fit his hands like it belonged there. They were part of history, he said, but did not know which part.

Before he finished belching up his lunch of peppered beef jerky and Jacksboro whiskey, Tennessee McClosky had talked Charley Moseby out of the double barrel, giving him twelve and a half dollars if Charley would throw a box of shells into the deal. For twelve and a half dollars, Charley Moseby would steal a box of shells, which he no doubt did.

Tennessee McClosky held the shotgun out for Wyatt Earp to admire. The shootist ignored him. He had seen shotguns before, even faced a few, and he was not particularly impressed.

"A shotgun's only good at close range," he said dryly. "I don't plan on gettin' that close to anybody who wants to kill me, unless I have no other choice. Given the choice, I'll wait out behind somebody's barn and shoot his fool head off."

"That don't seem to me like a very fair way to fight," Tennessee McClosky told him, scratching his whiskered chin with the barrel of the shotgun.

"I looked at the rule books," Wyatt Earp said with the wisp of a smile. "And there ain't but one rule. That's stayin' alive longer than the other fellow."

"I still say it ain't fair."

"It's worked for me."

Ike Rigby's belly blaster lay on the back corner table in front of me. I usually made it a habit of carrying some sort of weapon when necessary. With Ike Rigby gone, it was probably no longer necessary. But I did not plan on staying in Fort Griffin forever, maybe not past Monday, and the roads kept leading me farther west, leaving civilization farther behind. The ground in that territory, I'm told, is filled with the graves of strangers, but damn few strangers who had a belly blaster hanging from their side. Wyatt Earp said a shotgun, sawed off or otherwise, was only good at close range. Most card games are.

Besides, Charley Moseby said he only wanted six dollars, but I could have it for five, and, the last time I checked, my life was still worth five dollars. So I made Charley Moseby, by his own account, the richest man in Fort Griffin, Texas.

Wyatt Earp walked straight toward me, never looking either right or left, his jaw set firmly. He carried a new deck of cards in one hand, both shot glasses of whiskey in the other. He set one glass on the table in front of me and stacked the cards beside it.

"Shuffle," he said. "I'll cut."

"You can forget about the five hundred dollars," I told him. "You're not obligated to me in any way at all. I was merely playing with the judge's money and won a few more dollars than the judge needed. That's all."

"The judge wasn't real pleased with what you did." Wyatt Earp's eyes narrowed. "He hanged two Mexican sheepherders and a retired Wells Fargo shotgun guard by the time you got to Texas."

"What'd they do?"

"The sheepherders killed an old woman who had hired them to look after her sheep," he answered, "and the shotgun guard used his shotgun on a bank teller down in Cimarron, or some little town south of there."

"The bastards deserved to hang."

"Probably. But the judge wouldn't have strung all three of

'em up at the same time if he hadn't been mad at you."
Wyatt Earp slowly shook his head. "It was the greatest
spectacle Fort Smith had seen since Barney Jacobs burned
down a whorehouse because one of the girls got him drunk
one night and shaved every last hair off his body. It was a
lot of hair, too. Barney was a big man."

"Judge Parker must not have been real happy about
having to turn you loose."

"He thinks you stole from the church."

"God didn't care."

"Judge Parker sure as hell did."

I drained my shot glass of whiskey. Wyatt Earp did the
same.

"That's old water under the bridge now," I said, pushing
the cards aside, "and the bridge is washed out, and won't
neither one of us be going back to Arkansas. You don't owe
me, and I have no interest in collecting. So if you don't let
the bail money worry you, I certainly won't let it concern
me."

Wyatt Earp reached over, picked up the deck of cards, and
shoved them in my face. "Shuffle," he said. He spat the
word out as though it tasted bad, and his eyes were hard as
nails and almost as pointed.

I did, slowly, deliberately, letting him watch my every
move. I placed the cards back down on the table. "Cut," I
said.

Wyatt Earp, just as slowly, just as deliberately, spread the
cards across the table, turning one of them over.

A jack. Of clubs.

A faint, arrogant smile touched the corners of his lips.

Wyatt Earp was a decent man. He had steady nerves,
never backed down from a fight in his life, no matter how
crooked it might be, and most of them were. He would look
a man straight in the eye when he talked, could shoot just as

straight when he had to, but only when he had to, and was unfailingly loyal to any man, and probably any woman, who had been loyal to him. If you needed him, you could depend on Wyatt Earp being there, whether you asked him to come or not. The odds were never important to him. He would help you whip one man or an army. It did not matter to him. Friendship was the only religion Wyatt Earp ever understood or practiced.

But sometimes he could be a real pain.

This was one of those times.

I ran my fingertips lightly over the cards, never taking my eyes off him. His gaze met mine. The gunfighter and the gambler. He had already drawn and fired. Finally I rested my hand on top of the third card from the left. "You lose," I said.

I thought I saw his faint smile darken just a moment. "You don't know that for a fact," he said.

"You lose," I repeated.

"Let's see the card."

"I know we've agreed to erase the five hundred dollars from your ledger if you win. But I do not believe we have come to any understanding about what happens if you lose," I said, placing a heavier than normal emphasis on the word "lose."

"I pay double or I pay nothing," he said, "if that is agreeable to you."

I nodded and picked the card up between my fingers and slowly turned it around to face him.

A king. Of hearts.

He drew his Smith & Wesson with the deft quickness of a striking rattlesnake and shot the heart out of the king. I felt the card flutter like a faint pulse beat in my hand, nothing else.

Ben Carson dove behind the bar.

Tennessee McClosky blasted both barrels of his shotgun into the ceiling as he backed out the batwing doors of the Double Eagle. He wasn't aiming at anybody or any thing. It was just the reflex action from a frightened man who felt more comfortable with a wild horse under him than a shotgun in his hands.

One of the girls screamed. I had never seen her before.

Dora Hand tried her best to faint, but did not have much of luck. She finally sat down on a stool beside the bar and drank the rest of Tennessee McClosky's whiskey, and a braid fell from the top of her head and gently rested on her bare shoulder.

"I think you cheated," Wyatt Earp said.

"If you call a man a cheat in this game, you better be ready to kill him," I replied, calmly picking up the remaining fifty-one cards and stacking them in front of Earp. "If you don't, he's got every right to kill you."

"Is that a threat?"

"I don't threaten any man I can beat at cards," I said.

He stared at me. Hard. Every muscle in his face wound as tightly as barbed wire around a mesquite post.

Then Wyatt Earp broke out laughing. "I guess I owe you another drink," he said.

"Get an extra glass," I said.

"Why?"

"We'll drink one for old Fraley, too."

"I'll get the glass and the bottle," Wyatt Earp said. "You pay for 'em."

"I can afford it," I told him. "As soon as you pay me what you owe me, I'll have a thousand dollars."

"I thought you said you'd forget it," he said, picking up the king of hearts, missing a heart, and sticking it into the band of his hat.

"I will," I said. "But you won't."

"You think you know me pretty well," Wyatt Earp said, heading slowly toward the bar.

"I'm pretty good at reading cards," I answered. "I'm better at reading men."

We drank once to each other, once to old Fraley, and once to Judge Isaac Parker, may his rope never break unless our necks are in the noose.

Wyatt Berry Stapp Earp was what his mother named him. And his daddy said he was born to fight. It was his birthright, his heritage. He could not outrun it, and he never tried. Wyatt Earp acquired a resolute sense of justice from his father, but not the stern kinship the elder Earp had with the earth beneath his boots. Wyatt Earp never stayed on any patch of new ground long enough to call it his or feel at home there.

His father told him late one afternoon as they watched the blaze of a neighbor's house throw red flames into a darkening sky, after some outlaws had torched it, "It's a hard land we live on, son. It's overrun by a lot of hard men. We can't fight 'em all. But we can stand firm against those who ride against us. Sometimes, you're gonna look around and feel though the law is as unjust as the lawless. Maybe it is. But it's all we got. And generally the law expresses the will of the decent folks who are trying to build up this country. It'll do just fine until someone can offer a better safeguard for a man's rights. It's not enough to simply obey the law, Wyatt. It's every man's duty to uphold it and enforce it, or they've got no right expecting the law to protect them when things go bad. And sooner or later, they always go bad."

Most folks I know have five senses. Wyatt Earp had six. He had the instinct to survive even during the hardest of times, and those were the times he knew best and most often.

By the time he got to Kansas City after the Civil War, he was running in the company of Wild Bill Hickock, Billy Dixon, Bermuda Carlisle, Old Man Keeler and Cheyenne Jack. They had done their damnedest to tame the frontier, but the frontier, where mankind was dead set on fencing everything free but the wind, had not had any luck taming them. What impressed the impressionable Wyatt Earp most about these scouts, rogues, and buffalo hunters was their unmistakable mode of dress as they swaggered across Market Square. They wore black calfskin boots fashioned by hand, white linen shirts, and black broadcloth trousers. Their fancy vests were either silk or brocade and sometimes beaded buckskin. They dressed themselves in long-tail velvet-trimmed black frock coats, had black string ties tucked up under their chins, and used a broad-brimmed black sombrero to keep the sun off their faces. They fought renegades, Plains Indians, buffalo, gunfighters, rustlers, and each other. And Wyatt Earp learned one great lesson from them, one that prepared him for the rest of his life. They did not always win. But they seldom lost.

"A man ain't whipped as long as he stays on his feet," Cheyenne Jack told him. "He may be dyin', but he ain't dead till he hits the ground, and he ain't forgotten till they put him under it."

Wyatt Earp was barely twenty years old. But calendars did not mean much, not to him or anybody else who dared wander back and forth across no-man's land. They either grew up fast, or they generally did not grow up at all. They had a lot of acquaintances but few friends. The man who rode with you yesterday might shoot you tomorrow, provided you either had or didn't have something he wanted.

And they taught Wyatt Earp what it meant to stand eyeball to eyeball with a half-drunk gunslinger who had one thing on his mind, and that was to blow his head off, with or without his permission, generally without it.

"Both you an' him are standin' there nervous as a pig in a packin'house," an old gunfighter told him, and Wyatt was smart enough, even then, to listen to any gunfighter who had stayed alive long enough to grow old. He must have been doing something right. "He's gonna draw on you, an' you're gonna have to draw on him. And neither one of you are gonna hear more than one shot, maybe two at the most. He's thinkin' this may be it. And you're thinkin' this may be it. An' inside you're shakin' like a hound dog passin' a peach pit. There's gonna be one loser, maybe two. I've seen both men shoot each other to death, then one of 'em's gonna have to whip the other one just to see who gets through the pearly gates first. 'Course, the gates that let them in may not have any pearls on 'em. And occasionally, in a shootin' match, there's actually a winner. Let me tell you this, son. The winner is almost always the man who takes his time. His hand may be movin' faster'n a strikin' rattlesnake, but his mind ain't in no hurry at all. He takes it all in, deliberate and deadly. Then he points the barrel of that revolver like it was his finger, and by the time he squeezes the trigger, somebody's already callin' for the undertaker. If you ever get in a gunfight, son, what you want to do is make your first shot the last shot of the fight. If you have to shoot more than once, you generally ain't got the chance to shoot twice. I've seen a lot of gravediggers in my time, and they don't bury nobody who's still standin'."

After all these years, Wyatt Earp was still standing, the air around him pungent with the acrid odor of burnt gunpowder.

And I sat there slowly shuffling fifty-one cards.

One was missing, the king that lost his heart.

By the time the whiskey was only a harmless drop in the bottom of the bottle, Wyatt Earp motioned for Dora Hand, leaning against the bar, to join us. She walked slowly across the bar room floor, a big smile on her face, her hands on her hips. The dress grew tighter with every step she took.

"You know Miss Hand, I presume," Wyatt Earp said.

I nodded. "We've met," I answered, "though not under the best of circumstances as near as I can remember."

"I was more fortunate," Wyatt Earp said, slumping into the chair beside me and setting Miss Dora Hand on his lap, placing an arm around her tiny waist. "I can't recall the circumstances ever bein' any better."

"To the victor go the spoils," I said. It was a line I had read somewhere, either in school, in the Bible, or on the back of a cardboard fan from the Joplin Brothers Funeral Home in New Orleans.

"Miss Dora Hand is an actress." Wyatt Earp's voice was tainted with pride.

"Shakespearean, I believe."

"She's on her way to New York, you know."

"New York's a long way from here."

"Everywhere is a long way from here."

I turned toward Miss Dora Hand and asked politely, "Have you played New York before?"

"She has, I'm proud to say, performed on the world's greatest stages." Wyatt Earp turned the bottle upside down and waited patiently for the last drop of good whiskey to slowly inch its way down toward his empty glass.

"Maybe not all of them," Dora Hand interrupted, crossing her legs and laying her head softly against Wyatt Earp's shoulder. Her eyes were closed, and she wore a satisfied smile, which was the first one I had seen since arriving in Fort Griffin.

"She's going to sing tonight," Wyatt said proudly, spinning the empty glass on his forefinger, watching it reflect the golden glow from the flickering gas lamp that hung just above his shoulder.

"Where?"

"Here."

"The piano's broke. Shot to hell."

"Dora doesn't need a piano. She's got the voice of a songbird." Wyatt Earp leaned forward and grew serious. "It's her farewell performance."

I could not suppress my look of surprise. "I did not know Miss Dora Hand was going anywhere," I said.

"She's going with me." Wyatt Earp's eyes were as smug as his face.

"I've always had the distinct impression, Mr. Earp, that you were going straight to hell, riding a horse with a porcupine saddle." I wondered if the bottle in front of us had any whiskey left in it. "I'm not so sure it would be the kind of trip a young lady might want to take."

"She's going to be my wife." Wyatt Earp squeezed the last drop of sour mash from the bottle into a glass and handed the glass to me. "It is indeed a fortunate man who has that rare, once-in-a-lifetime opportunity to marry a beautiful actress who's been on the greatest stages in the world."

I smiled. I had a new, deeply profound respect for the lovely Dora Hand. She was undoubtedly a better actress than I had realized.

♠

♥ **12** ♦

♣

It was not the first time the ignominious Wyatt Earp had been in love, if he were indeed in love with a woman who had a beautiful face, a somewhat mysterious past, and private quarters in an upstairs room in the only bawdy house in Fort Griffin, Texas.

He had been only nineteen, if the calendar was right, when he stepped up before the preacher and wed Irilla Brummett, the girl just down the road and on the backside of his daddy's Iowa farm. The ceremony was a simple one, but strong enough, if the parson wasn't lying to them, to keep the couple together until death did them part.

She was as frail as an early wildflower that grew on the creek bank behind the bean patch, and she needed somebody to give her strength and warmth when the cold winds came rolling out of the Dakotas and stampeding across the prairie. Irilla decided that Wyatt was as solid as any rock on the family home place, and he worked alone for weeks, nailing together a little log cabin out where the scrub oak stubbornly held on to dirt that was as poor as he was.

He had not been able to give his bride a lot, not much more than his name. But he could damn sure keep her from having to live the way her mama lived and the way all of their neighbors were living. He could flat keep her bare feet off the dirt while she cooked and swept and cleaned the house. And Irilla told him that night she must be the richest—or at least the most fortunate—wife in all of Iowa. She owned the only wooden floor in the brakes and bramble bush of the Waukegan River valley.

Life was not an easy one, but nobody expected it to be. There were blisters and tears and a crop that wanted to die. But Wyatt Earp refused to let it. He kept the garden sprinkled with his own sweat and buckets of the muddy Waukegan water.

By next summer, he would have another little mouth crying for food. The thought of having a baby crawling around that wooden floor kept Wyatt Earp smiling and out in the fields working even when his muscles ached, and they almost always did.

Wyatt Earp did not know times were so hard, because he did not know anybody was having better ones, if, in fact, they were. He had staked his claim to the land, and he intended to keep it, even during those hot and dusty days when he was stricken with wanderlust, looking out over the handles of a plow and desperately feeling the urge in his gut to hit the trail again. Besides, nobody would ride away and desert the only wooden floor in the Waukegan River Valley.

Wyatt Earp and Irilla settled down, wrapped themselves against the winds of winter, and waited for spring. There had been clouds on the frost, so old-timers swore the ground was bound to be bad.

The ground froze.

And he thanked God for the wooden floor beneath his wife's tiny feet, and she thanked Wyatt, and together they dreamed of warm weather when another small voice would be added to their own.

The baby girl was born just about the time the first
tomatoes ripened on the vine. Wyatt Earp came running
from the fields, his heart pounding like a blacksmith
working over an anvil, when he saw the midwife step from
the door. From the stricken look on her face, the tear on her
cheek, he knew he would have no reason to ever smile
again.

That night, Wyatt Earp ripped up the only wooden floor
in the Waukegan River Valley. And from the boards he made
a pair of oblong coffins, one large and one small, though
neither were very big, and he buried all his hopes there
beneath the scrub oak that held stubbornly on to dirt as poor
as he was.

And just before sunrise, Wyatt Earp jammed the .44 pistol
his father had given him into his waistband, saddled up a
swaybacked old dun, too slow to run and too old to farm,
and rode west, headed to no place in particular, just west to
keep the sun out of his eyes. He never stuck another plow
point into the ground.

And, until that night, he had never let himself fall in love
again, if he were indeed in love with the woman who had a
beautiful face, swore she had graced the gilded stage
quoting the words of Bill Shakespeare, and did some of her
finest work for five dollars or less in the only bawdy house
in Fort Griffin, Texas. To be or not to be. She was what she
was, and that's all there was to it.

"You didn't strike me as the marryin' kind," I told him, as
Dora Hand, leaning against a piano that had not been played
since it got shot down in a barroom brawl, began to sing
some folk song that Scottish emigrants had brought over the
mountains with them years ago. It was a song my mother
had sung. The words were different, but nobody ever
listened to the words anyway.

"I've generally got no use for a wife, but Dora's different." Wyatt Earp settled down in his chair and closed his eyes. "My daddy always told me that you marry the first time because you don't want to live alone," he said, nodding gently to the rhythm of Miss Dora Hand's song. "You marry the last time because you don't want to die alone."

"You got a premonition?" I wanted to know.

"About what?"

"About dying."

He laughed softly. "Don't we all?" he asked. "The man who lives to be an old man out in this country is somebody who spends most of his days, and damn near all of his nights, by himself, is careful to always walk on the other side of the street, keeps his gun at home, is quick to apologize even when he's done nothing wrong, keeps out of sight either when there is a fight or there isn't, keeps his hands off another man's wife, cattle, or horse, not necessarily in that order, and doesn't ever make anybody mad, particularly not a woman."

"I don't think you're gonna be an old man," I told Wyatt Earp.

"If I reach thirty it's because there's a bunch of sumbitches out here who either shoot damn slow or damn crooked." Wyatt Earp absent mindedly pulled the Smith & Wesson from its holster and checked to make sure the chamber was full. "You ever think about it?" he asked.

"About what?"

"Dying."

"All I worry about is the next turn of the card."

"A gambling man can't expect to live long out here."

"He can if he doesn't cheat."

"A hard loser don't care if you're cheatin' or not."

I shrugged. "That's why I bought Charley Moseby's belly blaster," I said. "I can fire both barrels and reload by the time some two-bit card player has time to get to his feet, jerk an overweight pistol out of his holster, cock the hammer, and get off a shot."

"You never needed a belly blaster before."

"Maybe I've got a premonition," I said.

Wyatt Earp nodded, satisfied. "Maybe you ought to get married, too."

"I live with four queens in every deck," I told him. "I can't ever count on those women. There's no reason why I should have another one hanging around."

"In most towns, Mr. Smith and Mr. Wesson are the only friends I got," Wyatt Earp said. "At least, they're the only ones who'll take up for me when I get in trouble."

"That's the best reason I know why you shouldn't get married."

"That's why a man needs a wife," he said dryly. "Mr. Smith and Mr. Wesson are pretty good to have around when somebody's mad and gettin' madder all the time an' out tryin' to kill me. But I've slept with 'em fairly often over the last ten years or so, an' they don't make me feel any better when I wake up in the mornin' than I did when I went to bed the night before."

"A good woman's cheap," I replied, glancing up the stairway where each room promised a certain amount of pleasure, and men of all shapes, sizes, and odors paid a lot more when they were full of rotgut whiskey than they did stone cold sober. A drunk had no reason to hang on to his money. He wasn't expecting to see the sun rise anyway. A clear-eyed, clear-thinking man kept back enough dollars in the sweat band of his hat to come calling again, whether she asked him to or not.

"A cheap woman won't mourn me when I'm gone," Wyatt Earp said, drawing a deep breath. "A wife will."

"Miss Dora Hand might not."

"What makes you say that?"

"She doesn't even know you," I argued. "How could she be in love with you? Why do you think she would shed any tears when Charley Moseby, or somebody like him, carts your cold, stiff body up to the burying ground?"

Wyatt Earp smiled. "She's an actress," he said. "An actress can cry anytime she damn well wants to."

I wondered if she would want to, then decided it did not make any difference. A dead man doesn't know who grieves or who dances on his grave. And generally the only ones crying over a closed coffin are those he owed money to when he died. That's about the only thing I can say in favor of dying. It's a damn good way to get out of debt.

"Where is this wedding going to take place?" I asked.

"Here in Fort Griffin." Wyatt Earp shrugged, and his voice remained flat and calm. "It's where I met her. I guess it's where we're obligated to make it legal. Besides, Dora thinks the town's got a real pretty little chapel down at the far end of the street. I'd just as soon get married up there at the Double Eagle bar, but she says God don't come in here much, an' if we go to the trouble of tying the knot she wants to make doggone sure God's there to bless it and tie it tight." He shrugged again.

"Fort Griffin's got a church," I said. "It doesn't have a preacher man."

"I been thinkin' about that," Wyatt Earp replied. "You dress up decent enough, Hawkes. I guess you can marry us."

I thought about laughing out loud until I realized that Wyatt Earp was dead serious. "I've been accused of being a lot of things in my life," I told him, "but never a preacher man."

"Can you read?"

I nodded that I could, and he reached into the pocket of his black coat and pulled out a piece of wrinkled paper, filled with words that had been scrawled by a man who had not had any reason to write down anything resembling words for a long time.

"I jotted down some notes about love and honor, cherish and obey, and a line or two about death partin' us." Wyatt Earp's eyes grew solemn as he leaned across the table, his voice as solemn as a grand jury indictment. "Just read it pretty much the way I wrote it," he said, "and I figure it's solid enough to hold up in court, since there ain't no court in Fort Griffin, and damn few of 'em west of here."

"You've got the words down pretty good."

"It's not the first time I've said 'em."

There was, however, one thing troubling me. "Miss Dora Hand knows I've never been a preacher before," I said.

"That's all right," he answered. "She's never been a wife before, so I guess y'all come out about even."

If my lack of theology did not bother Wyatt Earp, it certainly did not bother me. "When's the wedding taking place?" I wanted to know.

"The day after tomorrow. Probably in the evening. Dora said it would take her that long to make her dress."

"White, I assume."

"Most wedding dresses are."

"I don't expect you to be wearing white."

Wyatt Earp shook his head and pulled his hat back low over his eyes. "I'll be wearin' the same suit they bury me in," he said.

"Who's your best man?" I asked, doing my best to think like a preacher man. "I'm not sure, but I think you're supposed to have one."

"I guess you are, Hawkes."

"I'm the preacher."

"You're also the only man who's gonna be there, as far as I know," Wyatt Earp said casually. "People don't show up for either a man's birthin' and his weddin' like they do to his funeral."

"Dying's permanent," I said. "I've seen ticks on a calf's belly last longer than most marriages do."

Miss Dora Hand hit a high note. I don't believe I had ever heard a human voice hit a note that high and wasn't particularly sure I wanted to hear it again. She threw her head back, clasped her dainty hands tightly together beneath her chain and hit it anyway. I wondered how long it would be before the coyotes started howling, too. They at least had the decency to wait for a full moon.

The morning after Wyatt Earp's sudden and unexpected announcement came sooner than Fort Griffin was expecting it, which was usually what happened in a frontier town where the saloon never closed, the girls upstairs never got to sleep until well after sunrise, and the pigs had a bad habit of laying down in the street with every renegade, rogue, buffalo hunter, cowboy, or drifter who found a warm wallow for his bed. It was a good way for a pig to lose his reputation, but a reputation, either good or bad, didn't mean anything to a hog.

Mornings were always peaceful in Fort Griffin. The train had come and gone, a day late as usual. Nobody got off, but nobody got on, so Fort Griffin was not better nor worse off than it had been the day before. Charley Moseby got bored and hiked up the hill, digging a hole in the ground just in case somebody might need it before he got back from Buffalo Gap, or if his blonde-haired Norwegian wife in Fort Griffin Flat found out about his dark-haired Tejano wife in Buffalo Gap.

The sun had flipped into the sky like a Mexican gold piece by the time Wyatt Earp escorted the lovely Miss Dora Hand out the front door of the Double Eagle and down to the freshly painted buggy waiting for them at the livery stable.

The man who shot Ike Rigby pretty much had what he wanted in a town that, only a day or so earlier, had found itself trembling whenever Ike Rigby raised either his voice or his skinning knife. He even had a wife in waiting that would mourn him when he was gone, provided, of course, the illustrous Mr. Wyatt Earp departed in a funeral procession instead of riding a fast horse.

Dora Hand was wearing a radiant smile that a grown man might have considered seductive if Wyatt Earp had not been holding her arm. The air around her was thick with the fragrance of a Parisian perfume, and her dress was cut a little too low to be classified as demure, although a ruffle of white lace did the best it could to keep her modesty intact. Dora Hand twirled a yellow parasol in her hand, obviously to keep the sun from touching and therefore damaging her lovely face. In her profession, actress or otherwise, too many wrinkles could put her out of business and on the streets. For whatever reason, old men definitely did not prefer old women.

"Mornin', Mr. Hawkes," she said in a soft southern drawl. "I understand from Wyatt that you used to be a preacher."

I glanced quickly at him. He shrugged. And I looked back at her again. "Yes, ma'am," I lied. "Back in Iowa. It wasn't a large church. But Pella wasn't a large town."

"What denomination, sir?"

"Baptist."

"A deep-water Baptist?"

"As deep as we could get till the river ran dry."

"Mr. Hawkes?" She arched an eyebrow.

"Yes, ma'am."

"You know what I think?"

"What's that, Miss Hand?"

"I think that when you and I found that poor preacher dangling from the chapel bells was probably the first time you've ever been inside a church." Her smile did not lose its radiance. I shifted my weight and wished that I had slept in with the hogs that morning. "You know what else I think, Mr. Hawkes?" she asked.

"I have no idea what you think, Miss Hand," I replied.

"I think I don't give a damn." She pulled the parasol lower to shade her eyes. "If you pronounce us man and wife, that's good enough for me."

What God joins together, let no man put asunder, is how I believe the passage goes. I did not know if it were scriptural or not, nor did I know if God had any intentions of joining together Wyatt Earp and the lovely Dora Hand, but I certainly was not going to stand in their way nor cast any judgments in their direction.

Wyatt Earp and Dora Hand understood each other.

She had slept with other men.

He had shot other men.

They might very well make it together.

Other men would do well to leave them alone. Charley Moseby might get rich if they didn't.

The sun was riding high in a cloudless sky, and the day had grown so hot the hog wallows were trying to dry up. The pigs had given up main street for the shade beneath the rotting board porch of the Double Eagle. An easterly wind had died fretfully away, and the red dust rising up south of town hung heavily in the air just above the treetops. The afternoon began to smell of sand and cow dung.

I saw the cattle before I heard them, longhorns rounded up from herds running wild below the Nueces, thin flanked and long legged, hundreds of them with sullen eyes and horns as sharp as military sabers, looking like a patchwork of yellow duns, jersey creams, browns with bay points, and bays with brown points. They had little meat on their bones, and most of that had turned to grit and gristle, but I guess those folks up north had so many hunger pains after the war they didn't mind gnawing a bone if it came out of a Texas cow.

Old-timers swore the cattle were tough, mean, and fast as horned jackrabbits, grazing undisturbed for centuries in dense thickets of mesquite, devouring the bloom stalks of the Spanish dagger and living for months on prickly pear when drought reaped the land and stole away their range of tall, dry grasses. They sniffed approaching danger in the winds, becoming, with the years, as wary as a wolf, but not nearly as hard to catch. Cattlemen said those raunchy old steers would run fifteen miles for water, then make one drink last them for two days.

That's why men, who it's presumed had more intellect than a cow, drank whiskey. On the trail north, nobody ever quite knew where the next creek might be, or if it still had water flowing through it, or if the water had been tainted with the rotting carcasses of dead animals or alkali poison.

The longhorns should have smelled the cowboys coming. It might have saved them a long walk to Kansas, where the only things waiting on them were rich fields of tall grass and a butcher shop.

The long-legged, thin-flanked cattle were being pushed rather nonchalantly down the lone street in Fort Griffin by a handful of long-legged, thin-flanked cowboys who had spent so much time in the saddle they felt naked when they climbed down for a chance to wash the dust out of their throat with a bottle of cheap whiskey. They weren't looking for Ben Carson's best stuff, which was just as well. He wasn't intending on wasting any of it on drovers who would pay as much for the rotgut whiskey as the good. As long as it was wet, no warmer than room temperature, and had the kick of a one-eyed mule, it would do just fine.

The upstairs queens of the Double Eagle had been bathing themselves in buckets of whatever they could find that smelled like a concoction of sin and sex as soon as they heard the first cattle bawling on the outskirts of town. Their lips were painted as red as Ezra Bodine's station house, and the powder on their faces was as thick as the dust of a cattle drive. The cowboys should be feeling right at home.

The number of soiled doves, who either made men feel at home or forget about home, was certainly beginning to dwindle. For the first time in a long time, the lovely Miss Dora Hand was not among them, which, if nothing else, meant the girls would be doing something other than singing that night. Thank God. Whatever else they did, I'm sure it was more tolerable and better received than their singing.

Trail hands all looked pretty much the same, regardless of which town they chose when it was time to kick the dirt off their boots. They were young, but growing old in a hurry, long before their time, squinty-eyed and rawboned with faces of sunburnt leather. Most had a week's growth of whiskers on their chins, and at least two of them had long, drooping mustaches. They had been on the trail for weeks, and smelled as though it might have been longer. They wore their revolvers like badges of courage, and the long trails north were littered with the unmarked graves of those whose courage was quicker than their draw.

In Fort Griffin, at least for a night, they had located a corner of paradise, the one their fathers had bragged about and their mothers had warned them about. The whiskey would corrupt their mind, mothers said, and the girls would corrupt their souls.

Though it wasn't noted for much else, Fort Griffin had

long been an honest purveyor of corruption bought, sold,
stolen, or traded at any price.

The trail boss had a different look about him. He was
young but clean shaven with raven black hair hanging down
thick upon his shoulders. His features were razor sharp, and
his eyes were the color of his hair. He was a tall man with
broad shoulders and thick hands, and he wore ivory-
handled, silver-plated forty-five-caliber pistols in holsters
that were slung low on both hips. He stood in the doorway,
looking over the Double Eagle, checking the faces, not
missing anyone, quickly looking past those he recognized
and lingering on those unfamiliar to him. He slowly
removed his rawhide gloves and stuck them into his belt. A
blonde swayed toward him, but his eyes looked past her, and
he followed his eyes toward the center of the room. He was
obviously in the mood for the unmistakable pleasures that
awaited him either upstairs or downstairs in the Double
Eagle. At the moment, he had other things on his mind. Ben
Carson offered to pour him a drink, but the young man
shook his head.

"I'm looking for a man who calls himself Wyatt Earp," he
said loudly, but to no one in particular.

A few patrons of the Double Eagle glanced at him, but no
one spoke. His own men were more interested in baptizing
themselves with whiskey and perfume. The very painted
women ignored him. They were open for business, and
business had been bad lately. They weren't concerned with
Wyatt Earp or anyone looking for Wyatt Earp. He was
occupied. They had turned their charms on the gallant
knights of the trail who had hard cash money in their
pockets and who would remain knights until the money was
all gone, which might take all night or fifteen minutes.

Ezra Bodine and I had been playing a two-handed game
of poker. He did not want to lose any money, he said, but did

have an interest in learning the game. As a rule, I never sat down at a gaming table at all unless men were in earnest about trusting their fortunes to cards being dealt by the hands of a stranger. Put a deck of cards in a dealer's hand when the chips are running high, and even a friend becomes a stranger. But, for the time being, I had nothing better to do, so I drank from Ezra Bodine's private stock of sour mash and tried to show him why a full house beats three of a kind and anybody who draws to an inside straight is known as either a fool or a pauper, usually both.

"I've been told a man who calls himself Wyatt Earp resides in this godforsaken little hellhole," the trail boss said again, louder this time, his black eyes flashing.

I pitched my cards on the table and stood up. "May I be of service?" I inquired, tightening my grip on the belly blaster. If he noticed, he did not let it disturb him.

"Are you by any chance Mr. Earp?" He frowned as he spoke, and I watched his hands instead of his eyes. They hung loosely at his side and did not seem to be inclined to reach for either revolver.

"Hawkes," I replied. "Brady Hawkes. But I happen to be acquainted with Mr. Earp. And if there is a message for him, I'll certainly make sure he gets it."

A strange smile curled across his lips. "I've been asked to deliver it personally," he said, and he gently rested the palms of both hands on the ivory handles of his pistols. "It's not the kind of message I would want to entrust to a stranger. I hope you are not offended."

"I'm afraid Mr. Earp is out of town."

"I'll wait for him."

"I have no idea when he'll get back."

"The cattle are in no hurry." The strange smile grew even more crooked. "And I have nothing to do until morning."

The trail boss reached into his shirt pocket and removed

a pouch of tobacco. He propped one foot on an empty chair and began rolling a brown paper cigarette. He had the penetrating eyes and the practiced hands of a gunfighter. He was looking for Wyatt Earp and would not say why, and that concerned me.

"Wyatt Earp is not a man I would draw on," I told him.

"I don't plan on killing him." The trail boss adjusted his hat. "If I did, I got plenty of boys in here who'd do it for me. All it'd cost is the price of a good woman. None of 'em have had a good woman, or a bad one for that matter, since leaving home. No, I don't have any reason to kill him." He shrugged matter-of-factly. "Of course," he said, "other people don't particularly feel the same way I do."

"Does Mr. Earp have a problem?" I wanted to know.

"That's entirely up to Mr. Earp."

"If I see him," I said, "may I tell him who's looking for him?"

"Kenedy," the trail boss replied softly. "James Kenedy."

"Then those are brush country cattle."

"Mostly from Matagorda."

I nodded. "I know your father," I said.

He shrugged, not impressed. "Everybody knows Mifflin Kenedy," he answered. "He's the biggest damn cattle rancher in south Texas."

"And, not counting Captain King, the richest, I assume."

"If my father had not taught Richard King which end of a cow you brand, the sonuvabitch would still be haulin' bales of cotton down the Rio Grande." The young trail boss walked to my table and, without asking, proceeded to pick up Ezra Bodine's bottle to pour himself a drink. The bottle was empty. "King's still roundin' up land, while my father's roundin' up cattle," he continued. "Kansas pays damn good money for Kenedy cattle. Captain King's land was poor when he stole it, and it's still as worthless as a four-card flush."

"I thought they were partners," I said.

"Who?"

"King and Kenedy."

"My father doesn't have partners." James Kenedy's eyes began to wander around the room again. "He staked King, then the drought came and killed the land, and the land killed everything on it. King came to the house beggin' for more money, but my father told him he could eat dirt, since he loved it so damn much."

"Did he?"

"What?" James Kenedy's eyes kept searching the room. He was swiftly losing interest in our conversation.

"Eat dirt."

"Maybe. I'm told it don't taste so bad in tortillas."

"I guess King had plenty of tortillas."

"I guess he did. My father sent him a bucketful of corn and told him he could either plant it and watch it die or have some of those hands from across the border use it for tortillas. It kept 'em from going hungry for a while."

"Mifflin Kenedy's a hard man," I said.

"There are only two kinds of men in south Texas," James Kenedy said. "Hard ones and dead ones."

Wyatt Earp walked into the room before anyone saw him coming. The silence hung between us for a few moments, then I told the young trail boss, "I don't think you'll have to wait much longer."

His eyes narrowed as he turned to watch the tall, lanky man in black trousers and a black frock coat amble toward us. "I would keep those revolvers where he can see both of them and your hands nowhere near them if I were you," I continued. "Mr. Earp's on edge at the moment."

"Somebody besides me looking for him?"

"Somebody's already found him."

"They out to kill him?"

"More or less."

"When's the showdown gonna take place?"

"Day after tomorrow as near as I can tell." I smiled. "I believe that's the day Mr. Earp is getting married unless, of course, he's changed his mind."

"That may be too late."

I frowned, and the belly blaster grew heavier in my arms.

"The bride may be a widow by then," he said.

James Kenedy squared his stance so Wyatt Earp could get a good look at both .45's, and he folded his arms. I started to make formal introductions, then decided there was neither any time nor reason for it. Ezra Bodine excused himself and hurried to another table, watching us out of the corner of his eyes, ready to dive for cover at the first sign of trouble. Trouble was a shadow that neither Wyatt Earp or myself had ever been able to escape.

"This gentleman's been looking for you," I said, as Wyatt Earp reached the table.

"Is he buyin' or sellin'?"

"He didn't say."

The shootist turned toward the young trail boss, a quizzical expression on his face. "I'm Wyatt Earp," he said.

"I understand you shot a man a few days ago," James Kenedy said bluntly without any formalities.

"I'm afraid that what you heard is correct." Wyatt Earp's jaws tightened. "Ike Rigby a friend of yours?"

"I never met him."

"Then what interest do you have in the matter."

"I'm a friend of Ike Rigby's brother."

"I trust that he was nothing like Ike."

"Frank's a career military man, stationed at Fort Richardson. He made it all the way to top sergeant before he got busted."

"The Rigbys are always looking for trouble. It appears like both of them found it and probably wished they hadn't."

The strange smile returned to James Kenedy's face. "It wasn't enough for Frank Rigby to simply kill Indians," he said. "He insisted on skinning them as well, and, on the record, the army took a real dim view of what he did."

"I'm surprised they didn't court-martial him," I said.

"They only took away his stripes." James Kenedy spoke with cold dispatch. "They let him keep his skinnin' knife." The young trail boss paused long enough to let Wyatt Earp carefully weigh his words, then he said softly, "Frank Rigby don't like what you did to his brother."

"I only had two choices," Wyatt Earp said. "Either he could die, or I could die. So I chose what I considered to be the most favorable of the two options."

"Frank Rigby still don't like it."

Wyatt Earp sighed as though he were suddenly weary of the whole affair. "He knows where to find me," he said.

"Frank Rigby's already found you. That's why I'm here."

I immediately looked behind Wyatt Earp's back. The faces had not changed. There were no weapons in sight. Still I felt uneasy, the way a man feels when he knows the guns may start blazing at any moment, and he's either the target or in the line of fire.

"He rode all night and most of the day with us," James Kenedy said. "He doesn't want to come bustin' in here and shoot up half of Fort Griffin just to get you. He'll meet you in the mornin'. Sunup. There's a grove of scrawny oaks outside of town about a mile south down Old Carver Road. Just you and him. Eyeball to eyeball. Draw and fire. Whoever walks away, walks away."

"What time does the sun come up?" Wyatt Earp wanted to know.

"A few minutes are five," I told him. "I don't know how many."

"It doesn't matter."

"What shall I tell Mr. Rigby?" James Kenedy asked.

"Just give him my card," Wyatt Earp answered. He looked at me. I fanned the cards on the table and withdrew a king of hearts. By the time I held it up, Wyatt Earp had drawn and fired once, his bullet tearing out the king's heart.

I handed the card to James Kenedy.

His hands trembled slightly as he took it.

"How many other brothers does Ike Rigby have?" Wyatt Earp asked.

"Frank's the only one," James Kenedy said softly, his eyes transfixed on the bullet hole in the cavity of the king's left breast.

"That's good," Wyatt Earp said nonchalantly. "I'd hate to have to keep doing this the rest of my life."

He turned to walk away, but my words stopped him cold. "You gonna tell Dora?"

"Is there any reason why I should?"

"She's bound to hear about it."

"Not till after it's over."

Wyatt Earp slowly ascended the stairs, removing his frock coat as he went. He looked older than he had earlier that day when all he had to worry about was the frayed rigging on his buggy. His head was bowed, his shoulders were bent as though he had been stuck behind a plow all day, trying to find new ground beneath the rocks. They say that it ages you a little every time you kill a man or know one's waiting to kill you.

The wise saddle up and ride away. That was not Wyatt Earp's way.

"We'll bury Frank beside his brother when it's done," I said to James Kenedy.

"Frank's a military man," the young trail boss replied. "He's fought a lot of battles, and he hasn't lost any of them yet. Give the United States Army a night to think about it, and they can always figure out a way to win."

He turned without another word and headed toward the bar. The blonde was still waiting on him, sitting on the edge of the piano bench, her bare legs crossed, the lace of her silk dress falling lightly off her shoulders. She could have already made herself ten or fifteen dollars. Maybe she was looking for something more than five dollars' worth of passion. After all, the lovely Dora Hand had gotten lucky and found herself a husband if he lived that long.

♠

♥ 13 ♦

♣

Charley Moseby had been digging for almost an hour, cursing every shovelful of dirt and mold and dried leaves he threw out from under the grove of scrawny oaks, their gnarled and twisted roots clinging precariously to the shallow soil that had been washed over a thick layer of caprock. He dug awhile and chiseled awhile, mostly hammering his way down into the narrow hole, as dark and ominous as the night around him. A half moon played cat and mouse with the treetops, and only occasional threads of light ever touched the ground. There was no hint of sunrise, not even the faint glimmer of dawn that sometimes crawls to the top of Wild Mule Mesa and begins pushing away what's left of the night.

No sound bothered to penetrate the early morning, with the exception of the gravedigger's shovel biting desperately into the earth.

Wyatt Earp sat leaning against the gnarled trunk of a live oak, as motionless as a dead man, his eyes closed, a Smith & Wesson dangling loosely from his grip. His black suit blended in with the night. At first glance, he wasn't even there.

The shootist had battled the demon of insomnia until shortly after midnight, then he arose and slipped quietly out of Dora Hand's bedroom, waiting, though not patiently, until she had been drowned by a deep sleep before making his way down to the Double Eagle bar. He sat there alone for an hour, maybe longer, oiling both his revolver and the leather holster that held it. Time and again he checked to make sure each chamber was loaded and the slug tightened on each cartridge. He stuck a pinch of graphite powder down into the spring that held the trigger. The difference between life and death, he had once figured, came to about three-sixteenth of a second. Everything must work in unison, his eyes, his brain, his reflexes, his hand, the trigger, the hammer, the firing pin, the aim, his nerve. If any of them balked or failed at the exact moment of truth, when all that separated him and Frank Rigby was three-sixteenth of a second, then Charley Moseby was digging that hole in the ground for him. Three-sixteenth of a second was a lifetime.

Wyatt Earp, Charley Moseby, and I had ridden out to the grove of scrawny oaks together. Charley Moseby, he had needed, if it can be said that a man needs his own personal grave digger. I, on the other hand, was a companion he had not anticipated in a country where mankind recognized a lot of faces in the crowd, but rarely a friendly one.

"There ain't no reason in you comin', Hawkes," Wyatt had said when he found me waiting for him out front of the Double Eagle.

"It's not much of a night for sleeping anyway," I told him.

"From what that young Kenedy said, I think it's expected of me to go alone."

"There's something else that young Kenedy said, and it's been botherin' me ever since he rode back to his herd."

"What's that?"

"He said to give the United States Army all night to plan

a battle, and they never lose. And Frank Rigby's had all night to plan this one."

"What do you make of it?"

"I think Frank Rigby is planning for you to show up alone. I don't think he'll be there by himself." I turned and stared at the dirt road leading south of town. It looked so empty, so lonely. It was leading a man to his death. "I figure you'll be up against three guns at least, maybe a half dozen of them. Who knows?"

Wyatt Earp thought for a moment, then said, "Ike Rigby never sought any help. He depended on his own fists, his own rifles, his own knife when he went to war either against man or beast."

"Ike Rigby was a loner." The night turned darker as a passing cloud snatched the moon out of the sky. "Frank Rigby's a military man. When he goes into battle, he's used to taking an army along with him."

Wyatt Earp's jaws tightened, but he forced a wry grin. "You think you can make a difference, Hawkes?"

"If nobody knows I'm there, I can."

"You never struck me as a gunfighter."

"Gambling. Gunfighting. There's no difference between the two." I shrugged and checked both coat pockets to make sure I had not forgotten every shell I could find that might fit the belly blaster. Ben Carson had a whole box of them, collected from rogues, renegades, and two-bit tinhorn gamblers who left them behind to pay off old bar debts when they made their final journey out of town under the care and the mercy of Charley Moseby. "It's not the hand you're dealt that wins or loses." I said. "It's how you choose to play out the hand."

"So how do you think we should play out the hand?"

"It's not very difficult," I said. "Frank Rigby thinks

you're only holding one card. He doesn't know you have a hole card. He certainly doesn't know what it is."

"You ever killed a man, Mr. Hawkes?"

"I've played a lot of hole cards, Mr. Earp."

At the edge of town, our horses slowed to a gentle walk. Sunup was an hour, maybe two, away. Wyatt Earp was in no hurry. He had seen sunrises before, but not often ricocheting off the gray metallic barrel of a pistol aimed at his head, his belly, or somewhere in between.

"It's a damn-fool time of the night for two men to go around shootin' at each other," Charley Moseby complained.

"It wasn't my decision," Wyatt Earp replied.

"It ain't right for any man to die before breakfast."

"You're just upset because you've got another grave to dig."

"I'm upset because I ain't had no sleep." Charley Moseby was slumped in his saddle, his shoulders sagging, a rusty shovel tied to his saddle horn. "It's a good three-hour ride from Buffalo Gap," he said testily, "an' I didn't get started home till way after sundown. And by the time I got back to Fort Griffin, there you was tellin' me it was time to go to work again. Hell, Earp, I been working too hard since you hit town. I'm just about ready for you to ride on somewhere else."

"I won't be around much longer."

"When you leavin'?"

"Who knows? Maybe about three-sixteenth of a second after sunup."

Charley Moseby coughed once to clear his throat. The parched summer sun was beginning to dry up his insides, and, other than a brief sip of tepid rainwater from Cripple Dog Creek, he had not had anything to drink for the past two

hours, which meant Charley Moseby, in his own words, was
beginning to shrivel up on the vine.

"I'm only comin' with you," the gravedigger said, "because I promised you a free grave after you shot Ike Rigby
and made me a rich man. If Ike Rigby's brother is faster'n
you, then the debt's paid in full. If he's too damn slow, I
hope to hell he didn't ride all this way with empty pockets.
If he ain't got no money on him, then he better pray he
keeps breathin' long enough to dig his own damn grave. He
sure as hell ain't gonna be sleepin' in none of mine."

We reined in our horses about fifty yards from the grove
of scrawny oaks. The trees rose up out of the darkness and
disappeared into the darkness. There was no sign of any
movement among the trees, no sound at all. It looked too
peaceful to me. At a gaming table, anything that looks
proper, orderly, and in its rightful place usually isn't. A
stacked deck never looks stacked until you're broke and
realize the card you need is probably up somebody else's
sleeve.

"You're a suspicious man," Wyatt Earp said.

"I've known several suspicious men in my time," I
replied, "and most every one of them has lived past the age
of fifty."

"What happened to the others?"

"They got married to suspicious wives."

Wyatt Earp laughed softly, but I think it was nervous
laughter. He was definitely in no mood for humor, which is
always out of place at weddings, funerals, and shooting
matches before the crack of dawn. We waited a good five
minutes. If Frank Rigby had already reached the oaks ahead
of us, he was doing a damn good job of staying out of sight.
A night bird, then two, swooped down past the half moon
and darted into the trees. Any sudden movement and they

would come exploding out of the oaks. The birds settled down in the darkness and stayed there.

"I'll check it out," Charley Moseby said, climbing down off his horse. "If there's anybody in there, they can tell by lookin' me over that I ain't no gunfighter, an' I sure ain't capable of killin' anybody as big as Ike Rigby even if I was."

The gravedigger hung his shovel over his shoulder and began shuffling toward the oaks, leading his horse, loudly whistling an old folk tune that pierced the silence of the night. He made sure he was heard. No one could ever accuse Charley Moseby of trying to slip up on them.

He was simply a man who had a job to do and was rapidly running out of time. It generally made everybody feel a little better if the hole was in the ground before the body turned cold.

Charley Moseby stepped into the cover of the trees and bramble brush and pulled the darkness around his shoulders like an old, familiar hand-me-down coat. There were no verbal outbursts, no barks of gunfire, no streaks of fire in the night. Charley Moseby simply walked his horse into the shadows and found no reason to walk back out.

He was down about six inches in the ground, jerking out roots, hammering on the layer of caprock and already cursing by the time we reached the grove of scrawny oaks.

I immediately glanced toward the east. It was as black as pitch.

The sun was going to take its own sweet time about coming up that morning.

Within thirty minutes, all of them crawling through the night with the speed of a runaway tortoise, Charley Moseby had grown tired of whistling. He had grown tried of digging. He slumped down against the live oak beside Wyatt Earp, breathing heavily. "A man that dies ain't got no pity for the gravedigger," he said.

Wyatt Earp had nothing to say.

His eyes were nothing but narrow slits, staring out toward the eastern horizon, watching for the sun, listening for footsteps of the man coming that morning to silence him for good. A bluejay began to squawk overhead, and a whip-poorwill cried in the distance. The day was gradually beginning to awaken. One moment, the trees were surrounded by darkness. In the next instant, the oaks began to take shape in the faint reflection of an early morning light. Nobody knew where it came from or how it got there. Light just suddenly appeared.

We heard hoofbeats echoing down the road long before we saw a lone rider, a cavalryman dressed in full military uniform with two stripes on his sleeve, break into the clearing just beyond the edge of the trees. He jerked his mount to a stop and stood in his stirrups, surveying the grove. His face was ruddy behind a red beard, and he leveled a Springfield carbine at the oaks, waving it nervously back and forth.

"Earp," he yelled in a voice loud enough to break rocks, "you in there?"

Wyatt Earp did not stir. "I'm waiting," he shouted back. "If you had gotten here earlier, this shooting would have already been over with."

"Are you alone?"

"I believe the appointment this morning is strictly between the two of us."

The grizzled old cavalry corporal nodded. "Then I'll go get Sergeant Rigby," he said. "He did not want to waste his time in the grove if you had turned coward and not shown up."

"I'm sorry, but I was under the impression that Mr. Rigby had been busted."

"He's missing his stripes. That's all. As far as his men are concerned, he don't need any stripes."

"He had better hurry."

"Why is that, sir?"

"It's almost sunup."

The grizzled old cavalry corporal laughed out loud. "Apparently there's something you don't know about Sergeant Rigby," he said. "The sergeant ain't never missed a good fight in his life."

"Give the sergeant a message for me."

"What is it?"

"Tell him to bring his skinning knife with him."

The corporal frowned. "Why should he be doing that?" he asked.

"You may need something to cut the bullet out after I'm gone." Wyatt Earp's voice was cold and distant. "I'm sure his men would want a souvenir to remember the good sergeant by since there are no stripes to cut from his sleeve," he said.

The corporal spat disgustedly, murmuring under his breath, and wheeled his horse around as a gold crease, no thicker than a muleskinner's whip, began to wrinkle the sky behind him.

"You're right, Hawkes," Wyatt Earp said in a voice barely louder than a whisper. "He won't be alone. Frank Rigby may not kill me, but he certainly wants to make sure he meets me in hell for breakfast even if he shoots a little too high or too low or too late."

I lay face down behind the bramblebush, pressing hard against the ground, looking out through wild buffalo grasses that had been beaten down by the rains. "At least we know what the honorable Frank Rigby has up his sleeve," I answered.

"And he's walkin' in here blind."

Charley Moseby sighed. "I just wonder which one of you sons of bitches is gonna be walkin' outta here."

"Whoever shoots first," I said.

"No," Wyatt Earp corrected me. "Whoever shoots the straightest."

Frank Rigby swung off his horse a good twenty-five yards from the grove of scrawny oaks, paused long enough to raise his revolver and check the chamber for one last time. He knew it was loaded. But old habits are hard to break. He was a big man, taller than his brother and several years older. His shoulders were broad, his arms thick, his gaunt face carved from hard granite. He walked with a slight limp, probably some old wound from the Comanche wars that had not healed. The gold from the crease in the sky bounced off his brass buttons.

He stared into the grove, a sardonic smile on his face. Rigby marched quickly out of the clearing and into the trees. The aging, red-whiskered corporal flanked him on the left. A lanky, sallow-faced private first class slipped into the oaks and knelt so near the thorny bramblebush I could have reached up and slapped him, which I was tempted to do. But there was no reason for the shooting to start until its appointed time, and it did, I had no doubt, have an appointed time. Both the grizzled old corporal and the sallow-faced private first class were carrying Springfield carbines, and they did not bring the rifles along to use for crutches.

Wyatt Earp stood at the foot of the grave, watching Rigby move steadily toward him. The busted sergeant grinned at his adversary, then he suddenly stopped his tracks. The grin dropped off his face as he pointed to Charley Moseby, still sitting beneath the tree, whistling a tune that could have either been a waltz or a dirge.

"Who the hell is he?" Frank Rigby demanded to know.

"He's a gravedigger."

"What the hell is he doing here?"

"Within the next few minutes, one of us, I'm afraid, is going to need a hole in the ground." Wyatt Earp smiled his most compassionate smile. "Charley couldn't bear the thought of just leaving either one of us around for the buzzards and coyotes to pick clean. Damn decent of him to get up at this hour, if you ask me."

"I thought you were coming alone," Rigby growled.

"Charley only digs graves. He doesn't fill them."

The sardonic grin returned to Frank Rigby's face. "That's my job," he said. He stepped up to the head of the grave and glanced down into the hole. The grin quivered slightly. The morning was still dark but nearly as dark as the long, narrow resting place that had been carved out of the earth.

"That's a cold place to be," Wyatt Earp said softly.

"I hear you put my brother in one of 'em," Frank Rigby said sullenly. "I hear you snuck up on him and shot him down in cold blood."

"He had killed a woman."

"She should've kept out of his way."

"And he was doin' his damnedest to kill another one."

"Most of 'em I know deserve killin'."

"Personally, I prefer old age as the preferable way to go."

"Then I'm afraid I'm gonna have to disappoint you."

Frank Rigby's muscles tensed, and his eyes were filled with fire and hatred. The two men stood, only the length of a grave apart, and a gentle wind swept off the ground and made its way out of the trees. Rigby glanced briefly toward the corporal, then back at the private first class.

Wyatt Earp's eyes never wavered. "Draw when you're

ready, Mr. Rigby," he said. "I don't mind waiting until you get up the nerve . . . even if it takes all morning."

Frank Rigby glared at him. His right hand was visibly shaking with either fear or anxiety. It was difficult to tell for certain.

His moment had come. There was no turning back now.

"I hope you have the decency to die like a man," Rigby said, cutting each word short as though he had whittled them with his skinning knife. "My brother. He knew how to die like a man."

"Your brother died like a dog."

Frank Rigby screamed and went for the long-barreled forty-five-caliber pistol hanging on his hip.

It was too heavy. The barrel was too long to clear leather clean. He may have been a damn good Indian fighter. He should have stayed away from a grove of scrawny oaks.

Both men drew. Only Wyatt Earp fired.

Frank Rigby, with a surprised look on his face, cocked his head toward the corporal, then back at the private first class. He stared with dimming eyes down at the cold barrel of his own pistol, wondering why in God's name it still had not fired, why he no longer had the strength to thumb the hammer or pull the trigger. It was a hair trigger. It would not take much more than a gentle wind to set it off. And yet he could not make it fire. He tried to curse, but no words were able to escape past his throat, and his throat was burning as though he had drunk from a cauldron of hot grease.

Frank Rigby could not figure out why daylight was suddenly turning so dark. It wasn't night. It was morning, early morning, and there was not a thunderhead in the sky. So why had the sky turned white and the trees black? His massive body was shaking, and he reached up to try and touch the hole that had appeared just above his left eye.

He could not find it. Frank Rigby crumbled into the grave.

The grizzled, red-whiskered corporal swung his carbine toward Wyatt Earp.

Charley Moseby pulled an ancient forty-four-caliber revolver out from behind the blade of his rusty old shovel and shot the corporal twice before his hammer jammed. The cavalryman fell rolling in the dried leaves, coughing blood and crying out in pain, either cursing or praying, but definitely talking to his Maker. I don't think his Maker had much to say about the situation.

The private first class never had a chance to move. He had been the smart one. He thought he had slipped into the oaks unaware. From his dense hiding place, he had a clear shot at Wyatt Earp, and the shootist would never even know from where the shot had come. The private first class was taking no chances. He took a moment too long to aim down the sight of the carbine.

I rammed both barrels of my belly blaster beneath his chin, did my best to shove them into his throat, and he turned white. Death was so close he could already smell the burnt powder. "If you want Rigby to go to hell by himself this morning, then drop what you're holding and lay face down on the ground," I told him.

His carbine had suddenly become too heavy to hold any longer. It hit the earth beside him, and I kicked it into the thorns of the bramblebush. "Jesus," he said with a raspy voice, "please don't kill me. I ain't got no business here, an' if you let me ride out, I'll keep on goin'. I didn't see nothin' nohow, an' I'll tell 'em I don't know what the hell happened to Sergeant Rigby. The devil's been chasin' him for twenty-some-odd years anyway."

"I hate to disappoint you," I said. "But I'm not Jesus."

He did not care. "Are you gonna kill me?" the private first

class asked, curling up into a fetal position, covering his face with his arms in a futile attempt to stop the bullets when they came, and he was definitely convinced that they would come.

"I'm thinking real hard about it," I answered.

"Jesus."

He was still looking for his savior. Maybe he had found him.

"Let him go," Wyatt Earp said, his voice as tired as his eyes. "I've got no quarrel with him."

"I don't know how you figure that. The sonuvabitch was doin' his dead level best to blow your fool head off," Charley Moseby growled, picking up the Springfield carbine, wondering how much it would bring back at the Double Eagle. Plenty, he decided, if the Texas trail drivers had not left town.

"Doin' your best don't count if you've got nothin' to show for your trouble," Wyatt Earp said. "Besides, we need somebody to haul the corporal out of here before he quits bleedin' and dies on us."

"You just lettin' both of 'em leave like they ain't been nowhere and done nothin'?" the gravedigger wanted to know.

"The corporal's gut shot. He won't last till dark, if he lasts that long." Wyatt Earp put an arm around Charley Moseby's shoulders. "I would hate to have you feel obligated to dig another hole out here. The ground out here's a might hard."

We stood above the narrow grave that held the carcass of Frank Rigby. He was taller than any of us had anticipated.

The grave was about ten inches too short.

"It was a helluva shot," Charley Moseby said.

I shrugged casually as though I began every morning standing beside a freshly dug grave in a makeshift cemetery.

"I don't know if Wyatt's bullet got him," I said, "or if he broke his fool neck when he fell."

Wyatt Earp glanced at me sharply, then grinned. "I'm glad there's only room for one in there," he said, and quietly walked away as Charley Moseby began scraping dirt and rocks and dried leaves onto the twisted body of Sergeant Frank Rigby who, as he suspicioned, had not made it to retirement.

The sallow-faced private first class was dragging the corporal to his horse. The grizzled old cavalryman was coughing every step of the way and blaspheming the wiry, harmless little man who had shot him while sitting down and holding a shovel. It just was not right. He kept struggling, trying to hold the blood in his belly with both hands. He knew he was dying. But the grizzled old red-whiskered cavalryman had never quit in the middle of a fight yet.

Frank Rigby had shown up with three of a kind.

The two wild cards were wasted.

Fort Griffin was sleeping late. The hogs had the street to themselves. And the stray dogs were fighting over a bone too small to be fighting over when we returned to the Double Eagle. Wyatt Earp's face was drawn, and he looked a little older, a little more wrinkled in the faint traces of daylight. He had ridden that long, winding mile back into town without speaking, and I let him wallow in his own conscience alone.

"Are you a religious man, Hawkes?" he asked at last.

"God and I have gotten to know each other on several occasions," I answered. "Usually when I'm in trouble. He's never called on me when He's had a problem."

"I prayed this morning before I went to the grove."

"It must have worked."

"No. I didn't pray for God to help me draw faster or shoot

straighter. I don't think He'd do that. I doubt if He hears those prayers anyway." Wyatt Earp's shoulders sagged, and his eyes looked with sadness at the ramshackle town around him. "I prayed that Dora would miss me if I didn't come back."

"I'm sure He listened to that one."

"Now we'll never know," he said, climbing down from his horse and walking with short, measured steps into the saloon.

James Kenedy sat in the back corner of the Double Eagle, playing five-card stud with two of his wranglers. Kenedy, as was to be expected, had all the chips. He raised an eyebrow in disbelief when Wyatt Earp strode into the room, still standing, still intact, free, from all outward appearances, of any holes that might have clotted on the way back. Kenedy laid his cards face down on the table, watching as the shootist headed toward him. Confusion clouded his eyes. At the moment, he did know whether to draw, fight, cut and run, or sit still and wait for the storm to pass. He tried to run a bluff instead.

"You lose your way?" Kenedy asked, his voice dripping with as much insolence as he could muster. "Or did you decide that facing Frank Rigby this morning would be bad for your health?"

Wyatt Earp withdrew the sergeant's skinning knife from his waistband and drove the thick blade into the old oak table. Kenedy flinched. His fists and his jaws both tightened. "Your friend won't be needin' this anymore," Earp said.

"Frank's too much of a man and too good of a shot to let you take his knife off him," Kenedy said caustically. "An' I don't believe you're good enough to kill him."

Wyatt Earp only gave a disinterested shrug. "If not," he said, "then we flat buried the son of a bitch alive."

I thought I saw Kenedy pale slightly, but it may have been the early morning sunlight crawling through a tear in the curtain and striking his face. He reached for his glass of whiskey and cursed softly because it was empty.

James Kenedy had two options confronting him. He could draw on Wyatt Earp with the avowed intention of avenging the death of a friend. Or he could ride out of town with his longhorn cattle, pushing north to Kansas, never looking back over his shoulder nor even remembering he had a friend named Frank Rigby.

He carefully weighed both options.

He ordered another whiskey to clear his mind.

James Kenedy emptied the glass of whiskey, licking the last drop off the rim. His hands were trembling slightly, and that had begun to bother him. He was scared and scared to death of being scared. The son of a wealthy Texas cattleman should not know the meaning of fear. That's what his daddy always said. But, of course, his daddy had never been scared a day in his life. He had ridden away from a few scrapes, but that was wisdom, he always said, never fright. It was better for a man to die with honor than live as a coward. James Kenedy silently cursed his father. It was worse feeling guilty than it was being scared.

Wyatt Earp had moved to the bar, his back squarely in Kenedy's line of vision. It was a target that even a man with trembling hands and a shortness of breath could not miss. All it took was enough nerve to draw his revolver and point it. No self-respecting cattle town would ever convict the son of Mifflin Kenedy for anything.

"Don't even think about it," I said softly to the young trail boss.

He glanced around, but his eyes refused to meet mine. Instead, he was trying to grow accustomed to the barrel of my belly blaster jabbing him somewhere between the sixth and seventh rib. It was a feeling nobody ever really grew accustomed to. I waited for Kenedy to speak, but he had nothing to say.

"You've got time for one shot if you're lucky," I said as casually and pleasantly as possible under the circumstances. "It's not enough."

James Kenedy did not argue.

If the whiskey had left any cobwebs lingering at all in his mind, my belly blaster cleared them away. He did not set his whiskey glass back on the table. He dropped it. He was on his feet without a word and heading toward the batwing doors of the Double Eagle, leaving Frank Rigby's skinning knife embedded in the table. He paused a moment behind Wyatt Earp, wiping the palms of his hands against his trousers, trying to get rid of the sweat.

James Kenedy was no longer suffering the discomfort of my belly blaster trying to separate his ribs. But he knew he still only had time for one shot, and one shot was still one shot too few.

♠

♥ 14 ♦

♣

Wyatt Earp paid no attention to James Kenedy's sudden departure. He had other things on his mind. He had walked away from his sunrise showdown with Frank Rigby in relatively good shape, which meant he was still alive and, by the time the sun packed up and left again, he would be walking down the aisle to become the lawful husband of the lovely Dora Hand. Or she would be walking down the aisle to become his wife. I had not been to many weddings, but I knew one of them was supposed to be walking down the aisle, which, I'm told, is not unlike the condemned in Judge Isaac Parker's prison walking that last mile to the gallows.

"I'm going up to see Dora," he told me as I laid the belly blaster on top of the bar beside him.

Ben Carson looked up sharply. "I wouldn't do that if I was you," he said.

Wyatt Earp's eyes questioned him.

"It's unlucky for the groom to see his bride on their wedding day," I said. "He's not supposed to see her face until he removes her veil."

"I'm not superstitious," he told me.

"Dora's busy," the barkeep said.

Wyatt Earp scowled, and his eyes darkened.

"She's up there with a paying customer," Carson continued.

Wyatt Earp's face grew as dark as his eyes. Every muscle in his body tensed. The fingers on his gun hand stiffened. "We're to be married tonight," was all he could manage to say.

The barkeep reached out and grasped Wyatt Earp's shoulder. "She's been a working girl a lot longer than she's been a wife," he said. "An' she'll be a working girl when she's a widow."

Wyatt Earp glanced to the top of the stairs. I had seen the look in his face before, but never on a human being.

"It's not worth it," I said to him.

"What's not?"

"Shooting Frank Rigby was self-defense. There's not a judge in the territory who'd convict you. What you're contemplating now is murder." I slowly and carefully removed Wyatt Earp's pistol from his holster and stuck it in my belt. "Judges don't have a whole lot of compassion for murder."

His eyes never left the staircase. "When are you gonna give me back my pistol?" he asked.

"When you calm down," I answered, "or when you get too drunk to remember what to do with it."

He turned to Ben Carson. "Give me a bottle," he said.

"You want the good stuff?"

"I want whichever stuff works the quickest."

"You think one bottle's enough, Mr. Earp?"

"How many bottles you got?"

The barkeep leaned down and looked under the bar to count them. "Twelve's all I got left," he said.

"I'll pay for all of 'em," Wyatt Earp said as self-pity slowly moved in to replace the anger that had gripped him. "You keep 'em till I need 'em."

"You need a glass?"

"All I need is a quiet little place where a man can drink in peace without some son of a bitch disturbin' him," he said.

Wyatt Earp cradled two bottles under each arm and headed for the batwing doors. He stopped suddenly and looked around.

"Hawkes?" he said.

"Yeah?"

"If you see Dora, tell her a drunk man's not responsible for anything he does."

"What are you planning on doing, Wyatt?"

A reckless light appeared in his eyes. "I haven't decided whether I'm gonna marry the woman or kill her," he said.

He stumbled out of the dimly lit bar and into sunshine so bright it hurt his eyes, if the sudden, painful grimace on his face meant anything. Wyatt Earp, carrying a bottle in each hand, ambled down the narrow street to the livery stable, renting a stall in the back, slumping down on stale hay between a roan gelding and a braying jackass and trying to determine how much cheap whiskey he could pour down his throat before his esophagus rotted out.

James Kenedy's south Texas longhorns shuffled past, as sullen eyed as the trail boss, headed toward the Red River, bawling because they were either hungry or thirsty or mad or because they did not have anything better to do than leave the one dirt street of Fort Griffin layered with dung and crawling with flies. Kenedy was riding out in front of the longhorns where the air was still fresh, which, I guess, was the birthright of the cattleman's son. It would be another two months before his herd grazed on Kansas grass.

Every hour or so, Wyatt Earp would stagger back into the
Double Eagle, grab another bottle from Ben Carson without
saying a word, then stagger back toward the stable. His eyes
were streaked with red, his clothes stained with dirt and
dung, not all of it dry. He was nursing his fourth bottle,
drinking awhile and sleeping awhile and snoring even when
he was awake. He had wadded up an old Mexican saddle
blanket and placed it under his head, and he was beginning
to smell as rank as the braying jackass, which, in retrospect,
may have been scandalizing to the jackass.

Charley Moseby had just pitched three deuces on the
table in front of me, which beat a pair of queens any way I
wanted to look at it, and pulled a dollar's worth of change
out of the pot. He was laughing softly under his breath,
feeling ten feet tall and bulletproof, dealing our twenty-sixth
hand of five-card stud when the short, feisty lieutenant, no
more than twenty-five years old, still green as an east
Arkansas gourd and wearing the starched blue uniform of
the United States Army, swaggered pompously into the
Double Eagle. He slowly removed his gloves and slapped
them hard against his leg, doing the best he could to look
like a battle-scarred veteran, although I doubted seriously if
he had yet seen his first bloody scalp dangling from some
warrior's belt. I wasn't sure he had seen his first warrior.
The young officer was flanked by a pair of bony-shouldered,
hollow-eyed, gaunt-faced corporals who must have been
elsewhere when meals were served for the past month. One
was chewing tobacco. The other appeared too tired, or
maybe too disinterested, to chew on anything.

The tobacco chewer pulled his revolver and fired once
toward the ceiling, which wasn't necessary but certainly got
everyone's attention, especially the girl in the upstairs
bedroom who came within a foot, maybe two, of losing her
best customer.

The young lieutenant glanced around the bar, a hint of confusion inching its way into his eyes. He wore the bars of an officer. No one was impressed. The lieutenant obviously had something to say and needed someone to say it to. One cowboy was sleeping at a corner table. Another had passed out in the floor. Ben Carson was awake, but he was up to his elbows in dishwater, and a man with soapsuds dripping off his sleeves seldom gave the appearance of authority. As soon as the corporal fired his revolver, Charley Moseby jumped to his feet and grabbed his shovel. Old habits die hard. And that left me, which, I guess is why the lieutenant headed in my direction.

I shuffled the cards again and watched him strut across the bar, wondering how someone so inexperienced could be so arrogant. Apparently he believed what the army told him about being an officer and a gentleman, which put him at the right hand of God.

"Your name, sir?" he asked.

I told him. "And yours?" I inquired.

"Second Lieutenant Anthony Hargrove," he said smartly and, for some reason, saluted. "I have a warrant for the arrest of one Wyatt Earp, a resident of Fort Griffin Flats, I believe."

"What's the charge?"

"Murder, sir."

"In Fort Griffin, sir," I replied without much concern, "murder is not necessarily a punishable offense."

"It is when you murder a sergeant and a corporal of the United States Army in cold blood," the lieutenant answered, a trace of emotion working its way into his voice.

"When did this alleged offense take place?" I wanted to know.

"Sometime late last night." The lieutenant leaned over the

table, gripping it with both hands, until his pale eyes were level with mine, and he said with a certain degree of confidentiality, "From the eyewitness report I have in my possession, Mr. Earp caught them sleeping and shot them both. The corporal lived long enough to reach Jacksboro. I have been ordered to retrieve Sergeant Rigby's body and return it to Fort Richardson for burying, along with Wyatt Earp for a trial and a hanging."

"It doesn't sound to me like it's going to be a fair trial," I said.

"The trial will be proper, and so will the hanging."

"You seem awful sure of yourself."

"I, sir, will prosecute the case myself."

"You interested in any other eyewitnesses?"

"One's plenty," he said, growing restless with our conversation.

"Did your eyewitness give you any motive for the shootings?" I asked.

"Robbery. No doubt about it." He stepped back and said, "Their pockets had been cleaned out, and Friday was payday. Earp probably got them in a card game, maybe even bought them a drink or two, saw the wad of money stuffed in their pockets, then waited to make his play until they made camp and went to sleep in a groove of oak trees on the way back to Jacksboro."

"Who, may I ask, was your eyewitness?"

"Private First Class Wilber, sir."

"How did he manage to escape this alleged wrath of Mr. Earp?"

"Private First Class Wilber was out gathering firewood at the time." Lieutenant Hargrove carefully measured each word as though writing an official report. "Sometime before sunrise, he heard gunfire and immediately returned to camp.

He found Sergeant Rigby and Corporal Sladecek both shot and witnessed the departure of said Wyatt Earp. Sergeant Rigby was dead where he lay, and Corporal Sladacek had suffered a pair of massive gunshot wounds to the abdomen. He was a twenty-year man, sir. Private First Class Wilber buried Sergeant Rigby in the grove and brought Corporal Sladacek to the fort with all due haste. Corporal Sladacek was pronounced dead two hours later by the post physician."

"That's a tidy little story," I said. "Did anyone check Private First Class Wilber's pockets for the missing money?"

"I don't understand . . ."

"I doubt if you would."

The lieutenant squared his shoulders and cleared his throat. "Wyatt Earp is the man named in the warrant," he snapped. "I had hoped someone here could tell me where I might find this Mr. Earp. Perhaps you, sir."

"I'm not so sure you want to find him," I said.

"It's my duty."

"How many men did you bring?"

"Twelve, including Corporals Sneed and Heller who escorted me in here."

"It's not enough."

Lieutenant Hargrove frowned and his face reddened. "I have enough firepower at my command to bring in any man alive."

"That's what Sergeant Rigby thought."

Lieutenant Hargrove's frown darkened. A faint trace of sweat appeared on his upper lip. He looked like a fine young man, in spite of his arrogance. The wisdom of growing older would take care of his cocky behavior. If he confronted Wyatt Earp, his chances of growing older dimmed considerably, and twelve armed soldiers wouldn't do a whole lot for the matrimonial future of Wyatt Earp and the lovely

Dora Hand, except, perhaps, make her a beaming bride and a grieving widow on the same afternoon.

"You seem to think that Sergeant Rigby and the corporal were not caught unaware," the lieutenant said.

"There are two sides to every story," I answered. "The living and the dead."

"Regardless, I still have a federal warrant for the arrest of one Wyatt Earp. I presume that you can tell me where I can find said Wyatt Earp."

"If that's what you insist."

"I have my orders, sir."

"Well, lieutenant," I said grimly, "there are two ways to take Mr. Earp. "One is an eyeball-to-eyeball, straightforward confrontation, where your thirteen army-issue weapons are pitted against his one revolver, if you choose to personally participate in the fight. If so, that makes the odds about right. He'll probably go down. No man can survive that kind of onslaught. But the question you have to consider, lieutenant, is how many of your men will go down with him, and whether or not you, sir, are among them."

"And what's the other way?" he asked.

Alternative one apparently did not appeal to the lieutenant.

"Take him when he's unarmed. Then none of your command gets hurt, and you have a man to hang, which may even mean a promotion. For you, of course, not Earp."

"Is that possible?"

I stopped shuffling the cards and dropped them back inside my coat pocket. "Tonight, sometime around seven o'clock, provided the liquor wears off in time, Mr. Wyatt Earp is going to take himself a wife in the chapel at the far end of the street," I said. "No man is any more vulnerable than when he's being married. He is obviously not thinking clearly or he wouldn't be in that position."

"How do you know Mr. Earp will be there?"

"I'm performing the ceremony. It's my job to make sure he's there."

Lieutenant Hargrove sized me up, which doesn't take long, then said, "You don't look much like a preacher to me."

"I'm not."

"Then what gives you the right to perform Earp's ceremony?"

I smiled. "I'm the only one left in Fort Griffin who's heard of God," I said.

"You don't seem to be too concerned about the fate of Wyatt Earp, who, I presume, is a friend of yours."

"In this country," I answered, "a man has to make provisions to survive not only tomorrow but the day after. The Wyatt Earps of this land ride in and about the time you get to know them, they've ridden on. I expect the army to be around a long time, and I certainly have no desire to spend the rest of my life running from you or anybody else with bars or eagles or stars on their shoulders. Wyatt Earp may get mad at me, but a hanged man doesn't hate for long."

"You've made a wise decision, sir," the lieutenant said.

I saluted him as he turned and strode briskly back across the room.

Charley Moseby stared at me with accusing and disbelieving eyes. "I didn't think you'd sell a friend down the river," he said coldly.

I shrugged again. "It's not seven o'clock yet."

"I knew it was a mistake," he said, throwing his shovel over his shoulder.

"What's that?"

"When you had your belly blaster jammed against the throat of Private First Class Wilber," he said softly, "you

should have gone ahead and pulled both triggers. Hell, I'd a
been damn happy to pull one of 'em for you. Saved all of us
a lot of trouble, specially Wyatt, specially when he ain't got
no better friends than you."

The shadows came limping across the prairie, shades of
purple and gray, and the wind began to die away as the day
found itself winding down to a restless end. Dust hung
above the town with a haze that threatened to turn the sky a
blood red. I had wandered on down to the chapel early,
lighting coal-oil lanterns on each side of the pulpit. A veil of
uncertain darkness began settling down around Fort Griffin.

I found an old Bible with frayed pages on the floor behind
the second pew and thumbed through it, trying to locate
some Scripture that had anything good to say about man and
woman becoming husband and wife. I finally decided on
the phrase, "God placed man and woman upon the earth to
live together as one and love together as one and become as
one in the sight of the Lord Almighty." It wasn't in the
Bible, but I figured it might have been if the author had
more time to think about it.

I wondered what he would have written about a groom
who would consummate his date with an army hangman
before ever bedding down with his wife, or if Wyatt Earp
would forgive me for what I had done that afternoon, or if
Lieutenant Hargrove and his command intended on taking
Wyatt alive or ending it there on the chapel floor.

With thirteen guns, he could certainly do whatever he
liked. I was gambling on the honorable Lieutenant Hargrove
going by the book and strictly by the book, just the way
West Point had written it.

The social wedding of the year in Fort Griffin had not
drawn much of a crowd. In fact, if I had not been in the
chapel, there would not have been a crowd at all. Ben

Carson did not close the Double Eagle for any occasion, and the church had never been able to compete with a saloon, not in Fort Griffin anyway. Bible toters had never been able to frighten anyone preaching hellfire, brimstone, and damnation. The rogues, renegades, and drifters who inhabited Fort Griffin just always figured the Hereafter, whichever one it was, would be a better place than where they were.

The lovely Dora Hand, however, was right on time, sweeping elegantly through the front door dressed in white satin and lace. She carried a bouquet of wildflowers, picked from alongside the tracks that ran northward from Ezra Bodine's railroad depot, and her smile did more to light up the sanctuary than did the lanterns. Two of the upstairs girls from the Double Eagle, two who didn't happen to be occupied that night, walked to the chapel with her. A bridesmaid and maid of honor, I guess.

The groom sat slouched in the corner of the church, his suit as black as her gown was white, his chin resting on his chest, his hat pulled low across his eyes to shield them from the lantern light, much too bright for the condition he was in. He had spent the last fifteen minutes grunting, then snoring, then grunting again, romance be damned.

Dora Hand moved toward the man who would be her husband, but I took her by the arm and stopped her.

"Not till after the ceremony," I said. "It's my duty to keep man and woman apart until they become man and wife."

"I don't know why you should."

I held up the Bible. "That's what it says in here," I answered.

Dora Hand could not dispute me. "I've broken most of the rules in my life," she said, laughing softly. "I might was well break this one, too."

"Not while I'm officiating." I opened the Good Book and

unfolded a piece of paper where I had scribbled a few notes, including the wedding prayer. "Hey, Wyatt," I shouted. "Get on up here and take your lady by the hand. Time's wasting, and the night's young. My fee goes up after the sun goes down."

The tone of my voice jarred him awake. His shoulders quivered, and I expected him to belch or worse. He rose uneasily, grabbed the back of the pew to gain his balance, and moved unsteadily toward his bride. She took his hand as the wind blew out the flame in the coal-oil lantern above her head, her smile beginning to fade, her eyes growing hard with disappointment, or maybe it was disgust.

I did not know whether the lovely Dora Hand was going to kiss him or slap him. Her decision was hanging in the balance.

"Please bow your heads," I said before she could do either one.

She bowed her head, both hands clasped prayerfully beneath her chin.

The maid of honor brushed back a tear that slipped out of her left eye, believing, I'm sure, that it is a God-given prerequisite for all maids of honor to cry. That's probably in the Good Book, too, or should be.

The bridesmaid was humming an old hymn under her breath.

The groom sighed, and the belch finally came.

"Dearly beloved," I prayed as solemnly as I knew how, "we are here today to join this man with this woman who are both old enough know what they are doing and wise enough to overlook if not forget what they know and don't know about each other. They have agreed to forgive each other's sins as You have forgiven them, so help us God, and we ask that you have mercy on their souls. . . ."

The front door burst open, and Lieutenant Hargrove, backed by twelve good men, stormed down the aisle. A carbine fired wildly over our heads, which gave me a reason to say amen, and the only lantern still burning in the chapel broke loose and dropped to the floor. I threw my hat on it to smother the flame, and the maid of honor began screaming, much differently than she did in her upstairs room at the Double Eagle. The bridesmaid dove for cover, modesty and dignity be damned. And the soldiers grabbed their prey and wrestled him to the ground before he ever knew he was in trouble.

"My God, what are you doing?" Dora Hand yelled, leaping into the midst of them, clawing and scratching, which was what an upstairs girl did best, elbowing and kicking her way through a sordid entanglement of arms and legs, battling to save her man from the clutches of soldiers who knew how to fight Indians, outlaws, and each other, but not women, especially not women dressed in white.

Lieutenant Hargrove grabbed her ankles and pulled her out of the melee, and Dora Hand emerged with a military issue forty-five-caliber pistol in her hand. She pulled the trigger twice, the bullets ricocheted off the walls and the fight came to an abrupt and an unceremonious stop.

Nobody breathed, much less moved.

A scared woman with a revolver in her hand is a killer, no matter how sweet and gentle and innocent she might be otherwise.

She had Corporal Sneed's pistol.

He wanted it back.

He had no intention of taking it away from her.

"Back up," she said, her voice shaking. "All of you."

Not a soldier disobeyed.

Dora Hand knelt beside the man who was within an "I

do" or two of being her lawfully wedded husband. He lay face down on the chapel floor. She slowly turned him onto his back.

And screamed.

The revolver fell out of her hand.

She screamed again.

Dora Hand was looking down into the gaunt, homely face of Charley Moseby. He grinned and licked his lips. And she fell to the floor beside him in a dead faint.

Somewhere out on the prairie, without a worry to his name, unaware that he and a braying jackass had parted company, alone again, Wyatt Earp was sleeping off a hard drinking bout he had lost with Ben Carson's cheap Jacksboro whiskey, dressed in the stained, shrunken clothes of a middle-aged gravedigger.

We had dragged him down to the depot as soon as Lieutenant Hargrove led his men to the grove of scrawny oaks. Wyatt Earp had neither argued nor complained. "Where you takin' me?" he mumbled.

"Straight to hell," said Charley Moseby, who had seen a few men on their way to hell in his time.

"That'll be two dollars," Ezra Bodine told us.

He shoved a ticket to Dodge in Wyatt Earp's shirt pocket, then hauled him like a sack of feed down the platform and deposited him inside the last passenger car of the first train to reach Fort Griffin headed north, which was the only train rumbling through town all day.

It was not a ride Wyatt Earp had commissioned.

But neither was the journey to the burying ground.

All he left behind was a woman and four bottles of whiskey Ben Carson still had stored beneath his bar.

He could always come back for them if either were worth the trip.

By the time the lieutenant's band of soldiers interrupted the pending marriage of the lovely Dora Hand to Charley Moseby, which probably would not have held up in court anyway, and I'm certain she would have taken it to court to get an annulment, the train carrying Wyatt Earp to hell or to Dodge, if there was a difference, had crossed the Red River and plunged into the oil pitch darkness of a moonless night.

♠

♥ 15 ♦

♣

Dora Hand spent the first two hours of her Sunday morning walking among the sunflowers that grew alongside the railroad tracks, wondering if the train that took Wyatt Earp away was ever coming back. By noon, she decided that it wasn't and had gone back to work again.

She had suddenly become the most talked about, most admired, and most wanted commodity in all of Fort Griffin, which is the kind of adoration that actresses pray for. It seemed that every man who rode through had heard about Dora Hand's unfortunate brush with fate instead of matrimony, and they sometimes drifted into towns miles out of their way just to see and partake of her lovely charms.

They all wanted to heal her broken heart.

And the lovely Dora Hand had enough broken pieces for them all.

But her eyes never left the railroad tracks, and the sound of each passing train, regardless of the hour, day or night, left her pale and shaken, sometimes remorseful and sometimes angry. The faraway wail of a lonesome whistle, piercing its way through the darkness, said everything that

Dora Hand felt now that Wyatt Earp was gone. It was as sudden, as unexpected, as sickening as a pistol shot.

"You should go to him," I told her on the morning I sat down at the Double Eagle for my last plate of fried eggs and ham gravy in Fort Griffin.

She stared at the window of the saloon blankly, and there were dark circles under her eyes. "I didn't run out on him," she said, her voice devoid of emotion. "There's no reason I should run to him."

"There is if you love him."

"I loved my mother, and she died on me," Dora Hand answered, a tear in her throat. "I loved Jack McClure. He took me out of the Tennessee mountains when I was barely sixteen years old, gave me something to eat, bought me the first new dress I ever owned, and taught me how to be an actress. He loaded up one morning and told me he was going down to Nashville on business and that he'd be back before the end of the week. I waited a month, and then they threw me out of the room because the rent was due and I was out of money. If you love somebody, Mr. Hawkes, they leave and never come back. If you don't love 'em too much, maybe they will."

"Wyatt didn't leave because he wanted to."

"Most men do what they want, or they don't do it."

"We were trying to save his life."

"Did it ever concern you, Mr. Hawkes, that you might be ruinin' mine?"

"We just decided you were a little too young to be a widow."

"Wyatt's not the kind of man to run out on a fight," Dora Hand said.

"Not from another man," I answered. "But this was different. The lieutenant had a federal warrant. That means Wyatt won't ever be safe, not as long as the United States

Army is looking for him. He can't travel far enough or fast enough to stay ahead of them for long or forever. Tomorrow. Next month. Next year. When he's sixty years old. The army will still be hanging that federal warrant over his head."

"Then there's no reason why I should go to Dodge," she said.

"How do you figure?"

"By the time I got there, more than likely he would be gone again."

Perhaps. I certainly could not guarantee that Wyatt Earp was in Dodge. I could not even assure her with a clear conscience that Wyatt Earp had stayed on the train long enough to reach Dodge. The army had been tracking him for just over a month now, and even a cold trail eventually turns hot. His was a known face. God might forgive, but the army never forgets. I could not even swear to Dora Hand that he had been able to escape the hangman, and the hangman, bless his soul, had been on Wyatt Earp's trail since the first day I met him.

The lovely Dora Hand pushed her chair away from the table and stood up. She straightened her hair, adjusted the white lace on her wedding gown, and gently smoothed the powder on her face, as unblemished as a porcelain doll. "If I went to Dodge, I'd just be another girl," she said, "and I'm sure a city as large as Dodge has plenty of girls and many of them younger than me." She smiled and cleared the tear from her throat. "I can't leave Fort Griffin. Here, I'm a star."

I watched her walk away and up the stairs, her bare, slender shoulders trembling but strong, doing her best to keep a stiff upper lip, her eyes moist but not a tear in sight, possessing the rare ability to meet and overcome the tragedies of adversity. I admired her a great deal. Grief is becoming in a lot of women, and Dora Hand was one of them.

I thought I was the only one leaving Fort Griffin that afternoon.

I was sitting on the bench beside the depot, watching a faint wisp of white smoke curling up beyond the grove of scrawny oaks, when the lanky frame of Charley Moseby slumped down beside me. He was carrying his shovel, and he dropped a small, ragged carpetbag on the ground at his feet.

"You leavin' town?" he asked.

I nodded that I was.

"I guessed as much," he said. Charley Moseby sat in silence, waiting until the locomotive had pulled around the bend past the oak grove before asking, "Dodge?"

"It's a place I haven't seen in a long time," I answered him.

"I've never been there," he said. "Of course, I've never been fifty miles west of Fort Griffin, as near as I can remember. They said I went to Pagosa Gap one time, but I was too drunk to remember anything about it, so that don't count."

"I appreciate you coming down to say good-bye, Charley."

"I ain't sayin' good-bye," he replied. "I thought I'd ride as far as Dodge with you."

"What's got you so all-fired-up anxious to see Dodge?" I wanted to know.

"I owe a man something."

"What's that?"

"I promised to dig his grave, and I figure it ain't gonna be long before he needs one." Charley Moseby sighed. He looked as though life had been nothing more than one bleak day after another. "Some people go out of their way lookin' for trouble," he said. "Trouble always knows where to find Wyatt Earp."

The train rattled to a stop. And the whistle blew loud and long. I wondered if Dora Hand had heard, and if the sound still struck her with the piercing force of a pistol shot. There was a time when she would run down to the depot and meet every train that arrived in Fort Griffin. Not anymore. There was no reason to.

Today was like any other day in Fort Griffin.

The train came. Somebody got on. Nobody got off.

♠
♥ 16 ♦
♣

Fort Griffin was a lot like the creek down in Sotol Flats, drying up and blowing away, just waiting for the next dust storm to consume what was left. And yet the town would be a thing of the past before those quaint souls who settled there and lived among its ramshackle buildings realized Fort Griffin had worn down and worn out, as worthless as an empty chamber in a gunfighter's .45.

Fort Griffin only thought it was wild.

Dodge City was bucking in eight directions at once. If God were still striking down wicked places with lightning, Dodge City would have been in the midst of a never-ending thunderstorm.

The town had a devil-may-care attitude, and, believe me, the devil cared a lot about Dodge City, particularly below the dead line, south of the tracks, where the streets and back alleyways were lined with dance halls, hotels, honky-tonks, picayune gambling houses and saloons. The only thing cheaper than a man's life was a woman's body, and the only thing more crooked than a woman's smile was a game of monte at Ab Webster's Alamo Saloon. There were three basic objectives to the game. The first was to cheat. The second was not to get caught at it. The third was shoot straight, shoot fast, shoot true, or run like hell if you didn't.

Deacon Cox was waiting for us at the Dodge House, though he had no idea we were headed his way. Deacon Cox was waiting for everybody. "Half the people are tryin' to get to heaven," he told us as the late afternoon sky lost the sun and turned a somber shade of purple. "The other half are doin' their damnedest to stay out of hell. An' the rest of 'em come to the Dodge House. When they get here, I'll have a room for 'em, and when they leave I'll keep their money."

Deacon Cox was a large man, dressed in a suit the color of Confederate gray, and there was a layer of lace on the sleeve of his white shirt. He had a big, round face, wide, inquisitive eyes, and a close-cropped beard, mostly red with a few stray strands of white. His rotund belly was the result of too much good food and too many glasses of French wine. He was never seen on the public thoroughfare without a beautiful woman hanging on his arm, and he made it a point to never be seen with the same woman twice in the same week.

Some men fight for power. Deacon Cox bought his. He owned and personally operated the largest, most respected, and probably the most expensive hostelry in Dodge. The governor kept a suite at the Dodge House, even when he wasn't in town. A king from some little country west of Russia had slept there during a wolf hunt. Whispered rumors in town said the president had discreetly spent a night in room 427 during the turbulent months after the Civil War, and he was not alone. It well could have been the First Lady, but the same rumors said that if it was, it marked the first time a First Lady had ever slid down the banister from the fourth floor wearing nothing but a pair of black garters and the president's tie dangling around her neck.

Deacon Cox catered to the wealthy and the powerful,

which was why he looked askance at Charley Moseby and me when we walked into the luxurious lobby, standing on a Persian rug beneath a crystal chandelier not unlike the one that was hanging in the foyer of Buckingham Palace, or so I was told. Sleeping in a railroad car from Texas had put a lot of wrinkles in our clothes, and we carried all of them into the Dodge House.

"You gentlemen misplaced for the night?" he asked.

"We need a couple of rooms," I said.

Deacon Cox frowned. "That will be cash in advance," he said.

"How much?" I wanted to know.

"Probably several dollars more than you've got," he replied.

I opened my coat and reached for a leather pouch, hooked to a gold chain around my neck. Deacon Cox suddenly became quite interested in me. The hundred-dollar bill I pulled from the pouch grabbed his immediate attention, then his eyes caught a glimpse of the belly blaster wedged into my waistband. He had seen a hundred-dollar bill before. He quickly dismissed it, turning a shade lighter than pale at the sight of the sawed-off shotgun, as ugly in the dim light as a rattler with his dander up.

"How many nights, sir?" he managed to say.

"Until the money runs out," I answered.

"What is your profession?" Deacon Cox asked, his voice shaken.

"I am a gambling man."

"I'm sorry, sir," he apologized. "I saw the shotgun and thought you might have other intentions."

"The cards are generally honest," I told him. "The men who handle them sometimes aren't."

He nodded in an understanding sort of way.

"For a gambling man, the money never runs out in Dodge, sir," he said.

"How about luck?"

He forced a smile. "Luck never runs out of Dodge either, sir," he said. "It just moves from table to table."

"And which table would you suggest I begin my business in Dodge?"

"Mayor Kelley's Alhambra Saloon," he said, "or Luke Short's Long Branch. Both are fine establishments, the finest you'll find west of the Mississippi, and they are always ready to welcome a new player to their table."

"Or a new player's money."

"It's all the same to them, sir."

Charley Moseby had slumped down into an English wing chair, propped his boots up on a small hand-carved mahogany table, and was looking at the lavish, ornate surroundings that engulfed him. Fort Griffin had been a concoction of slab boards, knotholes and rusty nails, whitewash and peeling paint. Dodge City was high-pockets rich; it reeked of money, not all of it honest, but spendable. Deacon Cox's hotel was large enough for Charley Moseby to put his Fort Griffin wife in one end and his Buffalo Gap wife in the other, and it might still be years before they ever stumbled across each other.

"You know what, Hawkes," Charley Moseby called out.

I turned around.

"This place sure would hold a lot of hogs," he said.

Deacon Cox turned red and probably thought seriously about turning us back out into the street, but he held the hundred-dollar bill tightly in his thick fist, and Deacon Cox had a difficult time turning loose of money once he had touched it.

He frowned with a certain disdain when he realized Charley Moseby had a shovel slung over his shoulder. He leaned over the counter and asked in a low, concerned voice, "What's your man holding?"

I whispered just as confidentially, "It's a shovel, sir."

"What does he do with that shovel?"

"Tell me about the people who come to Dodge," I said.

"What about them?"

"Do they live forever?"

"Seldom."

"Those who don't need Charley."

"What can Charley do for them?"

"He digs their graves."

Deacon Cox shivered. "That's a dirty profession," he said.

"I understand the governor stays here," I told him.

"His Excellency is here quite regularly," Deacon Cox said proudly.

"Then the hotel is used to it," I said.

"Used to what?"

"Dirty professions."

Deacon Cox curled his lip into a snarl. He wanted me to leave the premises, but not badly enough to give my money back.

I slid both room keys in my pocket, tipped my hat, motioned for Charley Moseby to follow me up the stairs, and all I could think about was a hot bath and scrubbing away the last residue that existed of Fort Griffin, Dottie Dembo, Ike Rigby, and the lovely Dora Hand who, at the moment, was probably in act three of her last performance. I began to wonder if the name of Wyatt Earp ever crossed her mind.

The night was just as dark in Dodge City as it had been in Fort Griffin, though not as bleak nor foreboding as it was in Judge Parker's Fort Smith prison. We walked down the plank sidewalks of Front Street, Charley Moseby and me, and there was excess light spilling from the doorway of every establishment to light our way. Horses stood calmly at the hitching rails, fighting an occasional fly or two with the flick of their tails, and, on every corner, big wooden whiskey barrels were filled with water, the only protection Dodge had against fire, the deadliest thief of all.

Pianos played. Fiddles whined. Men shouted. Women sang. Men grew tired of shouting and began to curse. Women screamed, a practice they never tired of. A stray gunshot echoed down one street. Pianos banged off-key. A meaningful gunshot erupted down another alley. A bottle broke. A window splintered. Fiddles scratched. Women laughed. Men paid the fiddler. A drunk crumpled face down in the mud. A gunshot hit the street lamp. The lamp went dark. And cattle started bawling for no reason. It was a lonesome sound, but cows didn't have any reason to be lonesome.

The noises of Dodge ran together. Running horses. Running men. A woman moaning with pleasure or pain. It was difficult to tell under the circumstances. Another curse. Another scream. Another fit of laughter. More pain. More pleasure.

A gunshot. A scream. This time it was a man. It was, I'm told, a normal night in Dodge.

I stood in the plaza trying to orient myself to new surroundings in a new town. I might be a stranger, but I would feel more comfortable if Dodge did not seem so strange. To the east stood the water tank, the depot, and the freight house. They all looked familiar. That's where the train from Fort Griffin had dumped us when the price of our tickets ran out. Just south of the tracks, ominous in the shadows, was a one-room house with floor, walls, and ceiling composed of heavy, solid timbers. It served as a jail, a place devoid of fresh air, a sanctuary that held August heat clear until the end of October, when it became an icebox. A man could age a year there in less than a week, or be dead for a week before anybody knew it. The stench of the living was as sickening as the dead.

Second Avenue loomed as the busiest and most popular street in Dodge City. It held Beverly's Store, the most important commercial business establishment on the plains, along with Delmonico's Restaurant, the City Drugstore, a barber shop, and the Dodge Opera House, which brought a rare glimpse of refinement and culture to a town that had a better grasp on the wages of sin. Whiskey flowed at the Long Branch, Alamo and Alhambra saloons, and grown men, some of them even sober, would step up to bet their hard-earned money at faro, monte, seven-up, or five-card stud, even gambling on chicken fights, horse races and foot races.

Dodge City had grown up around the tent George Hoover and Jack McDonald pitched back in 1871, hauling in barrels of aged whiskey they sold to Fort Dodge soldiers a watered-down glass at a time. Before the year ended, Henry Lovett, aware that the camp was stuck out in the middle of dust, heat, and prairie, but mostly dust, had staked out a second canvas saloon. That much dust could cause mankind to suffer a powerful thirst, and there was only one way to quench a thirst.

One sold straight whiskey.

The other stuck live rattlesnakes in the barrels and advertised that his whiskey had a real bite to it, and nobody doubted him for a minute.

Railroad tracks cutting along the banks of the Arkansas River, virtually in the ruts of the old Santa Fe wagon trail, brought a warehouse, a half dozen genuine saloons, and three dance halls. The town changed its name to Dodge City, in honor of the fort five miles away, and the saloons were crammed with railroad workers and buffalo hunters, soldiers, and Indian scouts. Cattlemen began pushing their great herds up the Plummer and Jones Trail, and Dodge accommodated them all with a rare opportunity to make money and lose it the same day. The corrals were stuffed with longhorn cattle, and the streets were crowded with wagons and animals for days at a time. Cattle owners and cattle buyers pitched their heated verbal battles about who owed who and how much in the refined confines of the Dodge House or over at Beebe's Iowa Hotel.

For the last several years, Dodge City had spent half of its time hiring a new sheriff and the other half wondering where the last peace officer had gone and who had chased him out of town. Upholding the law was a tough job. The bullwhackers and muleskinners did not like the railroad men, whose steel rails had pretty much put the teamsters out of business. The soldiers despised the buffalo hunters, accusing them of peddling guns and whiskey to the Plains Indians. Kansas liked the longhorn cattle better than the trail hands who drove them up the trail from Texas. The Texas drovers were ready to shoot any cardshark who had the gall to cheat them. Dodge City was not a hospitable place.

♠
♥ **17** ♦
♣

Spade Judkins, so I was told, had ridden the twelve long miles in to Dodge early that day, which was not unusual for a dirt farmer who cursed the dirt beneath his feet and spent most of his time out turning the rows of his garden, regardless of whether any seeds had been planted, just so the sharp plow point could rip open the earth he hated so badly. He vowed to give the good earth the same pain it had given him, and Spade Judkins was not a man of mercy. His lust for vengeance ran as deep as a taproot, as long as the harsh drought that hung like a suffocating shroud over his farm.

"This land didn't want me when I got here," he had a habit of saying, "an' it sure as hell don't want me now."

"It's pretty good land if you know how to take care of it," said Amos Fielding, a career military man who had retired his sergeant's stripes at Fort Dodge. "The trouble is, you ain't got no respect for it."

"It's done ever' damn thing it can do to break me."

"You're not givin' it a chance."

"I'm cuttin' it to the quick ever' day of my life, and the land's just too damn poor to even bleed."

Spade Judkins would plant a crop, then watch it die, then

get drunk for a week and lay in some back alley until his wife came to town and carried him home again. The whole town felt a quiet measure of pain and sympathy for Emma Judkins. She was a fine woman of good moral fiber and a strong Christian upbringing. And there was a time in her life when she might have been considered pretty, back before a few strands of gray troubled her long, black hair, and the Kansas winds hardened her face. She was always dressed in a black mourning dress, the only one she had. And the melancholy years had put a few too many pounds on Emma Judkins, but they had not dimmed the hint of fire that burned deep in her green eyes.

Unfortunately, the man who had given her his name had never given her anything else but misery when he was in a good mood and a bruise or black eye when he wasn't. Emma Judkins kept her head high and her chin firm anyway. And she always removed the ornery carcass of Spade Judkins from the wallows with as much dignity as she could muster under the circumstances.

No one ever tried to help her load the stout, whiskey-logged farmer into her wagon. Most tried to act as though they were totally unaware of Emma Judkins's plight. They merely crossed to the other side of the street and looked the other way. Emma was an independent woman and fiercely proud, and her chore was humiliating and demeaning enough without anyone trying to interfere. She never said it but the good folks of Dodge believed she appreciated them leaving her alone at a time like that.

"That Emma Judkins is a good woman," the white-haired Amos Fielding liked to say from his perch on the liar's bench outside the Long Branch Saloon. "A damn fine, handsome woman if I do say so myself."

"You best keep your filthy thoughts to yourself," Luke

Short told him. "What you're thinkin' is only about two acts shy of adultery, and the lady Judkins, she's been to church, an' she knows what the Good Book says about that, an' the Good Book, it ain't got nothin' good to say about it at all. She ain't go no use for retired Indian fighters with adulterous thoughts on their minds."

"I been studyin' about that somewhat," Amos Fielding said.

"About adultery?"

"No. About the lady Judkins bein' a Bible-readin' Christian." The old sergeant paused long enough to shove a few ragged stems of tobacco into his mouth. "I been doin' a little readin' myself, and, near as I can tell, the good Lord, He's a forgivin' sort of man. I don't think He'd hold it against her if she shot the sonuvabitch."

Spade Judkins was not hungry. There was no reason to be hungry, he said. That damn poor land of his wasn't going to grow enough to feed him anyway. When he needed rain, the summer sun scorched the earth. When he needed the weather to remain dry long enough to harvest those few crops that did manage to survive, the rain and hail and strong winds beat down, then blew away, whatever he had growing in the fields. Spade Judkins had trouble raising a good crop of weeds.

The lanky old longhorns from Texas had come ambling down Front Street about midafternoon, sullen eyed and leg weary after three months and a thousand miles on the trail. There had been one thousand, seven hundred and forty-three of them, unless Tom McMullen had lost a few stragglers during the past few days. The closer he drew to the railyards, the less time he spent watching out for his herd. The drive was nearing an end, and that's all any of his drovers were contemplating. The end of the trail meant a strong dose of whiskey, a hot bath, a soft bed, and a warm woman, usually one who still held the warmth of the last man to leave her arms.

Lord, how they had looked forward to Dodge City. Behind them were the painted deserts where the face of a tortured land never changed, flat and barren, condemned by miles of suffocating heat and thirst, and not even the nights could cool the ground. Cattle went blind, then mad. Men drank alkali water even though they knew it would probably kill them. At least they would not die with their throats dry. Lighting storms danced in the sky, and stampedes pounded the earth around them. Hard rains washed out the sky, leaving them without a North Star to guide their trails, and swollen rivers were more lethal than gunfire. A drover could walk away from a gunfight. The river had to be crossed. Tom McMullen had lost a few cattle and men along the way. Mostly they had stayed.

By night, the cattle would be sold, penned, and forgotten, and they would be rich cowboys in a rich town that wanted their money and usually got what it wanted. The only troubling question was whether Dodge City had enough strong whiskey, hot water, soft beds, and warm women. The cowboys could do without the hot water and soft beds, if necessary. By morning, they would be broke again, trying to figure out a way to get home and head north with another herd.

A night in Dodge made it all worthwhile.

Spade Judkins was in a surly mood by the time the drovers strode shoulder to shoulder into the Alhambra Saloon. He had been thrown out of the Long Branch after breaking off a table leg and beating a card shark who had the misfortune of holding one more queen than the deck allowed. Spade Judkins was not guilty of hammering the cheat unconscious. No jury of poker-playing, square-shooting, hard-drinking cowboys would ever convict him of that. The cheat had placed his own life into somebody else's hands when he slipped that extra queen of diamonds into his hand.

Spade Judkins, however, was charged with disfiguring a piece of fine furniture, and Luke Short needed legs under every poker table he could get, not that the early longhorn herds were beginning to drift northward out of Texas.

At the Alamo Saloon, Spade Judkins had thrown an empty whiskey bottle at a young lady in red velvet who sat atop the piano, singing every verse ever written about Home Sweet Home, and making up a few sad ones that would make any tender heart long for the homestead and family left behind. Judkins did not hit her, but the shards of splintered glass chased her off the piano. No one argued with the farmer that she had a voice not unlike a wild alley cat in heat. But she did have the best-looking pair of legs in Dodge, and no one had come to hear her carry a tune anyway. As long as she kept crossing her legs between verses, the lady in red velvet could sing all day and most of the night as far as they were concerned. She refused to return to her place of honor atop the piano until Spade Judkins was removed from the premises. He was out in the street, face down, a gash on his cheek, a knot just above his right temple, a pain below his ribs, chewing on a tooth that no longer had a place in his mouth, before he was aware that anyone had been disturbed or displeased by his actions.

He was spitting dirt.

And dirt had never been particularly good to him.

Spade Judkins dusted himself off, pushed his gray, stained hat back on his head, hitched up his faded blue trousers, and staggered on down the street. He glanced at the sky and caught a glimpse of a cloud growing darker in the

west. It looked like rain, but for the life of him, Spade
Judkins could not remember whether he was planting a crop
or harvesting one. So he forgot about the farm and turned
into the doorway of the Alhambra, which is where he sat,
holding an ace, his double chin quivering, when Tom
McMullen's Texas drovers hit town.

He ignored them, trying to talk himself into drawing to an
inside straight, which the odds said he would not be able to
do. But a farmer never worried about the odds. They were
always against him anyway. All he needed were two cards.

He raised the bet a red chip.

He tried but could not remember how much a red chip
was worth, only that he had one.

Bam Clifton eased his lanky body into an empty chair and
tossed a wad of bills onto the table. "I'm lookin' for easy
money," he said, then glanced at Spade Judkins and winked.
"Looks like I found the right place, if you have no
objections, sir."

"I got none," Judkins growled.

"What's the game?"

"Cards." Judkins belched and drained the last drop of
whiskey from its bottle.

Bam Clifton grinned. He had been foreman for Tom
McMullin's Circle Eight brand for almost two years now,
and it was his fourth trek to Dodge. He was barely thirty,
and he had the confident demeanor of a man who liked to be
in charge whether he was or not. A leather vest hung loosely
over a red-checked shirt, and Clifton's hat had obviously
been battered by too many sandstorms. His black trousers
were too short for his long legs, and his worn boots sported
new silver spurs with rowels as sharp as a knife blade.

No one who knew him ever believed that Spade Judkins
tried to cheat the Texas drover. He was certainly not above

it. But, frankly, Spade Judkins had never been able to figure out how to cheat anybody. He could not read written words at all, and he could not read cards any better. He just played what was dealt him.

He won sometimes, when the facts were kind to the ignorant, but mostly he lost because the fates did not treat him with any more respect than did his land.

Spade Judkins decided that he was dealt bad cards because God was punishing him for being such a poor farmer, or maybe God either burned or hailed out his crops to punish him for being such a poor card player. He had never been able to determine just which was which.

Spade Judkins was a sullen, irritable man all right. No one dared argue that point. He worked two mules to death and burned a squatter's shack when an old man settled down just beyond St. Joseph Creek and came sneaking into his barn one night to steal a chicken. Spade Judkins did not care about the chicken, but when he could look out in the early dawn and see smoke from a fireplace curling above the plains, then he reckoned that the old dirt digger from Indiana had definitely moved too damn close to the Judkins homestead, nailing his shack to vile land that was too poor to support one family, much less two of them.

Spade Judkins did have his problems when dealing with mankind. But he was definitely not a cheat. He was clumsy. That was his trouble.

Bam Clifton had taken ten dollars with a few hands that held a varied assortment of mediocre cards, and Spade Judkins was growing angry at his own inefficiencies. The madder he got, the more he trembled. And by the time he lay his last two dollars' worth of chips on the table, Spade Judkins was twitching and shaking like a wet dog stranded in a cold rain.

Bam Clifton laughed at him, which at certain times in certain circles would have been a deadly thing to do.

Poor old Spade Judkins knew there was only one way to shut the Texan up, and that was break him and send him home with pockets as empty as St. Joseph Creek after a long, dry summer.

And he might have beat him, too. The farmer had three eights showing in a game of five-card stud, and Bam Clifton was trying to decide whether to throw his cards in or gamble that Spade Judkins would make another stupid mistake, which he was prone to do when his nerves got to jumping like a frog leg in a frying pan, and the twitching and the shaking had become as irritating as a cockleburr under a horse's saddle.

All the drover needed was another ten. He had one showing and one in the hole. When Spade Judkins got ready to deal the final card to Bam Clifton, his nervous hands dropped it. That's all. He was twitching and shaking and jerking, and his fingertips were sweaty, and he dropped it.

The farmer immediately scooped the fallen card up and cut it back into the deck. No one paid him much attention. It happened all the time when drunks played cards. And professional gambling men earned their living, and some got rich, sitting at tables where drunks played cards.

But Spade Judkins had dropped a ten, the ten of hearts that Bam Clifton had been waiting for.

The drover's laughter was cut suddenly short. His eyes burned like flecks of brimstone. His voice was a cruel whisper. "You cheatin' sonuvabitch," was all he said.

They were the last words Spade Judkins ever heard.

He started to protest, but the Texan's first bullet slammed into his chest, jerking the farmer backward. Judkins began sliding out of his chair and onto the floor, reaching out to grab hold of something, of anything, to regain his balance, and nothing was there. His fingers were twisted, his face ashen. Spade Judkins tried to speak, but all that came out of his throat was a cough. And the spittle on his lips was stained the color of blood.

The drover's first shot had been hurried, fired in anger. He took his time before pulling the trigger the second time. He stood above the farmer and leveled his revolver between the farmer's eyes. Spade Judkins only had time to blink once before losing the top of his head.

Bam Clifton stood back and casually slid the .45 back into its holster. The Alhambra was as quiet as a cemetery plot. He looked quickly around and saw that he was surrounded by his own kind, Texans, trail drivers, mostly with too much whiskey in their bellies, men who had their own moral creed: "Blessed is he who has the fastest gun and the nerve to use it." The drover shrugged wearily.

"I don't mind bein' cheated," he said. "I've done a little of it in my time, and I've had it done to me. I just didn't like him being so damn obvious about it."

"It looks to me like the farmer's throwed his cards in," his drag rider told him.

"It certainly appears to me he has."

"Then I guess the money's all yours."

"I don't hear no argument from the farmer," Bam Clifton said as he leaned against the table and picked up the handful of chips. "Who's gonna cash these in for me?"

"I will," said the tall stranger, dressed in black, standing in the doorway of the saloon. His arms were folded. There was a look of boredom on his face, a silver star pinned to his coat.

Bam Clifton wheeled around and stared into the calm, lethal eyes of Wyatt Earp. "Who the hell are you?"

"I'm the man they hired to keep folks from gettin' shot around here," the stranger said. "Doesn't look like I did a very good job."

"You the sheriff?"

Wyatt Earp shook his head. "No," he answered quietly. "But they let me wear a badge anyway."

Bam Clifton gripped the handle of his .45 tighter. The farmer had been easy prey. The peace officer in black troubled him. The drover glanced down at the remains of Spade Judkins. "The sonuvabitch had it comin'," he said.

"I don't doubt that."

"He cheated me."

"Spade Judkins may have done a lot of things to irritate you," Wyatt Earp said softly, almost reverently. "But you'll never convince anybody that he cheated you."

"I don't have to convince anybody," Bam Clifton snarled.

"Only a jury."

"Hell," Clifton snapped, "you can't keep me here. I'm goin' back to Texas."

"If you try to walk out of here tonight," Wyatt Earp said matter-of-factly, "your friends will be carrying you home in a box."

"You threatenin' me?"

Wyatt Earp grinned the way a rattlesnake grins before he strikes. "No," he replied, "I'm merely letting your friends know they'd better start lookin' for a box. We usually use pine around here. It doesn't last long, but it's cheap."

Bam Clifton relaxed. The shock of the moment had worn off. He had been angry, then afraid, and now the old bravado that had brought him a thousand miles to Kansas was returning. "Can you count, lawman?" he wanted to know.

"Only up to six. Then I know a revolver's empty."

"The way I see it, there's only one of you," the drover

said. "There's twelve or thirteen of us Texans in here, maybe more. And I don't know how many more there are of us in out in the street behind you."

Wyatt Earp began strolling slowly across the barroom floor. "That's not enough," he said.

"How do you figure?"

"I've got no interest in them, sir. Only you."

Bam Clifton backed toward the wall. "They won't let you take me."

"They've got no choice."

"They'll cut you down before you get me out the door."

Wyatt Earp shrugged as though he were tired of the whole affair. "These trail drivers have come to Dodge for a lot of reasons," he said. "Some are lookin' for whiskey, an' some are lookin' for women, and some are lookin' for a good night's sleep out of the rain. I don't think any of 'em came to Dodge to die, sir. A man will give his life for a lot of reasons, for a lot of people. But frankly, sir, I don't think you're one of them."

Bam Clifton sneered. His back was against the wall. And the stranger in black kept coming steadily toward him. Time was running out. He had to make his move now while the peace officer's pistol remained in the holster.

"You only have one chance," Wyatt Earp continued.

"What's that?"

"That twelve of them stay around long enough to be on your jury." Wyatt Earp had a sneer of his own.

"They know I'm innocent."

"Your pistol fired the fatal shot."

"He was a cheat."

"And you were holding the pistol when it fired."

"Dodge ain't gonna miss the likes of him."

"Appears to me you're guilty as hell."

The Texas drover was digging deep, searching for whatever courage he had left beating in his heart. "A jury will never hang me," he said at last.

"You ever heard of a hung jury?"

"I've heard of it."

The sneer deepened on Wyatt Earp's face, creased by the shadows falling through the cracked window of the Alhambra. "We've got judges who'll hang the whole damn bunch if they don't come up with a verdict we like," he said.

"That's against the law."

The sneer softened into a smile. "I'm glad you're beginning to understand what is and what is not against the law," Wyatt Earp said. "Killing a man might not be against the law where you come from in Texas. But in Dodge, we don't approve of it."

Bam Clifton was not opposed to killing a man when he had to, and it looked as if he might have to. But he had never shot a man wearing a badge before. The lawman, damn his righteous soul, was daring him to shoot, and the stranger in black was a target Bam Clifton could not miss at that distance. Wyatt Earp was less than five feet away, moving closer, steadily closer. The drover could even feel the heat of the lawman's breath against his face. The palms of his hands began to sweat, and the weight of his .45 hung like lead on his hip. He could find out how fast or how slow he was, or the trail driver could run a bluff. "Maybe they'll help me. Maybe they won't," Bam Clifton said. "Are you willing to take that chance?"

"I don't have any choice either."

The Texas drover had been a brave man standing above Spade Judkins, firing that final shot into the farmer's brain. The courage departed him as quickly as does the soul of a dying man when Wyatt Earp shoved the cold steel barrel of his Smith & Wesson into the trail driver's mouth.

Bam Clifton heard the hammer cock and thought he was already dead. God, it was loud. His own revolver suddenly became too heavy to hold. His hand was numb and sweaty, and the .45 hit the floor. He pressed his back hard against the wall to keep from falling. Bam Clifton had not come to Dodge to die either.

Only Spade Judkins had been that foolish.

♠

♥ 18 ♦

♣

Charley Moseby and I had heard the gunshot as we left the plaza and ambled down Second Avenue, heading for the flickering lights of a whiskey-sodden acre that Dodge had bequeathed to hell. The pious Deacon Cox had suggested that the Long Branch or the Alhambra Saloon would be a good place for a man of my persuasion to survey the gambling landscape of the city. They weren't righteous places, but they had a reputation of being fair and honest, provided that a gambling man had the sixth sense required to read the face and the intentions of a stranger.

At first, I ignored the short, explosive burst of gunfire that echoed from down the street. In a Kansas trail town, the only time to worry about a gunshot is when it's aimed at you.

This particular shot missed its mark, or at least it missed me, and if it struck Charley he was not aware of it yet. Since there was no answering burst of gunfire, I dismissed the fray, concentrating instead on the game that awaited me.

On my first night at a new table, I always preferred the chair to the right of the dealer, which meant I could watch the faces of every gambling man at the table before I got my cards. That might not have meant much to some people, but it had always been a distinct advantage for me. And a man with an advantage was much better off than a man holding a pair of aces. By then, I would have a pretty good idea he was holding a pair of aces, and he had no idea what lay in my hand, good or bad. And I would know who was drunk or desperate, self-assured or just plain ignorant. Losers don't always lose, but they certainly play that way.

By the time we reached the doorway of the Alhambra, a curious gathering of armed and angry men had crowded into the street. They were Texas trail drivers, no doubt about it, lean and rawboned and as tough as buffalo jerky. For whatever reason, their night of wild, unbridled frivolity, wallowing in the dens of sin and iniquity that only the most stout-hearted of ministers even dared preach about, had come to a sudden and scurrilous end. Their mood was as disagreeable as a teased rattlesnake. The crowd had become a mob. There wasn't a word spoken among them that did not take somebody's name in vain.

"Looks to me like some poor bastard's gonna get himself killed over there," Charley Moseby drawled.

"Looks to me like some poor bastard already has."

"I've seen lynch mobs with a friendlier attitude."

"This one's not gonna waste its time hunting a rope."

"A bullet's quicker."

Charley Moseby wiped the tobacco juice away from the creases beside his mouth. "Whoever they're after's got two chances," he said. "He can duck or run."

"Or he can stand and fight 'em."

Charley nodded his head. "If he runs," he said, "he can probably live another twenty seconds. Twenty seconds is damned important to some men."

"It's time enough to pray."

"I never thought that God paid much attention to death-bed confessions or prayers on the run," Charley Moseby said with the theological wisdom of a bishop. "If he ain't already prayed up, then it's too damn late to start."

Wyatt Earp appeared at the door of the Alhambra, a silhouette whose face had been erased by the dark shadows of a hostile night. Every eye from the street was on him and the tall, lanky drover who was having trouble stumbling out onto the plank sidewalk. His hands and feet had been chained together with heavy manacles. A familiar Smith & Wesson was jammed against his neck. The drover was breathing in short, labored gasps. A gas lamp that hung from the side of the saloon reflected crisply off the silver star that separated Wyatt Earp from the rest of the rogues elbowing their way tightly around the batwings of the Alhambra.

The lawman in black was facing a dozen carbines, all cocked and ready to fire. At the moment, the only thing keeping Wyatt Earp alive was the collective conscience of the Texas trail hands. They would kill if necessary, but only if necessary. Most of the cowboys who drifted west had fought their way from childhood to manhood. Neither bumps nor bruises nor the taste of their own blood ever stopped them. They were not afraid to stand toe to toe with the biggest of men, nor ashamed to hammer the smallest into submission if their pride or their honor or their integrity was on the line.

But when it came to pulling the trigger, most had second thoughts, if there was time to think, provided they were not too drunk nor too stubborn nor too mean to think.

Their carbines had killed rattlesnakes, buffalo, wolves, coyotes, even a mountain lion or two. There was no conscience involved, only fear or anger or maybe hunger.

Taking a human life was not as easy.

Taking the life of a man with a star required some deep soul-searching. The question was not one they wanted to answer, but the tall lawman in black was giving them no choices.

They had to figure: Was the life of Bam Clifton worth risking their own?

Probably not.

But with a mob of thirty or forty men milling around on the street, one might just decide that it was.

Wyatt Earp was in no hurry to fight his way past the rifles. He was a man of patience, making quite sure that those who stood before him had plenty of time for second thoughts. It might make the difference between living and dying, then again it might not. He stood in the midst of a stormy silence, wondering if he could survive the thunder and the lightning of an unruly mob.

"Gentlemen," he said at last, "if you will be kind enough to let me pass, I have a certain duty to carry out. It has nothing to do with you, so I suggest that you just go on back to the pleasures you found here in Dodge. They're waitin' right where you left them. I can assure you that you do not want to go where this man is headed."

He waited for the crowd to back away.

No one moved, save an older, well-dressed, thick-shouldered cattleman with iron gray hair and a wind-worn, rock-hewn face, who was straightening his buffalohide coat, not unlike a trial attorney preparing to address the jury. The cattleman stepped up onto the wooden sidewalk, coming face to face with the lawman. His jaw was firm, his hands knotted into fists.

"I'm this man's boss," the cattleman said sharply. "Whatever he's done, I'll take care of it and see that he's punished appropriately. Now I'd be obliged if you go ahead and remove the chains."

"I don't believe we've been introduced," Wyatt Earp said, his voice wary.

"My name's Tom McMullen," came the reply. "Those two thousand Circle Eight cattle that came up your street this afternoon belong to me."

"Mr. McMullen?"

"Yes."

"On the trail, you're the boss," Wyatt Earp said. "You have your own set of rules. Your men obey whatever law you dictate to them. But when you rode past Aunt Katie May's whorehouse and entered Dodge City proper, then your law, your rules, your own private jurisdiction ceased to exist, Mr. McMullen. Bam Clifton owes his enormous debt to Dodge, and he'll pay."

Tom McMullen took a deep breath of exasperation. He pulled a leather pouch from inside his coat pocket and held it beneath the gas lamp. "What's the fine?" he asked. "I'll pay for what Clifton did."

"Are you sure?"

"The Circle Eight takes care of its own."

Wyatt Earp nodded. "I'm sure the judge would just as soon hang you as Bam Clifton," he said, "Just as long as somebody hangs for the killing of Spade Judkins."

It was difficult to tell in the darkness, but it appeared that Tom McMullen's red-veined face lost its color. His eyes went dull. His right hand dropped instinctively to the handle of his revolver, and he backed slowly down off the sidewalk.

"Nobody from the Circle Eight's gonna hang in this godforsaken hellhole," the cattleman growled.

Wyatt Earp pulled back the hammer on his Smith & Wesson and cocked it, which always sounded louder in the dark, especially when it was quiet enough to hear a man's heartbeat from the other side of the street. Bam Clifton's heart sounded like a runaway train. His eyes were pleading.

"I didn't murder anybody, Mr. McMullen," the drover

protested. "The damn farmer was cheatin' me, and it ain't no hangin' offense to shoot a cheat."

"In Texas, perhaps it's not," Wyatt Earp said. "In Dodge, we're doin' our best to get civilized. And shootin' some poor fool over a two-dollar card game is not what we consider to be civilized."

"I could have taken my cattle anywhere in Kansas, but I brought 'em here," Tom McMullin argued. "We're here at the expressed invitation of Mayor James Kelley. We're the guests of Dodge, and I expect for me an' my men to be treated like guests."

"You're allowed to bring your cattle here," Wyatt Earp replied. "You get top dollar in Dodge. But nobody gave you permission to shoot anybody. Now. Or next time. If you'll all be so kind as to step aside, I'll finish my business, and you and your boys can get back to yours."

A snarl etched its way across Tom McMullen's face. He drew his revolver and slowly raised his arm until the long barrel was eye level with the lawman. "If you refuse to listen to common sense," the cattleman said, "maybe you'll listen to this."

"Maybe I'll hear it. Maybe I won't," Wyatt Earp told him. "All I know for certain is that when Bam Clifton wakes up, he's gonna be shoveling a whole lot of coals into the furnaces of hell."

"He's sure as hell gonna have help, Mr. Lawman, and from what I understand, the devil furnishes his own shovels."

Tom McMullen was a tough old codger. He had fought to build his ranch and fought to keep it and buried anybody who ever got in his way. He had misplaced his conscience somewhere between the half dozen or so graves he had dug down amidst the mesquite thickets and palmetto fields of the harsh Texas valley.

He had had time for second thoughts, then and now.

It would not disturb Tom McMullen to pull the trigger. And if the boss man fired the first shot, then Wyatt Earp could expect to feel the blast of every rifle in the street, if that mattered. Usually a well-placed bullet from the revolver of an old gun handler, no farther away than four feet, was sufficient to cut a man down for good.

Wyatt Earp did not flinch. His gaze was steady and without compromise.

Tom McMullen cocked the hammer on his pistol.

They stood there, eyeball to eyeball, both ready to make the next move, neither quite ready to make the first one.

But the play would come.

Neither doubted it for a minute.

Bam Clifton began to pray softly beneath his breath. His boss would probably shoot down the lawman and live. Wyatt Earp would only have time for one shot, and it would enter the drover's throat just below his chin. The lawman's Smith & Wesson had never wavered. Bam Clifton's survival was no longer anybody's concern. Wyatt Earp only cared that the drover pay his debt. A bullet. A noose. It did not make him any difference. And the boss of the Circle Eight was preparing to go to war because his authority had been questioned, and Tom McMullen would rather lose the life of a good man than his authority.

"Damn it to hell, Jesus, get me out of this," Bam Clifton muttered. He had never felt so helpless and worthless in his whole life.

Charley Moseby spit the wad of tobacco from his mouth and leaned against his shovel. "Wyatt's doin' his damnedest to get himself killed," he said.

"He's running another bluff," I answered.

"Was he much of a card player?"

"He was never as good as he thought he was."

Charley Moseby sighed. "I was afraid of that," he replied.

"We can't stand here and watch Wyatt try to fight it out with a street mob." I told him. "We've got to do something to get him out of this mess."

"I was afraid of that, too," Charley Moseby said. He looked up at me with muddy eyes. "All I got is a shovel and a pistol my daddy gave me, and it didn't shoot straight ten years ago, and I ain't shot it since. And all you got is that half-pint shotgun. What good are we gonna be?" The gravedigger shook his head haltingly. "That's what I don't like about you, Hawkes. You take a problem, then you mess it up with a bigger problem. It's bad enough if one man dies, but when three die it's even worse, especially when the last two is me an' you, especially me."

"You can walk away, Charley," I said.

"That's the other problem," he told me.

"What's that?"

"I'd give ever'thing I own and half of what I can steal to be able to walk away from a friend in trouble." He shrugged elaborately. "But, hell, I can't do it."

"I knew I could depend on you, Charley."

"Which one you want me to shoot first?"

I grinned and winked at him. "Personally, I'm not planning on shooting any of them," I said.

Texas longhorns had always been considered wild animals by the vaqueros who chased them across deserts of catclaw and Spanish dagger. They were big and rawboned and as mean as anything with four legs. Their horns were like sabers, and they would turn on anything that smelled human and got too close to them. They were tough to catch and stubborn to drive, and longhorns became real jittery when they were crammed into those little old wooden pens down beside the depot.

A sudden movement could make them stampede.

They were scared of the dark.

Easy to spook.

And sudden bursts of thunder could turn them into killers.

I glanced at the sky. Not a cloud disturbed a quarter moon. No sign of a storm. Even a frisky wind had settled down for the night. That was all right.

I probably would not last two rounds of gunfire in a street fight.

But I knew how to make thunder.

Charley Moseby took his shovel and hammered out the wooden peg that held the gate, and the cattle began snorting and bawling, low and mournful, frightened and angry, stomping the ground, pawing the earth, pacing back and forth across the pen, their eyes as wary, as lethal, as a cornered bobcat.

He kicked the gate open.

And the longhorns pushed their way cautiously out of the pen and onto the back end of Second Avenue, sniffing the air, milling around in a tight circle, kicking up dust and beginning to fight amongst themselves. Charley Moseby grabbed the lead steer, a big brown-and-black dun, by the horns and turned him north, jabbing a boot forcefully against the longhorn's rump.

The steer was already as nervous as a pig in a packing-house. Now he was mad, too, and the rest of the cattle were angry if he was angry, and all of them were beginning to act as dangerous as a skunk with his tail up. All they needed was somebody to point them back toward Texas.

I fired the belly blaster once into the air. And they began to run.

I fired it again.

And they ran harder, a mass of flesh and muscle, horns and hooves, rawhide and raw power, thundering down

Second Avenue, pounding the earth, headed for God knows where and running with the devil himself.

They probably did not need any more persuasion. But I wasn't taking any chances. Not now.

I fired the belly blaster a third and last time.

Tom McMullen heard the cattle coming before he saw them, and there was no reason to look for them. They had already found him.

The longhorns, probably a thousand of them, bolted down the street like thunder drumming its way across a green and purple sky. When cattle get scared, they go crazy. When cattle get crazy, they tree or run down anything or anybody that crosses their path. By the time they passed the Alhambra, those longhorns looked as though they had come running out of the back door of hell on a hot day, and it was getting hotter.

Tom McMullen ran one way.

His drovers ran whichever way the cattle weren't coming, darting through doors, diving through windows, tumbling down back alleys, running as wildly as the longhorns were running loose.

And all they could hear was Tom McMullen screaming for somebody to stop that herd. There was an extra hundred dollars for anybody man enough to stop that herd, which was akin to slowing down a runaway train with an old rope. Hell, the boss of the Circle Eight yelled, he had just finished driving those damned old brush splitters a thousand miles to Kansas. He sure as hell did not want to chase them all the way back to Texas.

His men were on foot and losing ground.

They were scrambling down the street, coughing and gagging and choking on dust and dung, out of breath and out of luck. Those longhorns were payday. Without them, they would be leaving Dodge the same way they rode into town, so broke they'd all be scratching the bottom of the barrel, if they could reach that far down.

Wyatt Earp stood alone, with the exception of Bam Clifton who certainly was not going anywhere.

He watched the street until it grew empty and quiet. He had been one nervous finger away from dying. Now the guns that had condemned him were gone. And Bam Clifton was having a difficult time figuring out whether to be relieved or not.

He would live through the night, which meant he had another day to worry about the rope. A new day. A new rope. Already his neck felt raw. The sunrise might never be so bright again.

"You run a pretty good stampede," Wyatt Earp said when he saw Charley Moseby and me shuffling up the street. "You know there's a thousand-dollar fine for turning cattle loose in the streets of Dodge."

"That's pretty damn expensive," I told him.

"Cattle are pretty damn expensive," he replied.

"I wasn't talking about the cattle," I said. "I was referring to your life."

"I've been told my life's not worth a pile of cow dung."

"An enemy tell you that?"

"A woman."

"Sometimes it's hard to tell the difference," Charley Moseby said to no one in particular, squeezing another few chaws of tobacco into his mouth.

At the plaza, Charley Moseby and I turned toward the Dodge House, and Wyatt Earp headed for the cramped little building, fashioned from thick timbers, where he and Bam Clifton would wait for a judge to sentence the drover to death, provided, of course, the lawman could prove that Bam Cifton had sentenced Spade Judkins to death.

One thing was for certain. Spade Judkins would not be available to testify.

"Hawkes!" yelled Wyatt Earp.

I turned. He was merely another shadow among shadows. "Yeah," I called back.

"I didn't think I'd ever see you again."

"There's not that many trails out here," I answered. "Sooner or later, we all take the same one."

"You certainly came at the right time."

"Wyatt!" I yelled.

"Yeah," he called back.

"Were you actually going to shoot it out with the trail boss?"

"He thought I was."

"Was he right?"

"Tell me, Hawkes."

"What's that?"

"Have you ever drawn to an inside straight?"

"How many cards did I need?"

"Two."

"It's not a good bet."

"But have you ever done it?"

"Once or twice."

"Did the shark sittin' across from you think you had the guts to do it?"

"He thought I was a dead man."

"That's what Tom McMullen thought, that I was a dead man."

"You're saying that if I did it with cards, you could have done it with bullets."

"I'm a gambling man myself sometimes."

"You had a lot more to lose."

"Yeah." I could see Wyatt Earp grinning, even in the shadows. "My life's not worth much, maybe. But there was no way I was gonna lose my nerve, my dignity, or my reputation."

The shadows became one, and I heard the door slam behind Wyatt Earp and his prisoner. In the distance I could hear cowboys cursing and cattle bawling, and I wondered if either one of them had stopped running yet.

♠

♥ 19 ♦

♣

Morning and Wyatt Earp arrived at the Dodge House at about the same time, too early for civilized man, which, I presume, is why the first agony of daylight got to Dodge at such an ungodly hour. He had the clerk knock on my door while dawn was still just a faint glimmer in the east, and he was waiting on me, sitting in an overstuffed velvet chair, his back to the far wall, a cup of steaming coffee steaming in his hand, when I stumbled down the stairway.

"I've got to visit a lady this morning," he said, "and I wasn't particularly interested in going out there alone."

"You must be a changed man," I told him. "I never knew that Wyatt Earp needed a chaperon."

"I've got to inform a widow that she's a widow," he answered. "I don't mind deliverin' bad news. I've kind of gotten used to it. I thought you might be able to console her when she hears that her old man rode into Dodge, and he won't be coming back."

"Why me?"

"Preacher's are good at things like that."

I laughed, though it was bitter humor. "What makes you think I could pass for a preacher?" I asked.

"You were gonna marry me and Dora," he said.

Wyatt Earp had saddled me a horse, and we rode together the twelve long miles out across a flatland prairie to the lady Judkins's farmhouse. A morose Bam Clifton trailed along behind us. His hands were tied to the saddle horn, and a horsehair rope had been tied around his neck. Wyatt Earp held the other end of the rope. If the Texas drover tried to escape, he would not get very far without experiencing a dry, stinging sensation around his throat, which, I'm told, can cause a severe shortness of breath for which there is no known cure.

"Did you see Dora before you left?" Wyatt asked as we drifted across an endless sea of prairie grass, bent forward by the gentle morning winds.

"She mentioned your name a time or two," I replied, "but mostly the way people talk about vipers and sidewinders and other things that crawl in the desert and spit poison in the wound when they bite you."

"I don't think she would have made a very good wife."

"You haven't give her much of a chance."

"You didn't give me much of a chance, Hawkes," he said accusingly. "I didn't climb on that train by myself. Somebody put me there. The conductor said the culprit looked a helluva lot like you."

"The conductor didn't know me."

"No. But I sure as hell did."

The sun cut a crack in a ragged, purple cloud and touched the ground around us. I tried to think of some way to explain my actions that day in Fort Griffin, then decided the truth would be as good an explanation as any. "You're good in a gunfight, Wyatt, but you can't outfight the whole United States Army," I said.

"I did once."

"And you might do it twice." A covey of quail shot up out

of the grass and my horse shied for a moment. I settled him down, then said, "But the army doesn't just fight once, then quit. They keep sending men after you, and they never run out of men. Time and again. Sooner or later, probably sooner, one gets you. I know the difference between bad odds, long odds and impossible odds, Wyatt. The deck was stacked against you, and the army was dealing from the bottom. If you had stayed in Fort Griffin, you were already dead. It's just the bullet hadn't caught up with you yet."

"She was a whore, Hawkes."

"No," I told him. "She did what she had to do to survive. She's a lot like you, Wyatt. You've shot men. You've killed men. I don't consider you a killer any more than I consider Dora Hand a whore. She was what Ben Carson said she was, simply a working girl, nothing more, nothing less."

"I thought I loved her, Hawkes."

"Maybe you did."

"Maybe I still do."

"If the army ever forgets about you, Wyatt, you can go back and get her."

"By the time the army forgets me, she'll have forgotten me too."

"There's only one way to find out."

Wyatt Earp started across the prairie in a stony silence. He knew how to deal with men: fight them, cuss them, befriend them, kill them, or leave them alone. Women were totally beyond his comprehension. He thought that made him different. He would never understand that it simply made him a man.

"Why didn't Dora come with you, Hawkes?" Wyatt asked. "She had no reason to remain in Fort Griffin."

"She's a proud woman, Wyatt." There was no sense in being anything other than brutally honest. "You left her. Regardless of the circumstances, she believes you rode

236   Caleb Pirtle III and Frank Q. Dobbs

away and left her behind. She'd waiting until the day you come back to get her. She's not the kind of woman to chase you from one end of the country to the other."

"She's not a proud woman, Hawkes. That's not it at all."

"What do you call it?"

"Stubborn."

Maybe he was right after all.

Emma Judkins, dressed in a faded green gingham dress, looking older than her forty-two years, was standing in the shade of her sod house, her blue-checked apron filled with eggs, when we rode into her front yard. She frowned when she saw us. Wyatt Earp was new in Dodge. I was a stranger. Bam Clifton, a rope around his neck, had never been this far from Texas before. And the lady Judkins was by herself and uneasy because her husband was gone and her rifle, if she had one, was out of her reach, probably just inside the front door. She glanced quickly at the door, then back at us.

Wyatt Earp spoke first. "Emma Judkins," he said.

"That's right."

"I'm the chief deputy in Dodge," he told her, climbing down out of the saddle. "I'm afraid our visit isn't a social one."

"There's something wrong, isn't there?" The lady Judkins began to tremble and nervously rub her hands together.

"Yes, ma'am, I'm afraid there is."

"It's about Spade, isn't it?"

"Yes, ma'am, I'm afraid it is."

I dismounted and stepped toward her. At the moment, she was not aware that anyone existed on the plains of Kansas except her and Wyatt Earp. She did not want to hear what he had to say, and he did not want to tell her, and neither of them had any other choice.

"What's Spade done now?" she asked defensively.

"I'm afraid he's died is what he's done."

Emma Judkins turned white. She blinked once. Then twice. Then I watched her eyes roll up into her head, and she fainted dead away. I caught her before she hit the dirt and thought for a brief moment that the lady Judkins had gone on to join Spade. But they would no doubt be traveling in separate directions once they crossed over the River Jordan. Her breathing returned to normal, and we carried her inside the sod house, dark and cool, not yet touched by the morning sun.

I sat with Emma Judkins, rubbing her hands, cooling her forehead with a wet bandana until the color had returned to her face. "I'm sorry," she said when she finally opened her eyes. "I'm usually not that weak of a woman. I don't know what could have gotten into me."

"It must have been quite a shock," I said, wondering if that's what a preacher would have told her, figuring he would have had something a little more holy to say.

"I've been expectin' it," she replied with a touch of anguish in her voice. "When you live with a man like Spade Judkins, every day something unfortunate happens. You just never know what it's gonna be until it comes." Emma paused a moment, then asked, "How did Spade die?"

"A Texas man shot him."

"Over a woman?"

"Over a card game."

"Well," she said with a sigh, "that's some relief anyway."

"From what I understand, your husband died quickly. He never felt a thing," I told her, wondering if my words sounded as foolish to her as they did me.

Emma Judkins forced a laugh. "The way Spade drank his whiskey," she said, "the Texas man could have hit him between the eyes with a wooden mallet, and he wouldn't have felt a thing."

"You want to bury your husband in the Dodge cemetery or bring him back out here?" I asked.

"We can have the services there," Emma replied, the emotion drained from her voice. "Old Spade and the ground out here didn't get along very well. I'm afraid if we buried him out here, the ground would spit him out before spring."

I did not know whether to laugh or remain as pious as a hand-me-down preacher, so I nodded gravely and clasped my hands prayerfully against my chin. "I know this must be hard on you," I said as sympathetically as possible.

"Losin' Spade ain't much of a hardship," she said. "Not bein' able to get the garden plowed before fall sets in, now that's a hardship."

"Wyatt and I thought we might be able to help you get the ground turned before we leave here," I said.

"That's quite impossible," Emma Judkins replied.

"Why is that?"

"We've got no mules," she said. "They were old and worn out, and Spade worked 'em to death. He always said he was gonna buy some new ones as soon as he got ahead, but he couldn't make any money until he brought in a crop, and he couldn't make a crop without his mules. That's why he went to Dodge. Leastways that's what he told me. He took the last twenty dollars we had, hopin' for a run of luck at the gambling tables. But bad luck's all Spade ever had."

Her smile was as sad as any smile I've ever seen. She had pledged to spend her life with Spade Judkins until death parted them.

Now she was a free woman. Some women don't want to be free. It means being alone in the middle of a big, lonesome country.

"It's kind of a relief to me," Emma said finally, brushing her hair in a feeble effort to hide the strands of gray that crept among the black.

"Losing Spade?"

"Knowing it's over." She sighed. "Every time he ever rode away from here, I wondered if he was gonna come back. I thought he might get himself killed, or even kill somebody. Or, worse yet, find himself another woman and run away with her. Now I don't have to wonder about it or worry about it anymore."

"Life's not always fair out here," I said.

"It's as fair here as anyplace else, I guess," Emma Judkins replied. "At least God answers prayers out here. I wasn't sure he was listening to anybody in Kansas." She forced another smile, and not a tear had yet been squeezed from her pale blue eyes.

"Which prayer did He answer this time?" I wondered.

"He took Spade before Spade got into anymore trouble than he was already in," Emma answered placidly. "You see, Mr. Hawkes, I don't mind being a widow. It means that gettin' by just got a little harder. But I can keep my head up. People don't hold any grudges against you for being a widow. But if Spade had shot somebody, I don't think I could make it, knowin' he was in jail or hanged. Everywhere I went, people would say, There goes the wife of a murderer. I don't think I'm a strong enough woman to handle that, Mr. Hawkes."

"At least he left you with your name and your reputation intact." I looked around the bare rooms in the sod house and said, "You still have a place to live. It's not a big house, but it's good and solid. And with a little patience, you can grow enough to eat three square meals a day, and that's a better start than most people have when they reach Dodge. You do own the land, I presume."

"No. We just settled down when Spade lost the wheel of his wagon," Emma said. "Up till now, nobody's ever tried to run us off."

"If you can hang on a little while longer and don't mind a little hard work," I told her, "you can still make that crop you were telling me about, then get it harvested and sold before winter sets in."

"How will I get the ground plowed?"

I nodded towards the window. Emma Judkins sat up, eased off the bed, and walked across the small room. The wooden planks groaned beneath her feet.

Outside, she saw Wyatt Earp in the garden, turning rows that would soon be ready for planting. Bam Clifton had been hitched to the plow, taking the place of the cross-eyed Judkins mule, and his lean frame was bent double as he struggled forward, dragging the rusty plow point through the stubborn earth. The soil was matted with grass whose roots had been woven together for decades, for centuries. Sweat had plastered his clothes to his body. Dirt clung to his face. His back was breaking. He grimaced as the pain worked its way through his tired muscles.

Bam Clifton had never done anything in his life resembling hard work unless he had done it on horseback. He now had a deeper respect for work animals than he did when he had awakened that morning. The harness had dug into his shoulders until his skin was raw and bleeding.

The plow point banged into a rock, and the Texas drover pitched forward, off balance, clawing at the earth as he fell. He paused a moment to catch his breath, and Wyatt Earp popped a bullhide whip above his head.

"I don't understand," Emma Judkins said with another frown.

"You need a garden," I said with the righteous indignation of a prophet. "I promised you a garden. We'll get you a garden."

"But who's the poor man pulling the plow?"

"Looks like a mule to me," I said.

"You're gonna kill him."

"Sooner or later," I said.

By nightfall, Emma Judkins had pulled a sack of seeds out of the well house and begun pressing them into the soft earth. One by one, six inches apart. The ground was gunpowder dry and needed rain. The widow Judkins could not water the soil by hand. The creek was as dry as the garden.

A black cloud crawled out of the western horizon, and a spirited wind ricocheted across the prairie, promising rain. The sky had been known to lie. But at least the widow Judkins was being given a promise, which was more than Spade had ever had. Maybe she and the land could get along now that he was gone and no longer around to curse it anymore.

♠

♥ **20** ♦

♣

Dodge City had its seamy side of town where the bars and the brothels did not know the difference between day and night, especially not when Texas drovers herded their cattle northward to the rail yards. The cattle were worth twenty dollars a head in Kansas, sixty-eight dollars in New York, sixty-eight dollars in Massachusetts, and seventy-two dollars in New Jersey, which were ridiculous prices for steers that, one report said, "were not fit for people to eat. They will do to bait traps and catch wolves, but not feed people." Yet the rangy old cattle were making a lot of men rich. But only the rangy old cowboy, as lean and gristly as the steers that led him beyond any boundaries he had ever known before, risked his life to reach Dodge, then faced an even greater risk getting out of town in full possession of his money and his life.

The cowboy confronted the wilds and felt at home amongst them.

Dodge was doing its damnedest to keep the wilds south of town, while the city tried to shake off the tarnished, inglorious image of its past and become more settled, less treacherous, and more civilized. Mayor James H. "Dog"

Kelley was himself no rabid reformer. He owned a saloon, a dance hall, an opera house, a gambling parlor, and he bred greyhounds to race. He did not breed them to lose. Kelley would bet on a fast dog as quickly as a fast woman. But he was aware that Dodge was doomed unless somebody stepped forward to keep the lawlessness in check. Trail hands left their wages behind, but none stayed long enough to feel permanent, and those drovers who came to town and rode away seldom rode that way again.

The mayor vowed to establish a town where ladies could be ladies, and men could conduct their business in private offices, not over some whiskey-stained two-bit poker table in a picayune gambling house, although he certainly did not discourage their God-given right to participate at whichever table or bedroom they chose once the business at hand had been finalized and put out of the way, preferably without bloodshed.

The hard cash money it took to build Dodge, both the good side and the bad side of it, had been dragged up the cattle trails and down the steel rails of cattle trains working their way to and from Chicago.

The men who rode those trails would be the death of Dodge.

At least that's what the town council feared, and they had plenty of reasons, most of whom were buried within the five-acre cemetery that sprawled just outside of town. A white picket fence kept the curious coyotes away from the graves, even though the paint had begun to peel and the pickets were leaning southward with the wind. No one else ever came to disturb them. Those who had found a place of permanence up on Boot Hill were mostly drifters and wanderers and trail hands who took the wrong trail to the wrong town, men who simply left home one day and whose names were erased off the face of the earth. They no longer existed.

Dodge had laid its share of them to rest. The causes of their demise were varied and usually unreasonable. Few of them ever died of old age.

Mayor Dog Kelley was a big man who understood law and the need for law. He had a square face, thick, bushy eyebrows, and he wore a perpetual scowl, even when he was in a good mood. He liked smoking good cigars as much as he enjoyed watching his dogs run. He wore tailored suits, with a gold watch chain laced across his vest, and Dog Kelley never went anywhere without his ivory-handled hand-carved hickory cane.

He used the cane to pound the table when expressing a political opinion, of which he had many, to point out the comely young lady in a music hall burlesque show with whom the good mayor wanted to share the afternoon and maybe even the night, and the hickory cane became a powerful tool of persuasion whenever some unruly Texas drover refused to depart the premises of his saloon.

Dog Kelley had ridden those vast, empty plains as a sergeant in the United States Cavalry until he retired, serving for years as personal orderly to Brigadier General George A. Custer. The Indian wars had brought him to the western prairies. Cattle had kept him there. The art of soldiering, however, had given the mayor a distinct, almost holy, regard for authority. It was never debated, not openly anyway. It was never questioned. Dog Kelley did not allow it. As long as he ruled over the cattle empire of Dodge, his word was law, and his version of the law did not take a lot of schooling to understand.

Wyatt Earp was seated at a back table in the Alhambra, one card short of a spade flush, when the mayor sent T. J.

Ambrose scrambling downstairs with a message for the lawman to join him.

"Mr. Earp," the aging, white-haired Ambrose stuttered, "I sure do hates to interrupt you."

"Is there trouble?" the lawman asked without looking up.

"No, suh."

"You got a fight started you can't stop?"

"No, suh."

"Is somebody dead, dyin', or expectin' to?"

"No, suh."

"Then don't."

"What, suh?"

"Interrupt me."

T. J. Ambrose squinted his eyes and leaned over Wyatt Earp's shoulder, studying his cards. "Mr. Earp?" he said.

"What is it?"

"There ain't no reason for you to shy away from the interruptions. You ain't gonna be sittin' here much longer anyway."

Wyatt Earp sighed and threw his cards face down on the table. They were as worthless as his bluff would have been.

I winked at Ambrose, who showed the last three teeth he had when he grinned, and he was grinning like a jackass eating thistles. "You did Mr. Earp a big favor," I told him.

"How's that, suh?"

"You saved him a few dollars and a lot of embarrassment," I said.

"Mr. Earp, he's the best man with a gun I ever saw," T. J. Ambrose replied, his voice fairly crackling. "But his ability with cards would drive a preacher to cuss."

Wyatt Earp's eyes were hard, but his voice was soft when he turned to face the old man. "Now that you ruined a good hand of cards," he said, "what was it you had to tell me that couldn't wait until I had cleaned out the gambler?"

"The boss man, he wants to see you."

"When?"

"As soon as you can get that skinny butt of yours upstairs."

"Does the mayor have a problem?"

"Right now, he ain't got but one," Ambrose answered.

"What's that?"

"You, Mr. Earp. He wanted you two minutes ago, and you ain't there yet, and the boss man, he gets mad at old Ambrose if you don't hurry on up there and see what he wants." T. J. Ambrose lowered his cracked voice to a whisper. "When the mayor wants something, he don't want to wait for it."

Wyatt Earp sighed and flipped the old man a Mexican gold piece.

"What's that for, Mr. Earp?" Ambrose asked, rubbing the gold piece gently against his face.

"You might as well take it," Wyatt Earp said as he headed for the stairs. "I'd a' lost it to Hawkes, anyway. If he was holdin' spit, he would have beaten me."

When the lawman walked into the major's office, Dog Kelly was sitting behind an ornate cherry desk, imported from France personally by the president of the Cattleman's Bank of Dodge. The desk, heavily carved with angels, cherubs, and a toothless gargoyle, had been personally used by the president until the night he left from work late and walked head first into a Texas bullet meant for someone else. On the wall behind him was a case of books that Dog Kelley had never bothered to read. The single light from the desk lamp threw strange shadows across his face, virtually hidden behind a puff of cigar smoke.

"Have a seat," the mayor told Wyatt Earp as the lawman strode out of the dark hallway and into the office, his black hat in his hands.

The chief deputy of Dodge nodded without a word and sat down in a straight-backed chair with a caned bottom. It had been in the office when Dog Kelley moved in, and he kept it. The chair was hard and uncomfortable. It made visitors feel ill at ease, which gave the major a distinct advantage during any debate or discussion, regardless of the subject. Those who found themselves confined to the chair felt as though they were victims of some medieval inquisition. For Wyatt Earp, the chair offered the softest place to sit he had had all day. A borrowed saddle was giving him blisters.

Dog Kelley stared at him with dark, piercing eyes. He liked to measure the worth, the strength, the character of a man before doing any business. He had seen tough men wither and sometimes break beneath the stare, as cutting as the steel of a saber that had been left in the fire.

Wyatt Earp's chilled stare was calm and unconcerned, which made it even more deadly, and Dog Kelley realized it. He was not yet sure whether he liked it or not. But he certainly did realize the authority that lay behind the lawman's black eyes. Not many creatures could hold a steady gaze that long without blinking. A rattlesnake was all that came to mind.

Dog Kelley, during his days as a cavalry sergeant, had ordered men killed simply because Custer had deemed it the right thing to do. Wyatt Earp knew what it was like to actually pull the trigger. Dog Kelley had heard of men dying. Wyatt Earp had watched them take their final breath. He had snatched their final breath from them.

That made the two of them separate, and both were aware of the difference.

"You have quite a reputation," the mayor said, puffing again on his cigar.

Wyatt Earp crossed his legs, his hands folded placidly in

his lap. The Smith & Wesson hung heavy on his hip. Dog Kelly had not asked him a question. The lawman did not feel obliged to give him an answer. He waited.

"From what I've been told," the major continued, uneasy whenever a conversation was interrupted by long gaps of silence, "you were quite a renowned gunslinger before showing up in Dodge and putting on a badge."

"I have no idea where you got your information, Mr. Mayor, but someone is either lying, or he's sadly misinformed." The lawman spoke with calm, carefully chosen words. He also had no idea why the mayor of Dodge had requested a meeting, much less why Dog Kelley had such a sudden interest in his past. Perhaps the U. S. Army had finally gotten around to sending a wanted poster to Fort Dodge, one that bore his photograph and details of an early-morning duel in an oak grove thicket outside of Fort Griffin. Probably not. If so, the soldiers would have come after him themselves. They certainly would not have turned the chore over to an overweight politician with the jowls of a bulldog who knew how to handle a cigar much better than a revolver.

"You were arrested in Arkansas, I believe."

"It had nothing to do with a gun," he said.

"I understand you were under the care of Judge Isaac Parker."

"It had to do with a horse." Wyatt Earp began curling the end of his unkempt mustache. "I said I borrowed it. The owner said I stole it."

"Did you kill him?"

"Who?"

"The man who said you stole his horse."

The lawman in black frowned. "When I raise a gun against someone," he said, "it's because the badge says I have a right to keep the peace or because someone has a serious interest in shooting me down. I never use one to settle arguments or disputes."

The mayor raised his ivory-handled cane and laid it across his shoulder. He watched the smoke curling from the end of his cigar drift toward the ceiling and finally disappear in the darkness.

"Perhaps you're not the man I suspected you to be," he said.

"Perhaps not."

Wyatt Earp had learned long ago: the man who loses any discussion is usually the man who speaks first, speaks the loudest, and says the most. For the present, Dog Kelley was talking too much, and the lawman was content to let him circle around like a buzzard in flight until he finally got around to the reason he had called Wyatt to his office at such a late hour. Out in the bar, the night was still young. In the stuffy confines of the mayor's office, the night was growing more irritating by the moment. Wyatt Earp did not mind playing games, but only when money was riding on the outcome.

The clock on the wall behind the mayor said that midnight had passed seventeen minutes ago. It might not be entirely accurate. But it was close.

"I need a man who's damn good with his gun," Dog Kelley said, pounding the desk at last with his cane. The impact jarred the room like a pistol shot. Wyatt Earp did not flinch. "The whole damn town has to know he's good with a gun. But he's got to be tough enough and strong enough and nervy enough not to use it until he has no other choice. His revolver's his threat, and it's not an empty threat. But unless he's a second away from dyin', he's got to keep it sittin' snug in its holster. Does that make any sense to you, Wyatt?"

"You need somebody who's not afraid to die," the lawman answered.

"I'd never thought of it in those particular terms," the mayor replied, "but you're probably right."

"You need somebody brave enough to charge hell with a bucket of water."

"That's the exact man I'm looking for."

"You can't find him."

"Why not?"

"The sonuvabitch is already in hell, and his bucket's got a leak in it."

Dog Kelley leaned forward, propping his elbows up on the table. "Let me tell you the problem I'm facing," he said.

"I'm listening."

"The economic survival of Dodge City depends on Texas money," he said, chewing hard on the end of the cigar.

"Texas certainly spends a lot more in Dodge than it does back in Texas," Wyatt Earp admitted.

"But the unbridled lawlessness that Texas drovers bring to Dodge is ruining the town," the mayor continued, the staccato of his voice growing louder, more impassioned. "We've got shootings. We've got killings. We've got shootings even when we don't have any killings. We've got drunks in the street. And we've got drunks who get mean when they drink, and they can't get enough to drink, and we do damn well sellin' 'em whiskey. There are nights when Dodge is not fit for man nor beast, and it's damn difficult to even tell the difference between the two. We've got a helluva mess, and I need somebody who can talk tough when it's time to talk and shoot straight when it's time to shoot. I need a lawman in this town who's got the nerve to clean it up."

The mayor's final words hung in the air between them. His steady gaze was as pleading as it was demanding. Dog

Kelley waited for Wyatt Earp's response, afraid for a long moment or two that there would not be one.

The lawman in black was a practitioner of patience if nothing else. "You offering me the job, Mr. Mayor?" he asked, finally breaking the awkward silence.

"I was bettin' on you, Wyatt, because I thought you were a gunslinger who just happened to be wearin' a badge." Mayor Dog Kelley sighed. The tension was gone. The firm set of his jaw could not longer mask the weariness that had probed its way into his back like a stray bullet. "I guess I was wrong. Now I'm bettin' on you because I don't have anybody else."

"You have a whole staff of peace officers walking the street."

"I've got men wearin' badges and totin' guns, but I've seen 'em when the chips are down," the mayor said. He bit the end off his cigar and spit it beneath the desk. "I'm a pretty good judge of character, Wyatt. Some run when the goin' gets rough. Some don't. I'm looking for a man who'll stand his ground as though that piece of ground was his most precious possession. I don't need men who are content to follow orders. I'm lookin' for somebody who can give orders and make damn sure they're followed to the letter. No excuses."

"Just what is it that you want me to do?" Wyatt Earp asked.

Mayor Dog Kelley settled back down in his chair and tapped the ashes of his cigar into a glass tray beside him. "There are some folks on the town council who have grown so damn tired of the lawless elements runnin' in our streets that they want to close Dodge to Texas cattle. Keep the drovers out of town, they say. Send 'em somewhere else. If Dodge goes broke, so be it."

"There are some folks in Dodge who have a death wish."

"That's one thing you and I agree on, Wyatt." The mayor reached into a cherry cabinet beside the desk and pulled out an unopened bottle of imported whiskey, along with two crystal glasses. "Would you care to join me in a drink?"

The lawman in black declined. Some decisions needed to be made with a clear and sober head, especially decisions that dealt with law and order, particularly when it looked like he might be caught in the middle when the shooting started. And the mayor was right about one thing. The shooting had definitely already started.

Dog Kelley moistened his parched throat with a sip of the imported whiskey, then spoke again, softer this time. "We can't lose the Texas cattle," he said, "without closing the banks. And the Texas drovers are already welcome here. They're a little high-spirited and they cause more than their share of trouble, but they're always welcome. What I want you to do, Mr. Earp, is keep them from killing each other."

"There are two ways to do that," Wyatt Earp told him.

"Enlighten me, if you will."

"Put 'em in jail as soon as they hit town."

"That's hardly acceptable." The mayor grimaced and turned away. "Their money will do us little good if it's stuck in their pockets, and they're stuck in jail."

"The second way is by far the most difficult way, Mr. Mayor."

"What's that?"

"Take their guns away from them as soon as they set foot in town."

Dog Kelley raised an eyebrow, and a smile played at the edge of his perpetual scowl. "Can you do that?" he asked.

"It can be done," Wyatt Earp said defiantly. "Of course, it has its drawbacks."

"And what might they be?"

"I may have to kill one of 'em from time to time."

The mayor shuddered. "That's not good for business," he said.

Wyatt Earp stood and walked to the mayor's window, looking down on the street through the columns of a second-story balcony. "You pass the ordinance," he said, "and I'll do what I can to keep it as painless and as bloodless as possible."

Dog Kelley rose to shake Wyatt Earp's hand. A deal was a deal, he said. A handshake simply sealed it.

As the lawman in black opened the door to leave, the mayor said, "One thing troubles me. You've apparently accepted my offer and taken the job, but you haven't yet asked what the job pays."

Wyatt Earp shrugged as though the thought had not crossed his mind. "Those Texas drovers aren't gonna like leaving their guns with me," he said. "It's gonna make some of them mad and turn some of them into gunslingers, sure as the world. I didn't see any reason to worry about the pay until I found out if I was gonna live long enough to collect it."

Dog Kelley nodded. His face was clouded with cigar smoke. "We'll pay you fifty dollars a month base," he said. "If the drovers put up a fight or give you any trouble, we'll give you a bonus of two dollars for every man you bring to jail who's still alive."

"What if I have to shoot them?"

"We don't pay for damaged goods."

"Fair enough," Wyatt said as he stepped out into the carpeted upstairs hallway of the Alhambra Saloon and closed the door behind him.

A worried frown creased his face as he returned to the back table where T. J. Ambrose, Charley Moseby, and I sat, all in various stages of going broke over a game of Memphis

Shanghai that the old man had invented during one of his alcoholic binges on a Mississippi riverboat.

Wyatt Earp slumped into a chair beside us.

"I've seen the condemned in a more cheerful mood than you are," I said, absentmindedly counting the cards and realizing why I couldn't win. The king of diamonds was missing, which, as Ambrose explained it, had not been one of the rules.

The lawman sighed and shivered for no accountable reason. He removed his hat and ran one hand through his long, black hair. "Well, Hawkes," he said, "I'm out of the killing business."

Charley Moseby, whose attention had been distracted by the singing voice of a pretty painted lady whose eyes promised more than her song, suddenly jerked his head around as though he had been shot. "What'd you say?" he asked.

"I said I was out of the killing business," Wyatt repeated.

"Damnation, and damn it to hell!" he snorted.

"What in the world's wrong with you, Charley?" I asked.

"Hell," he said, his voice torn between anger and self-pity, "that means I'm out of business, too."

The gravedigger grabbed the deck of cards off the table and, in exasperation, threw them high above the table, whipping out his rusty old revolver and firing at them five times before the last card, a deuce of clubs, floated to the floor. He did not hit a card. He hit the ceiling five times, which is why Charley Moseby spent the night in the Dodge jail, wondering if his wife in Buffalo Gap and his wife in Fort Griffin had even realized he was gone, trying for the life of him to figure out why he had left them.

♠

♥ 21 ♦

♣

The seasons came and went as they were supposed to on the unbroken plains that rolled endlessly beyond the lights that hardly ever dimmed in Dodge City. By the time the snows blanketed the prairie grasses, the last of the longhorn herds for 1875 had rattled their way down the tracks toward Chicago's packinghouses.

Charley Moseby had leaned against the depot in the shank of the afternoon, his joints beginning to ache as the promise of colder weather hung like an angry cloud in the north sky, watching the gnarled oak corrals being emptied for the final time. The cattle had grown listless. Their eyes were dulled. They stood with their gaunt faces thrust into the wind.

Charley Moseby shook his head, his hair becoming as unkempt and shaggy, though not as red, as that of the longhorns. "Them Yankees ain't go no sense," he said.

I had no idea what he meant.

"They're payin' good money for them longhorns," he continued.

"All you see is hide and horn and manure," I told him. "What those people up north see is meat, and when you're hungry that's a pretty damn good sight."

"They're throwin' their money away," he argued.

"What makes you say that?"

"You can pack all the roastin' meat of a Texas steer into one of his horns." He spat a wad of tobacco he had been chewing since Tuesday into the dirt and bit off another plug. "I'd just as soon eat a pair of boots," the gravedigger said. "They're a helluva lot more tender, and they got a better taste."

"You ever eat a pair of boots?" I ventured.

Charley Moseby shrugged, threw his shovel across his shoulder and sauntered away. "They ain't bad," he mumbled, "if you remove the spurs first."

The Texas drovers had ridden home, at least those who had not fallen in love with some music-hall girl or settled down in their own private patch of ground inside the white and sagging picket fence of Boot Hill. The trail back beyond the Red River would not be nearly as long nor as treacherous as the drive north. Some were astride the same weary and sore-legged horses that had carried them to Dodge. Others had sold their mounts along with their cattle and boarded a train to Texas.

They were boys when they departed their mothers in Texas and men when Dodge got through with them.

One told me, "I left home wearing four dollars and eighty cents' worth of clothes and weighing a hundred and forty-six pounds. Three months later, I weighed a hundred and eighteen pounds, and I had two hundred dollars and sixty-eight cents in my pocket. Now all I got left is four dollars and eighty cents' worth of clothes on my back."

"Dodge wasn't very kind to you."

"It whipped me this year." The drover grinned. "Next year it's my turn."

"You coming back?" I asked him.

"If I can figure out how to get back to Texas," he said, "there ain't no doubt about I'll be back to Dodge."

"It's a hard life," I said.

"It beats no life, I guess," he said.

I guess he was right.

The last time I saw him, he was walking out across the plains on the south side of Dodge, bent forward, his saddle thrown across his back. He had lost his horse in a chuck-a-luck game, but not his saddle, never his saddle.

A cowboy without a horse was simply having a run of bad luck.

A cowboy without his saddle was through.

With the trail hands went the stock buyers, the pickpockets, the horse thieves, the snake-oil salesmen, the two-bit gamblers, the confidence men, a traveling medicine show with potions guaranteed to cure any ailment that might afflict a man on the trail, with the possible exception of a snakebite, gunshot, or noose, for which there was no known cure, gunslingers and gun toters, busted miners, bronc busters, and the editor of the *Dodge City Times* who said he would be back when the cattle hit town again and he had something worth reading to write about.

Wakes and wanted posters made news. Weddings and church socials and high soprano singers on the stage of the Dodge City Opera Houses did not. The editor had trouble sleeping at night without the sound of gunfire or the shattering of glass or the desperate wail of a woman's screams echoing up and down the streets. A dull town made for a dull newspaper, and nobody in Dodge City was willing to spend a nickel on a dull newspaper, which meant the editor could either go broke or pack up and move on out to the Rockies where, it was rumored, another wild and rowdy silver-strike boom town would give him plenty of news fit to print and a lot more that wasn't.

About all that was left in Dodge for the winter were the deadbeats, the drifters who had no place better to go, merchants with money in the bank, a gambling man with cash in his pocket, a gravedigger who lay awake worrying at night because the first snow had frozen the ground, making it too hard to dig, a mayor who bragged that Dodge was becoming the cultural metropolis of the western plains, a city marshal who took away more guns than he had given back, a police force that had fights amongst themselves when there was nobody else to fight, saloon girls who closed their shades and needed the rest, and a preacher man who stumbled into the Alhambra every Sunday morning sermonizing on the same topic: "He goeth forth in the morning full of bug juice and, lo, in the evening he is cut down by a Winchester ball."

Bigger Thompson was one of the deadbeats who had driven his wagon west from Illinois in search of silver or gold or anything of worth he could dig from the earth or steal from a sleeping drunk in the alley. To his misfortune, the cold had driven all the drunks inside, and Bigger Thompson was sitting at the bar of the Long Branch, drinking by himself, since there was no one else awake that Sunday morning who wanted to drink with him. He could tell with a quick glance that I wasn't looking for company, nor did I have any interest in passing the time of day with a stranger unless, of course, he had some wild idea that the cards might be good to him. His eyes were as red and streaked as a west Texas sandstorm. The dust, through the years, had turned his white hat gray, and he wore the tattoo of a snarling panther on the sinewy muscle of his right arm.

The sun had barely topped the balcony ledge atop the Long Branch when the Reverend Wilson A. Criswell bolted through the door, thumping his well-worn Bible with a gnarled fist. His eyes were dark and piercing, and a hawk nose wrecked an otherwise ordinary face. His black scissortail suit was much too large for a wiry, disjointed body that was almost birdlike in appearance. The preacher frowned and, without any warning, stuck a crooked, bony finger squarely between the red-glazed eyes of Bigger Thompson.

"Can you smell it?" he blurted out in that high-pitched voice of his.

"Get away from me," the miner growled.

"Can you feel it?" The voice had become a whine.

"You been drinkin', preacher?"

The Reverend Criswell curled his lips into a snarl. "It's all around you," he spit out, his eyes trying to cut deep into the soggy soul of Bigger Thompson.

"What the hell's all around me?"

"Hell!" The preacher's laugh had become a cackle. I had heard chickens sound the same way, usually just before some farmer wrung their necks. "Can you smell it? The brimstone's just like sulphur. Can you feel it? The flames are so hot around you, I can almost feel 'em. The devil's got you full of bug juice, now the Lord's gonna cut you down."

"I didn't know the Lord carried a Winchester," I said from my table in the back of the saloon. I had heard the Reverend Criswell's sermon before.

He ignored me.

Bigger Thompson could not ignore him. His face was flushed, almost the color of his eyes. I could see the tattoo begin to quiver on his arm.

"Confess your sins today, brother," the preacher man pleaded with heartfelt and genuine passion, "or you'll be forever doomed to those pits of hell when the day comes that you'll have to stand before your Maker."

Bigger Thompson studied the Reverend Criswell for a

moment, then asked, "You ready to meet your Maker, preacher?"

"I have a home awaiting me right this very minute in Glory Land."

A wry grin began to creep across Bigger Thompson's flat and sunken face. "You mean to tell me," he said softly, "that you're ready to die?"

"The moment I take my last breath on earth, I'll be sittin' in God's outstretched hands," the reverend replied smugly.

Bigger Thompson slowly removed a blunt-nosed revolver from his boot and jammed it hard against the preacher man's belly. "Then I guess it'd be best if you died right now," he said, "while you ain't got no sins draggin' down your skinny carcass."

All I could see were the whites of Reverend Criswell's eyes.

He tried to speak, but his tongue quit working.

Bigger Thompson cocked the hammer on the revolver. "I'd hate to see you hang around this godforsaken town long enough to get cross ways with some foul temptation and lose your soul," he said. "Looks to me like I'd be doin' you a helluva favor if I just pulled this trigger and watched the outstretched hands of God jerk you up 'fore you hit the floor solid."

The preacher man began backing up, holding his Bible for a shield. The words were still stuck in his throat like a broken chicken bone, but his eyes were pleading for his life. He stumbled and fell.

Bigger Thompson fired once.

The bullet splintered the floor between Criswell's legs.

The preacher turned white and tried to pray. His tongue wasn't working. But his legs were. He rolled to his feet and scrambled for the door. Bigger Thompson's second bullet removed the reverend's hat and sent it spinning across the bar. He fired a third time into the wall just to see which way Criswell would jump next.

The preacher man hit the street at a dead run, doing his best to keep both legs moving in the same direction at the same time.

"Hell," Bigger Thompson said to the empty doorway. "He wasn't no more ready to die than I am."

Wyatt Earp came into the Long Branch from the back alley. He stepped quietly behind the miner before Bigger Thompson realized he was no longer alone at the bar. He had heard no footsteps at all. That's why the lawman had never been concerned about handling drunks, no matter how mean they were. Drunks, he always said, can't hear a damn thing.

"I counted 'em," Wyatt Earp said softly. "That's three shots you just wasted. You got three left. I got six. Those aren't very good odds."

Bigger Thompson's grip never loosened on his revolver. Nor did he look around. "You the law?" he asked.

"I keep the peace," Wyatt Earp answered.

"You arrestin' me?"

"That's why I'm here."

"The preacher man, he ain't got no right comin' in here an' interferin' with me."

"You don't have any right shootin' at him."

"I didn't hit the bastard."

I stood up and walked toward them. "You're lucky," I told Bigger Thompson. "The city marshal's got a new policy out here."

"What's that?" he wanted to know.

"If you shoot at somebody and hit him, Mr. Earp hangs you with new rope," I answered. "If you miss, he uses old rope."

"What's the difference?"

"With any luck," I replied, "the old rope might break, depending, of course, on how many nights it's been left out in the rain, provided, of course, the country's seen rain in a coon's age."

Bigger Thompson turned ashen. Cold sweat beaded up on his forehead, but his face was flushed. He looked at the lawman with pleading eyes, and his right hand went instinctively to his neck.

Wyatt Earp sighed. "I'm not arrestin' you because you were a bad shot," he said. "In Dodge, it's not legal to carry a weapon of any kind inside the city."

"I didn't know that."

"We got signs posted on just about every building in town."

Bigger Thompson hung his head, and his shoulders were slumped. He laid the pistol on the bar. "I can't read," he said in a voice as empty as the cold, snow-banked streets of Dodge.

"There's no law against that," Wyatt Earp said. He picked up the miner's revolver and shoved it in his belt. A subdued Bigger Thompson offered no resistance. "You had anything to eat lately?"

"Not since Friday. Shot a jackrabbit on the other side of Lovelady Creek."

"Fried rabbit's not too bad."

"Didn't have no fire." Bigger Thompson shrugged with neither pity nor remorse. "It ain't bad raw if you're hungry," he said.

Wyatt Earp nodded as the miner stood and held out his hands. "You gonna put them steel clamps on me?" he asked.

"Do I need to?"

"You gonna hang me, marshal?"

"I don't even own a rope."

Bigger Thompson relaxed and wiped the sweat off his

forehead with the back of his sleeve. "I ain't goin' no-where," he said.

"I didn't think you were, not till after you got fed, anyway." The lawman grinned. "The biscuits are tough, and the stew's burnt, but they're both hot."

"How long you keepin' me?"

"You can leave in the mornin' if the preacher don't press charges," Wyatt Earp replied. "No reason to keep you any longer than that."

"The stew's punishment enough," I volunteered, leaning against the bar.

"Can I have my gun when I leave?" the miner asked, suddenly fearful that he might find himself walking around in a den of thieves and a pit of snakes unarmed for the rest of his life.

"I don't want your gun," the lawman said as he and Bigger Thompson walked out of the Long Branch. "But the three bullets belong to me."

"What'll I do if I need my pistol?" the miner asked.

"Smile a lot," I told him, "keep your mouth shut, and don't tarry where you're not wanted. Mindin' your own business is about the best insurance you can have out here."

It was damn good advice.

I wished I knew how to follow it.

The last time I saw the Reverend Wilson A. Criswell, he had a borrowed jackass hitched to a secondhand buggy, and he was making a new road across dried, snow-scattered prairie grasses, his back to the sun, heading east, back toward a more peaceable land where men feared the scriptural word of God and, even though they did partake of various concoctions of bug juice from time to time, they generally refrained from shooting at the holy messengers who had been chosen to deliver it.

Wyatt Earp released Bigger Thompson the morning after

he had collected his two dollars and fifty cents for the arrest, and Dodge settle down to confront the icy breath of a harsh winter in virtual isolation with neither an editor nor a preacher man to prick its conscience or torment its cold, hard heart.

The days were gray, the nights bitter.

The wind howled as though it had a broken heart. The tent city just below the dead line blew away. It was a week before anybody noticed it was gone or missed it. Whoever had been living there wasn't anymore.

The train slowed once or twice, but did not stop for more than a month, and only then to leave a bag of mail, mostly letters for folks who had moved on elsewhere or never arrived at all, and a young woman who came tracking up the snow-laden street, holding a stuffed valise with both hands, dragging it along in the ice and mud beside her.

Her cotton dress was blue with white stripes, thin and definitely made for summer or someplace a lot warmer than Kansas in January, and the wind cut straight through her. The young woman, bent against the chilled wind, staggered as the weight dragged her down, and she almost lost her balance. She might have fallen if I had not taken the valise from her grip and put an arm around her waist to hold her steady.

She looked up with eyes as blue as a limestone-bottom lake, and a faint smile played about her lips. She was shivering in the cold night air, and a light, icy mist had begun to fall around us.

Her skin was fair and unblemished even in the glow of the gas lamp that spilled from the window of the Alhambra Saloon. She could not have been more than twenty-five years of age, and her face was framed by long blonde hair, the color of wheat straw, that cascaded down upon her shoulders.

"You'll freeze yourself to death if we don't get you inside," I told her, leading her toward the saloon.

"Thanks," was all she said. Her hands, when she took my arm, were January cold and turning blue.

All I could hear was the sound of our feet crunching the frozen snow and the short, shallow gasps of her ragged breathing. A coyote barked in the distance. And Jeremiah Harper's wagon rolled past, its log chains clanking, its wheels moaning sadly against the rust of their axle.

"You're certainly not dressed for a night like this," I said as we stepped up onto the porch of the Alhambra. She shivered again as another knife of winter wind whipped around the corner of the building and slapped us in the face.

"I didn't know there was anyplace in the world this cold," she said, her voice shaking, her teeth chattering.

"You've never been to Kansas before."

She forced a timid smile. "I've never been farther north than New Orleans," she said as we walked into the saloon. She must have sensed every eye in the room staring hungrily at her, but she chose to ignore them. I escorted her to the brick fireplace behind the piano and ordered a straight whiskey, no water. She needed warming up in a hurry. The Alhambra whiskey came with a fire all its own.

"You do have a name, I presume," I said.

"Becky," she replied. "Becky Porter." She stood as close to the flames as she could get without smoldering her long dress, trying to rub the numbness out of her arms. Becky Porter's smile was angelic, which was disarming in a city like Dodge.

"We don't get many visitors to Dodge this time of year," I said. "I'd think you were lost if the train hadn't brought you."

She took a sip from the whiskey I handed her and coughed. It was either too strong, too bitter, or she had swallowed it wrong. I took a sip myself and found nothing wrong with it, which was just as well. I could stand a little fire myself.

Her deep blue eyes glanced awkwardly, timidly, around the saloon and its lavish trimmings, coming to rest on the larger-than-life picture that hung crookedly on the velvet-covered wall behind the bar. For more than a decade, the woman with big breasts and bigger buttocks, lying naked on a bearskin rug, caressing her cheeks with a turkey feather while a cherub with a queer smile danced in the sky beside her, had been the goddess of all who came to partake of the Alhambra's perverse pleasures.

"I came here to meet someone," she said. "I thought he would be waiting for me at the depot. He wrote that he would."

"Your father, perhaps?"

"My husband." There was that angelic smile again. Becky Porter laughed nervously and said, "Well, he's not my husband yet. But he asked me to marry him, and that's why I came."

"He's a most fortunate man," I said.

"Thank you, sir." She blushed, and it had been a long time since I had seen a woman of any age blush.

"Perhaps I know him."

"I'm sure you do," Becky Porter answered. "He must be very influential in town. He's the pastor of the Holy Ghost Methodist Church, Reverend Wilson Criswell."

I choked on the whiskey.

Maybe it was too strong and too bitter after all.

I spoke slowly, trying hard not to say the wrong thing. "How long have you known Reverend Criswell?" I asked.

"About a month," she said.

"When did you meet him?"

Becky Porter laughed nervously again. "Oh, I've never

met him," she said. "He ran an advertisement in the New Orleans *Picayune* looking for a wife. And I was looking for a way to leave New Orleans. Reverend Criswell sent me a train ticket and promised to love and cherish and do all those things that husbands are supposed to do. So here I am." She paused, and a worried frown darkened her face. "You don't think something might have happened to him?" Becky Porter asked.

"I'm sure nothing has," I said in an effort to comfort her. I must have looked quite foolish indeed. Here she was, the kind of innocent young girl who would be a minister's wife, and I had dragged her into a saloon and done my best to pour hot bug juice down her throat. God had always had trouble enough trying to forgive the things I did. This time, I had no right to expect any forgiveness at all.

"Do you know where I might be able to find him this time of night?" Becky Porter was beginning to feel uneasy. I could read it in her face. "Perhaps he did not get my letter, or perhaps he got his days mixed up."

All I could think about was the sight of the Reverend Wilson A. Criswell, hunched forward in the buggy, using a whip to beat the daylights out of his borrowed jackass, headed east in a dead run, the distant sound of Bigger Thompson's gunfire still echoing loudly in his brain.

I took Becky Porter's arm and led her to a chair, motioning for her to sit down. The frown deepened. She began to shiver again, and this time it had nothing to do with a January chill.

"There is something wrong, isn't there?"

"The Reverend Criswell doesn't live here anymore," I said.

Her blue eyes were suddenly pale, as bleak as a funeral morning. "I don't understand," was all she managed to say.

"He's gone," I told her.

"But he knew I was coming. I have his letter right here." Becky Porter began frantically rummaging through her valise. She pulled the letter from a small leather bag and handed it to me. I took it but did not bother to read it.

"I don't think he's coming back," I said softly.

She fought back a tear, then squared her jaw. She looked older than she had when I first saw here walking up the snow-laden street in the dark. Her soft eyes had a hardness that I had not recognized before. She rubbed her hands together until they no longer trembled. It was not the first time that Becky Porter had been hurt in her life. She hid her scars well, but they were there just the same.

"You can get a room here for the night," I said. "There's a train headed south in a week, maybe earlier. We can check the schedule in the morning. In the meantime, you'll be taken care of."

"That won't be necessary," Becky Porter said, her eyes suddenly calm but without expression. She stood, straightened her shoulders, and brushed her long, blonde hair with the palm of her hand. "I can make it just fine on my own." She smiled at me. It was still beautiful all right, but not nearly as angelic as before. "I was working in a New Orleans dance hall when the Reverend Criswell plucked my soul from hell. I know how to get by." The smile faded, but only for a brief moment. "I just thought I wouldn't have to anymore," she said. Her voice cracked slightly, but I acted as though I had not noticed, and she thanked me with her eyes.

Becky Porter walked toward the bar without looking back over her shoulder. All she needed tonight was a room and a chance to be alone. Tomorrow she could look for a job. Mayor Dog Kelley, if I knew the mayor, would never let her leave the Alhambra.

Reverend Criswell, God bless him, would never know what he left.

For Becky Porter, being in love with a dream would be a lot easier than being in love with the hawk-nosed face and disjointed frame of a preacher who had spent a lot more time wrestling with the devil than he had with a good woman.

The days grew shorter.

And colder. The wind blew as far south as Dodge, then stopped at the dead line. It wailed like a lonesome woman, and the back rooms of town were filled with lonesome women who knew how to find a smile when one existed and keep a man from knowing he was lonesome, too.

The moon at night was brighter and a good deal warmer than the sun by day. The streets were littered with loose pockets of unruffled and untracked snow, marred only by the footprints left behind by coyotes who had wandered into town and prowled the alley in search of food scraps that had been thrown behind Delmonico's Restaurant.

Art Delmonico knocked down two of them with his shotgun. And we ate venison for a week, wondering if it were indeed deer, or, possibly, four-legged scavengers that barked at their own shadows and howled at the moon with cold, bitter voices on cold, bitter nights. After the first bite went down, the rest did not matter. It was hot and greasy and heavily doused with brown gravy.

Sergeant Amos Fielding had ridden out to the widow Judkins homestead along about the time the first snowflakes reached down and touched the land. She had a hole in her roof, and the window facing north was broken, and not even a cow-chip fire could warm up the wind that blustered through the cracks and into the cabin. The mud chink in her chimney had busted loose, and the hand pump out beside the water well was frozen solid. The widow was a handsome woman, in spite of her years, and she had more to fix than she had hands to fix it. Amos Fielding did not have much to offer Emma Judkins, except an army pension, but he had a pair of callused hands that had not been busy for a long time.

It took the old sergeant all day to patch the roof, and by then a light mist was leaving icicles on his whiskers, and it was too cold for the twelve-mile ride back to Dodge.

"A man might run off into a snowbank, and nobody ever see him again," Amos Fielding said, laughing heartily.

The widow Judkins could not remember the last time she had heard Spade laugh. It was a sound forbidden in the cabin. He did not laugh. And, for too many years, she had had nothing to laugh about.

Emma Judkins gave the sergeant supper. He took her to bed.

And since the fire had burned itself out, and it appeared that the Kansas landscape was bracing itself for a severe winter, she crawled in under the covers beside him. Amos Fielding was older than Spade had been, and he was a good deal smaller. But he was stone cold sober, which was a relief to her, and he was definitely a man, and the Widow Judkins had not had a man, good or bad, for a long time.

She knew what she was doing was a sin. Then again, maybe not. Maybe it was just God's way of answering prayers. The Good Book did say He moved in slow and mysterious ways, and Amos Fielding was as mysterious as she could have ever imagined.

By morning, Amos Fielding found himself a married man.

"I ain't heard no preacher sayin' no words over us," he said, burrowing down beneath the extra quilt Emma had thrown over them after they quit sweating.

"Just the same," she told him adamantly, "we've gotten

ourselves married in the eyes of the Lord. You may not have said 'I do' during the night, but 'I did.' "

"Then, by gawd," Amos Fielding said with that booming laugh of his, "you can get up and get me breakfast like a good wife ought to."

The widow Judkins looked him over carefully. He might be wrinkled and scrawny, but he was definitely worth breakfast. Besides, there would be a circuit-riding preacher come through in the spring, and that was time enough to make them legally wed. In the meantime, the eyes of the Lord would have to be good enough to satisfy the both of them.

The chill gnawed at the bones of Dodge. Not even the flames from the log fire at the Dodge House had much luck biting through the winter air that hovered upon the plains, then cut its way through every crack that had lost its moss-and-mud chinking.

Charley Moseby grew lonesome and finally bored. He had a sudden urge burning below his belt to snuggle again beneath a buffalo rug with at least one, probably both, of his wives back in Texas. Sarah Jane offered to ease his pain. She had one of her own.

Sarah Jane still had a full figure and a warm smile. But Charley Moseby's eyes could never get past the ragged scars that Ike Rigby's skinning knife had left upon her face. And Sarah Jane understood. The hurt burned much deeper than the scars. But she was woman enough to understand.

Her life in the brothels were over. The red slashes of raw flesh had the ability to sober up even the drunkest of cowboys. An ear was missing, and part of her bottom lip had been peeled away. Spittle had an unfortunate habit of dripping out of the corner of her mouth without her being aware of it, especially when she smiled. And a smile was about all that Sarah Jane had left. The cowboys pitied her.

They could not love her. There was just not much whiskey left in Dodge, and the nights were never black enough to mask a face that Ike Rigby ruined.

So Sarah Jane took the only job left in town, working for Mayor Dog Kelley, cleaning his house, cooking his meals, reading to him late at night, staying out of sight when he brought visiting dignitaries, both male and female, to his home. He paid slave wages. But she ate well, even though she ate leftovers, and there was a roof over her head to keep the falling snow out of her bed.

Toward the dog days of summer, Sarah Jane received a new dress. It was not really a new dress, but she had never worn it before, which made it seem like new. One of the soiled doves in the Long Branch, barely seventeen, had been abandoned by a New Orleans gambler who paid twenty-two dollars and sixteen cents to buy her from a cotton farmer claiming to be her father.

Charley Moseby dug her grave in a lonely corner of the cemetery and inherited her clothes. Since he had no personal use for the dress, he gave it to Sarah Jane, which had prompted her offer of warmth on a cold night, any cold night, and there were plenty of them.

Charley Moseby cried because he did not want to hurt her feelings. But the nights just weren't that cold. Sarah Jane never asked again.

And Charley Moseby began talking more and more about Texas. It was too wild, too hot, too dry, too dusty, too poor, too big, too lonely, too windy for a common, decent man to ever settle down. And his wives were too old, too mean, too fat, too demanding, too cranky, too selfish, too stubborn. But, God, how he missed them both.

"You might as well go on back," I told him one morning. "I've heard so much about your wives, I'm beginning to think that one of 'em's mine."

"Can't," he answered.

"You left on good terms, didn't you?"

"They was both speakin' to me the last time I saw either one of 'em."

"I'm sure they're wondering what happened to you."

"They probably think I'm dead by now."

"Then go on back home and surprise them."

"Can't," he said again.

"Why not?"

"You stuck your head out lately?" Charley Moseby asked. "A horse would freeze before I got out of Kansas."

"You don't own a horse."

"I could steal one." He shrugged. "It's so damn cold out, nobody would miss an old horse till the spring thaw."

"Flag the train down," I suggested. "It got you here. It certainly knows the way back home."

"Can't."

"You don't like riding trains?"

"Can't afford the ticket," Charley Moseby replied.

I studied him for a moment, then asked, "What's it cost to get you back to Texas?"

"Five dollars will get me as far as Tellico. Then I can walk the rest of the way."

"In the snow?"

"I'd thought it'd still be warm there."

"We're talking about Texas," I said, "not hell."

"I didn't know there was a difference."

"How much does the ticket cost to Fort Griffin?"

"Five dollars and twenty-eight cents."

"How much you lack?"

"Four dollars and seventy-six cents."

"I thought you buried Sam Hastings last week."

"I did."

"You should have gotten something out of that."

Charley Moseby looked up with despondent eyes. "Sam was a well digger," he said. "All he had was a shovel. Trains won't give you no ticket for a shovel."

"Sell it," I offered.

"I'm the only man in town that's got use for a shovel," Charley Moseby replied, "an' I can't afford the damn thing."

I cut the cards, and the gravedigger and I involved ourselves in a game of stud poker. He played with pennies and only had sixty-seven of those. It took him twenty-four hands to win five dollars and twenty-eight cents, and, by three o'clock that afternoon, he was running madly down the track, slipping and sliding in the snow, waving a fistful of money in the air, trying to coax the conductor into slowing the train down long enough for him to jump aboard.

Charley Moseby had only been away from Dodge two hours before I wished I had gone with him.

The dead line was dead.

The saloons were as empty as the streets and just about as cold. The games with Charley Moseby offered the chance to play the first cards I had dealt all week.

Wyatt Earp could sleep on duty, and did. There was no law against shooting coyotes, provided nothing resembling a human being got in the way.

Maybe I should have gone back to Texas. Instead, I knocked on Becky Porter's door, woke her up, and, sometime long before daylight, my regrets had been absolved by the darkness, and I had misplaced everything I ever know about Fort Griffin, buffalo skinners, army deserters, card cheats, and a skinny little man who dug graves.

It was as good a way as any to wait for the thaw.

♠

♥ 22 ♦

♣

The cowboy had been riding hard for three days when he reined his big sorrel to a halt in front of the Long Branch Saloon. His shoulders were bent, weary from too many days in the saddle, and his unshaven face had been blistered by the sun. He was probably twenty years old but felt like forty, out of breath, with a dull ache throbbing in his back.

There was raw, unbridled excitement burning deep within the cowboy. He burst into the saloon, a serious thirst rattling around his dry throat, leaving the bright sunlight behind him and blinking until his eyesight became adjusted to the darkness.

"They're on their way," he said to no one in particular, although his words pricked the nerves of every human being in the place.

The men's cards grew warmer, almost as heated as the blush painted on the women's faces.

Luke Short walked out from behind the bar, rolling down the sleeves of his lace-collar shirt. "How far out are they?" he wanted to know.

"They was campin' on Margrove Creek the last time I

saw 'em," the cowboy answered, not yet able to catch his breath.

"How long ago was that?"

"Day before yesterday."

"How many of 'em was it?"

"Men or cattle?"

"Cattle."

"Close to a thousand, I guess," the cowboy said, stuttering. "I don't rightly know for sure. I can get to a hundred pretty good, but my countin' ain't too reliable after that."

Luke Short grinned the way he always grinned when the long winter and an empty spring was behind him. He had held on one more year. And God, or whoever was out there running the universe, had rewarded his patience one more time. He never knew when it would be the last time. He just kept betting on the next time.

Luke Short survived by sitting at the gaming tables for hours, maybe even days if that's what it took, breaking the cowboys and tin-horn gamblers who had come to break the saloon he ran. He and I had occupied the same room on a few occasions, but never the same table. A gentleman's agreement.

"I never try to take money off anybody who's capable of takin' mine," he said, which was about the highest compliment Luke Short had ever paid anyone.

I was welcome at the Long Branch, but Luke Short preferred that I ply my trade at another table in another saloon. "There's no use both of us fleecin' the same crowd," he had told me soon after my arrival in Dodge.

"I've never been known to fleece anyone," I replied.

Luke Short only smiled. "You do it your way," he said, "and I'll do it mine, just as long as we're takin' money out of different pockets."

I was suspicious of his methods, although no one had ever

called Luke Short a cheat, particularly if they were near enough for him to overhear them. He was quicker with the derringer he kept inside his vest than he was with the cards, and he could make a deck of cards dance, but only to the tune he himself played. Luke Short did not mind paying the fiddler as long as he owned the fiddle.

I could, however, not argue with his logic.

He poured the cowboy a drink of the cheap whiskey he kept in his most expensive bottle. "I figure your throat probably feels like a dust storm," he said.

"I ain't got no money," the cowboy told him.

"I'm not askin' for any." Luke Short handed him the glass, and the cowboy drank it greedily with one swallow. "When you think they'll be here?"

The cowboy licked the rim of the glass and studied the question a moment before asking, "What day is today?"

"It was Tuesday when I got up, and I haven't been to bed yet, so I guess it's still Tuesday."

The cowboy thought it over, then said, "Sunday. I imagine they'll be rollin' into town sometime Sunday."

Luke Short poured him a second glass of whiskey and turned toward the handful of grizzled men and painted women who had gathered around the bar. "They're on the way," he said in a loud voice, which made it official.

Come Sunday, the first Texas herd of the season would come thundering down the streets of Dodge, trailed by a dozen or more drovers who had not tasted nor touched any of the sinful refinements of civilization for almost three months.

Come Sunday, hell would be back in session in Dodge City.

If the calendar on the back wall of the Long Branch Saloon was not out of date, it was May third.

The year no longer made any difference.

Becky Porter and I stood on the balcony of the Alhambra and watched William MacArthur's JX longhorns make their way recklessly through the streets on an early Sunday morning, snorting like wild animals that would just as soon stampede through a building as walk around it. The herd was scrawny, all hide and horn, a lot of grit, a little gristle, hardly any meat at all. All early herds were.

The cattle were rocking gently as they walked, jammed together in a narrow street, tossing their broad horns into the air and nervously shaking their gaunt heads. Nostrils flared and their ears quivered. Before them clustered an unfamiliar sight and smell of human beings, animals, soured wood-and-mud buildings. They shuddered and shivered and marched on toward the railroad stockyards. The drovers were working hard to keep the herd together, yelling profanity, their ropes cracking like bullwhips. Only a few more yards, and it would be over. Only the drovers were aware of it.

But Mayor Dog Kelley had a five-hundred-dollar bonus waiting for the trail boss who pushed his cattle to Dodge first, and William MacArthur had been driving his rangy old longhorns across hardscrabble prairies where winter had stolen the grasses and not yet given them back, running without sleep for the last three days and nights to make sure he hit the saloons with an extra five hundred dollars that the back rooms of Dodge were quite willing to take off his hands.

This would be the year that William MacArthur broke the bank. This would be the year he rode home a rich man.

All cowboys lied to themselves, and some even believed it.

The JX trail hands were slumped dog tired in the saddle. One had taken a rope and tied himself to the saddle horn to keep from falling. The miles had threatened them, stomped them, tormented them, and stolen what was left of their youth. But it had not beaten them.

Their faces were sallow, their eyes sunken, their bodies shriveled. They were as scrawny as the herd, but, for the moment, not nearly as rambunctious. They all looked as though they were only a final breath or two away from the need of Charley Moseby's shovel, but Charley had taken it back to Texas. Beds were cheaper than coffins anyway, but not as permanent.

For the last few months, Dodge had faithfully observed the Sabbath. Saloons were closed and churches open. But not anymore. The Texas herd was in town. The preacher was gone.

Other herds would not be far behind. Luke Short swore he could already hear them coming, their hoofbeats pounding just beyond Margrove Creek like the rumble of distant thunder. It sounded a lot like spent money.

Becky Porter laid her head against my shoulder, closed her eyes, and sighed. Her hair brushed my face like a gentle wind in early spring. She smelled like summer roses still moistened by a morning dew.

"There's still time to take me away from here," Becky Porter said softly.

"Where would you like to go?"

"Someplace I've never been."

"Becky," I said.

"Yes?" She looked at me with upturned eyes, moist, not unlike the dew that could well have touched the roses.

"There is no place we haven't been."

She stared at me, a quizzical expression on her face. She started to argue, then thought better of it.

"The towns," I told her, "they're all alike. Some are a

little bigger than others. Some are a little tougher than others. But they're all just a collection of buildings trying to get by on a prairie that had just as soon they'd gone elsewhere. The faces, you've seen 'em all. The hopes, you've heard 'em all. The anger, you've felt it all. The saloons all serve the same whiskey, and whiskey all smells the same. The saloons have pianos out of tune. The churches have bells that ring only if there are any occasions to ring them. Jails have drunks, and worse. The stores have ladies' hats that don't fit and four with cockroaches in them. Gunshots sound the same. A grave is a grave."

"I guess that means we aren't leaving," she said.

I smiled and gently kissed her. "I guess not," I said.

She sighed deeper this time and glanced again at the JX cowboys climbing off their horses. "I guess it's time to go to work then."

Becky Porter turned sharply and departed the balcony before I could answer. I watched her go and wondered why I let her leave.

She was young and graceful, beautiful and gracious, a rose in the midst of thorns. All she wanted was a future, a man to call her own, a child in her lap, a cottage on the banks of an oak-shaded creek, a small garden on the sunny side of the cottage, food in her kitchen. All she wanted were the things that I was not willing to give her.

Once I could have. Once I might have.

It would have certainly been worth considering. But the years change a man, and I had already been a part of too many years, not many of them particularly good ones.

The south Texas herd of James Kenedy reached Dodge the final week in May. The cattle moved slowly northward after the snow had melted on the prairie. James Kenedy's daddy had money. He did not need that five hundred dollars

as badly as William MacArthur did. His herd spread
southward as far as the eye could see, three thousand of
them, probably more, virtually hidden in a veil of dust that
boiled and churned like a whirling dervish above the plains,
hanging low to the earth, too heavy to rise, too thick for the
hot, disinterested winds to shove aside.

Kenedy himself rode in front of the cattle, a sullen
portrait of money, prestige, and arrogance, none created by
his own hands, all of it handed down by a father who rode
into the Desert of the Dead in south Texas and refused to let
the parched brasada beat him or run him out.

He never tamed the land. But he learned to live on the
brush country's terms, and Mifflin Kenedy prospered beyond reason. He was as stubborn as the landscape that had
defied him to come and dared him to stay. Mifflin Kenedy
did not back down. It was not his nature.

The Kenedy name was power. Those who feared it
usually had every right to be afraid. They had crossed him,
or they had tried to take what belonged to him, or they had
stood against him, either right or wrong. It did not matter.
Occasionally a new mound of dirt mysteriously appeared in
the backwash of his vast ranchlands. No one mentioned it.
No one ever felt compelled to explain it. After the next
rainfall, the mound would flatten out and look no different
than the rest of the brasada, dry and dusty and the color of
spent gunpowder.

With an iron hand and an iron will, Mifflin Kenedy ruled
the mesquite and cacti kingdom that bred, then hid, the
longhorns of South Texas.

All James Kenedy had was his daddy's name. In most
places, that was enough. Mifflin Kenedy's cattle had helped
build the stockyards in Kansas. His name was as spendable
as a bank note. If Mifflin Kenedy sat down at a gaming table

and said he was good for a hundred dollars, no one questioned him. He was a gracious winner, a hard loser. But, before he left town, whether it was Abilene or Ellsworth or Dodge, and rode on back to Texas, he always looked up every man he owed money and paid his debts.

Mifflin Kenedy prided himself in his honesty. An honest man, he said, was generally only shot by mistake.

James Kenedy was a stranger in Dodge. Wyatt Earp had no interest in his name, only the revolvers he wore on both hips.

He was waiting for James Kenedy when the young trail boss swaggered down the mud-splattered plank sidewalk that led to the Dodge House. Kenedy's wide-brimmed sombrero was pulled low over his eyes, and a pencil-thin mustache the color of a sorrel horse occupied his upper lip. A bandana hung loosely around his neck, and a fringed leather jacket fit tightly around his broad shoulders. His boots were worn, but they had not lost their rich black luster. And his Spanish rowels had cruel razor points. Vaqueros had been known to cripple horses with the spurs. Losing a good horse had never bothered James Kenedy. There were always more in his daddy's corral.

Wyatt Earp stepped in front of James Kenedy, his face streaked by the shadows of sundown. His arms hung loosely at his side. There was a flicker of resentment in his eyes, confronting the man who had sent him out to die.

"Your guns," he said softly, his voice cold and dispassionate.

"What about them?" Kenedy snapped, trying hard to remember the face that looked so familiar.

"I'll take them now."

"Like hell you will."

James Kenedy stumbled backward defensively, both

hands resting on the handles of a matched pair of nickel-plated Colt revolvers. They had been specially made. His initials were carved just below the hammer.

Wyatt Earp emerged from the shadows, and James Kenedy recognized the tall, lanky drifter standing before him. He had not forgotten the face. Kenedy had merely been confused and confounded by the silver star on his shirt.

He was not prepared to see the man who had murdered Sergeant Frank Rigby wearing a badge.

"Your guns," Wyatt Earp repeated casually. "There's a law against carrying them in Dodge. It's posted. It's legal."

"You're crazy as hell."

"I'm afraid you're not alone in that opinion."

"There's not a law on God's green earth strong enough to take my guns away from me," Kenedy said, a growl crawling angrily out of his throat.

Wyatt Earp's shrug was one of disdain. "You can give them to me," he said, "or I can take them off your cold, lifeless body. It doesn't particularly matter to me."

"You're good at shooting men down in cold blood."

"It's not my choice."

"You never gave Frank Rigby a chance."

"That was Frank Rigby's choice. He could have stayed at the fort that morning and maybe still be around for full retirement." Wyatt Earp's voice was tired. "He didn't. He retired early."

James Kenedy glanced from Wyatt Earp's holstered Smith & Wesson to the lawman's empty hand. The ivory handles of his own matched .45s felt so tempting, so alive. The law could not prosecute him for killing a man with a badge. The silver star did not make Wyatt Earp either special or untouchable. Anybody could wear a badge, cowards, thieves, murderers, anybody. James Kenedy, the courts would say, was only defending himself, that's all, defending himself and his God-given, inalienable right to carry firearms in the streets of Dodge.

All he had to do was aim and squeeze the trigger. Wyatt Earp would be as dead as Frank Rigby and neither missed nor mourned by nearly as many people.

To hell with Wyatt Earp and the laws of Dodge.

They were meant for others, perhaps, but not for the son of Mifflin Kenedy.

James Kenedy's insolent smile gave him away.

The young trail boss had cleared leather with only one revolver when the long, heavy barrel of Wyatt Earp's Smith & Wesson struck his forehead. The sharp crack buckled his knees, and the lawman hit him again, harder this time. James Kenedy's head twisted around, and his eyes fluttered. Dodge began to grow black, and the sun was not even down. The third blow was the plank sidewalk slamming into his face when he fell.

James Kenedy waited for the pain. He could taste the salt of his own blood spilling from the gash in his head and into his mouth. It reminded him of sweat, only thicker.

Why didn't the pain come? Pain was the only sure way he could tell if he was still alive. James Kenedy did not feel a thing.

When he at last opened his eyes, the lawman was kneeling beside him. Kenedy blinked, but the cobwebs had gotten lost in his head. He tried to speak, but his tongue had been laid to rest. His mouth was the texture of aged cotton before the seeds had been removed. His throat had begun to wither away. He swallowed and choked on his own saliva, and his lungs had given up. They weren't sucking air at all.

"I've got the right to arrest you," Wyatt Earp said, "but I'm not gonna do that. You are an honored guest of Dodge, and we'll treat you like an honored guest as long as your weapons of any kind are locked away in my office. Do you find that hard to understand, Mr. Kenedy?"

James Kenedy nodded. Since he could not speak, it was the best he could do.

"Unless I'm mistaken, you're stayin' at the Dodge House?"

Again James Kenedy nodded. He blotted the blood on his forehead with the palm of his hand.

"You round up your men then," the lawman told him, "and have 'em in the lobby at eight o'clock. I'll drop by and pick up their weapons as well. When you depart Dodge, every revolver, rifle, shotgun, or knife I collect will be waiting on you. The mayor would rather see every man who rode in ride out than watch Boot Hill keep growing. We lose a little grazing land for every grave that's dug."

James Kenedy grimaced. The pain he had been waiting on finally struck him between the eyes with the force of a blacksmith's hammer. He had no response.

Wyatt Earp had not expected one. Holding a matched Colt .45 in each hand, he walked slowly back toward the dead line, leaving James Kenedy on the mud-splattered planks where he lay. The sun dropped behind the balcony of the Alhambra, and the gray shadows of an early darkness came again to slip like a waif down the street behind him.

Little Dave Little found an empty chair in the saloon, holding a hat that had been rained on, spit on, wind broke, and stomped on by a runaway horse. He was not quite sure where he was and wondering if he should stay any longer. Little Dave Little was barely sixteen years old, and the stubble on his face had never felt the prick of a razor.

He would have not weighed a hundred and ten pounds with his boots on, but he had made the thousand-mile trek to Kansas with Kenedy cattle, saving every nickel of the

wages he earned to carry home to Mama. He had lost his
father to consumption and an older brother to the war. The
garden out back had been a lot leaner than in the years past,
and she was depending on Little Dave Little to come home
with enough Kenedy money to feed her and the kids. He
was still a child, dressed in men's clothing much too large
for him, and trying his best to become a man.

Little Dave Little had just tasted his first sip of hard
whiskey. It burned his lips and seared his throat, and he
turned down the second glass placed on the table before
him, working with some difficulty to simply catch his
breath. A swallow of kerosene would have done him as
much good. Little David Little had just seen his first naked
woman lying on a bearskin rug in the picture behind the bar.
He was mesmerized, and his mouth was dry. There she was,
on the wall, not a shred of clothes to hide her breasts and
buttocks, and Calico Kate was sitting on his lap. Little Dave
Little suspected she looked much the same way beneath all
the ruffles that had been held together by yellow lace. She
brushed her face against his, and a wisp of auburn hair
touched his lips.

Little Dave Little would have told her his name. But at
the moment he could not remember what it was. He tried to
smile. But he could not get his lips to move. He wished to
God his mother was there to help him and damn glad she
wasn't.

Brush Face Summers emptied his glass and picked up the
one that Little Dave Little had barely touched. "You ain't
gonna need this," he said loudly. "It takes a real man to
drink a man's whiskey."

The boy wilted beneath the harsh laughter of the old drag
rider who was wanted in two states for robbery. Fortunately
for him, Kansas was not one of them. Brush Face Summers

had a black beard that touched the top button of his shirt. His hair was long and unkempt. The wind had tied it in knots. It looked as though he had ridden the trail from Texas in the same clothes, not bothering to change or wash them. If he had not ridden across a river or two, water would have never touched them. He packed almost three hundred pounds on a six-foot frame. A sawed-off shotgun dangled from a rope around his waist. Brush Face Summers was always grinning a sardonic grin, as devoid of humor as his eyes.

"You ain't got no use for that woman either," the drag rider bellowed. "She sure as hell ain't got no use for you."

Little Dave Little's face reddened. He clenched his fist.

Brush Face Summers only laughed louder. "What's the matter young'un," he said, "you gonna get up out of that chair and fight me?" He rolled up his sleeves and raised his fist, throwing a couple of short jabs to mock the boy. "Hell," he continued, "I've seen a three-legged jackass run faster an' a one-legged chicken kick harder 'n you." He threw another mock jab, stopping it only inches from Little Dave Little's nose.

"Leave him alone," Calico Kate said, her voice tainted with disgust.

"You gonna let a woman do your fightin' for you?" The drag rider's tone was one of humiliation. "Hell, boy, that whore's old enough to be your mother. She just don't lay herself down with as many women as your mama did." He drank straight from the bottle, spilling as much as he swallowed, ripping the bandana from the boy's neck and using it to wipe his mouth.

Little Dave Little struggled to get out of the chair. Calico Kate put her arm around him and refused to let the boy out of her grasp. She had gained a pound or two over the long winter and had him pretty well pinned to where he was sitting.

Brush Face Summers turned his attention to Calico Kate. "That's quite a cowboy you got under there," he said. "But I wouldn't let him touch me if I was you. He didn't do nothin' from here to Texas 'cept pick up cow chips. He cleaned out the rear end of every steer for the last fifteen hundred miles. Smells like it, too."

The drag rider laughed again, more vicious this time.

I looked over at a solemn-faced trail hand who was content to drink his whiskey alone. "What's the big fellow got against the kid?" I asked.

"Money," he answered. "Old Mifflin Kenedy splits the wages evenly among his drovers. Brush Face don't think the kid's worth that much, and he probably ain't. Brush Face thinks he'd a' made more money if Kenedy had left the kid home. We'd a' all made more money if Kenedy hadn't dragged the kid to Kansas. James sure as hell didn't want him. Mifflin's a hard man, but he's got a soft heart. The kid's mother needed the money, so Mifflin stuck the kid at the rear of the herd. Brush Face has been ridin' him pretty hard ever since we left Pleasanton."

"Are you bitter?" I asked.

"About what?"

"About the kid takin' part of your money."

"Shoot, mister," the drover said. "I'm just glad to have the job."

Calico Kate's face was drawn tight with scorn and rage. She had suffered just about all the insults she was prepared to take, and a painted woman in an upstairs room at the Alhambra seldom heard anything else. She stood and slapped Brush Face Summers hard across the face.

He did not blink. But the laughter stopped. His mouth

was twisted into an angry scar. "If you was a man, I'd kill you," he said.

"If I was a man," she shot back, "there would already be undertakers comin' to haul your body out of here. If you was a man, I wouldn't have to slap you."

"It might do me good to get rid of you anyway." Brush Face Summers glared at the upstairs matron of the Alhambra with eyes of molten metal.

"There might be a better way," I said, stepping between them, breaking open a new deck of cards.

Brush Face Summers eyed me suspiciously. His right hand dropped instinctively to the stock of the sawed-off shotgun at his side. "This ain't no business of yours," he said. "You know what I do with cockroaches that get in my way?"

"I have no idea."

"I step on 'em."

I ignored his comment and asked, "You play cards, Mr. Summers?"

"I've sat at a table or two."

"You good at it?"

"I've won enough to keep my belly full and shells in my shotgun."

I turned to Little Dave Little. "You play poker, boy?" I asked.

"No, sir."

"This is Dodge," I said.

"Yes, sir."

"There are only three reasons a cowboy comes to Dodge. And playing poker's one of them."

Little Dave Little glanced briefly at Brush Face, then back at me. "What are the other two?" he asked.

"One of 'em's whiskey, which you've had." I grinned.

"And the other one's a woman, which, I presume, you haven't had."

"No, sir."

I sat down at the table beside him. "It appears to me," I said, "that you and Mr. Summers have some kind of a conflict, and at least one of you, maybe both of you, want to settle it with a fight. Frankly, son, he'll kill you, and we'll have to ship you back to Mama in a box, which is a lot of trouble and expense to Dodge. And the city marshal will have to put Mr. Summers in jail and possibly even hang him, which is also a lot of trouble and expense. It seems to me that a good hand of poker would be a more civilized way to settle your disagreement."

"I'd rather kill the little bastard," Brush Face Summers growled.

"No," I told him, "you'd rather take the little bastard's money, some of which, you believe, belongs to you anyway."

The drag raider stroked his black beard and shrugged in agreement.

I turned again to Little Dave Little. "It's quite simple," I said, doing what I could to keep him alive. "Mr. Summers wants part of your money, probably all of it. And, unless my eyes deceive me and they haven't for a long time, you want Miss Calico Kate, who possesses the kind of mysteries you've dreamed about but never been able to solve before. My suggestion is this. Mr. Summers and you will play one hand of stud poker. If you win, Mr. Summers will pay for you to participate in a night's worth of pleasure with Miss Kate. If Mr. Summers wins, you will pay him a sum equal to one night's pleasure with Miss Kate. One hand, then it's over. Agreed?"

Silence.

I waited.

More silence.

Finally Brush Face Summers said, "I'd rather have Calico Kate for the night than the money."

"That, sir, is between you and Miss Kate."

I looked at Kate. She smiled. For once in her life, she was a winner either way, provided, of course, Brush Face Summers did not carry out his threat to get rid of her. Probably not. She was a master at soothing the wild, angry beast inside a man. Besides, Calico Kate kept a small, but potent, derringer under her pillow for those rare moments when a man went crazy and tried to mistreat her. The jury had never convicted her yet.

Little Dave Little muttered something I did not understand.

"Speak up, son," I said.

His jaw quivered. "I can't do it," he said.

"Why not?"

"He's yellow," Brush Face Summers blustered.

"I can't gamble none of Mama's money away. I ain't got much as it is."

"It's really not your decision," I told him. "It's your mama's. She can have the money, along with you in a box. Or she can see you come riding home again."

He thought it over for a minute, then said, "I don't know how to play stud poker."

"Don't worry," I said. "Mr. Summers will let you know if you've won or lost." I motioned for them both to take a seat at opposite ends of the table. Calico Kate leaned over my shoulder.

"It's been a while," she whispered.

"Since you've educated a boy?"

"Since I've shot a grown man."

I did not know whether she was referring to me or to Brush Face Summers.

Brush Face received a couple of aces quickly, which made him feel like a stud bull at breeding time. I gave him a four of hearts, a six of diamonds, then another ace just to tease him. The big man was grinning like a coon up a mulberry tree.

I could have dealt the boy four kinds. But I did not want Brush Face Summers to realize he was losing until he had lost.

Little Dave Little got a diamond flush instead. It was a harmless scattering of cards, nothing impressive, easy to overlook, but deadly enough to beat three aces any night of the week at any table in Dodge, especially this one.

The big man did not know he was a loser, and the boy certainly had no idea he had won until I told them.

Little Dave Little was shaking so badly he dropped his cards.

Brush Face Summers ripped his cards in two and tossed them over his shoulder. He sat for a moment like a keg of dynamite waiting for the short-burning fuse to touch the powder. His face darkened, his knuckles were white. He leapt to his feet, leveling the sawed-off shotgun somewhere between my eyes and throat. "This game's crooked," he yelled.

"It's the only game in town," I answered.

Calico Kate held out one hand and said softly, "Mr. Summers, I do believe you owe me two dollars."

Her other hand had jammed the derringer in his ear. Brush Face Summers could not see it. But he knew what it was.

Cold steel with a round hole at the end of the barrel all felt the same, regardless of the size. Derringers were useless from ten feet. They were deadly three inches away from a man's brain.

The drag rider, cursing under his breath, his eyes as red as those of a bull who had just found out he had been castrated, pulled a pair of silver dollars from his pocket and dropped them in Calico Kate's outstretched hand.

He started to threaten her again, but Wyatt Earp, who had been leaning against the bar, wearing a wry grin, watching me deal crooked cards, interrupted him. "I'll take the shotgun," the lawman said.

The solemn-faced trail hand glanced up from his whiskey and said, "Now that you've got him, marshal, Summers is wanted in Arkansas and Louisiana both."

"Then Arkansas and Louisiana can come and get him. I don't want him clutterin' up my jail and eatin' my food. I'd just as soon he ride out of town tonight as tomorrow."

As Wyatt Earp began walking away, Brush Face Summers stopped him in his tracks. "Hey, marshal," he said, feeling somewhat naked without the shotgun hanging on his hip, "if you got a law in town about carrying guns, how come you ain't took that whore's derringer away from her."

The lawman looked around, his eyebrows arched in mock surprise. "Why, Mr. Summers," he said, "I have no idea what you're talkin' about."

Brush Face Summers was gesturing wildly. "The whore," he said, "she stuck a little gun in my ear and would have blowed my head off, too, if I hadn't given her the two dollars. That's robbery, the way I look at it."

"That's business," I said.

"Mr. Summers," Wyatt Earp, "I'm afraid I didn't see a damn thing."

"Then go ahead and look for it now," he bellowed. "She's still got it on her."

"Mr. Summers," I told him, "a gentleman in Dodge does not frisk a lady unless she asks him to."

Calico Kate took Little Dave Little gently by the hand

and led him toward the stairs. "You never did tell me your name," she said.

He grinned a bashful grin.

"I will," he said, "as soon as I can remember it."

By the time the first rays of sunlight shyly slipped into Calico Kate's bedroom, Little Dave Little no longer cared if he had a name.

♠

♥ 23 ♦

♣

Wyatt Earp was prompt, if nothing else.

He walked alone into the lobby of the Dodge House as the grandfather clock in the foyer was striking eight o'clock. The great room was illuminated by a pair of tall candles, their flames dancing in a hot summer wind that slipped through the open window and painted an assortment of strange, crooked shadows on the wall.

The figures veiled by the darkness had no faces. They were shadows themselves, motionless and deadly, an army that had been assembled to fight for a cause no greater than the arrogance of their leader.

James Kenedy could not be seen, but his voice boomed out of the black hole in the lobby. "You're right on time, marshal."

"I came to do what I promised to do, Kenedy." The lawman's voice was calm and unhurried. "We don't have a lot of laws in Dodge," he said, "but we do our damnedest to keep the ones we do have, no exceptions, not even you, sir."

James Kenedy stepped out of the darkness, his arms folded with contempt. His matched Colt .45s, now hanging inside the back cell of the Dodge City jail, had been replaced by a bone-handled Smith & Wesson, not unlike the one Wyatt Earp wore.

"You came alone, I see," James Kenedy said.

"Collecting guns is not that great a task," the lawman answered.

"You may be able to outtalk or outshoot other cowboys who come to your town," James Kenedy told him, a smirk on his face, "but the Kenedy clan makes its own laws. Always has. Always will. And the first law is, nobody takes our guns. Nobody, marshal, especially not anybody in Dodge."

The trail boss removed the Smith & Wesson from its holster, polished the barrel for a moment on his shirt, spun the chamber once, then placed it gently atop the English cherrywood table that separated him and Wyatt Earp.

"That's my daddy's gun," James Kenedy said, his voice tinged with belligerence. "He's right particular about his gun. He wouldn't want anybody outside the family to touch it. If you do so, I'm afraid my men will be forced to stop you, and they outnumber you ten to one. I suggest, then, that you quietly turn around, walk out that door and leave the Mifflin Kenedy cowboys alone."

Wyatt Earp weighed the odds. Ten to one. They had been worse.

The lawman walked slowly, defiantly, toward the table, his eyes daring James Kenedy to breathe, much less move. He had less than five seconds to decide if the civilized law of Mayor Dog Kelley was worth his life. There were many who had said Kansas would be just as well off without him. Probably so. But, somehow, he had not quite been able to bring himself to agree with them.

Wyatt Earp lifted the Smith & Wesson off the cherrywood table and examined it as though he had all night, which he did. "Your daddy's got himself a nice revolver," he said.

"When you ride out of town, you can carry it back to him," He paused a moment, studying James Kenedy, trying to figure out what the young trail boss would do next, if anything. "I'll take the rest of the weapons now," he said at last. "Your men can pile 'em here on the table, one at a time. I'll treat them like they were my own."

Silence again.

A rifle cocked in the darkness. Wyatt Earp could not determine its location. He only knew that it sounded like the sharp crack of a gunshot echoing across the room. The noise was metallic and ominous.

"Kenedy," he said, his voice barely audible. "I've got all night. You don't. Tell your men to do what I've asked them to do. The night's young. There's no reason for them to waste it in here."

"If you don't put the pistol down," came the answer, "somebody in here's gonna shoot you. Is it worth dyin'?"

"That's a decision you and I both are gonna have to make."

"Mine's already been made."

"Then we're gonna leave the Dodge House in a helluva mess."

"You can't fight all of us," James Kennedy declared boldly.

"I don't have to."

"What do you mean?" There was a nervous twitch in James Kenedy's face. His eyes began to cloud over.

"When the shootin' starts," Wyatt Earp said calmly, "your daddy's gun's gonna make an awful big hole in your gut. I may not be so good from one side of the street to the other, but I assure you I never miss at this distance. And when the shootin' stops, they're gonna bury me and you in the same cemetery, and I'll be kicking your ass all the way to hell."

"Jesus, Earp!" Deacon Cox blustered his way into the

lobby. He was sweating profusely, not necessarily from the sultry summer heat that had squatted down around Dodge. "Leave 'em be. They're Kenedys."

"Who they are is not my concern."

"Kenedy's not causin' you any harm."

"He's breakin' the law, Deacon."

"It's only a minor law."

"It is until one of his cowboys shoots somebody."

Deacon Cox was rubbing the palms of his hands together, nervously glancing from side to side. "This is crazy, Earp," he said. "You're gonna kill everybody in this damn room if you have to just to keep somebody from gettin' killed."

"That's the way it's done sometimes."

"And in the process you're gonna wreck the Dodge House."

"It appears that way."

Deacon Cox mopped his forehead with a lace handkerchief. He looked around at his ornate handiwork. Even in the dark, it was impressive. By morning, there was a very good chance that it would be ripped up, torn out, cut down by a hail of gunfire. The finest hotel in Dodge would lie in ruins because of two stubborn and foolish men. He was not at all concerned with the fates of Wyatt Earp and James Kenedy at the moment. They could go ahead and kill themselves, which was fine with Deacon Cox, as long as they had the decency to march out into the street and leave his hostelry alone.

"There won't anybody ever stay here again when you get through with it," Deacon Cox said. "It'll take a year just to sand the blood out of the wood. I'll lose thousands of dollars. I'll be in financial ruin, Earp."

"Deacon," the lawman answered, "that's the chance you take when you rent your hotel to men who don't care about the law."

"But the Kenedy's are God-fearin' men."

"That's between them and God."

"Mifflin Kenedy's the richest, the most powerful man in south Texas, maybe all of Texas."

"He's gonna lose a son tonight."

"The Kenedys bring more cattle to Dodge than any other rancher in Texas." Deacon Cox was begging now, trying desperately to bring a sense of law and order to a man who had sworn to uphold law and order in Dodge. "The Kenedys aren't like everybody else. They deserve special treatment."

"If you insist then, we'll give James Kenedy special treatment."

Deacon Cox relaxed for a moment and forced a smile. Maybe he should have been an attorney, he thought. He certainly put up a damn good argument.

"We'll put him in a box that's a little more substantial than pine."

The smile dropped off Deacon Cox's face. "Jesus, Earp," he said again, "you don't give a damn about any of us."

Even though Dodge City lay in the grip of a sweltering heat wave, the fire in the Dodge House library fireplace was roaring like a furnace, and the blaze was getting hotter by the minute. I knew. For the past half hour I had been dragging rotten logs through the window and into the room, stuffing them into the hearth.

Earlier I had climbed out onto the balcony and pulled myself up onto the roof of Dodge's finest sleeping establishment, covering the chimney with the lid of a barrel I had picked up down at the livery stable. The smoke was inching its way skyward, then falling back down the bricks and spilling out into the library. It had no place else to go. In another minute or two, the smoke would be making its way across the hallway and into the lobby, thick and black and suffocating.

Deacon Cox was in midsentence when he first smelled the fumes. He whirled around as a pillar of smoke poured through the archway and engulfed the lobby. "My gawd," the emperor of the Dodge House screamed, "you're burning the place down on top of us."

He coughed. The smoke was thicker now. And smothering.

James Kennedy wrapped his shirt around his head to shield his face. His men came out of the darkness and crowded together around him. They had been prepared to fight a man. Fire was altogether different.

Wyatt Earp had not flinched.

From atop the second-floor balcony, I soaked a couple of rags in kerosene and tied them to the feet of an uneasy pair of Barred Plymouth Rock chickens that had been scratching in the yard of the hotel. I set the rags afire and dropped one old rooster and a half-starved hen over the railing, watching them descend in a haphazard spiral toward the lobby of the Dodge House.

They hit the floor, squawking and cackling, on a dead run, scattering in different directions, the burning strips of an old bed sheet fluttering and flapping and slapping the floor behind them. The Plymouth Rocks were scrambling around the room in drunken circles, tiny ribbons of fire slashing through the darkness.

The rags might scorch a few assorted furnishings, probably even blacken strips of the Persian rug beneath the cherrywood table, but I seriously doubted would set anything of importance on fire. A little scrubbing, and the Dodge House would be as good as new.

The smoke had been stifling. The blaze was disconcerting.

For good measure, I held my belly blaster toward the crystal chandelier above James Kenedy and pulled the trigger. The chandelier shattered, and rained tiny, fragmented shards across the lobby.

Kenedy's cowboys wilted in the faces of an unknown and unseen enemy.

They were trail hands, not fighters, anyway. They had only backed James Kenedy because they were on his payroll. Four quit on the spot. Three of them had no intention of heading back to Texas anyway. Two were in love with the same painted woman. And one had already sold his saddle.

They broke and ran as confused and troubled as a gaggle of rabbits in a coyote's back pocket, chewing at the fumes burning their eyes, coughing out the smoke that had gathered in their lungs, going through doors and windows without bothering to open them first, tumbling headfirst into the street, fighting each other for the next breath of fresh air as though it was the only air left. The Kenedy cowboys were on their hands and knees in the dirt, as repentant as any herd of trail hands I had ever seen. They had seen and tasted the fragments of hell, and, if a preacher had been around, he could have started a church on the spot.

Deacon Cox sat down in the middle of the lobby floor, his oversized head in his oversized hands. Everything he owned had been stuffed inside the Dodge House, the new, the old, the borrowed, and the stolen. If the hotel went up in flames, he might as well go up with it.

James Kenedy had not fled with his cowboys. He might have. The thought probably crossed his mind. But Wyatt Earp had jammed Mifflin Kenedy's Smith & Wesson into his throat.

"It's gonna cost you," James Kenedy said with a raspy voice.

"Everything I do costs me," the lawman answered.

"I should have had you shot." Kenedy broke out into a severe coughing spell.

"Your men didn't have a reason," Wyatt Earp replied, his eyes blinded by the smoke. "And you didn't have the nerve."

The lawman shoved the young trail boss through the doorway, and both of them stumbled into fresh air. The whole town had caught wind of the smoke. A few had seen glimpses of the flames galloping in circles through the downstairs of the Dodge House.

They came running with buckets. A fire, if it spread, could be the ruination of them all.

They were too late. The flaming rags had burned themselves out by the time the chickens came to roost atop the piano.

I had managed to take eight revolvers, two rifles, a shotgun, and three knives from the Kenedy cowboys when they came staggering and floundering out of the hotel and down the steps in a mild stupor. No one argued nor complained. As soon as they lost their will to fight, they lost interest in their weapons. I stacked them neatly in the wagon beside the stone steps and turned them over to Wyatt Earp after he tied James Kenedy rather rudely to the back axle.

"I want all the guns," he said.

"They're all there."

"I can't allow you to tote the belly blaster either."

"You sure as hell didn't mind me having the shotgun when you were in there doing your damnedest to get your fool head shot off."

He shrugged as though it were merely a night's work. "There's no law against buildin' a fire, startin' one, or frying chickens in Dodge," he said. "But I feel a lot safer when I'm the only man in town with a gun, any size, any shape, any caliber."

"I've had a couple of chances to shoot you," I replied, "and a couple of reasons to do it. But up till now I never thought you were worth the trouble."

"I'm not worried about you, Hawkes," he said. "But it would concern me if you lost the shotgun, and I didn't know who had it."

I studied his gaunt face for a minute. He looked tired. Wyatt Earp did not sleep much anymore. He said there was no reason to.

"I certainly don't recall you taking the derringer away from Calico Kate," I said. "If she can keep her gun, then it looks to me like I should be able to keep mine."

A faint grin stretched across the lawman's face. "I'm kind of partial to the place where she keeps hers," he said. "There may be a time when I want to look for it again."

I could not argue with that.

I walked back down the street and climbed the backstairs of the Alhambra Saloon. I ambled down the hallway and knocked on the third door from the back window. The piano down below was louder than I remembered. So was the laughter.

Becky Porter was awake. And alone. She cracked the door open and frowned when she saw me. My face was streaked with ash and sweat. My clothes were wrinkled, and I smelled somewhat like smoke and burnt feathers. I gave her the best smile I had left that night.

"What happened to you?" she wanted to know.

"Wyatt and I had a little business to take care of over at the Dodge House," I answered, figuring that was all the explanation she needed.

"I heard the commotion over there."

"There was more smoke than fire."

She looked at me curiously but did not speak for a moment. Finally Becky Porter said, "Brady . . ."

"Yes, ma'am."

"Come back when you want to take me away from here."

"Not till then?"

I thought she was teasing.

"No."

She wasn't.

"I was under the impression that entertaining men was your business."

Her smile was a sad and forlorn one, and I immediately wished I had not said it. "It is," she answered softly. "But I'm not in love with them."

I only caught the glimpse of a single tear on her cheek before she gently closed the door, and I heard the lock snap shut on the inside.

The night was blacker than it had been before. Even the moon had departed the sky. But that did not keep the coyotes from howling. Maybe they had invented lonesome. They sure seemed to know a lot about it.

When I walked into his office, Wyatt Earp was seated behind a desk piled high with a curious collection of pistols and rifles of assorted shapes and sizes and calibers, and some looked as though they had not been fired in years. Packing a gun gave men a certain sense of confidence whether they were tempted to use it or not. It was simply a part of their dress. Those who never had a reason to use a gun were usually those who never had the occasion to be shot by one.

"I need a place to stay tonight," I said. "Can you put me up in one of the cells, or do I need to go out and do some dastardly deed?"

"I thought you had a room at the Dodge House."

"I don't think I'm welcome there anymore."

"You'd probably complain about the smoke anyway," the lawman said.

"Deacons says I owe him for damages."

"Deacon better be careful." Wyatt Earp grinned. "I could arrest him for aiding and abetting a lawless element."

"Could you make it stick?"

The lawman shrugged as though it did not matter to him. "He'd be in jail a week before either of us knew for sure," he said.

I walked to the open window and stared out on the streets of Dodge. For some reason, they seemed less raucous than usual. Maybe it was because I felt less raucous than usual.

"What about Becky?" Wyatt Earp asked.

"What about her?"

"Her bed's a lot more comfortable than a cell."

"I think I'd have better luck at the Dodge House."

Wyatt Earp shook his head in an understanding manner. "She's lookin' for permanence, isn't she?"

I nodded.

"Sometimes that's not so bad," he said.

"For a gambling man it is."

"There's no reason why you can't settle down."

"There is when the money keeps moving west." I glanced back toward the gaslights of the saloons flaring on both sides of the street. "Right now Dodge is wild and wide open," I told him. "As long as the cowboy keeps coming, the tables will be piled high with chips, coins, bills, rings, watches, anything a man's got of value. I can find a chair at the Alhambra and won't have to leave till the cattle are gone. But times aren't what they used to be. The mayor's dead set on taming Dodge, and when he does the cattle will go elsewhere, or the cattle will go the same way as the buffalo. The saloons will dry up, and the whiskey bottles will be empty, and so will the tables. By the time I settle down, it'll be time to move on again."

Wyatt Earp closed his eyes and took a deep breath, a

pained expression masking his face. "I would have settled down with Dora," he said.

"Every man's different."

"That's the way it is with women and horses, too," he replied. "If you find a good one, keep it."

"You didn't," I said.

"If I had another chance, I would."

"You can go back."

"Life's not like that." His sigh was one of loneliness that only the coyotes could fathom. "You live one day, then another. And no matter how much you want it to, the trail you follow never goes back."

"The train does."

"The train never goes anywhere. It just keeps looking for a place to stop."

"And there is none."

Wyatt Earp stood, took a ring of keys off the wall beside his desk and unlocked the cell nearest the window. "Maybe you're right after all," he said. "Maybe none of us ever settle down no matter how hard we try."

By morning, I realized why some men would rather die than go to jail. The bunk was too narrow, too short, and too hard. The mattress was soiled with sweat and sour whiskey and an assortment of stains that I had no desire to decipher. I should have slept in the livery stable with the horses. It would have been more comfortable and not smelled nearly so bad.

My back felt as though somebody had slammed a nine-pound hammer between my shoulder blades when I walked out of the cell just as the summer sun was beginning to lift itself off a windswept prairie.

Normally I would not have been up so early.

Normally beds don't try to cripple me.

At the door, I looked back again at the stack of weapons

on the city marshal's desk. Only one intrigued me. I was tempted to take the belly blaster, stick it under my coat, and dare Wyatt Earp to take it away from me.

But he was apparently real serious about collecting the guns in Dodge City, just as the mayor had ordered, and he had no conscience about dealing with those who defied him. Wyatt Earp, as he said, made no exception. Spending another night in jail did not interest me, so I left the belly blaster where it lay.

Dodge was already awake. Maybe Dodge was always awake at that hour, and I had just never felt the need nor the inclination to verify it before.

The girls of the Alhambra were bent over their washtubs on the back porch of the saloon, heavily soaping their lace and linens. Their faces were plain and weary and already bored with the day. It would be another eight hours before they had to bubble again like expensive champagne. Paying customers were hardly ever around at this hour, and, if they were, they were simply crawling out of bed and going home, provided they had one.

Becky Porter ran her long, slender fingers through the blonde hair piled on top of her head and stared at me with those contemptuous blue eyes of hers. I smiled as warmly as I could, considering the hammer was still pounding my back. Her frown was one of disgust, or maybe it was disappointment, and she turned away. The door was apparently still closed.

Little Dave Little was sleeping on a bench outside the Alhambra. The bench was as hard as the cot in cell number one and not nearly as soiled. I envied him. He hardly ever left there anymore, not since he discovered what went on in those upstairs rooms with Calico Kate. Mama would still be broke when Little Dave Little found his way back home, provided he ever got that far. He swore he was going to remain in Dodge and be the love of Kate's life until his wages were gone, and they were going fast. He had taken a job at the livery stable, shoveling horse manure, which was about all he knew how to do, not counting what he had learned from Kate. The money he earned was slim, but it would keep him in Dodge a few more days, which, he decided, was better than being anyplace else.

Above the doorway of the Comique Theater, a pair of stagehands were nailing a large wooden sign announcing the pending arrival of the illustrious impresario Eddie Foy and his traveling troop of world-renowned singers, actors and dancing girls, featuring the New Texas Songbird, appearing in their first performance since returning from the great halls of Europe, hailed by critics as the greatest show to ever grace the stage of Dodge City. Both the words *impresario* and *troupe* were misspelled, which had probably never happened in Europe.

Most of the wagons crowding the streets were headed past the dead line and down to the track. They were driven by old men too weary and broken-down to do anything else. They were owned by the wealthy, sporting gentlemen from all over the country who had brought satchels full of money to wager on greyhounds running against Irish Count, the pride of Mayor Dog Kelley's stable.

The track itself, freshly painted, a carnival of blues and yellows, sprawled in a fertile river bottom that lay between the Santa Fe tracks and a pasture of Turkey red wheat, planted by a family of German Mennonite immigrants who had journeyed to Kansas from Russia the winter before, although no one had been able to figure out why.

By noon, more than two thousand had trekked down to the river bottom for a glimpse of the fastest dog flesh in ten counties, or maybe the world, if you listened to Dog Kelley, and everybody within spitting distance of the blue-and-yellow carnival tent was listening to the wit, wisdom, and diatribes of His Honor, the mayor.

It was the day Dog Kelley had been waiting for since early June when Judge Nathaniel Burgendorf from over in Haskell County casually mentioned that his prized greyhound, imported directly from the championship kennels of Germany, had never been beaten and would certainly never be beaten by any of the two-bit curs that ran in the river bottom of Dodge.

Dog Kelley had no problem suffering the slings and arrows of personal insult. He not even minded when pious politicians looked down their crooked noses at Dodge and referred to it, with disdain and contempt, as a cesspool of sin and den of iniquity. That was all right. He had even thought about nailing a hand-painted sign to the edge of his city saying, "If you want a dose of culture, keep on moving. It ain't here. But if you want entertainment, come to Dodge."

They could criticize him, his town, his taste in women. But no man alive would be allowed to call Irish Count a two-bit cur. Wars had been started for less than that.

"I've seen the dogs run at Dodge," Judge Burgendorf had said. "If they departed on catching a rabbit for supper, they'd all starve to death."

"Not Irish Count."

"Is he full-blood?"

"I've got the papers on him."

"Looks to me like he's got a little tortoise in him."

Was it worth five thousand dollars to find out? Dog Kelley inquired.

No, the judge told him, but it was certainly worth ten thousand dollars.

Dog Kelley knelt beside the kennel and admired Irish Count, as he had done every day that week. The big greyhound had never looked bigger, nor fitter, nor faster.

In ten minutes, he would have another ten thousand dollars to stuff in the upstairs vault of the Alhambra. He did not know which he would enjoy the most, the pure pleasure of winning or the sight of Judge Burgendorf heading back to Haskell County with an outrun and well-beaten imported cur tied to the back of his wagon.

James Kenedy interrupted his train of thought. "Mr. Mayor," he said.

"I'm busy at the moment."

"Not too busy to talk to me."

Dog Kelley looked up, a little perturbed, until he saw who it was, then a broad gin lit up his faced. He stood and slapped the young trail boss on the back. "I knew you liked our bars and our women," he said, "but I certainly didn't know you liked to see our greyhounds run."

"I ain't here to talk about dogs."

"If you're wondering about getting your cattle loaded, the Santa Fe tells me they'll be here and ready to start shippin' before the week's out," Mayor Kelley told him. "That was a great-lookin' herd you brought to town this year."

"I ain't here to talk about cattle."

The trace of a frown etched its way onto the mayor's face. "How's your daddy doin'?" he asked. "I know he don't drift too far from that ranch of his anymore, but we sure do miss him up in these parts. He and I have shut down and busted up a lot of saloons together in our time. The only thing harder than his fist was his head. Please give him my regards when you get home, James."

"I ain't here to talk about Daddy either."

Dog Kelley stepped back as his handler opened the kennel and led Irish Count toward the track. A glance at the big, sleek, easy-moving greyhound brought back the mayor's grin, but only for a moment. He turned his attention again to the son of Mifflin Kenedy. He had never seen the young man so tense. Drunk, several times. But never so tense, never so angry.

James Kenedy possessed the mood of a man who had either killed or was getting ready to. Dog Kelley knew the boy had a hair-trigger temper. It was a trait he inherited from his daddy. The Kenedys liked to fight and did not mind getting hurt if it gave them the chance to hurt somebody else a little worse. The Kenedys, frankly, did not lose. Mifflin Kenedy even refused to admit such a possibility existed.

"What's troublin' you, James?" the mayor asked, taking the boy's arm and walking him toward the track.

"That city marshal of yours."

"What's Wyatt done that displeases you?"

"He pistol-whipped me, for one thing."

"He must have had a reason."

"He wanted our guns, and I told him to go straight to hell and even gave him directions. Takin' our guns is akin to stealin'."

"That's his job."

"That's gonna get him killed."

"That's the risk he takes."

James Kenedy leaned against the railing, chewing on a straw. "I don't think you understand, Mr. Mayor."

"Explain yourself, then."

"The Kenedys ain't like common folks."

"I will agree with you on that point."

"We don't like people tellin' us what we can do and what we can't do, and we damn well don't like 'em taking things away that belong to us."

Dog Kelley squinted as he watched the two greyhounds approach the starting gate. He had never realized Irish Count was so small and short legged before. Judge Burgendorf's dog looked more like a horse. He felt a knot tighten up in his gut.

"What do you want me to do about it?" the mayor asked, though his mind was no longer particularly concerned with James Kenedy's problem.

"Tell Earp to treat us with the respect we deserve."

"And that means . . ."

"Give us our guns back."

"And if he doesn't?"

The greyhounds were off, flying around the first turn. Irish Count had fallen to the outside and was giving ground, trying desperately to get back to the rail. A roar rose up amidst the crowd, deep and rumbling like thunder before a summer rain, loud enough to scare bulls off the bed-ground.

"My daddy's gonna start trailing his cattle somewhere else. Abilene maybe. Ellsworth's growing. Wichita's not that much farther away." James Kenedy paused as the greyhounds bolted down the backstretch. "Mifflin Kenedy's got a lot of influence with other Texas cattlemen. But, hell, Mr. Mayor, you already know that. If Daddy goes someplace else, they'll all go with him. It means a lot of money to Dodge, Mr. Mayor. Hell, it means a lot of money to you."

The greyhounds were around the far turn and heading home. Irish Count had moved back into the lead. His head was down, his eyes peeled back, his ears laid flat. Dog Kelley had never seen him cover so much ground with so much determination. The screams around him were deafening.

It sounded like the whole town was there. And they had all wagered on his dog. And Irish Count was racing for the wire like the champion he was.

"I'm sorry," Dog Kelley said, trying to make himself heard above the roar.

"Then you'll get the city marshal straightened out."

Less than twenty-five yards from the finish line, Irish Count suddenly buckled. His legs gave way, and he tumbled against the wooden rail. The cheering died away. A hush descended upon the track. Irish Count crawled to his feet and tried gamely to reach the wire, dragging his back legs behind him. But he was too late.

Judge Burgendorf wore the triumphant grin of a winner.

The knot in Dog Kelley's stomach exploded, and, for a moment, the mayor thought he was going to throw up. "It's my law, and Wyatt Earp's following my orders," he snapped sharply. "I don't care if you ever get your damn guns again."

"My daddy ain't gonna like this," James Kenedy yelled, his voice quivering with anger.

"I don't give a damn what your daddy likes."

"He can ruin you."

"He can't do a damn thing that hasn't already been done."

"I'm gettin' rid of Earp one way or the other."

The mayor's anger boiled over. "Kenedy, you're all smoke and damn little fire," he yelled. "You aren't hardly fit to walk on the same ground your daddy does. You think you can run Dodge just because your name's Kenedy. Well, you can't. Wyatt stays where he is because he does what I tell him to do. You can't get rid of him without gettin' rid of me first, kid."

Dog Kelley stalked off, his jaws clenched tightly, his hands balled up into fists. Irish Count had failed him. He had no use for man or beast if they failed him. He walked past the fallen animal without bothering to look down.

"Mr. Kelly," the handler said anxiously, "the Count's hurt."

The mayor ignored him.

"What do you want me to do with him?"

"Shoot him."

"What?" The handler stared after Dog Kelley with disbelief lodged in his eyes.

"The damn animal's no good to me anymore."

"He did his best," the handler pleaded.

"It wasn't enough."

By nightfall, Mayor Dog Kelley was somewhat poorer, and word had crept into every saloon that lined Front Street and every picayune gambling house that clung to the dead line, spreading to every cow camp on the crooked trail to Dodge.

Wyatt Warp was not worth a plug nickel alive. Dead, he was valued at two thousand dollars. James Kenedy would personally pay the bounty. No one talked much about it. But everyone knew.

♥ 24 ♦

♣

Wyatt Earp did not eat like a condemned man.

The early-morning sausage at the Long Branch was stale, though not yet rancid, and the hardtack biscuits were tougher than usual, but he did not find them particularly disagreeable. The lawman put away three eggs and sopped an extra bowl of buttermilk gravy, washing it all down with a pot of coffee so thick he had to chew the grounds and spit them out beneath the table.

"What are you gonna do about it?" I asked, taking the last biscuit off the platter.

"About what?"

"The bounty."

He grinned as though he did not have a care in the world, and maybe he didn't. "One thing's for certain," he said. "I'm not gonna collect it personally."

"I know you're not concerned about Kenedy," I told him. "He's stood up against you twice and lost both times. I doubt if he has the nerve to try it again. But now he's got every gun in Kansas looking for you. Who knows? One of 'em might get lucky."

Wyatt Earp wiped his mouth with a napkin and leaned back in his chair. "It's kind of flattering, really," he said.

"To be shot at?"

"To be wanted."

I poured a cup of coffee myself, took a sip and picked the grounds from between my teeth. "A wise man wouldn't stick around," I said.

"I've never run from a fight in my life."

"I don't know how good a fight it's gonna be," I replied, "but I'm dead certain it won't be a quick one. The first one who comes to Dodge won't get you. You're too good for that. But there'll be another. And another. Always another man with a gun. The odds say you can't get them all."

"You're a gambler," Wyatt Earp told me. "You play the odds. I don't. I'd be foolish to worry about them. I don't recall them ever being in my favor. I don't expect they ever will be."

For whatever reason, the sunshine had lost its warmth, and the day was becoming dark and brooding. "Sooner or later," I said, "the possibility of walking out into the street and facing the same threat every morning will start to wear on your nerves. Back in Fort Worth, I saw it drive a good sheriff mad. He became suspicious of everybody, even his friends. He couldn't eat and couldn't sleep. He started shooting at shadows. He shot and killed a little girl one night simply because she dropped her doll in her daddy's wagon. He fired at the sound, and she was in the way. He was a blithering idiot when they carted him away to the asylum."

"A man who's scared ought to turn in his badge."

"Unless he's afraid to admit how scared he is."

Wyatt Earp's voice was calm, and there was no evidence of emotion on his face. "It's an odd thing about a man who's never shot anybody in his life but still thinks he's a gunfighter," he said. "If he knows you can kill him, he won't test you unless he's drunk. And if he's drunk, then he can't shoot straight. And if he can't shoot straight, then he's a dead man, and he knows it. So he damn well leaves you alone."

"He might not have to," I said.

"He might not have to do what?"

"Shoot straight." The cooler the coffee became, the more bitter it was. "You may wake up some night with a barrel of a gun shoved down your throat. Even a drunk can hit you at that range."

"That's why I don't sleep much anymore," the lawman said.

"You're gambling that all you have to do is keep your eyes open for a bunch of drifters, farmers, cowboys, ne'er-do-wells who think they can get rich with one pull of the trigger," I told him. "That's not your biggest concern anymore."

"What makes you say that?"

"The two thousand dollars makes a big difference,"

"Everybody's lookin' for a way to make easy money," Wyatt Earp said, frowning impatiently. "It might be a mistake."

"There'll be gunfighters coming to Dodge who had just as soon shoot you as a snake crawling on his belly," I said.

"There's no law against that."

"Shooting you?"

"Comin' to Dodge."

"You won't know who it's gonna be," I warned him. "Which face, which gun, which day, what time of day. But somebody's gonna try it."

"Maybe it's today," Wyatt Earp said, standing and straightening the holster on his hip. "Then we can get it over with."

"As long as you're alive, it'll never be over with."

"As long as I'm alive," he said, forcing a grin, "it doesn't matter."

Wyatt Earp adjusted his black hat and walked out into the
streets of Dodge with a certain stoicism, a human target with
a two-thousand-dollar price on his head, as alone as he had
ever been. Since I had nothing better to do that morning, I
went with him.

"You're a foolish man," he told me as we turned into the
plaza.

"How do you figure?"

"As crooked as these old revolvers shoot, they'll come
just as close to hitting you as me."

"My life's not worth anything."

"We got Boot Hill full of men who could say the same
thing."

Wyatt Earp waited until the wagon rolled to a stop beside
the mercantile, then helped the widow Judkins step to the
ground. She was still bedded down with Amos Fielding out
on land that had never grown a good crop, but she had not
changed her name. She smiled her thanks, but it was a sad,
worn smile.

Spring had come. And gone. And Dodge still did not have
a preacher man to officially and legally tie their knot for
them. If one did not get lost, take the wrong road and wind
up in town pretty soon, their knot might become too frayed
to stay tied. The widow Judkins was not particularly
troubled. She might be living in sin all right, but it did not
worry her as long as there wasn't a minister to stand in the
pulpit every Sunday and condemn her to hell.

After being married to Spade Judkins and living with
Amos Fielding for a winter, the brimstone of Hades might
be something of relief. From what she had read in the Good
Book, women weren't required to cook three meals a day in
hell. And at night, well, sin was no longer against the law,
which made it a lot like Dodge on a hot August evening
when the sun went down.

The train that steamed into Dodge City that morning was not encumbered with a mile of cattle cars and bound for the stockyards in Chicago. The Kenedy herd would have to wait another day, which meant James Kenedy would not be on his way home to Texas nearly as soon as I had hoped, which meant he was still around to pay off his blood money to any gun that dared face Wyatt Earp in daylight hours or hide in ambush when darkness descended again upon the hiding places of Dodge. There were many of them. Every window, street corner, or alley was suspect. I could feel eyes staring out from all of them, even when they were empty. Every rifle was cocked, every pistol primed, or soon would be. Wyatt Earp chose not to notice.

"I wasn't expecting to be born," he told me. "I'm not expecting to die. When it happens, it happens. If a man spends his every waking hour worrying about it, he dies a little each day of his life. Frankly, I don't have the time for it."

We ambled down the street toward the depot, as did the city marshal each time a train pulled into the station, especially those that were making unscheduled stops. He felt a little better knowing who got on and who got off, what motivated them to do either.

I survived my trade by reading faces, trying to determine who sitting at the table had the cards and the courage to beat me. Wyatt Earp read train schedules, and he worked under the assumption that every new face in Dodge was gunning for somebody. Now it was him, and the high-dollar guns rode trains.

The locomotive was hauling only two passenger cars and a caboose. The entourage that spilled out onto the platform was led by a small man, slight of stature, nattily dressed in a pinstripe cotton suit that did not have a wrinkle in sight. He had a pleasant round face, and his fair skin, almost pink, was obviously not accustomed to the sun. A black bowler sat perched on top of his head, and he carried a European-style cane, although he showed no sign of a limp.

Other than being out of place in a trail town that did not take too kindly to well-scrubbed, nattily dressed men, there was nothing particularly distinctive about him, other than the fact he had been foresightful enough to surround himself with a dozen or more women who were especially beautiful for that hour of the morning.

Their lips were freshly painted. Their skin had a golden hue. Their dresses were full, the colors of summer itself, and tailored to carefully reveal every enticing curve their bodies possessed, and they possessed every curve the law allowed and some the law was not too sure about. Not a blemish was in sight, not a hair out of place. If the nattily dressed man had come to town to open a new brothel on either side of the dead line, the Alhambra and Long Branch were in trouble.

He was smiling broadly with teeth much too white to have ever chewed on alkali water sucked from a tepid Texas stream when Mayor Dog Kelley stepped out of the depot and grasped his soft, puffy hand, shaking it vigorously.

"Mr. Foy," Mayor Kelley said, "let me be the first to welcome you to Dodge City. This is, I can assure you, a day we've all been waiting for. All of Dodge considers it a rare privilege for you and your troupe to include us in your tour of the west."

"And you are, sir?"

"Mayor Thomas Kelley, Mr. Foy, at your service."

"Well, thank you, Mr. Mayor," the nattily dressed man said, "but I doubt seriously if you have come down to the station this morning to see me."

"But you, sir, are the star."

"My name is at the top of the billing, Mr. Mayor." Eddie Foy laughed heartily. "But the young ladies are the stars. I tell a few jokes. I sing a few songs. But nobody has ever paid good money to see my naked legs. But then, I make a lot of money because good, red-blooded American men like to see the naked legs in the rest of the show."

Dog Kelley glanced at the ladies who had gathered with their luggage on the platform, content that all of the painted smiles he saw were meant exclusively for him, and he said, "That, sir, I have no doubt. I have no doubt at all."

Eddie Foy motioned to a young lady sitting atop a trunk, beckoning her to join him. She looked twenty-five, but was probably younger, with long black hair twisted around an oval, olive-complexioned face. Her eyes were black and moist, and they reflected the confidence of a young woman who had always known where she was going and had not stopped until she got there. Her features were soft and delicate, and she wore a pale yellow dress trimmed with white lace, twirling a yellow parasol that rested upon her shoulder.

"Mr. Mayor," Eddie Foy announced, "it is my pleasure to introduce you to the real star of our little troupe. She sings the way you've never heard songs sung before. Her sad songs can make even the toughest of men cry, and her love songs steal, then break, the heart of every man who has the misfortune of hearing her. She is a rare wonder indeed. I would like for you to say hello to the most stunning voice in all of America. Once you hear her, I can guarantee you, sir, that you will never forget her. We call her, with affection and admiration, the New Texas Songbird."

Wyatt Earp turned ashen. He grabbed the railing that encircled the depot to keep from losing his balance and falling. His body had been robbed of its strength. His eyes were waxen and hollow. I had seen men who looked that way before, but never outside a funeral parlor. He was staring into the lovely, exquisite face of Dora Hand.

She had done to him what no man—what no army of men—had been able to do, stripped him of his pride and dignity. Just the mere glimpse of her tore into his gut like a fragmented bullet, only more lethal. He had dreamed of her the way men dream of home when they will never see it again.

And there she was. As beautiful as ever. Perhaps even more beautiful than either of us remembered.

Dora Hand caught sight of Wyatt Earp, and her radiant smile flickered, but just for an instant. Her face was as soft as ever. There was a hardness in her eyes. Or was it fear? As she took the mayor's arm, the parasol dropped between her and Wyatt. As long as Dora Hand could not see him, then Wyatt Earp had ceased to exist.

Maybe she was right. Maybe he was just another stranger in town. But she had almost been his wife.

"Dora," he said as she walked past him. His voice was thick and raspy.

She did not turn around nor remove the parasol that shielded her face.

"Dora," he said again, the whisper louder this time.

All he heard was the music of her laughter when she called the mayor "darling," in much the way she had once talked to him.

"Miss Hand," Dog Kelley said, "we want to do everything we can to insure that your stay in Dodge is as pleasurable and memorable as possible."

"Why, thank you, sir."

"I'm afraid there was a fire last night at the finest hotel in Dodge. It wasn't destroyed, but, from what I'm told, the damages are rather severe."

"I'm so sorry to hear that, Your Honor."

"As a result, I wish that you and Mr. Foy would consider staying in my home for the duration of your visit here." He put his arm around both of them. "It would," he said quietly, "keep you removed from the rougher elements in town."

"We certainly don't want to be a bother to you," Eddie Foy told him.

"It's quite a large home," Dog Kelley responded, "with two bedrooms on the first floor and three on the second. So, you see, you'll certainly not be in my way, and you'll have all the privacy you require. If you need more, I'll arrange for that, too. Besides, I'm afraid I must leave after your performance tonight for a meeting with Judge Burgendorf over in Haskell County, so you'll have the whole house to yourself for the next couple of days. That should give you plenty of time to settle down and find your way around. Miss Hand, I would be sorely disappointed if you rejected my offer."

"Well, Mr. Mayor," she teased, "I've never disappointed a man in my life, and I certainly wouldn't want to start now."

Dog Kelley was not quite sure how to respond, so he laughed deeply and self-consciously, which was probably the right thing to do. Dora Hand was laughing as well, and Eddie Foy had ceased to pay either one of them any attention.

He was standing in the middle of Front Street, arms folded, staring at the columns that framed the doorway of the Comique Theater. The sun pounded unmercifully down on his head, and an uneasy sweat was beginning to take the starch and the creases out of his pinstripe suit. There was nothing in the world more stimulating and promising than a new stage in a new town. Dodge City was his to conquer.

But that challenge did not worry nor concern Eddie Foy. He had conquered the world, he and the Texas Songbird.

Eddie Foy hurried on across the street and disappeared

into the cool darkness of the theater. He might stay in the home of Mayor Dog Kelley. But this was where he lived.

Every man had his own code. The strong made their own rules. The weak followed those set down by others. Cowards were like the blind. Anyone could lead them. Somebody always did. They had no idea where they were going, and they seldom got there.

When Wyatt Earp pinned the silver star to his shirt, he went out to the creek bank behind the Long Branch, broke the last whiskey bottle he had stuffed in his bedroll and gave up strong drink for good. A man with a badge, especially if he walked the streets of Dodge, needed a clear head and a steady hand twenty-four hours a day, sometimes longer. Whiskey dulled the brain and deadened the reflexes. Whiskey made a man careless. A careless man made mistakes. Boot Hill was full of them.

The love of a woman, either good or bad, was oftentimes worse for a man than whiskey. Wyatt Earp was close enough to Dora Hand to reach out and touch her, to reach out and hold her again as he had done during those long, turbulent nights in Fort Griffin. But a whisper was the best he could do. She had looked at him, then through him, then past him. Not everybody liked nor even respected Wyatt Earp or the badge he wore. He was used to that. But nobody ignored him, nobody but Dora Hand.

She could just as easily have put a bullet in his heart. It might have been a more merciful thing to do.

The hard, lethal look in his eyes was replaced by a hollow, sunken stare. His face sagged and turned a pallid shade of gray. His hands trembled. His voice lost its vibrancy. Wyatt Earp was the prey of every two-bit gunman north of the Indian Territory, every one of them riding toward Dodge City with a bullet in chamber that could make them richer by two thousand dollars.

He was in no mood to fight back. At the moment, I'm not sure he was even capable of fighting back.

Only death, which wasn't so bad when you simply wanted to go to sleep without the fear of having to wake up again, could make him forget the lovely Dora Hand as she had forgotten him.

Wyatt Earp waited until Dora Hand had boarded the red freshly painted horse-drawn buggy that would take her to Dog Kelley's home, then he shuffled with his head down into the Long Branch and bought two bottles of Luke Short's strongest whiskey. He stuck one in his hip pocket, pulled the cork out of the other with his teeth, and walked back out into the street without paying for either one of them.

"That's a helluva note," Luke Short said.

"Wyatt's not himself this morning," I answered.

"He worried about gettin' shot?"

"I don't think it's crossed his mind."

Luke Short cleaned off the top of the bar with a wet rag, then asked, "Who am I gonna call now?"

"About what?"

"That sonuvabitch just stole two bottles of whiskey," he said, then shrugged as though he wasn't quite sure what he should do next. "The only man in town I'd trust arrestin' the damn thief is the thief."

"What's he owe you?" I wanted to know.

Luke Short told me, and I tossed the coins on the bar, watching the eagle heads spin until his big, beefy hands scooped them up and threw them into a drawer beneath the oil painting of a pair of naked cherubs running aimlessly through the Garden of Eden.

I had never seen Wyatt Earp run from man or beast. A fallen woman had whipped him like a farmer would a stubborn mule, then thrown him away and out of her sight, probably for good.

I found him down by the creek bank, propped up against the gnarled trunk of a scrub oak, pouring whiskey down his throat as though he were dying of thirst instead of merely dying inside. Splinters of shade left scars on his face. The first bottle was already half-empty.

"What the hell are you trying to do to yourself?" I asked, kneeling beside the scrub oak, staring out across a vast prairie where the grasses were long and green, fluttering in a gentle southerly wind.

"There are some days when I'd just as soon you'd get lost, Hawkes," he answered. "This is one of 'em."

"You want to die alone?"

"That's how it's usually done." He drained the first bottle and tossed it into the creek. It bobbed for a few moments on the strength of its own ripples, then sank to the mud below.

"She's not worth it, Wyatt."

He pulled the cork from the second bottle and spit it out. "You ever been in love, Hawkes?"

I thought a minute, then answered, "I've been there once or twice, Wyatt."

"You remember what it's like?"

The sun slipped behind a cloud, and I watched the ragged edges of a shadow racing across the prairie. "I try not to think about it."

"How'd you forget?"

"I sure as hell didn't drown myself in whiskey."

"How'd you forget?" he asked again, louder this time, demanding.

"Time, I guess."

"I ain't got time."

"Not if you're drunk on your feet when some Texas gunhand comes looking to put a bullet in you."

"He won't have trouble findin' me." Wyatt Earp pulled his hat lower over his eyes and closed them. "Besides, I'm not afraid of dyin' if my time's run out."

I reached over and pulled his Smith & Wesson from its holster. I checked to make sure there was a bullet in the chamber, then handed it back to him. "If you're not afraid of dyin', then why don't you just go ahead and save 'em a lot of trouble?" I said. "Lead poisoning, alcohol poisoning, it's all gonna catch up with you."

He stared down the barrel of his revolver, his hands still trembling.

"Go ahead," I said.

"And do what?"

"Pull the damn trigger," I said, standing up and walking away. "It's the coward's way out."

"I ain't no coward," Wyatt Earp replied, softly, slurring his words.

"You can face Dora," I answered, "or you can forget her. Or you can hide behind the bottle, which is what you're doing now, cloud your mind with whiskey and pretend Dora doesn't exist. But when you wake up, she'll still be there, and you'll still be here, lying in your vomit. Where I come from, cowards prefer the bottle."

"I ain't no coward," Wyatt Earp yelled.

"I can remember when you were a man," I said without looking back.

The bullet from his first shot struck the ground just behind my feet. His second shot slammed into the back door of the Long Branch.

Wyatt Earp was doing his damnedest to kill me.

He could not shoot straight anymore. The whiskey had blinded him, and he was having trouble holding the Smith & Wesson steady.

I turned around, and Wyatt Earp was grasping the

revolver with both hands, waving it awkwardly from side to side, aiming with the wrong eye, unable to see at all because of the tears burning his ashen face.

"Damn you, Hawkes," he yelled, his voice shaking. "If you'd be still, I'd blow your gawdamn head off."

I kept walking.

He fired again.

I have no idea where the bullet hit. I stepped into the back door of the saloon before he could pull the trigger again and, maybe, get lucky that time.

Luke Short looked up, his eyebrows arched, and asked, "What the hell's wrong with Earp?"

"He's feeling sorry for himself."

"He damn well better be. A Texas drover named George Hoyt's been in here asking about him."

"I suppose he wasn't a friend."

"The man had a stiff drink in his gullet and money in his eyes."

"You tell this George Hoyt where he could find the marshal?"

Luke Short grinned and wiped the sweat off his face with the same rag he used to clean the glasses. "All I sell is whiskey," he said. "And you know me, Hawkes. I don't give nothin' away."

I nodded and pitched another coin on the bar. "Wyatt sure doesn't need another bottle," I said, "but he's gonna want one. If I were you, however, I wouldn't take it out to him until he runs out of bullets."

"What are you gonna do about him?" Luke Short asked.

"Wyatt?"

"George Hoyt."

"If the man plays poker, I'll make damn sure he doesn't get out of Dodge with that two thousand dollars still in his pocket," I said.

"You think Wyatt's a goner?"

"There's only one man who can keep him alive, and that's Wyatt himself. And, unfortunately, he's not particularly interested in doing that at the moment. He'd rather lay out there in the hot sun, suck another whiskey bottle dry, and suffocate himself on a large dose of self-pity. I only hope it's quick, and he's asleep when they find him. And, sooner or later, George Hoyt or somebody else will find him."

Luke Short shook his head and shrugged elaborately. "I don't know," he said, "when Wyatt's got his back against the wall, he's pretty damn good with that Smith and Wesson of his."

"Right now," I said, "he couldn't hit a tree if he was sitting on the stump."

♠

♥ 25 ♦

♣

Culture did not come often to Dodge City, other than the
occasional melancholy lament of a brokenhearted whore
singing at the Alhambra about a lost love or a faraway
home, neither of which she ever expected to see again. The
traveling singing-and-dancing entourage of Eddie Foy had
created a mild uproar in the trail town. The curtain wasn't
scheduled to rise until almost seven o'clock, but the
canvas-covered seats of the Comique Theater were beginning to fill an hour before sundown had crept across Fried
Biscuit Creek and shuffled its way into Dodge.

Most of the cowboys dragged themselves up the short
flight of stairs to the balcony, its rails whittled by dulled,
hand-me-down pocket knives and scarred by old cigarette
burns, where they sat in the dark, long before it was dark,
passing a bottle of warm, stale whiskey among themselves,
out of sight and unable to interfere or disturb the genteel of
Dodge, who marched elegantly into the theater decked out
in their finest frock coats and long, ruffled dresses. It was
opening night in a town that did not have many genuine
opening nights. The riffraff performed from time to time,
secondhand actors in secondhand clothes, spouting second-

hand solioquies the way Shakespeare would have written them if he had been dead drunk at the time.

A singing troupe had wandered through a year or so earlier and hired a handful of the local girls for various roles in the show, which was probably how Eddie Foy had found Dora Hand in the first place.

During a dramatic moment in the performance, the villain had suddenly turned to a beautiful young lady, whipped out his revolver, just as the script required him to do, and fired three times. The blanks echoed through the theater like exploding dynamite caps. With a song on her lips, she grabbed her head, spun three times, rolled her eyes one final time toward the spotlight, and crumpled slowly to the stage. She jerked with convulsions once, then twice, and lay still. The villain again faced the audience, singing, "What have I done . . . what have I done . . . what have I done?"

A cowboy with a little too much stale whiskey staining his breath, leapt to his feet, grabbed his Colt .44, and put three bullets into the actor, just above his belt buckle. "I'll tell you what you did, you sonuvabitch," he yelled. "You shot the best-lookin' whore in Dodge City is what you did."

But that was before Wyatt Earp had been hired by Dog Kelley to take their guns away, which was one reason Dog Kelley hired Wyatt Earp to remove both their guns and any temptation they might have to plug either the guilty or the innocent. A good old-fashioned shooting, whether it was justified or not, had always been a little disconcerting to the wagons hauling civilization west. Dog Kelley wanted a quiet town, a peaceable town, a town where he could walk the streets at night, and not worry about a wayward slug finding its way to the back of his head.

Now the cowboys were sitting in the nickel seats, and they had come to catch a glimpse of those dancing naked

legs and maybe hear a song that would remind them of
someplace they had been before, although home was
probably out of the question. Home was where they put their
boots at night, usually on their cattle's bedding ground,
when they laid their head on a saddle and used their horse
blanket to keep out the chill of an early spring wind. It had
not always been that way. But it would probably never be
any other way again, at least not as long as they could ride,
and a man who could not ride had no place west of the
Mississippi and damn few places east of it.

Their clothes were wrinkled, stained, and slept in, as
usual. Their boots were caked with dirt and dung, as usual.
Not a cowboy removed his hat. A cowboy would have felt
himself naked without a hat on his head. The only cowboys
any of them had ever seen with bare heads had usually been
stuffed in a pine box.

The genteel were doing their best to refine the rough edges
of the trail town, but were badly outnumbered, and the wine
they drank smelled as though it had been plucked from the
vine a week or so before it ripened. The ladies had all
unpacked their finest jewels and draped the diamonds and
pearls elaborately around their well-wrinkled necks. The
men had combed their beards, kicked the mud off their
boots, and polished the brass on their suspenders. Their ties
were tied so tightly their faces had reddened, and they
wheezed when they talked. Many of them had been cowboys once, until some woman had showed them a better way
to live. God, how they missed the old way.

The genteel were all smiles and curtsies, full of reverence
and respect for the pudgy, pink-faced little impresario who
had chosen to grace the stage of Dodge just as he and his
troupe had done so many times before in London and Paris
and Rome.

"It's a grand night," I heard one gray-haired, matronly woman tell a friend as I pushed my way into the lobby.

"A night I'll always remember, to be sure."

"Dodge isn't like it was when Hamner and I lost a wheel to the wagon, and we settled down here because we couldn't get any closer to California. It was a wild place then, and a little scary, and I don't mind saying so."

She had obviously not ventured past the dead line lately. Most ladies never did. The real ladies of Dodge did not even admit there was a dead line.

"The city's definitely changing," her friend in the bright red dress replied. "I don't feel nearly as isolated out here as I used to."

"Eddie Foy certainly found his way to Dodge. Civilization just can't be that far behind. My husband works in the bank, you know, and he says Dodge has more money than it's ever had before, and a town with money is destined for greatness. That's what he says, and a man who works for the bank should certainly know a thing or two about money."

In spite of Mayor Dog Kelley's efforts, civilization had only gotten as far west as St. Louis, looked around, didn't see anything it liked, and gone back east. St. Louis couldn't even keep it very long. The road that civilization followed might have actually reached as far as Dodge, but it was washed out. Those who came to Dodge did not travel by road, and they usually arrived in the dead of night and tried to leave the same way.

The genteel, man and woman alike, did not begin their lives in Dodge City as members of a higher society. The only difference between the legitimate and the illegitimate was the amount of money somebody had stashed away in the bank's vault. It was earned or stolen in a variety of ways, known only in back rooms and poker tables and an empty bank or two. But once their cash reached a certain level, nobody asked them how they got it anymore, just as no one ever asked whether the names on their birth certificates and death certificates happened to match. Nobody cared. Money, at least in Dodge, washed away more sins than a good Baptist deep-water baptizing. I sometimes wondered how much money it would take to be legitimate, but not often. I never figured I had that much anyway, and if I did, there was always somebody else at another gaming table trying to take it away from me. And sometimes faces lied, and the cards did not always run the way they were dealt.

The south Texas drovers had elbowed their way down to the front row, which was the only place in the theater deserving of the Kenedy clan. James Kenedy himself was wedged into the center seat, a smug look plastered on his face. He kept looking back over his shoulder as though expecting someone or searching for someone who had not yet arrived. A frown finally crept into his eyes. He rolled his program tightly and swatted at a horsefly that came to rest on his leg. He missed.

I stepped behind the purple velvet curtain, and the theater grew considerably darker. A musty smell hung in the air around me. Backstage was virtually devoid of humanity, with the exception of a dancer tightening the cinch on her corset, making her waist much smaller than God had intended it to be, and Eddie Foy, gesturing frantically in an animated conversation with Mayor Dog Kelley. A slender streak of light from a gas lamp splashed across his face. Eddie Foy always knew where the spotlight was, no matter how dim and antiquated it might be, and he always figured it was up there just for him.

"The last time I was down in Weatherford, Texas, which is just outside of Fort Worth," Eddie Foy was saying, "I ran across the laziest man I believe I've ever seen. It was this farmer, and he was raisin' hogs, nothing but hogs, and all of his neighbors were out raising corn.

"I asked him, 'Do hogs pay better than corn?'

"And he said, 'No.'

"And I asked him, 'Then how come are you raisin' hogs?'

"And he said, 'Hogs don't need no shuckin'.'"

Mayor Dog Kelley laughed out loud, and Eddie Foy was obviously pleased with himself. He had made one man laugh. He could make an entire town do the same. The right word. The right phrase. The right gesture. The right smirk. Eddie Foy had them all, and he knew it. The curtain could not raise soon enough to suit him. He was already on fire, just like a circuit-riding evangelist, and he felt sorry for those poor bastards out front who would have to wait another fifteen minutes to hear him.

I found the lovely Dora Hand sitting alone in the darkness, prim and proper, her clasped hands lying limply in her lap. She was dressed in a long satin gown, buttoned to the neck, as soft and demure as the girl she had always wanted to be. Dora Hand was quietly humming a song that seemed faintly familiar, and her moist eyes were wide with anxiety. The warm red blush had fled her face. Her skin was the color of alabaster, pale and translucent.

She saw me walking toward her but did not speak. She turned away and looked toward a ragged spider web, cloaked in dust, hanging from the wall, brushing against the curtain. Each strand was illuminated in the pallid glow of a fluttering gas lamp, and the spider was only a crusty shell that had not been able to escape his own trap. The spider was not unlike the rest of us.

"Dora Hand," I said.

"Yes." Her voice was so weak it was barely audible.

"It's good to see you again."

She continued to stare at the web, mesmerized, her jaw taut, her shoulders rigid. "I'm sorry," Dora Hand replied, "but I don't believe we've ever met, you and I."

"Fort Griffin," I said to jog her memory.

Nothing.

"The Double Eagle Saloon," I said.

Still nothing.

"Wyatt Earp," I said finally.

In her own mind, the lovely Dora Hand was sitting alone in the darkness. It was as though I did not exist, nor had I ever existed. She turned at last away from the spider web and stood to face me, although her eyes were looking past me, maybe even through me, but never at me.

"Perhaps," she said softly, "it would be more appropriate to say I wished that we had never met, Mr. Hawkes."

The hardness I had seen at the railroad depot had not left her eyes.

But now it was touched by a hint of fear, the kind you witness when you walk up on a sparrow that has fallen with a broken wing.

She continued, "It's quite easy to pretend I've never been to Fort Griffin, never saw the upstairs of the Double Eagle, never heard of Wyatt Earp. I'm an actress, you know, and an actress can live in any world she chooses. I've chosen another world, a much better world. I don't really want anyone who reminds me of that other place, those other times, that other world, the one I left behind me, and I'm afraid that includes you, Mr. Hawkes. I am truly and deeply sorry. But in my new world, you and I have never met, and I would prefer to keep it that way."

Her smile was quick but not sincere.

It had a razor's edge.

"What about Wyatt?" I asked.

"It's only a name I faintly recall," Dora Hand answered.

"He still loves you." The words had no effect on her. I paused to collect my thoughts, then continued, "Wyatt's not the kind of man who loves easy or often. But when he does, he loves deeply and, I suspect, forever. You may not have asked to be the woman he fell for, but he fell for you anyway, Dora. He can't help it, and he can't stop it, and neither can you, I'm afraid."

"It must not be me he loves," she said. There was that quick smile again. "It must be someone else."

"She sure looks a helluva lot like you."

The smile vanished the way a cloud passing before the sun darkens the earth. "Mr. Hawkes," Dora Hand said, her voice as hard as her eyes, "all my life I wanted to be onstage. I wanted to feel the warmth of footlights in my face. I wanted to hear the roar of the applause and know the roar was meant for me. I wanted to feel important, to be some- body important, to be on top, to see my name on the playbill, to know that people were paying to see me perform. . . ."

"If I recall," I snapped, suddenly angry and not quite sure why, "you were getting paid to perform back in Fort Griffin."

She looked as though I had slapped her. Hard. Maybe too hard. It had not been a kind thing to say.

"Back in Fort Griffin," Dora Hand said, carefully choos- ing her words, "I told you that someday a traveling theatrical troupe would roll through town and take me away from all of that. I believed. I prayed for it. I would have sold my soul to make it happen. You thought I was a dreamer. Or maybe you thought I was crazy. And maybe I was. But it happened. We had a big snowstorm that nobody was expecting, and Eddie Foy got froze in on his way to Fort Worth. He couldn't get out of town for three days, and it gave him plenty of time to hear me sing, and he liked what he heard. He called me the Texas Songbird, and that's still what he calls me. He doesn't know anything about who I was or what I did or why I did it. As far as Eddie knows, I was just a stranger stranded in Fort Griffin like he was, a saloon singer looking for work, and a damn good one. Lord knows, the snow was so deep nobody else came to town. And the girls in the Double Eagle, they were just glad to know one of us finally had a chance to get away, so they didn't say anything, not even Kathy Marie, and Eddie roomed with her until the snow melted."

Dora Hand grabbed both my hands and squeezed them. The hardness in her eyes had cracked and was beginning to melt. She was pleading now, tears in her voice as well as her eyes.

"This is the chance in life I've always prayed for, Mr. Hawkes," she said. "Most people don't get more than one, and this is mine. If you or Wyatt or anyone else reveals my past, it would ruin me. Eddie would kick me off the train, and I'd be right back where I was. And, God, I don't want to go back there. Please don't do that to me."

"Are you in love with Eddie Foy?"

"He only has one love."

"She in the show?"

"Himself."

"He could do better."

She shrugged as though it did not matter.

"You must have known Wyatt was in Dodge when you came," I said.

"I was hoping he would be gone." Her smile was now one of self-pity, and she had practiced it until she had it down perfect. "Wyatt never hangs around any town very long. I thought maybe he had ridden on. God, I was praying that he had ridden on. I wasn't ready to come face to face with my days in Fort Griffin. They're not days I'm very proud of."

"Wyatt's the law in Dodge now."

The lovely Dora Hand nodded, casting her eyes to the floor. "When I saw him standing there beside the depot this morning, I almost died," she told me, nervously wringing the lace handkerchief in her hands. "I never expected to see him again."

"He thought you were a ghost."

She shrugged her dainty shoulders. "Maybe I am," she said.

"Wyatt wants to see you. He desperately wants to see you."

The fear returned to her eyes. "I can't allow that," she said frantically. "When Wyatt left Fort Griffin, he left my life for good. When I quite crying, I said I'd never cry over a man again, and I haven't, and I won't. I don't want Wyatt back. All he can ever do now is hurt me, and I've been hurt enough in my time."

"Right now, Wyatt is lying out there beneath the shade of a scrub oak, drowning himself in whiskey because he saw you again, and it rekindled all the feelings he had for you, Dora. He did the best he could to bury them, but some feelings just won't say buried. You didn't speak to him or even acknowledged he's alive, and it's killing him."

"I'm sorry he's taking it so hard. But there's nothing I can do about it."

"At least you can talk to him," I said. "In private. Tell Wyatt what you told me. He won't like it. And he'll probably go out, whip somebody, and get drunk again. But at least he'll understand it."

"I don't even want to be seen with him."

"Nobody will ever know."

"I can't take that chance," Dora Hand replied testily.

"He loves you, Dora."

"If Wyatt loves me, Mr. Hawkes, if he really, truly loves me, then he'll leave me alone." She turned and began walking slowly away, slowly across the empty stage. "I've got to go now and get ready for the show," Dora Hand said without looking back. "I'm an actress, you know, and the show is the only life I have anymore. I don't want to lose it."

She reached up and tore the dusty spider web from the wall as she walked past, then the shadows veiled her and swallowed her up.

The stage was as it had been before. Empty.

I no longer knew the lovely Dora Hand. Perhaps I never did. Had I been talking to the woman? Or the actress? Or was there any difference between the two.

Deacon Cox had never looked more fashionable as he swaggered down the aisle toward the front of the Comique Theater. His suit was black silk, no doubt imported from Europe, his riding boots created from the finest leather. His white shirt was ruffled at the collar, and he carried a top hat in his hand.

The two ladies hanging on to each of his arms, one a blonde and the other a redhead, both probably imported as well, had never met before. He only knew one of them by name. Deacon Cox had high hopes that they would all get better acquainted before morning. He wore the ladies like jewelry, resplendent and expensive. He doubted if Eddie Foy could produce any dancers with naked legs who were more beautiful than they. If he did, the cowboys in the balcony just might tear the theater apart. If he did, I just might help them.

Deacon Cox was one of the genteel, who, at least for a night, had managed to forget or ignore the fact that his fashionable Dodge House Hotel was in disarray, scorched and still scattered with the ash of embers long dead.

A bitter frown scarred his mouth when he saw James Kenedy chewing a cigar, perched on the first row of the theater, his boots propped up against the stage. The muscles in his broad back tensed. The veins in his neck turned a purple shade of red, and the pulse in his throat pounded hard like a farmer's hammer against the ruffled collar of his white shirt.

Deacon Cox stood for a moment without speaking, trying with a great deal of difficulty to regain his composure now that he was in a public place. Under normal circumstances, he might have paid a dollar or two to have had James Kenedy taken out back and shot no matter who the hell he was or what his name happened to be. But a certain decorum was expected of the genteel in a public place, especially on opening night at the theater. The ruffians did not belong, which was why, in Deacon Cox's eyes, James Kenedy had no business sitting where he was up front in the Comique. Let him go to the nickel seats with the rest of the malingerers.

"Pardon me," Deacon Cox said, as a gentleman should have said, "but I do believe you are sitting in my seat, sir."

"Hell," snapped James Kenedy, spitting on the floor tobacco he had gnawed from the cigar, "this ain't your seat. If it was, you'd have already been sittin' in it, and since you ain't, it belongs to the sonuvabitch who gets here early enough to get it."

The smirk broadened on James Kenedy's face.

Deacon Cox reached inside his coat and produced three tickets, handing them to the Texas trail boss. "These prove the seats do belong to me, sir," he said, his voice beginning to waver somewhere between anger and hostility.

James Kenedy tore the tickets in half and tossed them over his shoulder. "Those don't prove shit," he said.

"Must I have you thrown out, sir?"

The trail boss was on his feet instantly. The smirk had turned into a scowl, and James Kenedy's fists were clenched.

Deacon Cox dropped his top hat, which was of no real use to him anyway.

"Let's get a couple of things straight between us," James Kenedy said, his teeth clenched. "The Kenedys pay damn good money to stay in that rathole hotel of yours, and if we want to sit in your goddam seats, then we'll damn sure sit in 'em. And, by gawd, if I decide we want those whores of yours before the night's over, I'll come and get them, too. And if you say one more damn word about any of it, I'll cram this cigar so far down your damn throat I'll have to light it through your ass."

Deacon Cox had run out of choices. He could turn around and walk away and lose his dignity. He could fight a younger man, a stronger man, a man who was backed up by a half dozen rogues and might even lose his life. Or he could stand there speechless, which is what he did.

Mayor Dog Kelley stepped between them, eager to restore a little peace to the situation before it erupted into something ugly he could not control, and he had worked too hard to lure Eddie Foy to Dodge to let opening night, the most important night in Dodge since he was elected mayor, get out of hand.

"Gentlemen," he said calmly, "what seems to be the problem?"

"The little bastard's sittin' in my seats," Deacon Cox said, his voice hoarse. "I paid good money for 'em, and I've had 'em reserved for these two ladies and myself since we got word Mr. Eddie Foy and his follies were on their way to Dodge. I don't intend to lose 'em. I don't intend to have 'em stolen by a bunch of Texas cowboys who look like a pile of cow dung and smell worse."

Dog Kelley turned to James Kenedy, obviously perturbed. "What do you have to say for yourself, James?"

"If he don't get the hell out of here and leave us be, then
I'm gonna throw the sonuvabitch out of here," the young
trail boss spit out angrily.

"May I see your tickets?" the mayor asked James
Kenedy, remaining as calm as possible considering he was
standing between two kegs of dynamite, and the fuse of at
least one of them would burn down any second.

The rest of the early evening crowd was on its feet,
straining to see what the commotion was all about, aghast
that anyone would have the irreverent gall to disturb the
sanctity of Eddie Foy's traveling entertainment troupe. The
women were wringing their hands nervously. They were ill
at ease and embarrassed that two grown men inside the
Comique Theater had the audacity to act as though they
were drinking, or worse, at some picayune gambling house
south of the dead line.

Their husbands were quietly placing their bets, aware that
perhaps the best show of the night was about to commence
just as soon as the two men in question could decide who
had the nerve to swing first. Anybody foolish enough to
wager on the aging, slump-shouldered, soggy-faced Deacon
Cox had all the action he could handle.

"I don't have any of your damn tickets," Kenedy snapped,
throwing his cigar on the floor in disgust.

"Then you don't belong in these seats," the mayor told
him.

"A Kenedy belongs any damn place he chooses."

"Not in Dodge, he doesn't."

"You wouldn't talk to my daddy like that."

"Your daddy would purchase his seats like a Texas
gentleman ought to." Dog Kelley paused to make sure his
words had sunk in, then said, "He would not stoop so low as

to try and steal them, and he'd be damned upset that a son of his would be causing all this trouble."

The smirk returned to James Kenedy's face. "What the hell are you gonna do about it?" he asked.

"I'm not going to do anything," the mayor replied.

"I didn't think you'd have the guts to try."

"I don't have to do anything," the mayor continued. "Mr. Earp will do it for me. That's his job, in case you forgot."

Wyatt Earp slipped out of the shadows, a vacant grin on his face, his Smith & Wesson drawn and cocked, a spare bullet lodged between his teeth. The lawman spun the chamber once, and his eyes were black and menacing.

"Mr. Cox and the seats he bought are no longer your concern," Dog Kelley told the young trail boss. "Neither am I. I wouldn't even worry about Mr. Earp if I were you. But that revolver of his can put a mighty big hole in you, and it might be too big for any of us to plug. I don't know if you've ever heard the sound of a man trying to breathe when the air is sucking blood out of his chest. I have. And I'm not anxious to hear it again. Your daddy's a friend of mine. It would grieve me a great deal to have to send your empty saddle home to him."

The anger had whitened James Kenedy's face. "You're a real sonuvabitch," he said to the mayor.

"That's been the rumor from time to time," Dog Kelley replied, "but as of yet nobody's been able to prove it."

"You're through in his town, Kelley."

"That, my friend, is up to the voters to decide."

"That, my friend," mocked James Kenedy, "is a promise."

The young trail boss glanced again at Wyatt Earp. Light falling from the gas lamp was ricocheting off the revolver. The barrel looked longer than usual, the bore deeper, the muzzle bigger. He could already smell the acrid scent of gunpowder in his nostrils. And there was the bitter taste of black gall hanging in his throat.

The lawman hated him. James Kenedy was sure of that. Wyatt Earp would kill him and have no regrets. All the lawman needed was an excuse, any kind of excuse. Even the barest hint of a reason to pull the trigger was enough.

He would not need to get one tonight. James Kenedy spun on the heels of his boots and stalked out of the theater, followed by his drovers who were willing to pay a nickel a seat in the balcony whether their boss did or not. Naked dancing legs were always worth a nickel, especially if they were attached to real live breathing girls, which Eddie Foy's girls were rumored to be. Hell, there was no use going with James Kenedy. All he intended on doing was getting drunk anyway.

The vacant grin had not left Wyatt Earp's face. He was still leaning against the wall, scratching his chin with the muzzle of the revolver when I reached him. The odor of stale whiskey was rank on his breath. He had swallowed the spare bullet.

"He's gone now," I said.

"Who?"

"James Kenedy."

"Haven't seen him."

"You just chased him out of here."

"Who?"

"James Kenedy."

"Now, why the hell would I do that?" His words were slurred, his eyes as vacant as his grin.

I stared at him, trying to read his eyes. They were like a book with empty pages. Wyatt Earp burped, then coughed on the sour spittle working its way down his throat.

"You have no idea what just happened, do you?" I said.

"When?"

"Just now."

Wyatt turned to me, suddenly aware he had the revolver in his hand. "Did I shoot somebody?" he wanted to know.

"James Kenedy thought you were gonna shoot him."

Wyatt Earp's laugh was a reflex, nothing more. "Did I hit him?" he asked.

"He was afraid you were going to shoot his head clean off."

"I could have done it, too," the lawman said, "if I could have seen it. Damn, he's got a little bitty head. I couldn't see it 'cause his shoulders kept gettin' in the way."

"He was wearing a hat."

Wyatt Earp looked confused. "Why the hell did he have his hat on his shoulders?" he wanted to know. He burped again.

Wyatt Earp suddenly grew serious. "Did he hurt Dora?" he asked.

"Who?"

"James Kenedy."

"As far as I know he has not seen Dora."

"I thought that maybe that was why I tried to kill him."

"You didn't."

"What?"

"Try to kill him."

"I should have." Wyatt Earp looked helplessly around him, his brain, his reactions soaked with whiskey. "Have you seen her?"

"Dora?"

He nodded.

"She's fine," I said.

He kept nodding, unable to get his head back under control. "I want to see her," he said. "Where is she?"

"Backstage."

Wyatt Earp stumbled toward the curtain and almost fell.

I grabbed his arm to steady him. "You can't, Wyatt," I told him. "Not right now. It wouldn't be a wise thing for you to do."

"Why not?"

He waited for an answer. Then he answered it for himself. "Dora doesn't want to see me, does she?"

I thought about lying to him, but did not see any reason to. "No," I said, which I figured was simple enough for him to understand in his soused condition.

"I still love her, Brady."

"She knows that."

"She can't know that."

"I told her."

"You can't tell her like I can tell her, an', hell, she won't listen to you anyway, dammit. I'm the one that loves her, not you."

"It's been too long now, Wyatt."

He sighed and closed his eyes. For a moment I thought he was asleep. Then he said, "Dora doesn't love me anymore, does she?"

"You're part of her past, Wyatt," I said as gently as I knew how. "Dora is afraid of her past."

"She was almost my wife, Brady."

"Almost, but not quite."

"She should have been."

Wyatt Earp slumped against the wall, his revolver falling with a dull thud to the floor beside him. He tried to pick it up, his stiff fingers groping awkwardly in the darkness, and dropped it again. He looked as though he were about to start crying. I walked quickly away. If he cried, I did not want to know about it, nor would he want me to know about it. There were some things a man preferred to do in private, and this was one of them.

The curtain was late. It rose at three minutes after seven

o'clock, just when the crowd was beginning to grow restless, especially those who had already been waiting with great expectations for almost two hours, and for the next twelve minutes, seven dancing girls, their heavily painted faces a golden hue in the spotlight, showed off their long and naked legs for the first time, just a peek here and a flash of flesh there, but enough to make the cowboys know they had spent their hard-earned nickels wisely and for a good cause. I had seen lovelier faces in my time. I may have been the only one in the crowd to notice.

Eddie Foy was a master showman. He never sang alone. There was always at least one comely young lady on the stage with him, and she usually wore just enough to say she was wearing something, including a bashful smile as though her bare skin was being touched by other men's eyes for the first time, which made the other men feel as though they had ventured somewhere no one had ever gone before. Most of them were in love, or trying to get that way, and not even a heavy dose of whiskey could dim their sinful eyes.

Eddie Foy was out front, and he was saying, "Old Luther had a mule that balked on him, and the mule was sick, and old Luther was afraid the damned old mule was going to die. He called out the horse doctor, and the horse doctor poured a flask full of powder down the mule, and the mule was on his feet in a flash, kicking and jumping, and he was off down the road in a dead run.

"Old Luther turned around to the horse doctor and said, 'How much did that medicine cost?'

"And the horse doctor said, 'Fifteen cents.'

"And Old Luther told him, 'Well, give me two bits' worth, 'cause I gotta catch that mule.'"

He left the cowboys laughing.

The lovely Dora Hand brought a tear to their eyes. Her voice was as clear, as rich, as a silver bell on a cold, winter night. She sang of a home she had lost, a man she had lost, a family she would never see again, a child's voice she would never hear again, a life that had grimly passed her by and left her to face the morning alone.

Her heart was broken into enough pieces for every cowboy in the place to hold a fragment in his hand.

She was breaking every heart in the Comique Theater.

Wyatt Earp felt his heart being stomped on.

He pulled himself to his feet, blinked once or twice in a futile effort to clear his eyes and chase the cobwebs out of his brain, and crawled on his hands and knees up the steep stairway that led from the orchestra pit to the stage. Mesmerized, he reached out for the lovely Dora Hand, but she was too far away for him to touch her, and Wyatt Earp stood again, staggering across the planks with short, uneven, and uneasy steps.

The lovely Dora Hand was locked in the footlights, and every eye in the Comique was fastened on her, and every drover who had ever loved and lost, which was every drover in the place, was wishing to God he had one chance, even if it was his last one, to wipe away the hot tears that were streaming down her face.

Wyatt Earp was trying to free himself from the shadows as though he were a fly breaking loose from a rotten spider web, nothing more than a dark figure, the silhouette of a crooked-legged scarecrow emerging ever so slowly, ever so unsteadily, from a frayed cloak of darkness.

The lovely Dora Hand saw him out of the corner of her eye about the same time the big cowboy with a knife scar across the bridge of his nose came riding hell-for-leather into the theater.

He was yelling, the horse snorting.

He had a bellyful of borrowed courage. The horse was frantically stomping and screaming, doing his damnedest to

shake the bar bit from his mouth and tear away from his
rider, scared and skittish and not the least bit afraid to
admit it.

The piano player played on, never missed a note.

The song got caught in Dora Hand's throat, along with a
sudden shrill cry that sounded as if it came from a startled,
then frightened, animal.

The cowboy with the knife scar was waving a revolver
high over his head, an odd grin slashed across his face.

The horse reared back on his hind legs, fighting the air in
a maddened frenzy.

Wyatt Earp lunged for Dora Hand.

She screamed louder. And again.

The cowboy fired twice. Then again.

Wyatt Earp stumbled and pitched forward, falling face
down on the planks so recently adorned by the dancing girls
with naked legs.

The horse wheeled around and bolted out the door, the
cowboy firing again, this time over his shoulder, as the
distraught and distracted genteel of Dodge began fighting
and pushing and elbowing their way first one way, then
another, trying desperately to escape, though not quite sure
which way to run and trying to run in all directions at once.

Only one man in the Comique was carrying a weapon,
and he lay unconscious, maybe dead, on the stage.

The piano player was hunkered over the keys now,
pounding them faster and harder, a piece of one song, a bit
of another, an arpeggio that he made up as he went along,
chewing his gum harder and faster to keep time with the
music, never bothering to look up, hardly daring to move.
He had seen a piano player in a bar break and run during a
brawl one night, and the bullet had caught him just before he
jumped through a window and killed him before he hit the

floor. He kept playing and would have whistled as well if he had known the song he was beating out on the piano.

The lovely Dora Hand stood above the fallen Wyatt Earp, staring down at him, her hand covering her mouth, afraid to breathe, afraid to move. The Texas Songbird had lost her song and damn near her life. She made a frantic effort to scream. It was only a whimper and not a very good one at that.

I had leapt onstage, grabbed the lawman's Smith & Wesson, and was shoving my way down the aisle, battling to reach the front door of the Comique.

"Take care of him," I had yelled to the lovely Dora Hand.

She did not move. Perhaps she wanted to. Perhaps she couldn't.

I broke free of the teeming mass of frightened humanity, suddenly as uncivilized and selfish and unrestrained as a cattle stampede in a thunderstorm, driven crazy by the lightning and wild by the smell of burning sulfur, and stumbled into the street.

The fleeing cowboy had reached the plaza, cruelly cutting the flanks of his horse with a quill-tipped quirt, leaning low across the saddle, his face whipped savagely by the sorrel mane. Another fifty yards, and he would be gone and out of sight, just another rider in the night, heading out of town, whipping a good horse and riding fast, not a totally unusual sight for Dodge. Another twenty yards, and he would be out of pistol range. I kept waiting for someone to shoot, then figured it might as well be me. The rest of the guns in town were locked up in cell number one.

I shot once without taking a bead and heard the bullet ricocheting off the sign above Albert Hagerty's mercantile and careening from one side of the street to the other. There was no time to take aim. I shot a second time. Then a third, although I don't particularly know why. I didn't expect to hit

anything, but I had a revolver in my hand, and there was
nothing else I could do with it. It felt as heavy as my belly
blaster and nearly as deadly. I'm not so sure I could have
held it steady enough to do any damage with both hands.

Suddenly, without any warning, the horse reared and
pitched backward, throwing the cowboy to the ground. He
tried to stand, but his legs would no longer support him. He
took one step, then two, dancing with death, then crumpled
to the dirt ruts worn deep by wagon wheels and longhorn
cattle.

I ran toward him, wondering if I would have to shoot
again.

He lay motionless in the moonlight. His eyes were open,
but they did not see me. They were staring at the moon,
which hung like a silver dollar just above the top of the
Dodge House. He was fighting to hold his eyes open. If he
went to sleep, he would die. Nobody had ever told him that,
but it made sense at the time. The front of his shirt was wet
and soggy, and the cowboy knew it wasn't his sweat. So he
stared hard at the moon. As long as he could see it, he wasn't
dead. Not yet. And that was always a good sign.

Out of the shadows walked a familiar figure, lanky and
rawboned, his shoulders bent, his beard black and stuck to
his face like a prickly pear. He was as thin as an army
carbine, dragging a shovel along behind him.

Charley Moseby jammed the heel of a cracked boot on
the cowboy's neck, slowly feeding two shells back into the
rusty chamber of Ike Rigby's ancient shotgun. The beard
was longer and thicker than I had remembered, and his face
a little more drawn. Charley Moseby looked like he had
been hanging on to the back seat of hard times and finally
fallen off. He didn't die, so he came tramping back to
Dodge, although some I know would have sworn that death
was a preferable way to go.

From all appearances, the cowboy was on the verge of finding out. Blood was leaking out of his chest. He kept clawing at the wound as though surprised that anything had happened to him. His eyes never left the moon. It was turning yellow, and he wondered if the moon always turned yellow before somebody died.

I tore the faded blue bandana off his neck and pressed it hard against the wound to staunch the flow of blood. It spurted every time his heart beat, and his heart was beating faster than normal. The cowboy coughed, and his shoulders trembled. Pain will do that to even the strongest of men. Very few are as strong as they bragged about being when they contemplate dying, wishing they at least had the chance to face their Maker stone-cold sober. If the cowboy hung on until morning, he might very well get his wish. The whiskey was oozing out of his body, like the blood, with every drop of sweat that bathed his feverish face.

"You hit him," I asked Charley Moseby, "or did I?"

"You ever fire a revolver before?" he wanted to know.

"Only across a table once or twice. Never at that distance."

"You almost hit me twice," he said, "but you didn't come close enough to the cowboy to even put a good scare in him."

I nodded and knelt beside the hired gun. "I didn't know you were that good a shot, Charley," I said.

"I just fired off both barrels, and he ran into the buckshot," he replied.

"Why'd you shoot him?" I wanted to know.

"For whatever reason you were tryin' to knock him down," he answered. "Hell, if you was mad at him, I figured I was, too. Besides, I decided if I didn't stop him, you might be lucky or unlucky and blow my fool head off with the next shot."

Charley Moseby removed the cowboy's .45 from his holster, then asked, "What'd he do anyway?"

"He shot Wyatt."

Charley Moseby glanced over my shoulder before replying, "Hell, Hawkes, he ain't no better shot than you are."

I looked up as the feeble-footed, sodden Wyatt Earp staggered down the street toward us. The bullets had not done him near as much harm as the whiskey. If any of the slugs were embedded in him at all, he would not be aware he was dead or dying until he sobered up, which meant he might live forever. Even from a block away, his breath was as strong as coal oil, and his eyes were as glazed as the cowboy's.

Luke Short rushed from the Long Branch and reached us first. He grabbed the cowboy's hair and lifted his face out of the dirt, nodding as though it was someone he had seen before.

"Got any idea who it is?" I asked.

"Cowboy named Hoyt. George Hoyt," he answered. "Worked the Diamond D down in Williamson County, Texas. He had been in the saloon earlier looking for Wyatt."

"He found him."

"Didn't do him any good, did it?"

I shook my head in the negative.

"He dead?" Wyatt Earp asked, hanging on to Charley Moseby to keep from falling.

"No, but he's mighty uncomfortable at the moment," the gravedigger said.

"I shoot him?" the lawman asked.

"No, but if that horse of his hadn't reared when he did inside the theater," I said, looking straight at the disheveled figure of Wyatt Earp, "Mr. George Hoyt could have well been over with James Kenedy right now, toasting your bad

health with a glass of brandy and collecting his two-
thousand-dollar bounty."

"How come I didn't shoot him?" Wyatt asked. He had not
heard a word I said.

"You couldn't see him," I said, irritated.

"Sneaky little bastard, wasn't he," Wyatt Earp replied. He
tried twice to return his pistol to its holster before he
realized he wasn't holding a pistol.

"What are you gonna do about it, Wyatt?" Luke Short
asked.

"Well, if George Hoyt here lives long enough, I guess
we'll stick him in jail for a while and charge him with
discharging a firearm in a public place."

"What about attempted murder?" I wanted to know.

"I don't remember much about that," he said, "but I been
feelin' around, an' I ain't felt nothin' that feels like pain, so
I don't think he put any bullets in me. Hell, I don't think the
poor sonuvabitch came close enough to hitting me to call it
attempted murder. Disturbin' the peace maybe, but not
attempted murder."

"What about James Kenedy?" Luke Short asked.

"What about him?"

"He's the one that put the price on your head."

Wyatt Earp removed his hat and wiped the sweat from his
forehead. He thought for a moment, then said, "Near as I
can tell, there ain't no law against offerin' the bounty, only
collectin' it."

The cowboy coughed again. There were flecks of blood
in the spittle on his lips.

"He gonna make it?" Charley Moseby asked.

"It ain't up to me," Wyatt Earp said, staggering back
down the street.

Luke Short and I carried the cowboy into the Long
Branch and laid him across the bar, throwing away the

soggy bandana and shoving a rag into the hole that Charley Moseby's buckshot had carved in his chest, trying to stop or at least slow down the flow of blood. George Hoyt was still breathing when Doc Ferguson arrived and still alive when the doc left. The doc did not leave many that way. He was a lot better with horses and cattle than he was with people.

♠

♥ 26 ♦

♣

Wyatt Earp slumped in a chair behind the bar of the Long Branch, his head resting against the old upright piano, his eyes hollow and as yellow as the moon outside. At first glance, he looked to be in as bad a shape as George Hoyt, maybe worse. The cowboy did manage a soulful groan from time to time. Wyatt Earp was dead to world, which, he said, was the best way he knew to forget the lovely Dora Hand. Sleep blotted away thoughts that were better left alone, but George Hoyt could not sleep. His mistakes were burning like buckshot in his chest.

"Hell, Dora Hand's gotten rid of me," Wyatt Earp had said, his tongue thick, his mouth like cotton still full of seeds. "I might as well get rid of her. She ain't nothin' but a memory anyway, a good memory turned bad and gettin' worse ever' time I think of her."

We left him alone to wallow in his own misery, which was one quality mankind had learned to muster at an early age.

George Hoyt had taken his shot at Wyatt Earp and missed. The lawman might not be so fortunate next time. Drunks don't make particularly difficult targets.

At the moment, I wasn't so sure Wyatt Earp cared whether or not he ever woke up. Some hired gun would be more than pleased to oblige him. Luke Short said he would keep an eye on the lawman, who wasn't in no condition to uphold the law or keep the peace, but he wore the badge. Two thousand dollars, however, would fit in his pocket as easily as it would anybody else's.

I walked with Charley Moseby back down to the depot to pick up the cardboard suitcase that held his only change of clothes, an extra box of shotgun shells, and little else. The night was darker than usual. A yellow moon was stingy with its light. The Comique Theater lay silent. Nothing clears the streets like a good shooting. Eddie Foy had vowed to Mayor Dog Kelley that he would not let one minor incident spoil his visit to Dodge, but he had quietly checked the railroad schedule to determine how quickly the next train would be arriving in town. He planned to be on it while those naked dancing legs around him were still able to dance and he could still clear his throat without coughing up the spent remains of a bullet. The Comique might well lie silent for a long time. Only the dead line was in an uproar. The dead line did not yet know about the shooting. It had too many other things on its mind.

"Frankly, I never thought I'd see you again," I told the gravedigger. "I figured you had gone back to Texas for good."

"That was my intention."

"Something must have changed your mind."

"Fort Griffin did."

"Surely it hasn't gotten too rough for you."

"Fort Griffin's wastin' away to nothin'," he answered. "There ain't hardly enough people left for a good two-man poker game, and not enough money for either one of 'em to have an ante. The buffalo hunters are gone, but so are the buffalo. The old folks are movin' away or dyin' off, an' the new folks don't stop there anymore. Old Ben Carson ran out of whiskey. The good-lookin' whores all got married when a wagonload of Bible thumpers stayed around long enough to fill their barrels with water before headin' on out West. Three of 'em married the preacher man, who said it was legal and had the Scriptures to prove it, although I think he wrote some of 'em himself. The preacher man said he could turn 'em all into virgins again, as pure as the driven snow, but I don't really think that's what he had on his mind."

"What'd your wife think about your leavin' again?" I asked him.

"Which one?"

"The one in Fort Griffin."

"She kind of encouraged it." Charley Moseby paused long enough to make sure the knot was tied tightly in the rope that held his suitcase together. "What she said was, she'd take that shotgun away from me and blow me plumb to Buffalo Gap if I wasn't gone by mornin'."

"She found out about the wife in Buffalo Gap?" I guessed.

"She did."

"And she didn't like it."

"Not at all. Wives are real funny that way."

"What'd the wife in Buffalo Gap have to say about it?"

"She had her own shotgun."

"She know how to use it?"

"She did the first time she became a widow."

I shook my head and filled my voice with as much compassion as I could muster. "It's a terrible thing when love falls apart," I told him.

"Broken hearts ain't so bad," Charley Moseby said, "unless they're broken up by a shotgun blast."

That's what I always liked about Charley Moseby.

He understood life. It was never really bad because he had never really expected it to be any good in the first place, and the great thing about a new day was it got rid of the old one and usually just in time.

"You got a place to stay?" I asked him.

"These saloons still stay open all night?" he wanted to know.

I nodded.

"Then I got a place to stay."

"Saloons don't have very good bathing facilities," I said. "And the creek's running dry. It's mostly mud."

"There's just some things you don't have to do when you're not married anymore," he said.

When I first heard the noise, I wasn't quite sure what it was. Down beside the depot, the cattle were milling around in their pens, more restless than was customary this time of night, and they almost drowned out the sharp crack that so rudely disturbed the peace normally reserved for the midnight hour.

It was hollow. Almost an echo. Not in town, but on the edge of town. It was not an entirely unfamiliar sound.

"Somebody's been shot," I said.

"Wyatt?"

"Not unless he's out roaming some back street where he's got no business being."

Charley Moseby sighed heavily. "Then it's probably Wyatt," he said. "I knew I'd have to dig his grave sooner or later." The rope broke and he dropped his suitcase. He ignored it. "Where do you reckon it came from?"

There was only one dwelling in the direction from where the faraway crack of the gunshot had originated. It was large and imposing, two stories with gables, a white stone fireplace rising regally on each side, and six Corinthian columns lined up across the wide front veranda.

Only one man in Dodge could afford it, Mayor Dog Kelley.

I ran down the street, across the bridge that arched over Fried Biscuit Creek, through a stand of scrub oaks, and down a grassy lane that led to the mayor's manor.

I heard the screams before I arrived.

Sarah Jane was still screaming hysterically when I got there, standing beside the back door, her face awash with tears, shaking uncontrollably. She was frantically waving her arms, trying hard to talk, but all she could manage were screams, piercing wails that cut like a dagger.

I grabbed her shoulders and shook her, gently at first, then more vigorously. Sarah Jane was crying so hard she could barely catch her breath, gasping for air, pounding her tiny, clenched fists against my chest.

"Calm down," I whispered.

She couldn't.

"What happened?"

She tried to tell me. But no words escaped from her mouth. Only her eyes had something to say, and her eyes had witnessed one death too many, and death was about the only intruder who dared venture into the house of a man who enough wealth to keep everyone and everything else away.

Sarah Jane took my hand and led me quickly into the house and up the stairs. She was mumbling something I could not understand, but it sounded like a prayer, Thy kingdom come, Thy will be done . . . forgive us this day . . .

The bedroom door had been left open, and I saw her lying there, her face pale and translucent in the tattered splinter of yellow moonlight that spilled upon her lace and satin pillow. She appeared to be so calm, so restful. A faint smile lay upon her lips.

Her song had been silenced. For now. And for good.

The lovely Dora Hand was quite dead, a gaping bullet wound just below her throat, the goose-down mattress beneath her soaked with blood, still wet, still glistening in the frail light.

Eddie Foy sat crying on the floor beside her, his pudgy, pink face swollen and streaked with tears. Maybe they were real. Maybe he was merely an actor. Maybe an actor had a greater reservoir of emotion and was more willing to let it spill over than was the common man.

I looked immediately to see if he still had the gun on him, but his pudgy pink hands were empty, trembling but empty.

Sarah Jane had fainted in the hallway, lying in a twisted heap, by the time Charley Moseby trotted into the room. He looked at the bed, then at Eddie Foy, finally at me.

"It's her, isn't it?" he said.

I nodded.

"Jesus Christ," he said.

And he crossed himself.

♠

♥ 27 ♦

♣

Wyatt Earp awoke in jail just as the tattered threads of an early sunrise crept between the bars and fell across his bunk. The light hurt his eyes, stabbing them like a thin-bladed knife, but they weren't throbbing with nearly as much pain as his head, which felt as if it was ready to fall off, and the lawman was a little disappointed when it didn't. His back ached as though he had been shot at and missed, then ran over by a runaway horse and hit. His belly was a cauldron of hot grease, and the bile was sour, curdling in his mouth, before he spit it out on the cell floor.

He saw his desk piled high with paper that should have been thrown away weeks ago. He saw his hat hanging on the wall beside his revolver. And it was a mystery to him why he and his accoutrements should be on separate sides of the bars.

That, he decided, would take some deep contemplation. Wyatt Earp leaned back, closed his eyes, and began to contemplate about the good times, wondering why he had never had any, wishing that nightfall would hurry up and reach Dodge so the sun would get the hell out of his eyes.

What he needed was another drink.

But his bottle was as dry as his throat, which scratched like he had swallowed broken glass for supper, and maybe he had, for all he could remember.

In his mind, he kept seeing a beautiful woman who looked twenty-five, but was probably younger, with long black hair twisted around an oval, olive-complexioned face. Her eyes were black and moist, her features soft and delicate. She was wearing white and laughing, and no matter how hard he tried, Wyatt Earp could not decipher the face of the groom.

Sleep eased the pain but not the memory.

Mayor Dog Kelley had returned from Haskell County as soon as word of Dora Hand's death reached him, riding all night, appalled that his city, his dominion, could be responsible for such a heinous deed. Judge Burgendorf had not been surprised. Dodge was merely a town waiting to die anyway, he said.

The sudden shock that slapped Dog Kelley in the face had been replaced by sadness, then anger began to gnaw at his gut the way bad tequila finally shrivels, then kills, the worm trying to crawl to the bottom of the bottle.

By the time Dog Kelley's horse-drawn buggy bounced to a halt in front of his home, he was mad as hell and getting madder with every heavy breath that forced its way out of his lungs. His chest was tight, and the pain came in short bursts. His head was pounding as though someone was standing upon his shoulders and banging a blacksmith's hammer against each temple. He had not slept, and Judge Burgendorf's wine had failed to numb his conscience.

The cold-blooded murder of the lovely Dora Hand must not go unavenged, he swore to Doc Ferguson.

Somebody would have hell to pay. And the payments, by gawd, were due.

Dodge City might have been cursed with misfortune, but Dodge City would find the culprit, have him in custody, and deal with him in a proper, civilized manner before the sun rose even if somebody had to haul the sonuvabitch out to the creek behind the dead line, shoot him, and leave him for the dogs to drag off.

The town could weep for the Texas Songbird later. Now it had a debt to collect.

The grieving, the remorse, the regret could wait until Dodge City laid the lovely Dora Hand to rest, and, by gawd, Mayor Dog Kelley himself would make sure it was the biggest, the saddest, the most expensive funeral in the history of the town even if he had to pay for it himself.

At the moment, Dodge only had one suspect. For Dog Kelley, one was enough.

Wyatt Earp, for whatever reason, had exhibited a strange, impassioned fascination for the woman, as though he had perhaps known her before in another place, another time, although no one who knew was saying for sure.

Wyatt Earp, for whatever reason, had lost all control of his sensibilities. He had been drinking all day and most of the night. He would have made a fool of himself if James Kenedy had called the mayor's bluff in the Comique Theater. Thank God Wyatt Earp's reputation was intact even if the man himself had begun to shrivel up like that worm in the tequila bottle.

He was a wreck of a man.

Something was obviously bothering the city marshal, some sordid secret he had kept embedded down deep inside him.

The widow Judkins said she had seen him crying before Dora Hand's performance.

The genteel of Dodge had watched him try to attack the

Texas Songbird on stage, at least it looked like he was trying to attack her, and most would line up as witnesses for the prosecution if Mayor Dog Kelley had the nerve to drag Wyatt Earp before some reasonable facsimile of a judge. Why, Deacon Cox said, the lawman might have actually killed Dora Hand if that drunk-out-of-his-mind cowboy had not wandered into the Comique Theater on horseback, taking a little target practice at the footlights across the stage. It had been a fortuitous thing for the cowboy to do. Dora Hand might very well owe her life to George Hoyt, although she was only able to borrow a few extra hours before she had been taken from them forever. Deacon Cox knew. He had the best seat in the house.

Luke Short had even heard Wyatt Earp say, "I ought to get rid of her," only minutes after gunfire had erupted in the theater and in the street, and he would testify to the fact, and Luke Short's word would hold up in any court of law convened by Dog Kelley, and the mayor himself was ready to gavel the court in session as soon as he had a suspect in jail.

Dog Kelley deputized a dozen strong men, paid them ten dollars apiece from the coffee of the city's dwindling general fund, armed them with loaded shotguns from the city marshal's own office, and marched them to the Long Branch Saloon where Luke Short had been standing a nervous and tenuous guard.

A man who was asleep and immersed in a drunken stupor had never been difficult to capture and hogtie, and Wyatt Earp was no exception.

He opened his eyes once when he fell off the chair.

The faces were veiled by a queer haze, and their mouths were moving, but their words were only a distant roar. He did not recognize a soul.

Wyatt Earp thought he heard an angel singing but did not recognize the song or the voice either.

And he wallowed his way back down into the dark, comforting abyss of the stupor again.

Wyatt Earp awoke in jail, blinked at the faint, tattered threads of sunlight that jabbed at his swollen eyes like nails in a coffin, and had no idea where he was, how he had gotten there or what he was doing behind bars. There was no one around to tell him, or ease the throbbing pain in his temple, and he could not go ask anybody. The chains around his legs had been manacled to the bars in the window, and his ankles were already raw and bleeding. He tried to wipe the sleep out of his eyes, but his hands were cuffed to the chains, and there was a sharp pain in his right side as though somebody had rammed the toe of a boot between his seventh and eighth rib.

Wyatt Earp smelled something dead or maybe rotting in the August sun and almost threw up until he realized it was his own breath.

He had dreamed about old Fraley last night. And now he knew why. He lay back down on the bunk and waited in what was left of his drunken stupor for Judge Isaac Parker to come and hang him.

His sigh was hoarse and one of curious relief. At least it would be done right.

Wyatt Earp had the capacity to do a lot of things, not all of them particularly legal or moral or even defensible, but killing the lovely Dora Hand was certainly not one of them.

He did not possess a lot of love to give away. But what he had, she had gotten it all.

Now Dog Kelley was ready to try, convict, and execute Wyatt Earp before breakfast, if possible, for a murder that none of us who thought we knew him believed he was capable of committing. But when the mayor made his mind up, bowed his back and dug his heels in the ground, he no longer sought nor listened to reason. He was not particularly interested in guilt or innocence or even justice, only vindication for his town, which was already the most corrupt, depraved, and wicked trail town between Texas and Chicago. It was bad enough, the mayor believed, for a half-drunk drover to meet his Maker on Dodge City soil. It was downright licentious to lose the Texas Songbird before she had finished her song. Any hint of culture would take the long road or the wrong road before it ever took the main road to Dodge City again. Dog Kelley was sure of it. And he was incensed by the unfairness of it all.

"Where were you last night?" I asked Wyatt Earp when the self-imposed fog began to clear from his bloodshot eyes.

"I don't remember," he mumbled.

"It's important that you know exactly where you were and what you were doing and the time you were doing it," I told him.

"I don't even remember last night," he answered, his voice scratchy. He looked again at the chains that bound his hands and feet, glanced up with a drawn face and asked, "What the hell did I do to be locked away like this?"

"Nobody's told you?"

"You're the first soul I've seen all morning, Hawkes, and I'm not seein' you too well at the moment."

I studied his face. If there was anything in his eyes to read, it sure did not show.

"It's Dora," I said.

"What happened to her?" There was a sudden strain in his voice.

"She's dead."

Wyatt Earp's lips moved. He made no sound.

"She was murdered," I said.

He turned his face and buried it against the thick wall made from mud and wheat straw. His bloodless features were twisted in pain and agony. "Hawkes?" he whispered.

"What is it, Wyatt?"

"Did I do it?"

"Did you?"

"God, all I remember is her singing, then she wasn't singing anymore."

I left Wyatt Earp lying in his chains and confusion, a man in ruin, stopping beside the city marshal's desk where Luke Short sat cradling a long-barreled shotgun like a long-legged woman in his arms. His face was veiled by cigar smoke, and his eyes were flecked with red streaks from an obvious lack of sleep.

"I don't think Wyatt killed her," I said.

"He had every reason to," Luke Short replied.

"He had every reason not to."

Luke Short shrugged as though it did not make any difference to him either way. He exhaled another cloud of pungent smoke, tossing an unspent shotgun shell into the air and catching it. Wyatt Earp's badge hung crookedly on his vest. Luke Short was having a difficult time staying awake, but he was definitely the man in charge.

"When I left Wyatt last night, he had passed out in your saloon," I continued.

"Dead to the world, he was."

"I thought you were going to keep an eye on him."

"Wyatt don't pay me to protect him, just to pour whiskey down him."

"You do a damn good job of it, Luke."

"It keeps me in business."

I sat down on the edge of the desk, reached out, and

intercepted the shotgun shell Luke Short had tossed above his head. "You knew Wyatt Earp was the target of every gun in town," I said.

"That's what I've been told."

"Leaving him alone in the drunken condition he was in was like sentencing him to death."

Luke Short grinned coldly. "That's something I didn't have to do, Hawkes," he said.

"What do you mean?"

"Wyatt sentenced his own self to death when he stuck that pistol against Dora Hand's throat and pulled the trigger."

"Nobody's proved it."

His grin grew wider and colder. "Nobody's proved he didn't either," he said.

Luke Short had never spoken a greater truth.

It was another typical August day staring down on the sun-blistered fields of Kansas. The sun seemed closer than usual, and there were no clouds to spoil a deep blue sky that stretched out in all directions as far as the eye could see. The wind had come early and left early. August had never particularly liked Kansas.

Amos Fielding had fled the heat, the crops that would not grow regardless of how rich the soil might be, a well gone dry, and a sick mule that was too lazy to die. Most of all, he had fled the demands of Emma Judkins. She was a good woman, a strong and handsome woman, a Christian woman who could quote the Good Book from cover to cover and even understand what some of the Scriptures were talking about. But she was a woman, and spending the winter with her had caused Amos Fielding to remember why he had run away from his first wife and joined the army. Facing the Confederates at Shiloh, then the Apaches at Big Springs Run, had been a picnic by comparison. His first wife would have killed him by now, and he had left Emma Judkins considering the possibility.

He was sitting alone in the Alhambra Saloon, nursing the long, dusty neck of a bottle that held something akin to tarantula juice when I walked through the batwing doors.

"Hawkes," he called out.

I nodded to him, hoping he would not offer me a drink. I did not want to either hurt his feelings or wreck what was left of a worn-out stomach.

"Hawkes," he continued, "I thought there was a law in Dodge against totin' anything a man could use to blow the head off somebody else."

"There is. Signs are posted on every building in town."

"Then James Kenedy can't read."

"What makes you say that?"

Amos Fielding took another swig, sucking the bottle dry, before answering. "When I ran into him night before last, he was coming out of the Dodge House wearing two forty-four revolvers, and he had a Bowie knife a foot long stuck in his belt."

"Wyatt relieved him of those revolvers once."

"He either got 'em back or got himself a couple of new ones." Amos Fielding held the bottle up to the light to see how much bug juice, if any, was still left. "They ain't that hard to find, you know. A drover had just as soon sell his guns before he gets here as given 'em up when he rides into town."

It made sense.

"I don't think Kenedy was wearing those forty-fours because he thought they were pretty," Amos Fielding continued.

"He's had a hook in his craw ever since he hit Dodge," I answered. "He's got a rich daddy and thinks that places him a notch or two above the rest of you."

"His rear end stinks just like everybody else's."

"I try not to get close enough to find out."

Amos Fielding chuckled, banging the mouth of the bottle against his palm, trying to coax out that last drop or two of bug juice that had thus far eluded him. "Who're you scrappin' with? I asked Kenedy, and he said he wasn't lookin' for a fight. He said he was in town to kill somebody."

"Wyatt Earp, no doubt."

"Maybe."

"He's already tried twice."

"Some people ain't smart enough to know when they're whipped."

"Maybe James Kenedy decided to collect his two-thousand-dollar reward himself."

"Maybe," Amos Fielding said again. "Then again, he may be mad at a whole bunch of people. Some of 'em, he even thinks he can whip. Don't nobody with a rich daddy ever go to jail anyway."

I found Deacon Cox behind the front desk of the Dodge House. He had his sleeves rolled up and was trying to rub the scattered burn marks out of the mahogany escritoire where he kept his financial records. He scowled when he saw me.

"You ain't got enough money, Hawkes," he said.

"For what?"

"For a room here."

"I'm not looking for a room here," I said calmly. "I'm sensitive to smoke, you see."

The scowl deepened. "Get the hell out," he said.

"I will," I said, "as soon as I locate James Kenedy."

"He's not here."

"He is still registered here, I presume."

"Not since this morning." Deacon Cox pounded a heavy fist on the front desk. "The sonuvabitch left, and he still owes me a week's rent."

"He must have been in an awful big hurry."

Deacon Cox leaned back and folded his arms. Weariness replaced the scowl on his face. "He woke me up when I heard him running down the stairs about an hour before daybreak. I hollered at him. But he didn't say a word or even acknowledge I had followed him out on the front porch. He had his clothes under his arm, his saddlebag thrown over his shoulder, and the last time I saw James Kenedy, he was ridin' hell bent for leather back to Texas on that new horse of his." He paused to catch his breath, then added, "His daddy ain't gonna like what he did."

"No," I replied. "I don't think he will."

"Mifflin Kenedy never ran out on an unpaid bill in his life."

"From what I've heard," I said, "Mifflin Kenedy never ran in his life."

"You heard right."

Deacon Cox turned back to the escritoire, and I walked away, wondering why the facts did not add up.

James Kenedy was wearing a revolver, two of them, even though he knew damn well it was illegal in Dodge. That did not surprise me. He had departed Dodge in the dead of night. That did. And why had he bought a new horse? His daddy had the finest horse in all of Texas.

Dora Hand was dead.

Wyatt Earp was the only suspect.

Dog Kelley wanted to hang him as soon as he could find a new rope.

But James Kenedy was the man acting suspicious. He was the man on the run. Yet, as far I knew, James Kenedy had never met the lovely Dora Hand, only heard her sing, and he did not hear much of that.

Little David Little woke up when the sun did every morning. It was his job. The horses depended on him. Little David Little was spreading new hay in the stalls when I reached the livery stable, gnawing on a slice of beef jerky and remembering when he did not have that much to eat for breakfast.

"Mornin', Mr. Hawkes," he said between bites.

"I see you're up early," I told him.

"Sometimes I don't even mess with sleeping."

"The horses must take a lot of your time."

"The horses do just fine, Mr. Hawks," Little Dave Little said, jabbing his pitchfork into a fresh pile of hay. "They ain't no trouble at all. They just stand here and eat and shit and swat flies. Their owners, though, they ain't got no sense of time at all."

"Would James Kenedy be one of them?"

A curious smile played across the boy's face. "How'd you know that, Mr. Hawkes."

I winked at him. We all had our secrets. Gamblers just kept their secrets to themselves.

"Mr. Kenedy was down here this mornin', an' me an' the horses were tryin' to get a little shut-eye, an' he came in here like a mad bull with a thorn up his ass." Little David Little suddenly remembered what few manners he had learned in his short life and offered to cut me off a chunk of his jerky. I refused. "It was still dark," he said. "The moon hadn't even come out, an' he grabbed me by the neck and threw me into the stall, demandin' I saddle up that new horse he got—"

"When did he get the horse?" I interrupted.

"Early this week." He grinned in admiration. "It was a helluva horse, Mr. Hawkes."

"What kind?"

"Big thoroughbred, I think it was. A race horse anyway, that's what it was. Solid black with one white foot and a white scar on his forehead."

"What in the world did James Kenedy need with a race horse?"

"I don't think he wanted anybody to catch him."

"Who was he running from?"

"I didn't see nobody chasin' him."

"What was he running from?"

"Beats me." Little David Little shrugged, scratching the carbuncle on his neck. "If a man's got enough money to buy a high-dollar race horse, I didn't think he had to run, unless there was a woman he was tryin' to get away from."

I walked back out into the sunshine, and the boy followed. "Where was Kennedy headed?" I wanted to know.

"I didn't ask him, an' he didn't tell me."

"Was he alone?"

"Hell, yes, he was alone," Little David Little said, squinting as he looked into the sun. "There ain't no other horse around here that could keep up with him."

"Thanks, son."

"You bet, Mr. Hawkes."

I pitched him a fifty-cent piece.

"What's that for?"

"If a man loses sleep, he needs to be paid for it."

Little David Little stood admiring the slab of silver in his hand. "I sure wish Mr. James Kenedy had knowed that," he said.

He was whistling when he returned to the pile of hay. I had not felt like whistling in a long time.

The facts were there, staring back at me, but still they did not add up, or maybe I was just not smart enough to add them up.

Becky Porter was sitting at the back table of the Alhambra, her head in her hands, her frail shoulders shaking as though she were crying. She had not seemed particularly anxious to see me for days. She would not answer her door when I knocked. She turned away when she saw me. Becky Porter was tired of being temporary, and I figured I would be temporary for the rest of my life, such as it was. On that morning, she appeared to be so lost, so alone. She looked like she needed a friend, even if she no longer cared to be in his company.

I sat down beside her. She did not notice. I gently placed a finger under Becky Porter's chin and tilted her face toward me, sickened at what I saw. Her right eye was black and almost swollen shut. Her cheeks were puffy and bruised. I could almost see the marks a closed fist had made, the marks she had felt, and a new rage boiled inside my gut.

"What happened, Becky?" I asked softly.

"Just the risk of the trade, I guess." She choked back a sob.

"Who did it to you?"

"It doesn't matter."

"It damn well matters to me."

Becky Porter lowered her eyes. The guilt she felt was worse than the pain. The scars would heal long before the grieving, which would haunt her forever.

"Who did this to you?" I asked again, taking her hands in mine.

"He busted into my room sometime after midnight," she answered, her voice dull and lifeless. "I was asleep, and he threw me like a rag doll from one side of the room to the other. That's all he wanted, to hurt somebody."

"Who busted into your room?"

The tears came, then the sobs, wrenched from deep inside her. "All he wanted to do was hit me. I tried to fight him off, but he wouldn't stop. I never saw a man in my life burnt up with that much hatred. All he could talk about was killing somebody. I thought he was talkin' about me, but he wasn't. He just wanted to hurt me or anybody he could get his hands on, and I happened to be handy. He was crazy, Brady, a crazy man who wanted to kill somebody."

"Give me a name, Becky."

She cried until the tears would not come anymore, then whispered, "James Kenedy's who it was, Brady. A crazy man who wanted to kill somebody."

"He succeeded, Becky."

"What?" Her hand shot to her face, and her eyes were suddenly wide with fear and aflame with apprehension.

"Dora Hand's dead."

Her eyes grew cloudy. The fear was erased from her face, supplanted by a look of disbelief and confusion. "Why Dora Hand?" she asked.

"I have no idea."

"I doubt if James Kenedy even knew Dora Hand."

"That doesn't keep her from being dead."

Becky Porter sadly shook her head, lost again in a savage whirlwind of bewilderment. "James Kenedy was after Mayor Kelley," she whispered.

Damn. The facts had been there all along. They suddenly added up.

Mayor Dog Kelley was leaning against the bars of Wyatt Earp's cell, his arms folded defiantly, a smug look etched on his face. "I've already rounded up a jury," he was saying. "Since there's no judge in town, the mayor will preside. Near as I can tell, I've got that right. I hired you to keep the peace in this town, not destroy it, so it's gonna go hard against you, Wyatt. You can either order your last meal now or after the trial. It makes no never mind to me."

Wyatt Earp sat morosely on the bunk, his wrists and ankles bleeding.

"Turn him loose," I said entering the room.

Dog Kelley spun around. His first glance was toward to my hands to make sure they weren't carrying anything capable of hurting him. He relaxed when he saw they were empty. "It'll be a cold day in hell before I do that," he snapped.

"Then hell just had its first snow." I walked straight toward him. "Wyatt Earp did not kill Dora Hand," I said. "Turn him loose, and we'll bring back the man who did."

Dog Kelley eyed me suspiciously, then nervously. "You don't know what you're talkin' about," he told me.

"James Kenedy shot Dora Hand," I said bluntly.

"That's impossible," the mayor snorted. "What did James Kenedy have against Dora Hand?"

"Not a damn thing," I answered, feeling my temper rising.

"Then why the hell would he kill her?"

"Think about it," I answered.

"About what?" He was obviously grasping for answers that lay outside of his reach.

"Where was Dora Hand sleeping last night?"

"She was at my home."

"In whose bed was she sleeping?"

"Mine." Dog Kelley was growing more perplexed now. "You know I had to leave town on business last night after that fiasco in the theater. My bed was the largest and most comfortable. Miss Hand obviously chose to sleep there."

I nodded. "The room was dark, Mr. Mayor," I said. "All James Kenedy saw was a figure asleep in His Honor's bed."

Dog Kelley's eyes narrowed. "What are you trying to say, Hawkes?"

"The bullet that killed Dora Hand was meant for you."

The mayor slumped against the desk, almost falling into Luke Short, still wearing the badge, still holding the shotgun. "You're just guessing, Hawkes."

"It's a damn good guess."

"I don't believe it."

"Who took Kenedy's guns away from him."

"Earp did."

"Who gave Wyatt his orders."

"I did."

"James Kenedy had made his play against Wyatt twice. A third time might cost him his life. He would just pay to have Wyatt taken out. Two thousand dollars was no problem to him. But you, Mr. Mayor? James Kenedy did not consider you a threat. He could take care of you himself. Dora Hand was merely an innocent victim."

I picked the keys up off the desk and walked toward the cell.

"Who knows about Kenedy?" Dog Kelley asked.

"Why?"

"Dodge needs Kenedy cattle and Kenedy money," he said. "Hell, we'll just hang Earp, and it'll all blow over, and, after a while, what happened won't mean anything to anybody."

"It'll mean a helluva lot to Wyatt Earp."

"He's expendable."

I unlocked the cell door, then turned and faced Dog Kelley. "An innocent man has never been expendable," I said. "Keep the cell ready. We'll need it when we get back."

Dog Kelley grabbed Luke Short's arm, and he pointed to me and Wyatt Earp as I turned the key in the lock holding the chains around the lawman's feet. "Don't let 'em get out of here," he said savagely.

"You put me here to guard Wyatt Earp," Luke Short spit out, "not shoot him."

"I'm payin' you good money to follow my orders," the mayor yelled.

"It ain't enough," Luke Short said, throwing the shotgun to the floor, standing up, and walking out of the jail ahead of us.

♠

♥ 28 ♦

♣

We rode out of Dodge while the sun was still tilted high in a turquoise sky, Wyatt Earp, Charley Moseby, and me, heading south toward the frayed makings of a thunderhead that was hanging awkwardly above the tree line like a bad bruise.

James Kenedy had an eight-hour lead, he was riding a race horse, and he had every reason in the world to keep moving, day and night. His was the panic felt only by desperate men. James Kenedy had a murder on his hands, if not his conscience, and not even a trail town with the sordid reputation of Dodge would tolerate the murder of a woman who moved in the higher realms of society.

"If we don't get him before he gets back to Texas, we won't get him at all," Charley Moseby had said. "His daddy'll be waitin' for him on the Texas border, an' his daddy'll have ever' gun he can ridin' with him."

The bowels of Texas were definitely James Kenedy's final place of refuge, perhaps his only place of refuge. But Texas lay four days away if his race horse didn't go lame, and if Little David Little could be believed, and I had no reason to doubt him, James Kenedy was flogging the race horse pretty good when he left town.

Wyatt Earp had poured Luke Short's hot, greasy coffee down his gullet for more than an hour, trying to chase the haze from his eyes and out of his head. A two-day growth of whiskers clung like a grim shadow to his face. His breath still smelled like coal oil, only more deadly. But his hands were steady, and he was no longer wallowing in self-pity. There was no reason to cry for the lovely Dora Hand anymore.

There was no Dora Hand anymore.

James Kenedy had a debt to pay, and Wyatt Earp would be the man to collect it. An eye for an eye. A tooth for a tooth. A life for a life. Vengeance is mine. That's what the Scriptures in the Good Book said, more or less. Those were the only Scriptures Wyatt Earp could quote, the only ones he believed in, the only ones he needed.

If James Kenedy had not done his praying by now, it was too late. God might forgive him, but it was Wyatt Earp who wore the gun.

Charley Moseby had been wrong about his assessment of James Kenedy's triumphant return to Texas. Texas might well be his holy place of refuge. But Wyatt Earp would trail him to hell, if necessary, and generally it always was.

Mifflin Kenedy might well be on the border to protect him.

Charley Moseby could dig two graves as easily as one.

"If he follows the cattle trail, and that seems like the sensible thing for him to do," Wyatt Earp said, "I reckon he'll swing wide along the Plummer and Jones Trail, then ford the Cimarron down near Wagon Bed Springs. From there, he can pick up the Texas Trail and it'll lead him through the Indian Nation. That's the route trail bosses have been takin' ever since they started pushing those damned old longhorns northward. The river's narrow there, fairly predictable and almost always shallow enough to get across without the risk of losin' your horse."

"He's got a big head start on us," Charley Moseby said.

"It doesn't matter."

"How're you gonna catch him?"

"We're gonna get to Wagon Bed Springs before he does."

"You're gonna kill our horses," I told him.

"Maybe."

"Then what the hell are you plannin' on us doin'?" Charley Moseby asked.

"Walk, if that's what it takes," Wyatt Earp said dryly, "then crawl if your feet wear out. But, by gawd, we're gonna camp on the Cimarron before he does."

"We can't make up that much ground," I said. The sweat was beginning to trickle down between my shoulder blades. My skin stung as though I had backed into a bull nettle. The heat was stifling, and it was rising in great, suffocating waves off the plains of dead grass.

"We can if we forget the Plummer and Jones Trail," Wyatt Earp answered.

"An' head straight south?" Charley Moseby wondered.

Wyatt Earp nodded.

"But that's across the desert," I told him.

Wyatt Earp nodded again. "We'll save seventy-five miles goin' that way," he said. "I'm bettin' James Kenedy can't go two days without sleep. He's a rich man. He thinks he's a free man. When he looks back at sundown and doesn't see the dust clouds from running horses behind him, he'll forget to worry about us, and careless men don't last very long in this country."

"It's a hard seventy-five miles," I let him know.

"There are no easy miles."

"The desert has no rivers, no creeks, no wells, no water of any kind," I said. "Nothing but vultures."

"The vultures have to drink somewhere," Wyatt Earp said, undaunted. "Keep your eye on the vultures, and, sooner or later, they'll lead you to water."

"It's probably alkali water," Charley Moseby spit out.

"That's all right. It's wet."

"Alkali water will rust your boilers," Charley Moseby told the lawman.

"Or kill you," I threw in.

"I've seen a kildeer get the wet runs just flyin' over a creek of gyp water," Charley Moseby said.

"It'll keep me alive until I find James Kenedy," Wyatt Earp answered.

"What happens after that?" I wanted to know.

"It depends on who rides away from Wagon Bed Springs, and who's left behind."

Traversing the desert of lost souls was a gamble any time of the year. In August, it was purgatory.

Gambling, though, was what we did best, all except Charley Moseby, and he only came along in case there was a grave to be dug. He was running a little short on hard cash dollars anyway, and James Kenedy should have plenty of them stuffed in his pocket. Charley Moseby would break his back digging in hard rock and go broke if he had to put either me or Wyatt Earp away.

The thunderhead grew darker, ominous and foreboding. A bolt of lightning cut through a purple seam in the cloud. The air around us smelled like dust, nothing but dust kicked up by the horses and a hot wind that burned its way across the land.

There was no reason to try and reason with Wyatt Earp.

His eyes were fixed firmly on the old wagon rut that led toward the desert of lost souls. Many Conestogas had started across the plains of dead grass. The empty prairie that lay far south of Dodge in the Indian Territory was littered with their weathered and rotting skeletons.

The rolling landscape looked so peaceful. It had deceived many a man. And man had become part of the land itself, dust to dust, ashes to ashes.

Darkness came early to the plains of dead grass. The thunderhead, boiling out of the south, a batting of incensed clouds all wadded up and twisted together, torn apart by an angry wind, then stitched back together by lightning, reached up and snatched the sun out of the sky. The evening shadows turned the prairie gray, and the dry grasses crackled beneath us as we rode on toward a rough, treacherous country where the rivers ran dry and not even rattlers left their imprints in the dust. The horses were dancing nervously, as worried about the desert below them as the storm above them.

The belly blaster hung loosely from my saddle horn. Wyatt Earp had a Winchester carbine shoved into a saddle scabbard. And Charley Moseby was carrying a Big Fifty, an old fifty-caliber Sharps rifle. It was long and unwieldy, too heavy for a common man to shoot. But no one doubted its accuracy, and it was deadly from three hundred yards. Most men could not even see three hundred yards. None of them ever saw death coming from that distance. Wyatt Earp had planned to deal with James Kenedy from long range. There was no sense of honor in the anger he felt, no reason to give the killer an even break. Still, it was more of a chance than he had given to lovely Dora Hand, whose face, in death, had found the innocence she had lost.

The wind had picked up. And it smelled like a far-off rain. The lightning fairly crackled, bending low to the ground, bouncing along the grasslands, glowing red, then orange, like fox fire, casting light without shadow on the prairie.

Charley Moseby removed his hat, took a pouch out of his shirt pocket, and began stuffing a handful of aged beeswax inside the crown of his hat. He tossed the pouch to me.

"Lightnin' don't strike beeswax," he said. "Bees leave the flowers by themselves when the lightnin' starts and crowd back around the hive."

"The lightning's getting mighty close." I said, watching the sky grow black, then white, then black again.

"As soon as it starts rattlin' off my horse's ears, I'm gonna throw my gun away."

"You may need it," I replied.

"Not where I'm goin' if the lightnin' gets inside my pants."

His eyes were as nervous as those of his horse. His eyes were as nervous as mine. Only Wyatt Earp rode that night without fear or hesitation. The rain was splashing against his face before he was aware of the storm, and the rain appeared to be dragging the thunderhead clumsily across the prairie toward us. The gully washer kept pounding the earth around us long after the agony was gone from the skies.

"I didn't think it rained much in this country," Charley Moseby said, his head bent low against the wind.

"It doesn't."

He shrugged and pulled the collar of his jacket tighter around his face. "Then this is the damnedest dew I ever saw," he said.

We rode all night, drenched by rain, battered by hail, slogging along without a trail or a star to guide us. The rain fell hard enough to strangle a good-sized frog. It wiped away the skyline, then the prairie itself.

We would have taken shelter. But there was none, not even a tree, not even a dead one. Wyatt Earp was depending solely on his wits and intuition. Buffalo hunters had survived those same rolling grasslands. He figured he could do the same.

The rest of us were depending on Wyatt Earp. He could have led us in circles or straight to hell, and we would have followed without knowing the difference. Maybe he already had.

The night was wet. But it smelled of brimstone.

Long before any likeness of light fought its way onto the plains of dead grass, the rain stopped as quickly as it had begun, and with it went the wind. The clouds rolled back. And steam sizzled off the parched earth.

By morning, the soil was dry. And dust was dancing in the sunshine as though the rain had merely been a bad dream. By noon, it had become a forgotten dream. The heat soaked through our skin, and a wicked sun seared the marrow of our bones. We had drank the rain, even chewed on the hailstones, but had found no water since the skies dried up.

Charley Moseby opened a can of tomatoes and passed it around. We pressed the cool meat of the tomatoes against our blistered lips to moisten them.

Above, there were black dots circling, and they looked a lot like buzzards. They did not appear to be particularly bothered by thirst, only hunger, and they began descending down toward us, waiting, in no hurry, merely content to wait, possessing infinitely more patience than mankind.

Around us were piles of bleached buffalo bones and the rotting carcasses of old Conestoga wagons that had carried the dreams, the hopes, the promises of stubborn and wayward families only as far as the desert of lost souls.

I reined my horse to a halt long enough to unloose my canteen and take a short swig of cool water turned warm.

Wyatt Earp turned in the saddle and looked back at me.

"Don't waste the water," he said. "Right now you're only thirsty. By night, you'll be thinkin' you're gonna die."

"We need to rest the horses," I said.

"We've still got a long way to go."

"If the horses don't get some rest pretty soon, you'll wind up walking to Wagon Bed Springs if you get there at all."

He thought it over a minute, then nodded.

We dismounted and began southward on foot, leading the horses. It looked like we might have to walk to Wagon Bed Springs after all.

"Any of this look familiar?" I asked Wyatt Earp.

"I've never been over this country before."

"You sure we're still headed in the right direction?"

"I'll know for sure when we get there."

"If we get there."

Wyatt Earp tilted his head back and gazed up squinting toward the sun. "We'll get there," he said.

"The question is," I told him, "will we get there before James Kenedy."

"He won't beat us to the springs."

"You're pretty damn sure of yourself."

Wyatt Earp grinned through cracked lips. "James Kenedy is a rich man," he said. "James Kenedy don't have any better sense than to stop and rest his horses."

My back had begun to ache. My feet were finding new places for old blisters. I would have grinned, too, but I no longer felt like it. I just keep putting one foot in front of the other and waiting for the sundown.

It came, and not a minute too soon.

We rode all night, chewing on Indian jerky and corn dodgers to beat back the sharp, biting pangs of hunger that kept gnawing at our stomachs. The jerky was hard, the dodgers burnt. Nobody complained.

And Charley Moseby's old bay horse lay down on him

and died. Thirty minutes later, he would have been drinking the muddy, tepid water of Wagon Bed Springs. Maybe, after all those years and all those miles, it just wasn't worth his trouble.

Wyatt Earp and I walked our weary horses the rest of the way to the Cimarron River, then sat atop a sand bluff above the ford and waited for daylight. The sun had already begun to crease the sky by the time Charley Moseby reached our camp. He was not moving too swiftly or too easily in the sand. He had a Montanta rig saddle slung over his shoulder, grumbling with every step he took, and he had already taken too many to suit him.

"You'd just as soon leave a man to die out here as not," he said to no one in particular.

"You should have took better care of your horse," Wyatt Earp told him.

"He was the oldest damn horse in the pen," Charley Moseby replied.

"And the cheapest."

"I ain't makin' it too good now that you don't let nobody wear their guns in town," Charley Moseby said, unpacking his canteen. "Folks are livin' too damn long, and the longer they live, the hungrier I get, an' the harder it is for me to get by. Your law didn't do a damn thing to help the gravediggers."

He ambled on down toward the Cimarron.

"If I were you," I told him. "I'd go on back to the springs. The water's cleaner there. The river looks pretty muddy."

"It don't make me no never mine," he answered. "Hell, I'm plannin' on drinkin' all of it anyway."

Wyatt Earp and I spent much of the morning checking out both sides of the Cimarron. Most of the tracks we found were our own. There did not appear to be any signs of a rider having forded the river within the past day or two, but tracks in the sand can sometimes be deceiving. The sand is a restless soul, shifting every time the wind changes its mind. A man could walk across in the morning, and by nightfall footprints would be gone, as though no one had ever trod there at all.

Over his shoulder, I glimpsed the faint glimmer of a light flickering in the distance, barely visible on the far side of the draw. As the gray of an early dawn rolled back across the deserted wastelands, we could see a slender thread of smoke curling up from a rock chimney. There was life upon the desert after all and in the oddest of places.

We rode to the dilapidated log cabin, talking loudly amongst ourselves, making plenty of noise, making sure our horses made plenty of noise.

A man who lives isolated on the edge of purgatory does not like to be startled when he is not expecting anyone, especially not in the early morning before his coffee has had time to settle on his stomach. It makes a man angry. And an angry man has a bad habit of shooting first, then going out later to see what he shot at and if he hit it.

The door was cracked open, and someone was watching us. There was no movement, no sound, nothing.

I could not see anyone or anything, with the exception of the dull metal barrel of a carbine looming out of the shadows. It was leveled in our general direction.

"Anybody home?" Wyatt Earp called out.

"Maybe. Maybe not," came the reply. "Who be you?"

"Marshal Wyatt Earp," the lawman said loudly and distinctly.

"Never heard of you," came the reply. The voice was old, cracked.

"I'm from Dodge."

"You're a helluva long way from Dodge."

"May we talk with you a minute?"

"I got plenty of time."

Wyatt Earp started to dismount.

The shot fired over his head stopped him.

"I can hear you just fine from where you're standin'," the voice without a face said. "Don't need you to get any closer."

Wyatt Earp's face was hardened with a growing indignation. He was a dutifully appointed lawman. He expected to be treated that way. "It's against the law to fire on the city marshal of Dodge City, Kansas," he said coldly.

"It ain't against the law around here unless I hit you," the voice said with a cackling laugh. "An' if I don't know you, I'm just as apt to hit you as not. An' if anybody else comes around here, they won't none of 'em give much of a damn, which means your law ran out somewhere 'twixt here and Dodge."

"That's not a very neighborly attitude," I said, trying to keep from ruffling his feathers. If the man was as old as his voice, the finger on the trigger should be getting worn and weary by now. When that happened, he would simply set the carbine down in the corner of his cabin if he trusted us or put a bullet either between us or through us if he didn't.

"It's kept me around for fifty-three years." He laughed again. "Besides, I ain't got no neighbors. Had one once till I caught him stealin' my chickens."

"He move on?" I wanted to know.

"He sure don't steal no chickens no more."

Wyatt Earp got down to business. "Have you seen any rider passing this way in the last day or so?"

The voice became a man, as a thin, stoop-shouldered, white-haired Warren Ward eased through the narrow crack in the doorway and stepped out onto the porch of the cabin. He took a sip from the coffee cup he was holding. "I ain't seen nobody since the Rockin' B cowboys came back through," he said, "an' that must've been a month ago if I been countin' my days right. I measure their feet when they ford the Cimarron, make 'em their boots while they're gone, and they pick 'em up when they ride back through." The old man paused to adjust the wire-rim spectacles that had slid down to the tip of his nose. "Got one pair left over," he said. "A gunfight over a card game, I guess. You can have 'em for seven dollars and thirty-eight cents, as long as you got the correct change. I make boots, but I don't make change."

"The cowboy we're looking for would have been riding alone," I told him.

"What'd he do?"

"Killed a woman."

"He ain't been by here, an' it's damn good thing he hasn't." The laugh was more of a cackle. "He sure wouldn't be killin' no women no more. No, sir."

"You got any more of that coffee?" Wyatt Earp inquired.

"Maybe."

The lawman fished around inside his vest pocket and pulled out a silver dollar. He pitched it onto the porch at the old man's feet. Warren Ward picked it up and looked the coin over closely, spitting on it to make it gleam. A toothless grin stretched across his wrinkled face. "If you got another one of them," he said, "I'll sell you a pair of boots."

"We haven't slept since Thursday," Wyatt Earp said. "Right now I'd rather have the coffee."

We had finished one cup and were working on the second when Charley Moseby came scrambling over the bluff and stumbling down a steep slope that led toward the cabin. "He's on his way," he yelled.

"Kenedy?"

"Hell, all I can see is a little dust kickin' up on the prairie." Charley Moseby was out of breath and wheezing heavily. "The dust ain't got no name, but it looks awful familiar, an' it's headed toward the river, an' he's comin' on the run."

Wyatt Earp pulled an old army spy glass from his saddlebag and trained it in the direction where Charley Moseby had pointed.

The horse was black. A white streak scarred his forehead. His right foreleg was white.

Wyatt Earp did not need to make out the features of the rider, hidden in the midst of a whirlwind of dust. The race between the hunter and the hunted was almost over, and it would end upon the banks of Wagon Bed Springs.

The race horse was worn out, lathered in sweat. His legs gave way, and he stumbled. And James Kenedy, standing tall against the sun, struck him again across his flanks with a leather quirt, urging him toward the Cimarron. Across the river, and he would be within smelling distance of Texas. Across the river, and he would find his sanctuary and home.

Wyatt Earp took the carbine out of his saddle scabbard and cocked it. He knelt on one knee, braced himself against a boulder and took aim toward the whirling dervish of sand, waiting for James Kenedy to ride into range. The lawman was in no hurry. He had watched the vultures and stolen their patience.

James Kenedy was less than two hundred yards away when he apparently saw something that obviously disturbed him a great deal. No one will ever know what it was. The sharp glint of sunlight off a rifle barrel. A shadow that looked out of place or too much like a man. A face. A horse. Smoke curling skyward from a rock chimney. The lone figure of Warren Ward shuffling up the bluff behind us. Instinct. Fear. Suspicion. The craving for survival.

James Kenedy jerked his race horse to a stop, and the big black stood there, his legs quivering, snorting and blowing hard. The son of the Texas cattle baron stood in his stirrups

and shielded his eyes from the sun with his hand, methodically surveying the barren landscape that stretched out
before him like an artist's canvas, filled with browns and
grays and little else. He was a statue on the prairie,
motionless, wary, cautious. He was careless about other
people's lives, but damn careful about his own. The shadows, he knew, would lie to him, and he did not trust them.

Wyatt Earp's patience wore thin, then wore out. He would
not have made a decent vulture after all. He had his prey in
his sight, a nervous prey, as skittish as a jackrabbit in a
prairie full of coyotes, ready to run, afraid not to run and
nowhere to run. He fired.

The range had fooled him, as distances tend to do when
the prairies are flat as a tortilla and just about as burnt. The
bullet kicked up the ground beside the race horse's white
foreleg.

"Damn," the lawman muttered.

He fired again, the slug tearing through a bush of thorns,
scattering a covey of quail from its cover.

James Kenedy wheeled his race horse around and dug his
spurs angrily into the animal's heaving flanks. The horse
reared and screamed, the leather quirt cutting deeply and
cruelly into his broad, lathered shoulders.

I had taken the fifty-caliber Sharps rifle away from
Charley Moseby, pointed in the general direction of James
Kenedy, and pulled the trigger. The jolt staggered me
backward. The big gun roared like a cannon on the third day
at Shiloh.

There was no way I would be able to get off a second shot
in time.

I did not have to.

The ball slammed into Kenedy, spinning him around in
the saddle. He swayed back and forth, losing his grip of the
reins. He was still frantically grasping for the saddle horn

when he pitched forward and tumbled to a harsh and unforgiving earth.

I waited for him to rise again.

James Kenedy lay folded in a heap, a pile of twisted bones and sunburnt flesh.

I would have considered him dead if he had not been screaming.

"Helluva shot," Charley Moseby said.

An enraged Wyatt Earp busted the carbine on a boulder behind him and threw the remains into the dirt. It had failed him when he needed it most. He had no use for the Winchester anymore. "Hawkes just pulled the trigger," the lawman said, a cutting edge in his voice. "That damn fool on horseback ran into the bullet."

"That's generally how it's done," Charley Moseby told him.

"He's down," was all I said.

Him being down was all that Wyatt Earp cared about.

He walked toward the fallen James Kenedy. He lay writhing in the dust, clawing the ground with his fingers, screaming and cursing.

His right shoulder had been shattered by the Big Fifty, his arm almost torn from its socket. It lay useless beneath him, the bone in splinters.

James Kenedy was praying to die and praying that he wouldn't, praying for anything that would ease the piercing, excruciating pain and erase the anguish that tormented him. His forehead was burning. His eyes had sunk back into his head, and his face was waxen, the color of hog tallow.

Wyatt Earp knelt beside him, reaching down to brush the dirt away from his mouth.

James Kenedy's voice was almost a whisper. "I should have known it was you," he said.

"You can't do what you did and get away with it."

"How'd you get here so damn fast?"

"Trouble was," Wyatt Earp told him bluntly, "it appears I wanted to get you a helluva lot worse than you wanted to get away from me."

"You may have got me, you sonuvabitch," James Kenedy said, coughing, "but not before I got that bastard who started all the trouble."

Silence.

"I hope I blew his goddamn head off," Kenedy spat out, along with a throatful of dirt he had swallowed when he fell.

"Who?" Wyatt Earp asked softly.

"That bastard Dog Kelley." James Kenedy's body shook with a sudden convulsion. The groan came from deep inside of his belly.

"What you did," the lawman said with a faint chill in his voice, "was kill somebody else."

Silence again.

It seemed to last forever.

James Kenedy was staring at the lawman with eyes that could not quite comprehend the words he had heard. Finally, he said, "What do you mean, I killed somebody else? Hell, I couldn't have missed Kelley that close. I could have reached out and touched him."

"The mayor was out of town."

"Then who in hell got in the way that night?" James Kenedy was angry, not repentant, full of resentment, not remorse.

"It was Dora Hand."

Silence.

James Kenedy grimaced, and the blood drained from his face. I did not know whether it was from pain for disappointment. For a moment, I thought he was going to pass out. He fought to keep his eyes from closing and said bitterly, "I don't even know a Dora Hand."

"That's a shame," Wyatt Earp said quietly. "I did."

James Kenedy ignored him. He was looking at me now, specs of red floating in his eyes. He was staring at the Sharps rifle, the Big Fifty, cradled in my arms. "You damn sonuvabitch," he grunted. "You ought to have made a better shot than you did, an' I wouldn't be hurtin' this damn bad."

Wyatt Earp answered for me with a voice as cold, as dead as winter. "You damn murderin' sonuvabitch," he said, "Hawkes did the best he could."

Charley Moseby touched the shattered arm.

James Kenedy jerked, and his eyes rolled back.

"He's losin' a lot of blood," the gravedigger said.

"That's his problem," Wyatt Earp replied.

"You gonna finish him off right here?"

"I'd rather see him hang."

Charley Moseby sighed. "Then I guess I better go ahead and try to get his arm bandaged up. Hell, Wyatt, it'd be a lot less trouble if you just let him lay here and die."

"I'll pay for the rope myself," the lawman said, walking back toward the Cimarron, looking up at the widening circle of vultures who had been wasting their time that day.

We loaded James Kenedy up with Indian Whiskey Warren Ward was selling for a dollar a bottle and strapped him to a stretcher Charley Moseby had fashioned from an assortment of weeping willow limbs he had cut down along the river's edge.

We took the easy road home.

James Kenedy spent the first night lying beside a campfire, cursing us. He would never hang, he said. His daddy would never let it happen. He would be a free man before the week had ended, then, by gawd, none of us would ever sleep in peace again. Sooner or later he would get us all, and if he didn't, his daddy's gun hands damn sure would. His shoulder had numbed, the pain was only a dull ache, and the

Texas trail boss was feeling a good deal meaner now that he knew he was not going to die.

It was the last night he cursed us.

It was amazing how quiet he became when Charley Moseby rammed the muzzle of the Sharps rifle into Kenedy's mouth and slept with his finger lying heavy on the trigger. James Kenedy did not get much rest that night. But he sure did not keep us awake with his obscenities.

♠

♥ 29 ♦

♣

Wyatt Earp soaked in a tub of hot water for almost an hour, then shaved, put on his black suit, and went up to the knoll at sundown. He stood, his head bowed, while the last splinters of daylight played out their time on the earth, then knelt and placed a white rose atop a fresh mound of dirt.

Amen. Dora Hand lay among strangers. Such had been her life.

No preacher had come to deliver any final parting words for Dora Hand. But Eddie Foy had sung two verses and the chorus of some song about not crossing Jordan alone, and he quoted her favorite passage from the Good Book, something about the Lord being gracious and full of compassion, slow to anger, and of great mercy, and he said the world had lost a great voice, a great talent, a great woman.

He would miss her immensely. The stage would seem dark without her. But the show must go on. And he left her among strangers.

Wyatt Earp had returned to Dodge and his grieving. He

had told me, "It doesn't matter what a woman does when she's alive, as long as she's a lady when she dies."

And then he went up to the knoll at sundown. He sat there in the darkness beside her until morning came. It was, I believe, the longest time they had ever spent together.

♠

♥ **30** ♦

♣

The summer had not been kind to Amos Fielding. The land around the old Judkins place was worse than he had expected. But then, he had not quite lived up to the widow Judkins's expectations either, and she had become quite an expert at chunking firewood. As soon as she had replenished herself with what was left of his manhood, she threw him outside with the hogs, which did not in any way improve the condition of the hog wallow. Amos Fielding's seeds went bad, then his crops withered. Only the weeds prospered. The well water turned to gyp, then it soaked itself back down into the ground and wouldn't come out again. The mule that was too lazy to die finally got around to dying. And the shrapnel he had carried in his chest since the First Battle of Pea Ridge broke loose and started working its way into his lung. Amos Fielding coughed a dry hacking cough for most of August, then when the days grew hotter, it became more difficult for him to breathe. He felt he was drowning in a land that had no water.

Amos Fielding gave up trying to sleep early one morning and crawled out of the widow Judkins's bed. He did not bother to wake her. She had not been talking to him for days anyway, not since he left the gate open, and the family's only milk cow had wandered away. He found the cow by noon and drove her home, but Emma Judkins was not in a forgiving mood, so she kept her mouth shut and spent her spare time memorizing the second chapter of Romans as though it were a letter written to her personally by one of the apostles.

Amos Fielding looked down on his sleeping wife, who would have been his wedded wife if a preacher had ever come to town, and every breath was a strain, threatening to be his last. He might have been roped to the cow, but he certainly wasn't carrying her brand. He was too weak to put on his clothes, so Amos Fielding staggered butt naked out to the shed behind the ramshackled old barn and sat down atop a water bucket, slowly feeding four cartridges into the chamber of his army revolver, about the last thing of value he could call his own.

He shot two of the hogs just to see if the rusty old pistol would still fire.

He shot the goat grazing on a hillside to see if he could still hit anything at that range.

He spent the last bullet on himself. It entered just below his left eye and splintered the back of his head. He fell back in the hog wallow, his blood mixed with the mud, and that's the way the widow Judkins found him when she came out to check the henhouse for eggs.

"He must have been murdered," she told Wyatt Earp.

"It don't look that way, ma'am," he said.

"Amos wouldn't take his own life."

"What makes you say that?"

"He had so much to live for."

"What about the hogs that were shot, ma'am?" Wyatt Earp asked.

"I'm gonna miss those hogs," she said.

Burying Amos Fielding was a nuisance. Charley Moseby hitched a borrowed horse to a wagon, loaded a pine box, and drove out before daybreak, removing the old man from the hog wallow and laying him to rest atop a knoll alongside Spade Judkins. The widow had not bothered to prepare the body for him, which had always seemed to be the Christian thing to do.

"He didn't bathe none while he was livin' here," Emma Judkins said, "he best not expect me to wash him when he's gone."

Charley Moseby walked back down to the cabin and asked her if she might want to read a Scripture or two above the grave since he had finished packing the dirt around the pine box, her being the last living Bible believer south of the dead line.

"He didn't listen to 'em when he was livin' here," Emma Judkins said, "he best not expect me to read any to him when he's gone."

"God might appreciate it," the gravedigger told her.

"God erased Amos Fielding's name from the Book of Life a long time ago," she said. She thought it over a moment, then asked, "Where'd you put him?"

"Up there beside Spade."

The widow frowned. "Dig him up," she said.

"I can't do that, Emma."

"Spade was my lawful wedded husband," she said. "Amos was just a drifter who passed through and stayed awhile. That's all. He ain't got no business up there beside Spade." She looked at Charley Moseby with cold, piercing eyes. "Move him," she snapped.

Charley Moseby was not the kind of man to argue, especially not with a woman.

He rode back to Dodge just as the sun sat itself above the Dodge House, leaving Amos Fielding where he found him, lying in the wallow, one eye and the back of his head missing. He brought the pine box back with him.

As soon as Charley Moseby reached town, he hurried straight to Wyatt Earp's office. Amos Fielding was the last person on his mind.

"There's trouble headed this way," he said breathlessly, bursting through the doorway.

The lawman was not particularly concerned. "When wasn't trouble headed this way?" he wanted to know.

He was seated at his desk, working on the one-handed border shuffle I had taught him the night before, irritated that he had not been able to master it. He had a fistful of cards in his right hand. The rest were scattered on the floor, and Wyatt Earp was trying to decide whether to pick them up again or throw the rest across the jail and leave the gambling to me.

He instinctively glanced out the window behind him, his eyes running down the street from one end of Dodge to the other. It was empty.

"It's Mifflin Kenedy," Charley Moseby said.

Wyatt Earp's eyes narrowed as he glanced toward the cell where a surly James Kenedy lay staring at the ceiling. The prisoner's shoulder was heavily bandaged, his arm in a sling. His hand was turning black, and Doc Ferguson said that if the young man's circulation had not improved by the week's end, he would probably have to take the arm.

James Kenedy had cursed Doc Ferguson, too.

A man with one arm was only half a man in a land where those with two arms had to struggle to survive, and James Kenedy knew it.

Wyatt Earp finally answered. "Mifflin Kenedy's a law-abiding man," he said.

"He's bringin' five men with him," Charley Moseby spat out. "I saw 'em camped down on Nickerson's Crossing."

"Mifflin Kenedy's come a great distance," Wyatt Earp replied calmly. "It stands to reason he would not travel alone."

"These ain't cattlemen that's with him."

"Then who would they be, Charley?"

"Hired guns. I seen their eyes. When I rode past, they was sittin' there cleanin' their Colts, and cattlemen don't sit around cleanin' their guns before breakfast. Hell, most of 'em just wear their pistols for show anyway. That's why so many of 'em get themselves killed. They don't know what the hell to do with a gun when they think they have to use it. Mifflin Kenedy's men, they know what to do with a gun. They've flat used 'em before. I seen their kind. They're hard men, Wyatt."

Wyatt Earp carefully stacked the cards on top of his desk. He arose and ambled to the front door. Opening it, he stood on the threshold, staring at the road making its way to Dodge from the southern end of town. It was the road that would bring Mifflin Kenedy and, if Charley Moseby were right, his hired guns to town.

"Mr. Kenedy has every right to see his son," the lawman said, "as long as he comes unarmed."

"I don't think that's what he's got on his mind."

"Then we'll change his mind."

"How you gonna do that?"

Wyatt Earp glanced across the room at me. I had left my cell and walked to the window, wondering why the day suddenly felt warmer than it had before. My back still ached from sleeping on the jailhouse bunk. But a man does not complain when it's the only bunk in town he can afford.

"You want to tell him, Hawkes?" Wyatt said.

"It's like any high-stakes game," I answered, turning to face the gravedigger. "We've got the edge. Thanks to you, Charley, we know Mifflin Kenedy is on his way. He does not know that we know he's anywhere near Dodge. Thanks to you, we know he's bringing five guns with him. He does not know that we know he's hired guns or how many of them he has. That means Mifflin Kenedy is at a definite disadvantage."

"So what are you gonna do about it?" Charley Moseby asked.

"We're gonna let Mr. Kenedy visit his son," Wyatt Earp answered, "hire himself a good lawyer, and have a front row seat at the trial."

"He ain't gonna appreciate your hospitality."

Wyatt Earp's mood grew dour. "I've never seen a daddy yet that could stomach a hangin'."

"What about those hired guns he's got with him?"

"If they come to Dodge, then their guns are gonna be stuck over there in that cell next to James, just like everybody else's."

"They ain't gonna like that."

"I haven't found anybody yet who does, with the possible exception of those who haven't been shot at."

James Kenedy had risen from his bunk and was leaning against the bars of his cell, an insolent grin plastered on his ashen face. He was thin from lack of food and sleep. The throbbing ache in his shoulder had taken away his appetite for both.

"You might as well let me out now," he said, drawling out his words.

"I've got no reason to do that," Wyatt Earp said.

"It'll save you a helluva lot of trouble later on." James Kenedy grimaced and grabbed hold of the bars with his good hand as a spasm of pain, then nausea, swept over him. His knuckles were white, his hand quivering. A weaker man would have cried out. James Kenedy only groaned. He steadied himself, then said, "My daddy's gonna get me out of here, and there's not a damn thing you can do to stop him."

"Only one man can get you out of here," Wyatt Earp said. "And that's the judge."

"My daddy can."

"Only if he buys the judge."

"He's done it before."

"If he does, then it'll damn sure be the judge's last case."

James Kenedy laughed sardonically. "A two-bit lawman can't get the judge thrown off the bench," he said. "You don't have enough power, prestige, or money."

"No," Wyatt Earp answered. "But there's an empty plot of ground up there beside Dora Hand that's just about the right size for most judges I've seen."

"That'd be murder," James Kenedy spit out.

"No," I said quietly, "that would be justice."

James Kenedy swallowed his laughter, and the grin died on his face.

Dodge City was seldom a beehive of activity in the hot afternoon of an August day. Nobody felt like moving in the sweltering heat, and nobody did. The faint sound of a honky-tonk piano slipped out of the Alhambra. A farmer's wagon was headed back out of town. A carpenter was replacing the scorched roof of the Dodge House with a new one. A pair of horses were tied to the hitching rail outside the Long Branch. A Closed sign was being nailed above the box office of the Comique Theater, and I wondered if it had been closed for good or just until the good Mayor Kelley could lure another troupe of dancers and singers west. From my perch atop the Alhambra, Dodge City seemed as quiet as a preacher pouring bourbon while the rest of his congregation was sipping communion wine. I lay behind the balcony corner post, the Sharps rifle tucked under my arm. It felt as out of place as I did.

A lone rider came walking his horse up the street from the south.

He was a big man, well over six feet tall, with a drooping black mustache framing a square-jawed face. His shoulders were thick, and he wore a black vest over a white shirt that had not seen too many washings. His black hat shaded his eyes, and he rode easily, confidently, his right arm dangling loosely at his side, never far from the bone-handled Colt on his right hip.

He reined his bay to a halt in front of the jail below, calling Wyatt Earp by name.

The door opened, and the lawman stepped outside.

"You Wyatt Earp?" the rider wanted to know.

"That would be me."

"I have a message for you from Captain Mifflin Kenedy," the rider said.

"If you've been hired to deliver it, then I'll be willing to let you do it."

"Captain Kenedy wants his son."

"Captain Kenedy's son is wanted for murder."

"Captain Kenedy doesn't think he's guilty."

"Then the captain can wait and see if a jury agrees with him."

The rider glared down at the lawman. He said, "I've come to carry James Kenedy home. If he's done anything wrong, it will be dealt with in Texas."

"Where Captain Kenedy owns the judge and the jury?" Wyatt Earp smiled a lethal smile. "I don't think so, sir."

"Captain Kenedy has authorized me to pay to the city of Dodge twenty-five thousand dollars, which, he believes, should be sufficient to cover whatever fine his son might owe for the deed you claim he has committed." The rider looked around him. "It appears that Dodge could use twenty-five thousand dollars. It might look like a city then."

If his words had been intended to insult Wyatt Earp, he should not have gone to the trouble. Wyatt Earp could care less whether Dodge lived or died, whether it became a thriving metropolis or rotted away like the Conestogas we saw scattered on the plains of dead grass.

"Tell Captain Kenedy his son is not for sale."

The rider frowned. He pulled a watch from his vest, glanced at the time, and said, "It's now sixteen minutes past three o'clock. If James Kenedy is not returned to his father by sixteen minutes after four o'clock, then he's coming in to town to get him himself. And, Mr. Earp, you do not want to do business the way Mifflin Kenedy does business."

"Captain Kenedy is welcome in Dodge anytime he wants to come," Wyatt Earp said. "But you, sir, are not allowed in town wearing that Colt. Remove it with your left hand and drop it on the ground beside your horse. Move slowly enough for me to count the hairs on the back of your hand. We don't do anything in a hurry around here, with the possible exception of building the gallows necessary to hang a woman killer."

The rider did not move. His defiant stare was one of arrogance.

"They say you're fast with that pistol of yours," the rider said. "And you may be. But you don't know who I am, or how fast I am, and I don't think you want to die just to find out. Believe me, Mr. Earp, you can't beat me." His argument was as convincing as a spade flush.

"Maybe not," the lawman replied, his eyes moving up the face of Alhambra Saloon. "But he can."

The rider jerked his eyes upward. He was now staring into the muzzle of the Big Fifty. It looked like a cannon, and I was feeling like a man gambling on a twenty-five-thousand-dollar pot with two deuces showing, nothing in the hole, and praying that no one at the table would be vain enough to call my bet.

The rider's gunhand went rigid. And Wyatt Earp gently removed the Colt from its holster without a shot being fired.

I was tempted to shoot the rider's hat off just to prove I could do it but figured I would probably blow his head off instead, so it was a temptation I resisted and always regretted that I did.

The rider did not argue with either the Big Fifty or the Smith & Wesson.

A good gunfighter knew when it was wise to wait and fight another day. His day would come, if not in Dodge, then someplace else. Besides, Captain Mifflin Kenedy was not paying him to die. That was one job he had never taken. For the time being, he had to be satisfied with a cell of his own.

His only question to Wyatt Earp was, "When is supper served?" He said he had been riding all day and was hungry enough to eat a chicken, feathers, beak, cluck, and all.

"When we go out and kill something," the lawman answered.

"Rabbits?"

"Usually dogs."

The rider wasn't quite so hungry anymore.

Mifflin Kenedy had not sent one rider to Dodge and one rider alone. He was an odds player. If one hired gun could free James Kenedy, so be it. If not, he could at least occupy the city marshal along enough for two other hired guns to slip unseen into Dodge and take up advantageous positions within the town. They would be there when he needed them, and chances were he would need them before the day ended. Mifflin Kenedy left nothing to chance.

He had not counted on us having the edge.

We owed it all to Amos Fielding. If he had not put a bullet

through his brain, and if Charley Moseby had not ridden out early in the morning, then we would have all been sitting there in total ignorance.

Mifflin Kenedy and his hired guns could have struck, struck hard like a chain of blue lightning, broken James Kenedy out of jail, and been gone on their way back to Texas before any of us knew they had swept into Kansas and were camping on the banks of Nickerson Crossing.

The edge is everything.

One of the hired guns had eased into Dodge from the west. He was a small man, thin as a razor blade, with a face so white some doubted it had ever been touched by the sun. He arrived like a ghost, his face as white as his hair. No one heard him. No one saw him coming. He was sure of it, and he preferred it that way. The ghost had loco camped out in his eyeballs, and he crept into the livery stable and waited beside the window, one that gave him a clear view of the whole street. He carried a Winchester rifle and would strike as quickly as a rattlesnake, only more deadly, and no one would ever know he was there. No rattle. No warning. Those who gave warnings seldom lived long enough to give many of them.

Dodge was not the first city he had taken.

He had wiped streets clean with gunfire, then departed, and no one had ever learned his name. He had no name, only a reputation among those who could afford to pay what he was worth, which meant he worked a great deal for Mifflin Kenedy.

A peculiar smile worked its way across his face.

He could not have asked for a better vantage point.

Mifflin Kenedy would be pleased.

The ghost was still smiling his peculiar smile when Charley Moseby slammed him across the back of his head with a shovel. The first blow only stunned him. The gravedigger swung again. The impact drove the ghost's well-battered head through the window, breaking it and scattering glass fragments among the piles of hay.

Little Dave Little quickly grabbed the fallen Winchester and scampered to the back of the stable. "You want me to shoot him?" he yelled.

"If he gets up, you do whatever you have to do to knock him down again." Charley Moseby was ready to hit him again, the shovel cocked over his right shoulder, but the ghost crumpled face first into the hay.

"You kill him?" Little Dave Little asked.

"I damn sure tried."

"I think he's still breathin'."

"Hardheaded sonuvabitch, isn't he?"

Charley Moseby and Little Dave Little led three horses into the pen out back. They methodically tied the ghost's left leg to the gray, his right leg to a sorrel and both hands to the neck of an old bay that had a mean, cussed look in one eye, was blind in the other, and had a wild streak in his disposition. The hired gun was dangling between all three horses when he awoke at last, startled, then angry and somewhat bewildered.

"What the hell's goin' on?" he asked.

"I'd be careful if I was you," Charley Moseby said, walking out of the pen without looking back. "If you was to spook them horses, they might run off in all directions at once. Horses are bad about that, you know."

The last word he heard before stepping into the street was the ghost hollering, "Whoa," and he wondered how many times the hired gun would yell it before the horses finished the oats Little Dave Little had left for them and decided it was time to head for greener pastures. There weren't any that time of year, but the horses did not know it.

The third gunman could have been anybody. Dodge was

full of unfamiliar faces. A stranger today might be a friend tomorrow. A stranger today might be your killer tomorrow. There was a reason why they were strangers. They were usually running from something or someone, and they seldom stayed for very long. They seldom had any reason to.

The third gunman only planned to hang around an hour or so, no longer. He, too, was a stranger. But Charley Moseby knew who he was.

He had a large, puffy face with a patch over one eye. He was older, less daring. He carried two revolvers in their holsters and another stuck in his belt, and he was not wearing his guns for ballast. He had torn down the sign that outlawed guns in Dodge before walking into the Alhambra. By midnight, it would be in an uproar. But in the middle of the afternoon, the third gunman had the place virtually to himself. He stopped by the bar, ordered a whiskey so as not to arouse any suspicions, then sat down at a table by the window.

He could see the street. He could see the jail. The whiskey sat before him untouched. He could drink it later, when there was no reason for his head to be clear, his hand steady.

He glanced up at the clock above the bar. Only ten more minutes he would have to wait before Mifflin Kenedy reached town. It would have been a lot easier if that damn city marshal had just given up the captain's boy without a fight. But, hell, without a fight he wouldn't have a job.

He was still staring out the window when I dropped the five cards on the table in front of him.

Aces. And eights. A dead man's hand, and he knew it.

The third gunman tried to turn his head, but he jammed it into the muzzle of my belly blaster. He knew what that was, too. He had either felt one or used one before.

Charley Moseby removed all three of his revolvers. "We got a law against wearin' those things in town," he said.

"It's a damn stupid law," the third gunman said testily, his stinger out, irritated because an old gravedigger and a gambling man had gotten the drop on him.

"Most times we give them back," I said, smiling pleasantly. "But in your case, we may make an exception."

"Captain Kenedy's gonna have your head for this," he said.

"Maybe." I shrugged as though it did not matter. "But he sure won't have his son."

The third gunman spit on the floor.

He spat again when we marched him into the back room of the saloon and wedged him inside a half-empty barrel of whiskey.

He tried to spit on Charley Moseby. The gravedigger had had enough. He fired once, using the gunman's own revolver, and the slug tore into the barrel.

I could tell by the sharp pain that tore across the gunman's good eye that he had been hit, but I did not know where or how bad, and Charley Moseby did not care.

Promptly at sixteen minutes past four o'clock, Captain Mifflin Kenedy rode into Dodge, flanked by two of his hired guns. He was older than I had imagined, slumping wearily in the saddle as though the years, and the long ride from Texas, had been particularly difficult for him. His face was as gray as the country around him. A thousand miles worth of dust had worn itself into the long-tailed coat he wore. It had been fashioned for dances, for the good life, the good times. He had worn it to watch his boy die.

Mifflin Kenedy was a study in contrasts. He was known as a quiet man, a devout man, a Quaker, who had traveled to south Texas from his home in Florida. He settled on the crooked, cranky waters of the Rio Grande, and he watched a conflict between Mexico and the United States rage around him. The language was foreign, and the tempers were hot as gunfire.

He looked around him and recognized the need for good rivermen. General Zachary Taylor and his army would be stranded, even lost, without them. He fought the war behind the helm of his boat. And when the last soldier had marched away, he stayed behind in that uncharted country and built an empire out of hide and horn.

The Mexican War had made him rich. The War between the States had only added to his fortune as he survived the Comanches, Mexican raiders, draft dodgers, guerilla fighters, and the Union Army that all plundered the Nueces Strip.

He fought wars, not men, and he could not understand why anyone, even so far removed from Texas, would deliberately defy him. It just did not make sense. Mifflin Kenedy was generally a good man not to mess with. If you were going to beat him, it would be after the fight when he wasn't looking.

The captain's hired guns were young and rawboned. The young were clean shaven and fearless, carbines lying across their saddles, the muscles in their faces not unlike those in a coiled rattlesnake. The sullen one had a ragged scar on his chin, carved by a Jim Bowie knife. The other had eyes that did not match, hard eyes. The devil had a mortgage on both their souls.

The miles had not bothered them. They had miles farther to go once that day had ended. For them, the miles would never end. Life was one day after another, one town after another, one death after another until it was their own.

Wyatt Earp, keeping the sun to his back, stepped into the street to meet them.

Mifflin Kenedy jerked his horse to a stop and leaned over

his saddle horn. "I've come for my boy," he said. He had a gravel voice that sounded like a crow with the croup.

"I've got him now," the lawman answered. "You can have him when the undertaker gets through with him."

"He belongs to me, marshal."

"Not anymore, Mr. Kenedy."

"He belongs back at my Laureales Ranch in Texas," Mifflin Kenedy reasoned. "He's a little young, a little reckless, a little wild, I guess, but we all are or we wouldn't be here, Mr. Earp, either you or me."

"He's a killer."

"Aren't we all?" Mifflin Kenedy threw up his arms as though he was momentarily at a loss for words, then said, "This is a rough country, Mr. Earp, and we've all lived through some rough times. None of us would have gotten where we were if we let people run over us. Sometimes you have to fight back. Sometimes, fighting back gets somebody killed. It's unfortunate, to be sure, but it happens. It's happened to us all."

"James Kenedy killed a woman."

The captain glanced quickly away. His face hardened. He was a proud man, a man who had suffered many times in his life, but he had never suffered a defeat. No matter what his son had done, be it good or evil, James Kenedy was still his son, and he would be damned before he left his son to rot or die on Kansas soil.

Mifflin Kenedy dismounted. "I'm comin' in to take my boy home," he said.

"You'll take him home in a pine box."

The captain ignored Wyatt Earp. "You can't stop me, Earp."

"I'll do my damnedest."

"I'm afraid you don't stand a chance." Mifflin Kenedy shielded his eyes from the sun and scanned the rooftops,

the back alleys, the porches, the balconies of Dodge, his
squinting eyes pausing at each window, searching for any
glimpse he could find of the three hired guns who had
ridden to town before him.

Dodge was silent. Empty.

"If you're lookin' for help, Mr. Kenedy," Wyatt Earp told
him, "there won't be any."

Kenedy stood motionless, full of contempt, waiting for
his gunmen to appear. "This town is mine," he said.

He waited.

Nothing.

"Texas may belong to you," the lawman answered. "But
in this town, you're just riding through. You may visit with
your son as long as you'd like, spend the night here if you
want. But when you leave, you'll be leaving alone."

The old man sighed. He no longer looked like the legend
he was.

"I didn't want it to end this way," he said.

"You don't have a choice."

"No." He sighed again, as he had sighed so many times in
the past. "I don't reckon I do."

He removed his hat, wiped the sweat from his forehead
with the back of his sleeve, and as he abruptly lowered the
hat, both of the young guns raised their carbines toward the
lawman.

Wyatt Earp shot Hard Eyes before he had time to cock the
lever of his Remington. In the same motion, he slapped the
rump of Scar Face's horse. The horse reared back angrily,
then spun around, bucking wildly, tearing the reins from the
gunman's grip. Scar Face lost a stirrup, then his balance,
finally his rifle. He was clinging desperately to the big
horse's mane when Wyatt Earp's second bullet knocked him
from the saddle.

He fell in the dust beside Hard Eyes, instinctively

reaching for the revolver in his belt. I kicked it away. He looked first at Wyatt Earp, then at Mifflin Kenedy, the dust beneath him thick and heavy with the color of blood, then he looked at nothing at all.

It had not been a good day to come to Dodge or to die.

Wyatt Earp slid his Smith & Wesson back into his holster, saying to Mifflin Kenedy, "It's over, Captain. There's nobody left."

Mifflin Kenedy glanced down at his own .44 jammed in the belt beneath his gray coat. It was old like he was. It had not been fired in anger for a long time, not since the war when guns became so cheap to hire. There was a time it had kept him alive. But he was younger then, quicker of mind and of body both, back before the rheumatism had crept into his joints and crippled his shooting finger.

"I know what you're thinking," Wyatt Earp told him. "You're thinking there's only one thing left you can do for your boy and that's draw down on me with that pistol in your belt and die for him. Believe me, Mr. Kenedy, it's not worth it. He's guilty. He pays. Pull that pistol, and you'll pay right along with him. And, from what I've been told, you're too decent a man for that."

Mifflin Kenedy's fingers gingerly stroked the butt of the .44, only inches away from the trigger guard. He had always considered himself a decent man. And a decent shot. How good was Wyatt Earp anyway? He had heard the lawman was a drunk. Had the whiskey slowed him? Had age slowed him down? It was time to find out.

He did not have to.

"There is no man better than Mifflin Kenedy," Mayor Dog Kelley said, hurrying down the street toward us. He stepped precariously over Scar Face and Hard Eyes, ignoring them, barely glancing down at them. They were no longer a problem, just a nuisance.

"Hello, Kelley," the captain said, though the energy had fled his voice.

Dog Kelley grabbed Mifflin Kenedy's hand and shook it awkwardly. "I did not know you were coming, Captain."

"They got my boy, Kelley."

"It is indeed an unfortunate incident," the mayor replied, "one I regret very much."

"They're gonna hang him." Mifflin Kenedy sighed a beleaguered sigh. "A man can't just stand around and watch his boy bein' killed like that, it's inhuman is what it is, and there's not a damn thing I can do about it."

"You should have let me know you were coming, Captain, and come to see me as soon as you arrived in Dodge."

"What good would it have done, Kelley?"

The mayor stepped back over Scar Face and Hard Eyes, staring down at them for the first time. "These boys would have been alive if you had," he said.

"I bet they had daddies, too," I told him.

Mifflin Kenedy jerked as though he had been shot, and I knew my words had sunk in.

Dog Kelley turned to Wyatt Earp, wearing the stern face of a politician. "I've been spending a good deal of time reviewing the charges you have levied against James Kenedy and the case you are bringing to court against him," he said. "You don't have a lot."

"We have enough," I said.

"It doesn't appear that there's enough incriminating evidence to even hold him in jail," Dog Kelley said.

Mifflin Kenedy brightened. "What are you saying, mayor?" he wanted to know. "Are you considering turning James loose?"

"I've already considered it," Dog Kelley replied pompously. "He's free to go back home with you as soon as Mr. Earp unlocks the cell."

Wyatt Earp's face was granite, his eyes suddenly filled with loathing. "You don't have the authority to do that, Kelley," he said.

"I'm the official duly elected mayor of Dodge City. I can do anything I damn well please in this town."

"Not as long as I'm town marshal."

"I hired you," Dog Kelley snapped. "By gawd, I can fire you, and I can do it any damn time I want to. And if I do, the first person I'll hire is a town marshal who's got enough guts to walk in there and unlock that cell before night gets here."

Wyatt Earp clenched his jaw. He reloaded the Smith & Wesson. "I don't aim on losin' James Kenedy," he said, "to you or to the captain or to anybody."

"What I don't want to lose is business," the mayor declared. "What I'm doing, I assure you, is best for Dodge. As you know, Captain Kenedy is a very powerful and persuasive cattleman back in Texas. Dodge City needs Texas cattle or it won't have a chance in hell to grow and prosper. Without them, we're ruined. If Captain Kenedy and those other cattlemen turn their back on us and take their herds elsewhere, then Dodge City will dry up and wither away. I can't afford that, Wyatt. You can't afford that. Look around you. Look at all the people in this town whose very lives depend on Texas cattle. What good is hanging James Kenedy, if they lose their town and their homes and maybe even their lives in the process? In my job, I have to figure out what will do the most good for the most people, then do it. And what I have to do, Wyatt, is let James Kenedy go. That rifle shot damn near took his arm off. He's been punished enough."

Silence.

Wyatt Earp's voice was as soft as a newborn day. "So what you're gonna do is just let James Kenedy kill a woman in cold blood with a bullet meant for you and walk away from it."

"Dora Hand is dead," the mayor said. "I'm sorry, but there's not a thing we can do for her anymore. My job now is to keep Dodge from dyin', too."

Mifflin Kenedy placed an arm on Wyatt Earp's shoulder. His voice was strong and sincere. "I deeply regret the woman's murder," he said. "But I did not see my son kill her, so I don't know if he's guilty or not. And you, sir, don't know that for a fact either."

I spoke up. "James Kenedy admitted killing Dora Hand," I said.

"Not to me, he didn't," Dog Kelley snapped.

Wyatt Earp grabbed the mayor's coat and yanked him back across the bodies of Scar Face and Hard Eyes. "If you want to keep Dodge from dying, then you're too late," he said coldly. "It isn't dying anymore. With your sense of law, your sense of justice, it just died. A year from now, the only thing you're gonna have left in your street is dust and a few boot prints that the wind forgot to wipe away. You keep rantin' and ravin' about the coming of civilization to Dodge. Well, civilization goes where men respect the law. They may break it, but they damn sure respect it. And you, Mr. Mayor, you just spit on it."

He cast a sharp glance back at Mifflin Kenedy. "You want your boy?" he asked, his words as explosive as a pistol shot. "You come a thousand miles to take a killer home? Well, hell, then you can do whatever the hell you want with him."

A bitter Wyatt Earp stalked away down the street, through a narrow alleyway that ran alongside the Alhambra and back across the hog wallows to the livery stable. Dog Kelley, frustrated, and Mifflin Kenedy, confused, followed, never more than a few steps behind him, not wanting to lose sight of the lawman, fearful that he would change his mind again.

He led them through the mud and dung and into the barn.

And there, in a light so dim it seemed as though the day and its trappings had already departed from them, they came face to face with James Kenedy. His face was drawn and twisted crookedly to one side. His eyes were pale as an early moon. He was sitting astride his horse, his hands tied behind his back, a noose around his neck. The rope was attached firmly to a high beam that hung across the roof of the barn.

Those pale eyes were wide with fear. And pain. There would be no trial, no judge, no jury. Only judgment.

Wyatt Earp took the reins of the horse from Charley Moseby and handed them to the trembling hands of Mifflin Kenedy. He said adamantly, "You can have the boy's horse and take it on back to Texas with you, Mr. Kenedy. But James is staying right where he is."

"God, what are you doing?" Dog Kelley yelled.

"They're hanging my boy." Captain Kenedy's knees grew lame and almost buckled under him. He reached for the top rail of a horse stall to keep from falling. A weaker man would have fainted.

"No," I replied, "we're not hanging anybody. But if you want his horse to remember him by, you can certainly have him."

Wyatt Earp jerked on the reins, and the horse took a couple of steps forward. James Kenedy stood in the stirrups, the rope stretched tight. He was having trouble breathing.

"Stop, dammit!" Dog Kelley yelled.

Mifflin Kenedy lunged for the horse, grabbing his big neck, hanging on to his thick mane, frantically trying to keep him from simply walking away and leaving James Kenedy dangling by his neck from the high beam in the barn.

"Help me, Daddy," James Kenedy whispered, his voice barely audible. The insolence, the arrogance had deserted him.

Mifflin Kenedy tried to answer his son. He searched for the right words but could not find them. He wanted desperately to hug the boy's neck but was suddenly fearful he would never get that chance again. Where had the time gone? Why wasn't James just a colt running around the ranch, chasing calves by day and fireflies by night? Why had he grown up? Why couldn't he have been a little boy forever? Why had he ever taught the boy to fire a gun and drive cattle and chase women and follow that long, crooked trail to Kansas? Why couldn't they just go home and start over? One more time. One last time. It would be different next time.

Mifflin Kenedy died a little that afternoon. He would die a little more during each passing day. Until then, he had never thought he would die at all.

Dog Kelley reached for Wyatt Earp. "I'm takin' that badge off you," he said.

"You can fire me," the lawman replied, "but nobody takes the badge off me."

I mounted my faithful old white-faced sorrel. He had carried me to Wagon Bed Springs across the plains of dead grass and desert of lost souls. I figured he was strong enough to take me anywhere. Charley Moseby climbed to the top of the stall and slipped the noose off James Kenedy's neck. I took the reins from Captain Kenedy and began to lead the condemned man's horse out of the barn.

"What the hell are you doin'?" Dog Kelley demanded to know.

"I'm riding till I find a judge who can't be bought," I replied, "and then we'll find a jury that's not afraid to hang the son of Mifflin Kenedy."

"Where the hell do you think you can find anybody that foolish?" the mayor asked.

"I know Isaac Parker," I said. "Near as can I recall, he owes me a favor, whether he remembers it or not I don't know."

"Every man has his price, even Isaac Parker."

"His gallows have been worn out by people who believed that."

"Parker don't have jurisdiction over a crime committed in Kansas," Dog Kelley argued.

I grinned. "Parker's rope reaches a long way," I said, and we turned down a deserted street just as the sun climbed down the far side of the Alhambra.

Mifflin Kenedy had cast a long shadow. But now it was swallowed up in the shades of early evening. The captain had run out of options. He was a law-abiding man. He was a God-fearing man. His son was on his way to the hanging tree. It was time, he knew, to shoot or give up the gun. Shoot Earp. Me. Charley Moseby. Dog Kelley. Hell, it did not matter anymore. Mifflin Kenedy had to shoot somebody, anybody. He reached for the pistol that had been stuck just inside his coat.

Wyatt Earp rammed his Smith & Wesson into the old man's ribs.

"I'll have you arrested for that," the mayor yelled at Wyatt Earp.

Wyatt Earp only shrugged as though he was not a bit surprised by the mayor's words. "That's just what *I* was aimin' to do," he said, dragging Captain Kenedy toward the alley that led to the jail. "Of course, he'll probably be out in time to make it to the funeral."

Darkness was chasing the last vestiges of light from the prairie as we rode out of Dodge, past the fresh mound of dirt that covered the remains of the lovely Dora Hand. The white rose had wilted, but the winds had left it alone.

James Kenedy cried like a little boy lost until the purple shadows of sundown caught up with us, then he cursed Dog Kelley, Wyatt Earp, Dora Hand, his daddy, Dodge City, Texas, and finally me for being such a poor damn shot. He was a man possessed, raining out a string of profanity so hot it would fry bacon. He cursed the jerky I gave him, the coffee I brewed on a campfire, the coyotes howling at a new moon. He cursed the hard ground he lay on, the saddle blanket under his head, the wind because it blew, then the wind because it didn't. He cursed most of the night and was still cursing me when the August sun came again to bake the prairies around us. He cursed until his throat was sore and his voice dry and hoarse as a coyote chucking up brimstone. He begged for water, then cursed because I would not give him any, cursing the land because it had no rivers and the sky because it would not rain.

We had miles to go, and most of them were hard ones. James Kenedy could curse all the way to the gallows as far as I was concerned. I watched the vultures ride the wind overhead and wondered how long it would take before Charley Moseby had stolen a horse and found us. He was a good man to have around during times like these.

He made damn good coffee and dug damn good graves.